Praise for G.A. McKevett and *Murder in Her Stocking*

"For a glimpse into small-town life, where the neighbors squabble, gossip flies, everybody knows your business before you do, and when times are hard but everyone pulls together, this Christmas tale will warm your heart."
—*King's River Life Magazine*

"McKevett gives us a sometimes sassy and sometimes stern yet always relatable protagonist in Stella, whose juxtaposition of strength and vulnerability beautifully embodies the complexities and dynamism of real, everyday women. Be forewarned: You'll laugh, you'll cry, and you'll probably curse the fact that you have to wait a year for the next book."
—*Criminal Element*

"Readers will look forward to Stella's further adventures."
—*Publishers Weekly*

Books by G.A. McKevett

Savannah Reid Mysteries

JUST DESSERTS
BITTER SWEETS
KILLER CALORIES
COOKED GOOSE
SUGAR AND SPITE
SOUR GRAPES
PEACHES AND SCREAMS
DEATH BY CHOCOLATE
CEREAL KILLER
MURDER À LA MODE
CORPSE SUZETTE
FAT FREE AND FATAL
POISONED TARTS
A BODY TO DIE FOR
WICKED CRAVING
A DECADENT WAY TO DIE
BURIED IN BUTTERCREAM
KILLER HONEYMOON
KILLER PHYSIQUE
KILLER GOURMET
KILLER REUNION
EVERY BODY ON DECK
HIDE AND SNEAK
BITTER BREW

Granny Reid Mysteries

MURDER IN HER STOCKING
MURDER IN THE CORN MAZE

Published by Kensington Publishing Corporation

G.A. McKevett

MURDER
In Her
STOCKING

A GRANNY REID MYSTERY

KENSINGTON BOOKS
www.kensingtonbooks.com

KENSINGTON BOOKS are published by

Kensington Publishing Corp.
119 West 40th Street
New York, NY 10018

All Kensington titles, imprints, and distributed lines are available at special quantity discounts for bulk purchases for sales promotion, premiums, fund-raising, educational, or institutional use.

Special book excerpts or customized printings can also be created to fit specific needs. For details, write or phone the office of the Kensington Sales Manager: Attn.: Sales Department. Kensington Publishing Corp., 119 West 40th Street, New York, NY 10018. Phone: 1-800-221-2647.

Kensington and the K logo Reg. U.S. Pat. & TM Off.

First Kensington Hardcover Edition: November 2018

ISBN-13: 978-1-4967-1628-6 (ebook)
ISBN-10: 1-4967-1628-0 (ebook)

ISBN-13: 978-1-4967-1627-9
ISBN-10: 1-4967-1627-2
First Kensington Trade Edition: October 2019

10 9 8 7 6 5 4 3 2 1

Printed in the United States of America

*This new series is
dedicated to all of Savannah's friends,
who have loved Granny Reid for so long.*

I would like to thank Leslie Connell for the many hours she has spent over the years reading and proofing my work, giving me suggestions, and noticing when characters arrive in two cars and leave in one or change eye color halfway through a book. I am even more thankful for her loving friendship.

I am also most grateful to Wanda and Charles Johnson, Arden Massie, Jim Hinze, and Jerry Pierce for their generous research assistance. I pronounce you honorary members of the Moonlight Magnolia Detective Agency.

A warm thank-you goes to my Facebook friends who helped me remember what our lives were like in the 1980s. What fun we had strolling memory lane together.

I also wish to thank the fans who write to me, sharing their thoughts and offering endless encouragement. Your stories touch my heart, and I enjoy your letters more than you know. I can be reached at:

sonja@sonjamassie.com
facebook.com/gwendolynnarden.mckevett

Prologue

"This has to be the absolute best Christmas ever."

"With Granny here in California and the new baby, too, it doesn't get better than this."

"Just don't get between me and that plate of fudge. I'm warnin' y'all!"

Stella Reid settled into her granddaughter's most comfortable chair, which sat beside the glittering Christmas tree, and propped her feet on the overstuffed footstool, between a couple of warm, purring black cats.

Ahhh, her spirit whispered. *Nothin' quite like a kitty foot massage.*

Hugging the latest addition to her family close to her heart, Stella listened to her loved ones chattering among themselves.

She breathed in the familiar holiday fragrances: the rich pine smell of the tree, the spicy bouquet of the gingerbread house on the kitchen table, the lingering aroma of chocolate from the fudge making that afternoon, and, most importantly, the sweet scent of the infant in her arms.

Baby Vanna Rose snuggled against her chest, the child's tiny fingers wrapped tightly around her great-grandmother's thumb. Her eyes glistened, reflecting the splendor of the tree's twinkling lights and shiny ornaments.

Stella looked around the room, adoring each friend and family member in turn. Her grown grandchildren, Savannah and Waycross, were nibbling on generous squares of her famous fudge, while their spouses, Dirk and Tammy, helped themselves to a punch bowl of eggnog.

The family's closest friends, Ryan and John, had just arrived and were placing gifts, wrapped in elegant silver and gold foil papers, on the glittery, fluffy "snow" beneath the tree.

But as deeply as Stella Reid loved everyone present, she had to admit that her favorite, at least this year, was Vanna Rose, Tammy and Waycross's tiny, red-haired imp and Stella's youngest great-grandchild. There was nothing quite as beautiful as a baby at Christmastime, a reminder of the reason for all the celebratory uproar.

As Stella listened to her family members express their joy and appreciation of the holiday, she had to agree with them. Christmas *was* a wonderous time, and *this* was the best one yet.

Well, the *second* best.

As delightful as this one was, there was another Christmas that held a special place in Stella Reid's heart and that none could ever eclipse.

"The night is darkest just before the dawn" was a quote Stella had often heard and had frequently recited herself. That year had been especially dark, its night long and deep, filled with trials and worries galore.

When the dawn had finally broken, its warming light was badly needed and most welcomed by all.

No Christmas, no matter how bright the tree, fragrant the food, bountiful the gifts, or merry the fellowship, would ever be as sweet, as soul satisfying, as that one had been more than thirty years ago. . . .

Chapter 1

"**A**in't Christmas just the best, Gran? It's like the magic in fairy tales, only *real*!"

Stella Reid looked down at her eight-year-old granddaughter Alma, whose eyes sparkled with holiday wonderment as she gazed at the same old battered tinsel stars and ragged streamers that were strung across Main Street every year in tiny McGill, Georgia. Since it took so little time and money to decorate the dinky three-blocks-long town, Stella wondered, not for the first time, why the town council didn't splurge and shell out a few bucks for some new ones once every quarter of a century or so.

But the glow on her grandchild's lovely face gave Stella reason to rethink her position. Magic, the real kind, was born in innocent, open hearts, who sought it everywhere. And found it. Even in tattered tinsel decorations.

"Yes, Alma sugar, Christmas *is* the best," Stella told the child as she squeezed her small, warm hand. "It plumb dazzles the eyes and the heart alike. A time when most anything can happen."

"Good," piped up Marietta, the restless eleven-year-old who was tugging at Stella's other hand. "Maybe I'll finally get them sparkly dress-up high heels I been asking for. Ever' year I write Santa a letter and tell 'im I want 'em, but when I look under the tree . . . nothin'! Diddly-squat! I don't know why. Lord knows, I'm always good as good can be."

Stella heard a throat clearing behind her. Her oldest grand-angel, Savannah, whispered, "Yeah, Miss Contrary Mari's good, all right. Good for nothing."

The third oldest, Vidalia, clapped her hand over her mouth to stifle a giggle. She almost always agreed with Savannah about Marietta's shortcomings, but she knew a reprimand was forthcoming.

Casting a disapproving look over her shoulder, Stella said, "I heard that, Savannah girl. If you can't say something nice, then—"

"I know. Sorry, Gran."

Marietta stuck out her lip and whirled around to face her accuser. "What're you saying sorry to Gran for, Vannah Sue? I'm the one you insulted! Gran, make her say sorry to me, too. I'm the one who was wounded."

Stella halted the entire entourage of her seven grandchildren in the middle of the sidewalk and cringed a bit to see her fellow McGillians having to walk around the blockage.

Stella had just collected her grandchildren from their mother's house and hadn't had a chance to give them baths or wash their hair and clothes, as she usually did once she got hold of them, a time or two per week.

She saw the disapproving looks of some of her neighbors as they passed the Reid gang, and she couldn't blame them. From the chocolate that was smeared on the face of the youngest, little Jesup, who had just turned six, to nine-year-old Waycross's wild mop of dirty red curls and second grader Cordelia's torn blouse, they were a motley mess, to be sure.

The oldest, twelve-year-old Savannah, did her best to keep them clean and neat, but it was a heavy burden and a losing battle for any child.

Stella's daughter-in-law, Shirley, had surrendered long ago— if, indeed, she had ever fought at all. She possessed a talent for bringing children into the world, at the rate of one per year, and she had a knack for naming them all after towns in Georgia where she had lived at one time or another. But that was where her mothering skills and maternal interests ended. No one who knew her could say they had ever seen her pick up a hairbrush, a bar of soap or a bath towel, or, heaven forbid, an iron.

Shirley's time and life energy were spent sitting on a barstool at the Bulldog Tavern on Main Street in downtown McGill, beneath a picture of Elvis, listening to sorrowful jukebox songs and bemoaning her perpetual rotten luck.

Stella tried to keep the anger she felt for her daughter-in-law to a minimum. After all, Stella's own son, the children's father, did even less for his brood than his wife. A truck driver who came home only a few times a year and stayed just long enough to impregnate his extremely fertile wife, Macon Reid wasn't the sort of son that Stella bragged about at church socials. She was fine with him driving a big rig. It was honest, hard, skilled work. But she'd be a lot prouder if he hadn't stashed a girlfriend or two in every port of call. Or if he'd put out at least a little effort to be home for the important stuff. Like Christmas.

Wondering how Macon had turned out so badly when he'd had such a fine daddy kept Stella Reid awake at night. It also kept her from judging her daughter-in-law too harshly.

Stella liked to think that most people tried the best they could. Some came up a mite light on the All Things Virtuous side of the scale, but Stella refused to believe that anybody started out in life determined to be good for little, if anything, to their fellow man.

At least, that was what Stella told herself when she collected her seven grandkids from Shirley's filthy house, with its empty refrigerator and unused washing machine. When she was carting the youngsters out the door and wishing Shirley well with the brightest fake smile she could muster, Stella was often enjoying the fantasy of snatching her daughter-in-law off that barstool, shaking the daylights out of her, and then finishing the job with a smack upside the noggin.

Stella felt guilty about entertaining such violent imaginations, but just a little. She figured it was better to *think* it than *do* it.

Hey, whatever works, Stella frequently told herself while indulging in those satisfying daydreams. Resisting temptation was an art that took many forms.

Stella drew a deep breath, summoning her patience, and told Savannah, "Tell Marietta sorry, too, darlin'. Nobody should ever be called 'good for nothin',' because the good Lord made ever'body good for somethin'." She added under her breath, "Though it's sometimes more obvious what certain folks are good for than others."

She turned to Marietta, whose lip was back in place and curled into as ugly a sneer as Stella had ever seen.

"Miss Marietta," she told her second oldest, "you wipe that nasty look off your face. If you don't cotton to bein' called 'good for nothin',' you might try bein' good for *somethin'* come dish-dryin' time. Hear me?"

The lip shot out again as the child gave her grandmother a

hateful glance that could have peeled the paint off a freshly polished fire engine.

"You stick that lip back in, girl," Stella added, "before a crow flies overhead and poops on it."

Demanding sparkly plastic high heels and showin' a heap o' disrespect to her elders, indeed, Stella thought. *Lord, have mercy. That young'un's not even a teenager yet, and she's already giving me fits. I can see trouble comin' a mile off.*

With some effort, Stella got her troops reassembled, and they continued their march down the Main Street sidewalk, toward the drugstore.

History had taught Stella that taking her grandchildren from their mom for an "overnight" usually meant a week's worth of Grandma babysitting, at least. The medicine chest was low on Merthiolate, castor oil, and bandages. In a house filled with active, accident-prone children, a well-stocked bathroom cabinet took precedence over holiday shopping.

The army of Reids rounded a corner, and too late, Stella saw him.

Elmer Yonce. One of her least favorite McGillians.

He was between the Reids and the drugstore, blocking their path. Something told her that he had been waiting there for quite a while, intending to do exactly that.

It wasn't the first time she had tangled with Elmer.

She noted with some amusement that his hands were on his hips in what might appear to be a grandiose and authoritative stance. But Stella had known Elmer since elementary school, and she could tell he was taking the opportunity to hold up his britches, which were in danger of heading south, due to him sucking in his belly overly much.

For her benefit, no doubt.

An unsettling thought.

Any guy in the habit of pullin' in his gut and puffin' out his chest to impress womenfolk should probably invest in a pair of suspenders, she decided as he approached their group.

"Merry Christmas, Sexy Stella. You're lookin' ever' bit as sweet and tasty as a plate of your best fudge," he said, waggling his right eyebrow in what was, no doubt, an effort to appear flirtatious and irresistible. "Got plans for Christmas Eve? If not, I could slide down your chimney and leave a little something in your stocking, if you know what I mean."

Stella bristled. This was a bit over the top even for the town degenerate. If she weren't surrounded by her wide-eyed grandkids, ol' Elmer's left cheek would be glowing red and her palm would be tingling.

"Reckon I know exactly what you mean, Elmer Yonce, you filthy-minded peckerwood," she told him. "You best watch what you say to me. Specially when my grand-young'uns are within earshot." She reached out and pulled her brood close, like a hen gathering her chicks when a hawk soared overhead.

"Yeah!" snapped Savannah. "Her name's not Sexy Stella. It's Gran or Granny, or Sister Stella, or Mrs. Reid."

"That's right," Marietta chimed in. "She's pretty, but she ain't sexy. She's our *grandma*!"

"Well, I . . ." Elmer coughed and stared down at his mud-caked boots. "I knowed your grandma for years, kids, and I always thought she was mighty, um . . . Oh, never mind. I didn't mean no disre—"

"Our gran's strong, too," nine-year-old Waycross added, equally indignant. "If she decides to smack you upside the head with her big ol' black skillet, you'll know you've been beaned one for sure!"

"Yeah, Granny's fierce. She'll work you over good fore she's done with you," threatened little Alma, with the fury of a much-riled second grader, "and we won't lift a finger to save your mangy hide when she does it, neither."

In her peripheral vision, Stella caught sight of a figure, a large figure in a sheriff's uniform, moving toward their sidewalk assemblage.

"Have we got a problem here, folks?" asked a deep, rich male voice—the voice of law and order in McGill, Sheriff Maniford Gilford. Though, the citizens whom he protected and served knew better than to call him Maniford.

Born as he was on Saint Patrick's Day, rumor had it that his daddy had been deep in a bottle of Irish whiskey when he saddled his innocent baby son with that awkward handle. Those whom Sheriff Gilford arrested on a fairly regular schedule opined that this might be the source of his contrariness.

Though, Stella had never thought of her old schoolmate as difficult. Quite the reverse. For as long as she could remember—which was her entire life, since both of them had grown up in McGill—Manny Gilford had treated her with only kindness and respect.

Since Stella's husband had passed away six years earlier, the sheriff had developed an almost uncanny talent for appearing out of nowhere the moment she needed a friend. Especially one with a badge.

"No, Sheriff Gilford. We got no problem a'tall," she said, deciding to cut Elmer some holiday season slack. "Mr. Yonce here was just wishin' us a Merry Christmas. He'd 'bout wrapped it up and was fixin' to move along."

The sheriff fixed his pale gray eyes on Elmer, causing the older guy to squirm. Under the lawman's suspicious, unwavering gaze, Stella's wannabe suitor withered like a well-salted slug and slithered away. He limped slightly from an old war wound—a battle that had raged many years ago between himself and a mule he had attempted to harness. Elmer had consumed the better part of a six-pack. The mule, on the other hand, had been stone sober, so he'd won the fight with one well-placed kick, which Elmer was too inebriated to dodge.

Gilford watched Elmer until he disappeared around the corner, then turned back to Stella. "If that knucklehead brings you grief, Mrs. Reid, you just let me know, and I'll put a stop to it right away. I know how he is. I get complaints on him all the time."

"He called Gran 'Sexy Stella,'" Alma piped up. "That's *not* her name!"

"But we fixed his wagon," Waycross added proudly. "I warned him how good she is at skillet smackin'."

Sheriff Gilford's gray eyes twinkled. "Yes, son, your grandmother's skill with a cast-iron frying pan is pretty much legendary in these parts. If I could do what she does with a skillet, I wouldn't need to carry a gun."

Savannah stepped forward. Her bright blue eyes glowed with admiration and something akin to infatuation as she looked up at the sheriff, who, even though he was in his fifties and had silver hair, was still an attractive man who cut a handsome figure in his sharp, crisply pressed uniform. "He said something downright disrespectful to my grandma," she said solemnly, "but we stuck up for her."

"I'm glad you did," Gilford replied, with a sober expression that matched the child's. "We have to look out for each other, and especially our kinfolk. What did he say that was outta line?"

"It doesn't matter," Stella interjected. "You can't take anything a weasel like that says to—"

"He said something not nice about coming down her chimney and leaving something in her stocking," Savannah replied with a knowing look that, sadly, was beyond her tender years. "We don't have a chimney, and I'm pretty sure ol' Elmer knows that. So, I reckon he meant something naughty."

It hurt Stella's heart to think of the environment her granddaughter was being raised in, one where she would understand a double entendre at her young age. The girl was growing up far too fast, thanks to her mother and the characters Shirley exposed her children to on a daily basis.

A look of anger crossed the sheriff's face, and it occurred to Stella that he was thinking the same thing.

Gilford reached over, placed his big hand on Savannah's shoulder, and gave her a quick reassuring pat. "Thank you, young lady, for reporting that offense to me. Now that you've given your statement to a law official, you don't have to worry about it or even think about it anymore. I'll deal with it now, and I assure you that Mr. Elmer Yonce will regret that he showed your grandma any disrespect. In fact, after I get done givin' him a proper talkin'-to, I reckon he'll be scared to say boo to a fine lady like your grandmother anytime in the near future."

Satisfied and happily reassured, Savannah slipped back in place behind her precious gran.

Stella was about to thank Sheriff Gilford when she saw a familiar figure sprinting up Main Street in their direction.

"Pastor O'Reilly," Gilford said when the out-of-breath runner reached them. "What's going on? Is the church on fire?"

"Worse than that," replied the minister, trying to catch his breath as he leaned on one of four municipal garbage cans evenly distributed for shoppers' use along the three-block-long city center.

"Worse than the church bein' afire?" Stella said, trying to even imagine such a thing.

"Reckon it's not quite as bad as that," Hugh O'Reilly admitted, wiping an overly abundant amount of perspiration from his brow, considering the chilly nip of winter that hung in the air. "But it's a sacrilegious felony that's been committed. That's for sure! You've gotta come see for yourself!"

The pastor and the sheriff took off down the street toward the town square two blocks away. Stella could see that a group of her townsfolk had gathered near the gazebo, with more joining by the moment.

Whatever felonious mayhem had been committed, the much-revered town square appeared to be the scene of the crime.

She felt one of her grandkids tugging at her sleeve. When she turned to them, she saw a look of nearly rapturous excitement and curiosity on her oldest grandchild's face.

"Please, oh please, can we go see what it is, Granny?" Savannah begged. "Pastor O'Reilly said it's felonious! We don't hardly ever have anything *felonious* to look at here in McGill!"

"No!" Waycross shouted at his sister, his ruddy face flushing red. "We was on our way to get Merthiolate and bandages. Gran said so."

Savannah gave her brother a suspicious look and said with all the grim authority of an FBI agent questioning a suspected serial killer, "Since when, Mr. Waycross Reid, did you get all hot 'n' bothered about buying Merthiolate?"

He scowled up at her. "Ain't hot 'n' bothered 'bout nothin'.

Just sayin' we should tend to our own bizness fore we go tendin' to other people's."

At that moment, Stella saw one of her two best friends, Elsie Dingle, join the knot of lookie-loos gathering in the square. She could tell by the way feisty Elsie was elbowing her way through the crowd to get a better view that she considered the sight to be worth the effort. The diminutive black woman might be only five feet tall, but Elsie knew how to use her otherwise abundant proportions to her advantage in a rambunctious crowd.

Anything Elsie took an acute interest in was something Stella had to see firsthand. Elsie Dingle might be the second nosiest woman in town—or *inquisitive*, as Stella preferred to call it—but Stella Reid was the Queen of Curious.

"Okay. We'll go take a look at whatever it is," Stella told her brood. Other than Waycross, who had developed that new-found hankering for medical supplies, they were eager to investigate the commotion. "But," she added in her sternest grandmother voice, "if it's somethin' awful and not fittin' for young'uns' eyes, I'll tell you to close 'em, and y'all better snap 'em shut then and there. Understand?"

Heads bobbed in eager acquiescence.

In an instant, the Reid clan was off and running, with Stella and Savannah leading the charge and Waycross bringing up the rear.

As they neared the crowd, Stella caught bits and pieces of the gossip flying about.

"Blasphemy!"

"That's what it is, all right. Plain and simple."

"A crime against Christmas itself. I can't stand it."

"Whoever would do such a thing?"

"I can't even imagine, but when the sheriff catches them, they should be horsewhipped right here in the town square, in front of everybody."

McGillians by the dozen were gathering in a tight semicircle in front of the new gazebo, their eyes wide, mouths gaping at the carnage before them.

Stella reached the front of the crowd a few steps behind Savannah, who was smaller and nimbler at darting among the sightseers.

Stella heard her granddaughter gasp. The child whirled around and looked up at her grandmother with a mixture of horror and mortification on her face.

"Oh, no! Oh, Gran," she whispered as Stella put an arm around the girl and pulled her close. "Lord help us. We're in deep doody now!"

Stella looked past her granddaughter to the town's pride and joy, the new gazebo and, more importantly, the recently acquired nativity scene, elegantly displayed for all to enjoy, with real hay and everything.

The sacred depiction of the first Christmas had been bought with monies raised by schoolchildren selling candy, teenagers washing cars, moms baking and selling cakes and cookies, and dads contributing their Christmas bonuses, and with the generous donations of members of the McGill Chamber of Commerce. All six of them.

The display was an old one, its paint faded, a few figures chipped, a couple of shepherds' fingers broken off. But without those minor flaws, the people of McGill could never have afforded such a luxury. The town council had decided that since the sheep had a broken leg and was, therefore, well behaved, the shepherds didn't need ten fingers to corral it.

Stella's next-door neighbor, Florence Bagley, had once taken a correspondence art course that she'd found advertised in the back of a magazine, so she had been given the chore of restoring the figures to their original glory. Other than one of the wise men being decidedly cross-eyed and the Virgin Mary having a downturned mouth, which made her look more disgruntled than "blessed among women," Flo had done a pretty good job.

Overall, McGillians had been thrilled with their lovely acquisition. No other town in the county had anything to rival their beautiful, darned near life-size, nativity scene.

But now . . . the unthinkable had happened.

Vandalized!

No wonder everyone was in a dither.

As Stella gazed upon the destruction wrought by desperately perverse roguery, she thought her heart had surely stopped.

Every figure, from the Virgin Mary herself to Joseph, from the shepherds and wise men to the sheep and the donkey, and even the angel hovering above them all—every single member of the holy entourage was sporting a mustache.

And not just a simple under-the-nose dusting of whiskers, either.

The elaborate, long, sweeping black mustaches curled upward at the ends, then around and around in a series of ever-tightening spirals.

It was truly a sight to behold.

Even baby Jesus himself was thus adorned.

"I wanna know who did this!" Sheriff Gilford exclaimed as he stood next to the manger, pointing at the ruins. "Whoever you are, step forward and own up to it right now. If I have to come after you, you'll be in a whirlwind of trouble."

Stella could scarcely breathe. She could almost feel the mustachioed Virgin gazing at her with painted eyes that were filled with disappointment and sorrow.

Having been born with the divine gift of Preeminent Nosiness, Stella had solved many crimes in McGill. Single-handedly, she had uncovered the villain who had plundered Miss Abigail's fine flower garden on the evening before the county rose competition. She had solved the cases of the Ex-Lax-laced brownies at the church social of '69 and the unsettling appearance of outhouses on the tops of barns on homecoming night in '78.

But Stella Reid didn't need to use any of her finely honed detecting skills to solve the crime at hand.

Far too many times before, she had seen this particular artist's distinctive work. Facial hair adornment was his stock-in-trade. His signature flourish—mustaches with tightly wound spiral ends.

His artwork had adorned the newspapers and magazines in her home, a few books and, one dark night, even a page in her precious family Bible. Yes, Adam and Eve's wardrobe of fig leaves had been accessorized by these unique spiraled cookie dusters.

Much to Stella's and the young artist's distress.

Her distress when she had discovered the unwelcome adornment. *His* when she had taken him behind the henhouse and introduced the seat of his britches to a freshly cut switch.

Not because of his art, but because he had lied about it when questioned.

There was one thing that every Reid kid knew: Granny didn't abide lying.

As Stella looked down at Savannah, she could tell by the look on her granddaughter's face that she, too, had solved this mystery in an instant.

In fact, all her grandchildren had turned and were staring at their brother, whose face was flushing nearly as red as his mop of curly hair.

He looked like a fox caught in the corner of a henhouse, with a flapping chicken in his jaws.

Stella took one step toward the nine-year-old culprit, and a second later, all she saw was a copper streak as he wriggled through the crowd and darted down the closest alley between the tavern and the pool hall.

Someone grabbed Stella's arm. She turned to see Elsie standing next to her, a look of concern on her round bronze face. But her coffee-colored eyes sparkled with good-natured humor as she said, "Go tend to your scoundrel of a grandson, Sister Stella. I'll haul the rest of your crew back to your house and get some supper on the stove for 'em."

"Would you mind much?" Stella asked, knowing the answer. When it came to helping her fellow man, Elsie didn't mind a bit. She'd do anything for a friend, and if Elsie had an enemy in the world, Stella was sure she'd do right by him, too.

Elsie Dingle was one of the few people Stella had met who actually worked hard at living the life everybody talked about in church.

"Wouldn't mind a bit," was the generous answer.

Elsie expertly herded the Reid youngsters into a manageable huddle. Stella wasn't surprised at her skill. Elsie had been present the day Savannah was born, and although she had never been blessed with children of her own, she had performed the services of a surrogate grandma for the gang more times than Stella could count.

Elsie glanced toward the now-empty alley in which Waycross had disappeared. "I recognized your little booger's handiwork the minute I saw it," she said with a wave of a hand toward the nativity scene. "You best go grab him before he reaches the Mexico border."

"Naw," Stella replied with a soft chuckle. "I know right where that child's headed. 'Tain't as far as all that."

Chapter 2

During the more than half a century of her life spent in McGill, Georgia, Stella had often wondered why her hometown had more cemeteries than grocery stores, schools, churches, or even taverns.

At first glance, it might seem that people did more dying than living in McGill. But in the end, Stella had decided that she'd seen far more people leave McGill than arrive. It wasn't the sort of town that people relocated to, seeking a better way of life for themselves and their families.

When the population of McGill wavered, it generally dropped rather than rose.

To the consternation of parents and grandparents of grown children, most of their offspring moved away after graduating from high school. Either they escaped to college campuses out of the area or they designed more anonymous lives for themselves in the cities of Atlanta, Chattanooga, or Nashville.

Then there were the others who left McGill by establishing a permanent residence in one of several cemeteries outside of town.

The oldest of those graveyards was St. Michael's, situated just out of town, on a hill overlooking the river. St. Michael's was established before the Civil War, and its population included soldiers who had died fighting in that bloody conflict and their wives and children who had died when Sherman cut his bloody path through Georgia. Those tombstones showed the gradual but inevitable ravages of time, their inscriptions becoming less readable with each passing decade.

Even as a child, Stella had walked the rows of that cemetery, smelling the rich mustiness of the place, feeling the too seldom groomed grass swishing against her ankles, reading the names on the stones, most of which she eventually memorized. Entire families had perished during those dark years, and smaller towns, like McGill, had never fully recovered.

The gnarled oaks dripped their gray Spanish moss onto the weathered stones, adding a feeling of graceful melancholy to the place. The lacy moss softened the hard look of the tombstones, as though lending a maternal, feminine touch to the otherwise cold and forbidding setting.

The elegant draping graced every tombstone, ancient and recent, without partiality, sharing its gentle beauty with all who rested in that peaceful place. It touched the large, imposing statues of weeping angels and those of soldiers brandishing their battle swords, as well as the simple headstones of the poor, less celebrated, but just as loved sons of Georgia.

Like Arthur Reid.

The sun was beginning to set as Stella passed through the wrought-iron gates and entered the graveyard. She gave her customary brief nod to the statue of Michael the Archangel, who, for as long as she could remember, had been fighting and subduing the mighty dragon serpent at his feet by piercing its head with a sword that was longer than the angel was tall.

In her time, Stella had seen far too many acts committed by the likes of that old serpent. She figured that any being, like Michael, who could keep Satan under control—even for a season—was all right in her book.

With a heavy, troubled heart, she headed toward the rear of the cemetery, where the dates on the gravestones were the 1900s rather than the 1800s.

Where her Irish father and Cherokee mother were buried.

Where her husband, Arthur, had been buried six years ago.

Where Stella knew she would find her grandson.

The small-for-his-age, copper-topped boy was right where she knew he would be, in front of the simple tombstone that bore the inscription:

ARTHUR REID
AUGUST 7, 1928–OCTOBER 26, 1976
BELOVED HUSBAND, FATHER, AND GRANDFATHER
AT LAST, A WELL-DESERVED REST

The child sat on the dew-damp ground, his knees drawn up to his chin, his thin arms wrapped around his shins. He was shivering from the cold, and from more than a little fear, Stella suspected.

A curious, energetic, and highly creative child, Waycross had pulled off some doozies in his life. *But no doubt about it*, Stella thought as she approached the boy, *this one plumb beats all*.

Her heart softened when she realized he was crying. Sobbing, even. His small shoulders were heaving hard and fast. His face was pressed against his knobby knees.

He wasn't even conscious of her presence until she knelt on the grass beside him.

When she touched his shoulder, he jumped and pulled back,

then looked up at her with eyes the same shade of brilliant blue as her own and wide with alarm.

"Don't worry, little one," she said. "We're just gonna talk, you and me. We've got us a problem, and between the two of us, we're gonna figure out the best way to solve it. Okay?"

"Okay, Gran."

Stella watched as relief took the place of fear on his delicate features.

After sitting on the ground, she pulled him onto her lap and began to gently rock him. As he snuggled in, she couldn't help thinking of her husband, six feet beneath them, and how sad it was that he was the closest thing to a male figure that this little boy could turn to in a time of trouble.

Six years ago, Arthur had left them, taken in a terrible tractor accident while working their small farm on the other side of town. Stella and everyone who loved him had thought their lives had ended along with his.

The townsfolk of McGill had never seen a funeral with so many attendees or so many tears shed. It had been an enormous outpouring of grief for the gentle man who had quietly touched so many lives with his acts of kindness.

"Art Reid pulled my car out of a ditch with his tractor one cold night in the pouring-down rain. Wouldn't take a dollar for it, neither," one mourner had said.

"He spent a whole Saturday helping me pull the automatic transmission outta my old Buick, and you know what a hateful, backbreaking job that can be. Didn't even cuss when it slipped and danged near tore off three of his knuckles, neither."

"He's the 'friend that sticks closer than a brother' that Proverbs talks about," another said. "He gave me five dollars for gas when I needed it bad. Found out later it was the last money he had in the world. What's more, when I tried to pay him back, he wouldn't hear of it."

"Didn't tell ever'body in town he gave it to you, neither," someone added, "like some do. They help you out one time, and you never hear the end of it. But Art 'tweren't like that. He wasn't the sort to do you a favor, then throw it up to you later on."

Indeed, Arthur Reid had been well loved, respected, and missed. But his chief mourners, by far, were his wife and grandchildren.

Little Waycross had been only three years old when his grandfather passed. But, although the boy had no distinct memories of him, he cherished every good word, every kind story he had ever heard spoken about Gramps. Waycross Reid was fiercely proud of the man who had been his grandfather.

Perhaps, Stella surmised, his attachment to his grandfather was because he had so few reasons to be proud of his own father. Sadly, the boy and all the Reid family members were reminded of Macon Reid's shortcomings daily. Such were the trials of living in a small town filled with people who had plenty of opinions but precious little common sense about when, where, or how to state them.

She brushed the auburn curls from the boy's forehead, placed her hand beneath his chin, and forced him to look up at her. "You out here talkin' to your grandpa?" she asked.

He sniffed. "Yes, ma'am."

"I thought so. Bendin' his ear 'bout all your problems?"

Waycross shook his head. "No. That'd take way too long. I was just lettin' him know 'bout this last one. The worst one."

"What'd he have to say 'bout it?"

"Not much. I'd just got done fillin' 'im in when you showed up."

Stella suppressed a chuckle. "Sorry. Didn't mean to interrupt an important conversation like that."

"It's okay. Gramps don't mind. He likes it when you come to see him. He misses you somethin' fierce."

At first, Stella thought her grandson was teasing. But when she looked into his eyes, she saw a level of sincerity that shocked her.

Could there be more to Waycross's graveside visits than she had considered?

"He told you that?" she asked. "Gramps told you that he misses me?"

The boy nodded vigorously, setting his curls abob. "All the time."

Stella gulped, trying to swallow the lump forming in her throat. "Well, ain't that interestin'. What else does your grandpa tell you?"

"He said he likes your new hairdo. It reminds him of the way you wore your hair back when you and him was courtin'."

A shiver skittered down Stella's back, and it had nothing to do with the damp earth she was sitting on or the brisk twilight air. She had, indeed, worn her hair in much the same fashion when she and Art had first started keeping company. Back then, she had worn it long and loose about her shoulders, because that was the way he preferred it. Now the carefree style was born of necessity and a lack of time to primp and crimp while providing part-time care for a herd of grandkids.

But there was no way for little Waycross to have known that. Only a couple of old black-and-white photos remained of that era of her life, and she was pretty sure her grandson had seen neither of them.

"I didn't know you came here to have actual conversations with your grandpa," she said. "I thought it was just so you could be close to him."

"That too," he replied. "But Gramps is a smart guy. He gives good advice. You should try it yourself sometime."

Stella tried to get her mind around the idea that her grandson had some sort of spiritual connection with her departed husband. But she reminded herself that she shouldn't be surprised. Art had always put his family above everything, helping them in every way he could. It wasn't so hard to believe that he would continue to do so from the other side.

"What sort of advice does Gramps give you?" she asked.

"Mostly, he tells me to mind you and always do what you say, 'cause you're smart and won't lead me wrong."

"That *is* good advice."

"But he tells me I shouldn't do everything that Mama says to do, 'cause some of it's against the law, and I could wind up in the hoosecow."

"I think that's *hoosegow*. It means 'jail.'"

"I know what it means, and I don't wanna go there."

"Why would you go to jail for doin' somethin' your mama tells you to do?" she asked, suddenly quite concerned.

"'Cause Sheriff Gilford takes a dim view of stuff like snatchin' cigarettes at the service station."

"Your mama told you to . . . what?"

"She told me to act like I need to use the station's toilet, and then she'd pretend she was having problems pumpin' the gas so that ol' Mr. Warren would come out to help her. Then she wanted me to go in and take some of her favorite cigarettes out from behind his counter."

Stella felt her blood pressure rising by the second. She ached to get her hands on her daughter-in-law and, at the same moment, was thankful she couldn't. How dare that woman involve this innocent child in her own illegal shenanigans!

"Have you actually done that, sweet cheeks?" she asked the boy. "You can tell me the truth. It's okay. Have you gone and snatched cigarettes from ol' Mr. Warren? If you have, I won't hold it against you, 'cause it weren't your idea."

"Nope. I told her a little fib. Pretended I couldn't find her brand. She was mad, but at least I didn't get a whuppin' for not doing what she said."

"She would have whupped you for not doing it?"

He nodded.

"How do you know that?"

"'Cause she told me so, and she had that look in her eye. The kind she gets when she means business."

For the child's sake, Stella fought to keep her temper under control. The last thing he needed was to have the adults he loved at each other's throats. But that was exactly what she wanted to be. At Shirley Reid's throat, strangling her until her eyes bugged out on stems like those of some cartoon character who had just seen something startling.

"I know it's a sin to lie," Waycross said, continuing his confession, "but I figured it was better than stealin'. I could've got in bad trouble for thievin', but all I got was one smack on the head for not doin' what she told me."

"You done good, darlin'. Real good. I'm proud of you." Stella fought back tears as she pressed a kiss to his forehead and promised herself that she would deal with this problem as soon as she settled the issue of the Holy Family's unsightly facial hair.

She drew a deep breath and said, "Speakin' of wrongdoings, we need to address the problem at hand. The one you created when you decided to take a paintbrush to—"

"A marker."

"What?"

"I used a marker. Paint works okay for beards, but a marker's better for mustaches."

"I shudder to think of how you became such an expert."

"You said it was okay to draw them. You said it looked funny."

"I said it was okay for you to draw them on magazines and newspapers after I'd done read 'em. But, as I'm sure you remember, I draw a line at Bible folk. Remember the Adam and Eve incident?"

"Yes, ma'am." Tears filled his eyes.

"Then why did you do it, punkin? Those figures belong to the whole town. Why would you think it was okay for you to deface public property like that?"

He shrugged. "I didn't know I was defacin' nothin'. I just wanted to make people laugh. You laughed when I put mustaches on the president and Queen Elizabeth."

"Yes, but that was in my magazine, not the town's manger scene. What do you reckon we oughta do to set this situation straight?"

He looked up at her with wide, frightened eyes. "We gotta *do* somethin'?"

"Sure we do. We can't just pretend nothin' happened, and that we don't know squat about it."

Tears began to stream down his face, and she could feel his small body trembling against hers. "Do we have to tell them, Gran?" he asked. "Do I have to fess up?"

"That's usually best under circumstances like these."

"But it wouldn't be the best. Not this time. It would be plumb awful."

"I don't think it'd be so bad. Most folks hold a body in high regard if they admit they did something wrong and want to set it right."

"Not me," he said, shaking his head. "Nobody in this town is ever gonna hold none of us Reids in high regard, no matter what we do."

Stella felt like someone had just shoved something cold and sharp between her ribs. "Why would you say such a thing, Waycross?"

"You know," he said, with eyes too old for his years. "Because of my mom and my dad. Because of . . . the way they are."

"How's that, darlin'?" she asked, dreading the answer. Of course, she knew better than her grandson what her son's and daughter-in-law's reputations were, but she needed to know how much he knew and understood.

"They say," he began, "that my mom's afraid that barstool— the one under Elvis's picture—is gonna float away if she ain't holdin' it down night and day."

"What do you think of that, sugar?"

"I think it's dumb, 'cause that stool's bolted to the floor. I checked myself one night, when I went in there to tell her to come home."

"I see."

"And they say my dad's always keepin' the road hot in his truck, drivin' all over the country, 'cause he'd rather be away from his wife and kids so's he can chase skirts."

The feeling of something sharp and cold stabbed even more deeply into Stella's chest. She was sure it was piercing her heart. "What do you reckon that means," she asked him, "when they say that?"

He shrugged. "I don't know. That sounds dumb, too. He's a guy. What would he want with a skirt? Besides, skirts don't run down the road on their own, now do they? Why would anybody need to chase one?"

"I agree, sweetheart. In all my born days, I've yet to see a skirt of any kind hightail it down a street." She kissed the top of his head, breathing in the precious boy smell of him. "It sounds to me like whatever folks in this town are sayin' 'bout us Reids is a bunch of hooey and not worth gettin' ourselves in a dither about. Okay?"

"I just don't want to confess my crime to anybody, 'cause it'll add to all the hooey."

Stella thought it over long and hard, weighing the value of teaching the child the consequences of a transgression versus adding to the burden of shame he already carried.

Finally, she said, "I think I've got a solution to this problem. A way you can atone for your crime without the town gossips gettin' all in a tizzy."

He looked up at her, painfully hopeful. "What way's that, Gran?"

"You'll see. It requires you putting that artistic flair of yours to work, and some old-fashioned sneakiness on both our parts. Reckon you're up for it?"

Grinning broadly, he said, "Yes, ma'am. Let's git 'er done!"

Chapter 3

Before Stella could begin the process of helping her miscreant grandson atone for his felonious behavior, she decided to stop by her house and see how Elsie was faring with the rest of the horde. Elsie had used Stella's old Mercury panel truck, as the rear had been outfitted with seven seats and was the only vehicle in McGill, other than the town's one school bus, that could transport all the Reid young'uns at once in a halfway safe manner.

Therefore, Stella had the pleasure of driving Elsie's red 1965 Mustang on her way home. As she pulled onto the dirt road leading to her small shotgun house, Stella marveled at the ease of driving a smaller vehicle with good brakes and only one quiet child inside it.

But even as she enjoyed the simpler, easier scenario, she reminded herself that there wasn't a single one of those seven kids she would trade for their weight in gold. Or for a ton of the stuff, for that matter.

"Simple" wasn't always the sweetest.

"I thought we was taking me to a place where I can right my

wrongs and amend my evil ways," Waycross said, a bit concerned, when he realized where they were headed.

"We are," Stella assured him. "But first, we gotta run inside and make sure that Elsie's got things in hand. Plus, you might need a potty break before we get down to the nitty-gritty of you payin' your debt to society."

Waycross giggled. "I'm a boy, Gran. I can take a potty break anyplace, anytime. All I need's a bush that's thirsty."

"Be that as it may. We ain't heathens. You'll use the outhouse like proper, civilized folk."

She drove the Mustang to the front of the house and carefully parked it next to her old truck. "Besides," she continued, "I thought we'd asked Savannah to join us. Might be good to have her along. That girl has a knack for skullduggery."

"Savannah digs up skulls?"

Stella laughed. "Not that I know of, but I wouldn't put it past her. *Skullduggery* means 'bein' tricky and crafty.'"

"Sneaky?"

"That too."

"Then Savannah's perfect for a skullduggery job. She's sneaky as they come, and then some."

"Now, now." She reached into the back seat and grabbed her purse. "Keep your words kind and soft when describin' your sister. Miss Savannah *is* downright gifted when it comes to bein' sneaky. But she uses her powers for good. Most of the time. Once in a while, a body's gotta use their God-given wiles and cunning when they're fightin' on the side of the angels."

Together, they hurried up the rickety steps and onto the porch, where the chains on Stella's beloved bench swing were creaking as an ever increasingly cold wind rounded the corner of the house and blew against it.

"You grab Vidalia's warm coat, too," she told him. "You're gonna need it."

"I don't wanna wear that thing," he whined. "It's a girl's coat. It's *purple*!"

"I understand, but that wind's pickin' up somethin' fierce. It's gonna be dark where we're goin'. Nobody'll see you."

"But what if they do and they laugh at me? I get laughed at enough for my hair being red and my freckles."

"If anybody sees you and dares to laugh at you, I'll give 'em a smack upside the head. Okay?"

He grinned up at her with a snaggletoothed smile that set her heart aglow in spite of the winter wind.

"Okay," he said. "It'd be worth havin' 'em poke fun at me just to see you whack 'em." As they opened the door and started to walk inside, the boy paused and said, "You gonna bring your skillet, Gran? Just in case?"

"Not this time, grandson. If the need should arise, the good Lord will supply a weapon."

"'Cause you'd be fightin' on the side of His angels, right?"

"Exactly right."

Stella looked around, and as always when she left the children in Elsie's care, the house was quiet, orderly, and filled with a gentle peace, which seemed to follow Elsie Dingle wherever she went. That was one of the things that made Elsie a great friend and occasional babysitter.

Another was her ability to bake the best coconut cakes and apple pies in the county.

Stella and Waycross made their way through the long, narrow house, which was built in typical "shotgun" fashion, without the luxury of hallways, one room leading into another. The style was rumored to have been given its name because one could fire a gun through the front door and the bullet would exit through the back door without striking a wall.

They passed through the living room, Stella's bedroom, then the children's bedroom, and made their way to the kitchen, where the other six grandchildren sat at Stella's chrome dining table, with its red mother-of-pearl Formica surface and matching leatherette chairs. On the wall nearby, a clock the size and shape of a black cat, with green rhinestone eyes, twitched its tail, marking the passage of time in the Reid household. The clock was one of Stella's treasures, as her oldest grandchild had bought it for her with money she had earned doing menial labor for her neighbors.

Savannah had always demonstrated a generous nature and a willingness to work hard, to go along with her nosiness and crafty wiles. Stella considered it proof that most people were a combination of saint and sinner.

Savannah sat at one end of the table, Elsie at the other. Elsie was calmly dishing up seconds of mashed potatoes and thin slices of meat loaf served Elsie style, with plenty of catsup sweetened with a bit of brown sugar.

The table was uncharacteristically quiet, with each child shoveling in the food, as though it might disappear at any moment, before they had their fill.

Stella couldn't help wondering how long it had been since they had enjoyed a nutritious, hot meal. Too many times she had looked into Shirley's refrigerator, only to find beer and condiments that were long past their expiration dates.

The moment Elsie saw Stella, she jumped to her feet and offered the chair she had been occupying.

"Here you go," she said. "I was just finishing up. I'll get you a fresh plate and—"

"No, no. You just sit still and finish your dinner peaceful like. We are in no rush. Unless you need to get home . . ."

A slight look of sadness crossed Elsie's round, childlike face. "I got nobody and nothin' much to rush home to, if it's all the same to you," she said.

"That's good, 'cause I was gonna ask if I could impose on you to hang around awhile longer. Mr. Waycross and me, we got us some business to attend to, if you wouldn't mind holdin' down the fort a bit longer."

Elsie brightened in an instant. "Oh, I can stay all night, if you want. I could sleep on the couch if needs be."

In her peripheral vision, Stella saw Waycross flinch. She smiled to herself. The couch was Waycross's bed—at his expressed request. A few months ago, he had laid down the law and proclaimed himself "too old to sleep in a room full of girls anymore."

Considering the tough evening he had endured so far, Stella couldn't bear the thought of ousting him from the "bed" he was so proud of. Even a gentle-natured fellow could take only so much trauma in a twenty-four-hour period.

"That's okay, Sister Elsie." Stella put her hand on Elsie's shoulder and eased her back onto the chair. "It won't take all night, this little chore of ours. We'll get 'er done lickety-split and be back before you know it."

"Unless Waycross gets his butt arrested," Marietta interjected, speaking around a mouthful of mashed potatoes.

"Don't talk with food in your mouth, Marietta," Stella told her. "And don't use strong language at the dinner table—or anyplace else, for that matter."

Marietta made a big show of swallowing the potatoes and rinsing them down with a gulp of water, then restated her case with haughty authority. "Unless Waycross gets his *hind end* thrown in prison and rots there for the rest of his life, 'cause we ain't got enough money to bail him out with."

"That does it!" Savannah reached over and grabbed her sister by the front of her shirt and shook her soundly. "You shut your mean, nasty mouth, Marietta Reid, or I swear, I'll slap you neked and hide your clothes!"

In an instant, a shirt-yanking, hair-pulling affray was well under way.

"Girls!" Stella exclaimed as she rushed to separate her beloved grandchildren before they could do serious bodily harm to each other. With no Merthiolate or bandages in the house, bloodshed simply wasn't to be tolerated.

But before she could reach them, Elsie had taken control of the room in her natural gracious way. "Anybody want some apple pie? There's ice cream to go with it. But only if you're sittin' in your seat quietly and not tearing your sister's hair outta her head or ripping her clothes off."

In a heartbeat, complete and utter silence reigned.

Gentle smiles decorated both Savannah's and Marietta's faces.

The little boogers look plumb angelic, Stella thought. *Ah, the power of pie à la mode.*

"For everybody's information," she said, "Waycross ain't going to no jail. He's just got a little chore he needs to do, and it's nobody's business but his own."

She gave Waycross a nudge toward the empty chair, where he usually sat. "Park yerself over there, grandson, and shovel down some of Elsie's good meat loaf and mashed potatoes while you got the chance. I'm gonna run next door to Flo's house and pick up a couple of things. When I get back, you and me's gonna address that issue that nobody needs to talk about. Not one solitary word."

She looked around the table at the curious faces, which included Elsie's.

Turning to Savannah, she said, "If Miss Elsie don't need you here to help with dishes, baths, and such, Waycross and me would like to have you join us for our little excursion."

Savannah brightened, her deep blue eyes twinkling, at the prospect of an adventure. She looked pleadingly at Elsie.

Waving a dismissive hand, Elsie said, "Oh, she can go along, if she's a mind to. We can get by without her for once. Miss Marietta can give me a hand with the little 'uns."

Instantly, Marietta scowled, dropped her fork onto her plate with a clatter, and propped her hands on her hips. "How come stupid, ugly ol' Savannah gets to go, and I have to stay here and do her work?"

"She's goin' because *I asked her to*," Stella replied, her voice soft and low, but stern. "And the next time you let an ugly word come out of your mouth when addressing one of your siblings, Miss Marietta, you're gonna find yourself chewin' on a bar of Ivory soap. As you may recall, you ain't fond of the flavor."

"No," Vidalia said with a snicker, "Mari's partial to Camay, 'cause it's for bee-u-tee-ful women."

"Then how come *she* uses it?" chimed in usually docile Alma.

"'Cause Marietta thinks she's sooo bee-u-tee-ful, like the women in the magazine pictures," Vidalia explained, striking a glamorous profile pose for all to appreciate.

"Not another word, any of you, if you want some of Miss Elsie's pie." Stella leaned across the table and passed the platter with its one remaining slice of meat loaf to Waycross. Her own tummy rumbled at the sight. She reassured her empty stomach that there were plenty of mashed potatoes left.

As though reading her mind, Elsie said, "I'll put you back a piece of pie, Sister Stella, and I'll save you some ice cream for when you get back from your . . . uh . . . chore."

"Thank you, darlin'." Stella patted her friend's shoulder. "I'll look forward to that. See you all later, and you young'uns best mind your manners. If I hear you've been naughty for Miss Elsie, we'll be havin' us a mighty *serious* reckoning first thing tomorrow mornin'."

Stella didn't recall ever having to actually deliver a "serious reckoning" to any of her grandkids. In fact, not even she herself knew for sure what such a thing would consist of. But considering the ferocious gleam in her eye when she announced the threat, they lived in mortal terror of receiving one, and that was usually enough to keep them from maiming one another.

Years ago, Granny had decided that the proper disciplining of children was 99 percent love and 1 percent making sure they were terrified to cross you.

Chapter 4

Leaving the children in Elsie's more than capable hands, Stella hurried outside into the winter darkness. She debated about whether or not to drive the truck, since it was a bit colder than usual for a December night in Georgia. But she had left her purse in the house, and having no keys handy, she decided to just walk across the small field that separated her house from Florence and Bud Bagley's home.

As the Bagleys had been Stella's nearest neighbors for more than thirty years, and Florence had been her close friend since childhood, Stella knew the couple well. Too well, when it came to being privy to their frequent squabbles and occasional knock-down-drag-outs.

Mostly, it was Flo who got knocked down. Stella dreaded the day she might hear that her neighbor had also been dragged out.

Bud wasn't popular in the town. Too many people had been on the receiving end of his temper—a temper that was bad on a good day and worse on a bad one.

Liquor consumption didn't help.

Bud wasn't a happy drunk. Alcohol brought out the worst in

his surly, troublesome disposition. Most folks in McGill were leery of him and gave him a wide berth.

Some were downright afraid of Bud Bagley.

Stella wasn't one of them.

One day shortly after Arthur had died, when Stella was in the depths of her grief and fresh out of patience, Florence had come running across the field, her nose bleeding profusely, half scared to death, seeking help.

Stella had promptly called Sheriff Gilford, but before he could arrive, an angry Bud had come to retrieve his wayward, disobedient wife. When pounding on the back door hadn't worked, he'd kicked it open.

Unfortunately for him, Stella had been cleaning the skillet she'd just fried the Sunday chicken in and had it in her hand when Bud burst through the broken door and into her kitchen.

By the time the tale of the "Stella Reid Skillet Massacre" had been passed along to every household in McGill, it had been revised, embellished, and amended until there were several versions of the "gospel truth."

By some accounts, Bud had rushed into the house and, as bad luck would have it, had run face-first, several times, into Stella's fourteen-inch cast-iron skillet.

The stories on the other end of the spectrum included her chasing him out of the house and across the field to his home, skillet bashing him all the while, and doing so much damage that it took Doc Hynson four hours and over a hundred stitches to close him up.

Some more creative eyewitnesses swore that when they saw him stumbling into Doc's office, part of his brain matter was hanging out of his right ear.

Stella knew that the actual, honest-to-goodness truth lay somewhere in the middle. But most importantly, she knew that Bud Bagley was a bully, plain and simple. When she'd walloped him upside the head with that frying pan, she had seen real fear in his eyes.

Terror, in fact, and more than a little surprise.

Bud Bagley wasn't used to being stood up to.

Especially by a woman.

A couple of good, solid whacks and he had backed right down. But then, most people would have, she recalled as she walked up the Bagleys' driveway, toward their house. That particular skillet was the one she used to fry chicken for seven hungry kids. It was mighty heavy, and she hadn't exactly held back when she clobbered him with it. Twice. There in her kitchen.

Since that day, Bud had avoided his utensil-wielding neighbor and, better still, had backed off a bit on his wife thumping. So, all in all, Stella figured that giving Bud a bit of what he had coming was time and energy well spent.

The memory brought a smirk to her face as she approached the large brick home, with its wide veranda and fine paved driveway. It was a far cry from her little hovel of a house, rickety porch, and dirt road.

But Stella didn't mind. She hadn't minded when she and Arthur bought the place from the Bagleys over thirty years ago. It had been her first adult home, her only adult home, and she wouldn't have had it any other way.

More than once it had occurred to her that she would have much preferred to spend her life in her shotgun shack, with Arthur Reid sitting at the breakfast table with her and sleeping beside her on their humble featherbed, than to live in this elegant brick home, with its fancy shutters, wrought-iron fences . . . and Bud.

Even without Art, her life was better than her friend's.

No, Stella Reid wouldn't trade places with Florence Bagley for the world.

As though to reinforce her convictions, as she approached the house, Stella saw the front door crash open and Bud Bagley rush out. Yelling crude insults over his shoulder at Florence, who was standing in the open doorway, her hand over her mouth, Bud made his way to his oversize pickup, parked in front of the house. Bud was famous for his monster pickup, with its custom bright blue metal-flake paint job.

The townsfolk could see Bud Bagley coming a mile off, and that was just the way he liked it.

He yanked the door of his ugly big truck open, climbed inside, and seconds later came roaring down the driveway toward Stella.

She barely had time to scramble to the side to avoid being hit.

For just a moment, she caught a glimpse of Bud's face, glowing green from the lights of his truck's dashboard. The view was brief, but it was clear enough for her to tell that he was drunk and furious.

Both were all-too-common conditions for the well-off man who owned the town's largest gas station, not to mention its only grocery store and pool hall.

Once Bud was out of sight, Stella turned her attention to her friend, who was still standing in the doorway, holding her hand over her mouth. By the porch light, Stella could tell that Flo was crying. She could also see that her friend had spotted her approaching the house and didn't look happy about it.

Stella chided herself for not phoning Flo before dropping by. Folks in McGill seldom called to ask permission before stopping at one another's houses. Southern hospitality favored an open-door policy toward all.

But Stella reminded herself that the Bagleys' home wasn't as hospitable as most.

Houses that harbored secrets of a violent nature seldom were.

"Evenin', Flo," Stella called out. Her cheery tone sounded fake, even to her.

"Hey, Stella," was the lackluster reply. "How're you this evening?"

Stella stepped up onto the veranda, and Flo opened the door wider, inviting her inside. Though she still had her hand across her mouth.

Stella noticed that her eyes were red and swollen from crying, and her usually perfect hairdo was badly mussed.

"Actually, we've done better," Stella told her as she walked into the foyer and Flo closed the door behind her. "That's why I'm here. I was wondering if you could help me out with somethin'. Me and mine are in a bit of a pickle."

Flo lowered her hand from her face, and Stella was alarmed to see that her lip was bleeding.

"Oh, darlin'. That's gotta hurt."

"No. It's nothing much."

Stella gave her a sad, understanding smile, but Florence looked away and headed toward the back of the house and the kitchen. "I hit myself with a cupboard door a while ago, when I was taking down some plates. It's no big deal."

Following her into the kitchen, Stella weighed the pros and cons of once again getting involved in her neighbor's marital problems. It didn't take long for her to make her decision. Stella

Reid had never been one for standing in the bleachers and watching life play out on the field below.

Right or wrong, wise or foolish, she got involved. Even if it meant that from time to time, she paid a penalty.

"You didn't smack yourself in the mouth with a door, Florence," she said as she watched her friend tear a paper towel from the roll, wet it, and dab at the blood. "You and me both know it, so don't go insultin' my intelligence. That man of yours slugged you in the mouth, and that *is* a big deal. A real big deal."

Florence tossed the bloody paper towel into the garbage. "This one was my fault," she said sheepishly. "I knew this morning that he was low on beer, but I forgot to bring some home with me from the store. He works hard. He's under a lot of stress, and he really looks forward to his beers when he gets home."

"That's a heap and a half of hooey. If anybody's under stress in this household, I'd say it's the one who gets beat up for something stupid like forgettin' to restock a grown man's beer. You work as many hours in that store as he does. Most days, even more. Why can't he remember to cart his own beer home if it's that all-fired important to him?"

"That's not how things work around here," Florence replied in a voice so flat and lifeless that it broke Stella's heart just to hear her words.

She could remember when Florence was young and positively bubbling over with the joy of life. She was the prettiest and most popular girl in town.

Because she was so pretty and lively, she had nabbed herself the "richest" man in town. Florence's mother had been overjoyed!

Florence and Bud had had the fanciest wedding that McGill had ever seen, with real white doves flying as they drove away. They had even honeymooned at Niagara Falls.

Florence had been miserable ever since. Every year, her life energy appeared to be seeping out of her at a faster and faster rate. Stella couldn't remember the last time she had seen Florence smiling and carefree.

Stella walked over to her friend, placed her hands on either side of Florence's face, and turned it toward the light so she could see her wound better. "Your lip's busted, sugar," she told her. "It's gonna leave a scar."

Florence gave a bitter little laugh with no mirth in it and shook her head. "Bud's getting sloppy in his old age. Used to, he was careful to hit me only in places it wouldn't show. Under my clothes."

"Yeah, that so-called out-of-control temper of his. The one he got from his no-good daddy and says he can't help. If he was smart enough and in control enough to hit you where it wouldn't show, he'd be able to just go for a walk or somethin' to work off his anger and not hit you at all."

Florence sighed, suddenly looking tired and annoyed. "We've had this talk many times before, Stella. We wind up going in circles. You need to stay out of it. Bud still hates you for hitting him that time. He'll never get over you making him a laughingstock like that. He still gets teased about it, folks making skillet jokes and such."

Stella couldn't suppress a little snicker. She had to admit that, in her opinion, beaning Bud Bagley with a frying pan was one of the ten top accomplishments of her life, and the memory never failed to bring a smile to her face and a ray of sunlight to her spirit.

"Don't laugh about it! There's nothing funny about it!" Florence said with a degree of fear and urgency that startled Stella. "My marriage isn't your business, and if you don't stay out of it, you could get yourself hurt. Bad."

Stella thought long and hard before she answered. When she did, she fought to keep her face as blank and her voice as even as she could, hiding her own emotions of anger, frustration, and helplessness.

"You're right, Flo. It's *your* marriage, *your* business. If you truly want me to stay out of it, I'll just bite my tongue and not say another word to you about it ever again."

Florence gave her a small, sweet smile filled with affection and even a bit of good humor. It softened her face, and just for a moment, Stella caught a glimpse of her old friend, the happy-go-lucky girl who had made everyone laugh every day at school.

Before she had met the "love of her life," the richest man in town.

"You couldn't keep your mouth shut if you had to, Stella Reid. You'd bite that tongue of yours clean in two, and knowing you, you'd still be able to state your piece, loud and clear, with just half a tongue."

Stella couldn't help laughing. That was one good thing about having a friend you'd known your whole life—she knew you better than you knew yourself . . . and loved you, anyway.

Florence grabbed another paper towel, walked to the refrigerator, and took an ice cube from the freezer. She wrapped it in the towel and pressed it to her wounded lip with such practiced expertise that Stella felt a chill just watching her.

"Don't fret," Florence told her. "Looks like things may work out exactly the way you'd like them to between me and Bud."

"What's *that* supposed to mean?"

"Lately, he's been talking about leaving me. He threatened to just now. That's what the big fight was about."

"I thought it was over beer."

Florence shrugged. "Most of our fights start off about something little, then slide into the bigger things. He told me that if I don't shape up, he's going to leave me flat. Can you imagine? After all these years, to just walk away from a marriage?"

Florence started to cry, and Stella couldn't imagine why.

"Let him walk! It'd be the first good thing he's done for you since he shoved that ring on your finger."

"This is you not stating your opinion, not telling me my business?" Florence chuckled, tears streaming down her face. "Ten whole seconds you held out. That has to be some kind of record for you."

"Oh, hush up. You stand there mashin' an ice cube against your busted lip and tell me it'd be a bad thing if that man walked away from you? Go ahead and see if even you believe it."

Anger flashed in Florence's eyes. "He wouldn't just leave me. He'd take everything with him. Everything we worked for. He'd kick me out of this house, *my* house. The house I dreamed up all on my own and told the contractor how to build. The house I decorated. I chose every pillow and curtain and every picture on these walls. But it's his name that's on the deed, and I'll be the one on the street, looking for some ratty house to rent and not being able to afford even that."

"But you have the store. You've worked there forty years, putting in more hours than he has."

"The store's in his name, too. His daddy left it to him, long before Bud ever married me." Florence began to cry even harder.

"I'm telling you, Stella, if he kicks me out, I'll have nothing. Absolutely nothing."

For a long time, Stella stared down at the floor, considering her next words.

Florence was right; she couldn't withhold her opinion and act like one of her closest friends' problems weren't her own.

A wiser woman probably could, she decided. A smarter woman could turn her back on a lifelong friend and still look herself in the eye the next morning in the bathroom mirror.

Unfortunately, Stella knew she would never be that wise.

She wasn't even sure she wanted to be that smarter woman.

"You'll have absolutely nothing," she said softly, "except maybe . . . safety, peace, freedom, self-respect."

Florence sniffed and shook her head. "Self-respect doesn't pay the bills."

"Unpaid bills ain't the end of the world, Flo. Lots of folks have those. Hell's bells, I've got a stack of 'em myself."

Florence turned her back to Stella, walked to the garbage can, and tossed the ice cube and paper towel into it. When she turned back around to face her friend, her eyes were cold, distant.

Stella knew the conversation about Bud was over. Again, they had talked in circles and wound up at the same sad place.

Nowhere.

Florence couldn't imagine her life without Bud and all the material things he represented. Apparently, she wasn't ready to even try to imagine such a life.

Stella knew there was absolutely nothing she could do about it, and maybe that was the way it should be. After all, who was she to advise another woman on what to do with her marriage?

What kind of world would it be if one person made such decisions for another?

"You should probably tell me why you ran over here," Florence was saying to her. "Bud could come back at any time, and when he does, you really shouldn't be here."

Stella thought of little Waycross, back at her house, waiting with fear and trembling to find out what sort of price he was going to have to pay for his transgression.

Her precious grandson was her responsibility. Not her friend Florence—lost and struggling as she might be.

For certain, Bud Bagley wasn't her burden to carry.

"You, um, might've heard . . . there was a bit of excitement in the town square today," she began.

"Waycross painted mustaches on everybody in the nativity scene," was the curt reply.

"Oh. Yes. You know?"

"I painted every one of those figures myself. At least twenty people called to tell me as soon as the vandalism was discovered. I had to take my phone off the hook."

"And you knew it was Waycross?"

"Of course."

"How?"

"Remember when Waycross took over the paper route for the Mitchell boy, after ol' man Wisecarver ran his Buick into him when he was delivering papers on his bike?"

"Yes, I recall. Waycross took that route for over a month, while the Mitchell boy's leg was in a cast," Stella said, fearing where this was leading.

"Every day of that month, whenever I picked up my paper on the front step, I was treated to your grandson's artistry."

"Oh, no."

"Oh, yes. Not even President Reagan or the First Lady was spared."

Stella couldn't help giggling at the thought of Nancy Reagan wearing one of Waycross's elaborate curly mustaches.

"It wasn't funny," Florence said, completely giggle free. "It was highly annoying. But I tolerated it because, well, because he's yours. But I wasn't the least bit happy to hear that all the hard work I did on that beautiful manger scene was wasted because your grandkid went crazy off his rocker with a black marker."

"None of us are happy about it, Flo," Stella assured her. "Least of all Waycross. He's plumb beside himself with grief and remorse about it."

"Really?"

Stella thought of how her grandkid had looked when she'd last seen him. He'd been happily gobbling down Elsie's meat loaf and mashed potatoes, gleefully anticipating apple pie topped with ice cream. "I reckon he *will be*, once I'm done with him."

"Whatever punishment you've got planned, it won't fix the damage that's been done."

"Actually, it will. That's the punishment. To fix the damage that's been done. I came over here to see if you've got any of those paints left over—the ones you used when you did the figures. We don't need much. Just a bit of flesh tone for the humans and some brown for the donkey and white for the sheep."

"You're going to have a fourth grader paint the town's nativity scene?"

Stella shrugged and grinned a bit sheepishly. "He's a very good little artist for his age, and I'll be there to supervise. I'll make sure he just covers up the mustaches. That's all. Nothing else. I promise."

Florence motioned for Stella to follow her to a guest bedroom, which she had converted into an art studio. "Okay," she said. "I'm going on the record as telling you that it's a very bad idea. If you don't keep a close eye on that little ruffian, I swear, the holy Christ Child will be wearing ruby-red lipstick and arched black eyebrows."

Chapter 5

"**H**old that flashlight steady, Savannah, darlin'. Your little brother's gettin' more paint on me and his sister's coat than he is on the Virgin Mary's face," Stella told her granddaughter as the stealthy trio labored in the cold December darkness, trying their best to set the world right and balance Lady Justice's scale.

Though eager to get to work and have the task all done and dusted, Stella, Savannah, and Waycross had postponed their chore until after nine o'clock. Figuring they were less likely to be discovered in the performance of their covert mission with the streets dark and deserted, they had waited in the truck, which Stella had parked discreetly across the street from the pool hall.

Upon hearing the stroke of nine from the belfry of the First Baptist Church on the corner, they had emerged from the truck, paint cans and brushes in hand and deadly serious looks on their faces.

By then, all the stores along Main Street had closed, even the ones that had stayed open late for holiday shoppers.

Most of the straggling die-hard patrons of the pool hall and tavern had gone home. Stella figured the few who remained would be so inebriated they wouldn't make reliable witnesses, even if they discovered the threesome working away on the figures in the crèche.

The nativity scene was dark, as all the municipal holiday decorations had been turned off at 8:00 p.m. to conserve electricity, out of respect for the town's limited budget. While the lack of light made the artistic aspect of the job more difficult, at least they weren't likely to get nabbed and thrown into jail for life for the vandalization of public property—as prophesized by Miss Doom-and-Gloom Marietta.

By the time the church clock tolled the half hour, notifying Stella that she and her family had been at their task for thirty long minutes, she was beginning to question the wisdom of forcing Waycross to do all the painting by himself.

During his confession, the child had stated that he'd managed to bewhisker the Holy Family in less than three minutes flat. But, unfortunately, permanent marker was the mini-artist's medium of choice, not acrylic paint. De-whiskering was proving to be far more difficult and time consuming.

Besides, he had performed the first act of artistic expression while in the throes of gleeful inspiration. Now he was not only obliterating his own work but paying penance, as well.

Waycross Reid was quickly learning that it took far longer to accomplish something one was forced to do than it took to follow one's own creative vision.

By the time the clock tolled ten, the threesome had made considerably more progress.

"Okay. Mary, Joseph, the wise men, the donkey, the sheep, the angel, and the shepherds are done," Stella said, wiping sweat from her brow onto her coat sleeve.

Who'd think a body could sweat so much on a cold winter night? she wondered. *Especially when their hands are numb with cold.*

"All that's left now is baby Jesus," she told Waycross. "You did say you wanted to do him last."

"I figured I should practice on the others first," he said, "so I'd be good at it by the time I got to him."

Savannah shifted her position and shone the ever-weakening flashlight beam onto the infant's face. "You'd better make it snappy, little brother, as this flashlight's about to give up the ghost any second now."

"Don't say that!" he shot back. "Don't rush me. I'm nervous enough as it is. This is serious business. I reckon God's mad enough at me already. I don't want to mess up his baby son's face and get in worse trouble than I'm already in. It's bad enough having the whole town hate you. I don't need God Almighty hating me, too."

Stella moved closer to the manger, too, as she was holding paints and brushes, assisting the artiste. "I wouldn't worry too much, if I was you," she told him. "I'm sure God doesn't hate you. I don't think He's mad at you, neither. I think He knows exactly how many hairs are on that curly red head of yours and how many freckles you've got on your nose. And I believe He loves every single one of them, hairs and freckles alike."

"But I thought this here was a mortal sin, what I did," the boy said, looking confused.

"More like youthful mischief, and not done with any sort of malice or evil intent. Believe me, Waycross Reid, there are a lot worse deeds committed every day in this sad ol' world of ours."

"Then why are we sneaking around like this," Savannah asked, "doing it in the dark and freezing our bee-hinds off?"

"Because your little brother has a hard enough time being the only carrot-top boy in town. He doesn't need to grow up with this nonsense on his head, too. He'd never hear the end of it."

Savannah nodded thoughtfully, and even in the dim light, Stella could see that she understood. In a town as small and intimate as McGill, a person's reputation was everything. Earned at an early age, it stuck for life and tended to determine one's destiny.

When it came to reputations, thanks to the shenanigans of Shirley and Macon Reid, the family's name was beat to shreds.

Savannah understood all of this. Stella couldn't help being enormously proud of her. The child was wise beyond her years. Always had been.

"I reckon you're right about that," Savannah said, jiggling the dying flashlight. "People here in town already have plenty to say about us Reids. We don't need to give them even more to wag their tongues about."

Waycross dipped Florence's best brush into the light peach–colored paint, swabbed off the excess on the edge of the can, then turned to the infant in the manger. With his tongue protruding from the corner of his mouth, his brow furrowed with concentration, Waycross knelt beside the Holy Child's improvised cradle and began his final and most important act of reparation.

But the instant he touched the brush to the baby's upper

lip, a bright light bore down on them, exposing them and their furtive activities with its harsh glare.

"Hit the deck!" Savannah exclaimed as she ducked behind the manger, dragging her little brother with her.

Stella took cover as well, behind a sheep. Peeking between its legs, she could see a vehicle coming straight toward them. It was a large car, and for a moment, Stella thought it might be the sheriff's cruiser.

"Uh-oh," she heard Savannah say. "The jig's up."

"Hit the deck? The jig's up?" Waycross whispered. "Vannah Sue, you gotta stop reading so many of them Nancy Drew books."

"Shh, both of y'all," Stella told them. "If it's the sheriff, you two keep mum and let me do all the talkin'. Ya hear?"

"You ain't gonna tell him, are you, Gran?" Waycross asked tearfully. "Marietta said he'll toss me in jail with all them real bad guys, and I'll have to stay there, hangin' out with hoodlums, till I rot."

"Marietta's full of bull-pucky. Pay her no mind and keep quiet," Stella whispered. "Sheriff Gilford ain't gonna throw no little kid in jail. Least of all you, Waycross Reid. He's a better man than that." She took a closer look at the oncoming vehicle. "Besides, I don't think it's the sheriff, anyway. There's no lights on the top of that car."

As the automobile drove by, they were all three relieved to see that Granny was right. It wasn't the dreaded police cruiser. It was a big Chrysler station wagon with wood-grain panels on the sides.

Since there was only one woody wagon in McGill, they instantly knew whose car it was.

"Oh, my goodness! It's Principal Neville," Savannah whispered. "What's he doing down here this time of night?"

Yes, what is *he up to?* Stella thought. Suspicions leapt to mind, but she kept them to herself. They weren't the sort of stories a self-respecting grandma shared with her grandkids.

Rumors concerning Jake Neville and his wife, Allison, had been flying like chicken feathers in a cyclone all over town the past week and a half.

Ten days ago Allison had been seen tossing Jake's computer and a pillowcase full of his clothes out the front window of their house and onto the sidewalk. The clothing had fared better than the computer, which had shattered on impact. But the pillowcase had come open, and a stiff wind had blown Principal Neville's underdrawers down the street.

In and of itself, that wasn't such a dreadful thing. Most folks understood that a school principal wore underwear . . . or at least they hoped he did. But one pair of Jake's boxers was particularly festive in nature, with a Grinch face over the crotch. The character's otherwise small green nose was greatly exaggerated and strategically placed, and the word *naughty* was emblazoned on the rear.

Had Jake Neville been the local plumber, an electrician, or the town dogcatcher, his reputation might have survived the event. But the combination of knowing that the town's high school principal wore silly and slightly risqué underwear and that his wife had tossed him out on his ear, and he was now living with his mother, was simply too tantalizing not to be shared.

And shared it was. Over and over and over again.

From the time Principal Neville's knickers hit the sidewalk until everyone in town knew about his marital conflict and his exotic taste in male lingerie, only an hour and seventeen minutes had passed, establishing a new all-time record for the McGill gossip chain.

Now, a week and a half later, Stella watched the disgraced school administrator's Chrysler cruise down Main Street, and she considered the various rumors she had heard thus far concerning Allison Neville's reasons for pitching her husband out of their house.

Some said he had been playing poker for money in Andy's barbershop after hours. Again. After her warning him that she wasn't putting up with his gambling nonsense anymore.

Others claimed they had heard him call her a particularly nasty word just before his eviction. While no husband had actually been murdered for using that word in the history of McGill, a few *had* been hopelessly maimed and rendered unrecognizable to their loved ones after uttering that unfortunate syllable. So, there could be some truth to that account.

However, the most common rumor, and the one Stella favored, was that Allison Neville had caught her husband in the act of tickling the fancy of the town's premier floozy, Priscilla Carr.

Miss Prissy Carr resided at the bottom of the barrel of McGill society. She had no husband of her own, which wasn't, in and of itself, a fatal social faux pas. But Prissy wasn't the least bit adverse to borrowing someone else's for an hour or two, when she had the notion.

It was widely believed by the women of the town that Miss Prissy Carr had the morals of an alley cat or, worse yet, of a man. Some said she even accepted money from time to time in exchange for performing certain actions that no self-respecting wife would do.

Except, perhaps, for an especially well-behaved husband. On his birthday.

If he promised not to tell anybody.

Considering all the evidence stacked in that direction, Stella wasn't a bit surprised when she saw the Chrysler take a sharp turn and head into the alley behind the Bulldog Tavern . . . the tavern with the second-story apartment where Miss Priscilla Carr lived. The apartment with a staircase that led from Prissy's apartment right down to the dark alley.

No doubt, it was a most convenient setup for a woman with overactive hormones, a cash flow problem, and an insatiable need for male validation.

Not to mention the wayward husband seeking a cheap thrill and not wanting to have the whole town find out about it, even before he could get his britches up and his belt buckled.

"Hmm," Savannah said, scrambling to her feet and switching the flashlight back on. "Guess we know for sure now."

"Know *what* for sure?" Waycross asked as he grabbed his paintbrush and resumed his restoration of the infant.

Savannah gave her grandmother a knowing grin. "Why the poo hit the fan at the principal's house, and why his drawers hit the street."

Stella gave her a stern look . . . as stern as she could muster through a grin. "You should pay less attention to grown-up gossip," she told her precocious granddaughter.

"'Twasn't grown-ups I heard it from. The fifth graders were talking about it at recess. They favor the Prissy Carr theory, too."

Stella slapped her hand to her forehead. "Lord, have mercy. What's this world comin' to?"

Waycross stood, stretched his tired back, and surveyed his handiwork. His face was as peaceful and full of grace as the Virgin's.

A freshly cleansed conscience is a fine thing, indeed, Stella told herself, looking at her grandson and feeling a surge of pride.

Some kids would have pouted and been resentful through the entire process. But, to his credit, Waycross had shown grace, dignity, remorse, and a willingness to make restitution. His grandma couldn't have been more pleased with him.

"Waycross Reid, you did a fine thing, the right thing, making a crooked line straight here tonight. And I've no doubt that you've—"

Her words were cut short by a cry, a terrible scream that echoed through the alley and into the street, chilling the soul far worse than any winter wind could freeze the body.

Stella set the paint can on the ground and instinctively reached for her grandchildren and pulled them to her.

"What was that?" Waycross asked, his voice shaky.

She could feel him trembling as she hugged him tight against her side.

"I don't know," she replied honestly, searching her mind for a memory of that sort of scream and finding none.

She had heard cries of fear, pain, and surprise. But this was different—more intense, urgent, and harsh. Like nothing she had ever heard before.

"Was it a man or a woman?" Savannah asked, her own arms tight around her grandmother's waist.

"I'm not even sure it was a person," Stella replied. "Maybe an animal or . . ."

But she knew in her heart it was not a beast of any sort. Someone, a human being, was in trouble.

Terrible trouble.

There, in the dark, lonely street, Stella knew there was no one else who could help that person. No one but her.

She looked down at her grandchildren, who were staring up at her with wide, frightened eyes.

Her first responsibility was to them. To keep them safe. Anything and anyone else was secondary.

"Come on," she said. "Let's go."

"No, Granny! We have to help them," Savannah exclaimed, resisting. Then the child said exactly what Stella was thinking. "I'm afraid they might be dying!"

Stella grabbed the girl's hand and her brother's, too. "I know, Savannah girl," she said. "I think so, too. But I'm gonna make sure you kids are safe and sound first. Then I'll go back and help them as best I can."

Waycross tugged at her sleeve. "You can't, Gran. You might get hurt, too."

"I'll be careful," she replied as she pulled them along, racing toward the end of the block and the sturdy two-story brick box of a building—the sheriff's station.

Fortunately, it was a short block, and in less than a minute, they had arrived at the station.

"Listen good," she told them, shoving them toward the rusty screen door. "You hightail it inside. Tell whoever's on duty what we just heard. Then you stay there. Sit yourselves right down and don't go *nowhere* until I come back to fetch you."

"But you might need our help and—" Savannah argued, but her grandmother interrupted.

"No! The sheriff or one of his deputies will come help me. You stay put right there in the station. Promise me, Savannah, that you'll keep your little brother safe inside there."

Reluctantly, Savannah said, "I promise, Granny."

The girl grabbed Waycross by the hand, and together they raced inside the station, the door creaking then slapping closed behind them.

Stella waited until she could see them through the window, speaking to the deputy at the desk. Then she turned and ran as fast as she could back to the square, back to the alley where that unfortunate soul was in terrible trouble.

Her heart told her they weren't just in trouble. They were dying.

Unless she was too late, and they were already dead.

Chapter 6

What if it's an accident, and you just wasted precious time taking the kids to the station house? Stella thought, tormenting herself, as she raced back toward the town square. *What if somebody bled to death back in that alley, and you could have stopped it?*

Yes, that might be, and if it's true, that'd be awful, and I'll have to live with it, she told the condemning voice. *But what if I took two innocent children into a violent situation, and they were hurt— or even worse? There'd be no living with something like that.*

By the time she reached the nativity scene, the matter had been decided in her own mind and heart.

At this point in her life, Stella Reid was many things: a widow, a mother, an alto in the church choir, an excellent gardener—especially when it came to roses—and as good a neighbor as she could manage to be, considering that she had the likes of Bud Bagley living next door.

But, primarily, she was a grandmother.

Those children were her life, her mission, her calling. If someone had died in that alley because she'd put her grandangels' well-being first, then she would find a way to live with it, believing in her heart that the tragedy was somehow meant to be.

The peace of mind that her decision gave her was fleeting, though.

As Stella passed the crèche and headed down the alley behind the tavern, a dark sense of foreboding swept over her. A shiver trickled down her back and into her limbs, and it had little to do with the chill of the night.

Stella recognized the sensation all too well.

Three times before, she had experienced that same ominous, oppressive feeling. It was as though something evil and menacing was enveloping her, pressing in on her from all sides, robbing her of breath, draining the strength from her body, until she thought her legs might buckle beneath her.

The first time it had happened, Stella had been only a child. As her precious mother died in her arms, that malevolent presence had surrounded her, crushing her, until she thought that she, too, would die.

The second instance occurred on a day six years ago, when Stella had looked at the kitchen clock and realized that her husband was thirty-three minutes late for the midday dinner she had prepared for him.

Arthur Reid knew how hard his wife worked at preparing his dinner, knew all the loving care that went into her meals. He never came home late from tending their fields.

Never.

Except that day.

The third instance had been mere seconds before two men wearing army uniforms and somber faces knocked on her front door. Stella hadn't needed to open the door to know why they were there. They had come to "regretfully inform" her that her oldest son had been killed in action.

They had told her that she should feel proud of her boy, because he had given his life for his country. But Stella hadn't felt proud that day. Her heart had been too broken to feel anything but agony.

The pride had come later, much later, when she reached out her hand and touched her son's name engraved on the wall of the Vietnam Veterans Memorial.

Death.

This black, oppressive feeling that gripped her heart and sent fear cascading through her bloodstream—it meant death.

Not the peaceful ending of a life well lived. An untimely death.

Someone had been taken violently. Before their time.

For a moment, Stella froze, unable to move. Hidden in the shadows of the silent alley, she considered the fact that if she wasn't careful, the untimely passing she was sensing might turn out to be her own.

Be careful, girl. Watch yourself, she thought. *We can't let nothin' bad happen to you. You've gotta stay alive and help raise those children. Heaven knows, Shirley can't do it on her own.*

As she strained her eyes to see in the darkness, she wished she had Savannah's flashlight with her. Dim and fading as it might have been, it would be better than nothing.

She listened intently for anything and everything. Movement, voices, even the sound of breathing.

She heard nothing but the wind's whining complaint as it swept leaves and litter from the street, between the buildings, and into the alleyway.

She debated the wisdom of announcing her presence versus remaining quiet and, hopefully, undiscovered.

Why did you come running back here then, if it wasn't to help somebody? she asked herself. *How much help do you expect to render by just standin' around, with your teeth in your mouth, and nobody even knowin' you're here?*

"Hello?" she called out, timidly at first, then a bit louder. "Hello? Is anybody there?"

She heard a slight scratching, scurrying noise off to her right, but during her childhood, Stella had listened to enough rats scampering around in barns and along the rafters of her house to recognize the sound of a rodent scrambling for cover.

Shivering, she took a few steps in the direction of the tavern's rear entrance. "Is anybody back here?" she called out, louder this time. "It's Stella Reid. I thought I heard somebody. Are you hurt? If you need help, I . . . Oww!"

At first, she thought someone had slugged her shoulder. The impact knocked her backward and nearly off her feet.

Self-protective anger rose in her, replacing her fear. "Hey! What do you think you're doin'?" she shouted at the figure that had struck her and was now running away.

But her indignation quickly faded as she mentally processed what had just happened and realized that they hadn't hit her but had simply slammed into her while running out of the alley.

She watched as the person rushed past the manger scene, and tried to recognize them. But they were nothing but a graceless, anonymous shape attempting to make a clumsy getaway.

Once the offender reached the street, she could see them more clearly by the glow of the town's one and only traffic light. A flashing four-way red light at the corner of Main and Madison.

There was no mistaking that face or the limp. No one else in town walked like that, except—

"Elmer Yonce," she muttered. "You lop-eared scalawag. What

were you up to back here? No good, I'll betcha. That's what you were up to. Same as you've always been."

That was when Stella heard it.

A faint gasp.

A moan and then a terrible guttural gurgling that sounded like some kind of macabre percolator, perking a bitter, deadly brew.

She turned and hurried through the darkness toward the sound. It seemed to be coming from an area near the rear of the tavern.

"I can hear you," Stella said. "I'm coming. Where are you?"

"Here," came the weak, hoarse reply.

Feeling her way rather than seeing, Stella stumbled along until her foot struck something soft. Something that was moving. But barely.

She was horrified to realize it was a body. Someone was lying at the foot of the staircase that led to Priscilla Carr's second-story apartment.

"Stella?" the person said in a harsh voice between awful gurgling gasps. "Stella . . . Reid?"

"Yes. Yes, it's me. I'm here, and I'm going to help you."

Stella knelt on the ground, and as her eyes finally began to adjust to the darkness, she could see just enough to recognize the person lying there.

The permed blond hairdo was way too big, even by 1980s standards. Her shirt was low cut, exposing far more than the average McGill woman would have shown, even to her husband on an anniversary night.

No one in town showed that much skin or had hair so large except the town "bad woman." Both were her trademarks.

"Priscilla, I've got you, honey. Don't worry. You're not alone anymore," Stella told her. "Can you hear me?"

She cupped Priscilla's face in her hands and felt the woman give a slight nod.

"I know you're hurt, sugar," Stella said, feeling foolish for stating what was so terribly obvious. "Try not to worry. The police are coming. We're gonna help you, so don't be scared. Everything's gonna be okay."

Don't lie to her, the condemning voice in Stella's head told her. *It's not okay, and you know it. She's dying. You're lying to a dying woman.*

Oh, shut up and go away, Stella countered with a calmer voice, a wiser voice from deep inside her spirit. *We don't need your two cents' worth at a time like this. Even if she dies, everything will* be okay. *Death is just another part of livin'.*

The awful gurgling was getting worse by the moment. Stella could feel a wet, warm stickiness on her fingers and palms, and she knew it was blood. Quite a lot of it.

"Did you fall, darlin'?" she asked. "Did you take a header down those stairs of yours?"

There was no verbal reply.

Stella had the distinct feeling that Priscilla was now past speaking. But she was certain she could feel a slight shaking of her head from side to side, as though in denial.

"You didn't fall by accident?"

Again, a small but distinct side-to-side movement, signifying a no.

"Did somebody do this to you, Priscilla? Did somebody deliberately hurt you?"

She felt a faint but definite nod.

"Who was it that hurt you, honey? Can you tell me?"

When Priscilla didn't respond, Stella asked again, more loudly. "Prissy, who did this to you? Please tell me. Try hard, sweetie. It's important."

Stella listened, straining to hear any word of response, but there was nothing. Even the terrible liquid breathing was slowing and becoming less pronounced by the moment.

"Oh, Sheriff, you best get a move on!" Stella whispered into the darkness. Then she added a quick but heartfelt and desperately sincere prayer. "Lord, please get us some help here pronto! She's gotta have medical attention right away! Please, please, please!"

Stella sat down on the ground next to Priscilla Carr and gathered the woman's damaged body into her arms. She held her tight and rocked her in the same tender way she soothed her grandchildren when they had suffered some injury either to their flesh or their spirits or both.

The accusing voice in Stella's head decided to weigh in once again, shouting at her. *You shouldn't move her! You might hurt her, damage her even worse! If her neck's broken, you could paralyze her, even kill her, and then you'll be in a heap of trouble!*

But Stella was listening to her heart, not the dark voice in her head. Her heart assured her that the worst had already been done to Priscilla Carr.

Cuddling and comforting wouldn't cost Prissy her life. Sadly, they wouldn't save it, either. But a kind embrace from someone who truly cared, someone offering unconditional love— that just might ease her fear of passing from this world into the next.

Stella had a feeling that Prissy Carr hadn't received a lot of cuddling, comforting, and unconditional love in her short lifetime.

Sex—whether paid for with a twenty-dollar bill or freely given in exchange for a moment of feeling desired by a fellow human being—was a poor substitute for the real thing.

* * *

Within only a few minutes, Stella's prayers were answered.

Sheriff Gilford arrived, and he brought help with him: Doc Hynson and the doctor's van, which was the closest thing McGill had to offer for emergency transport if its only ambulance was already in use.

But by the time they came, Stella Reid was the only one remaining in the cold, dark alley.

Just Stella and Priscilla Carr's body.

Prissy had already left.

Chapter 7

As Stella sat on the cold metal folding chair next to the front desk in the sheriff's station, it occurred to her, and not for the first time, that for a basically honest person who tried to abide by the laws of God and man, she'd spent more than her share of time in that station house.

She wasn't particularly happy about it, either.

Most of her visits to the old but sturdy two-story brick building had been to post bail for her daughter-in-law, whose addiction to liquor resulted in her being charged with a lot of petty offenses, like public intoxication and disturbing the peace.

On a particularly bad night, Shirley Reid's offenses were less petty, like assault. Usually, with a beer bottle or her purse.

Once, she had used her boyfriend's cowboy boot. While he was still wearing it.

Long ago, Stella had stashed a coffee can in the back of the cabinet beneath the kitchen sink, and any time she could, she added some coins to the can. She told the grandchildren that it was the "for emergencies only" can. But in her mind, she called it the "bail Shirley's butt out of the can" can.

Unfortunately, Stella had lost count of the times she had emptied the contents of that can into a pillowcase and then lugged the pillowcase into the station to secure her daughter-in-law's release.

Stella did not perform this ritual for Shirley's sake. Quite the contrary, Stella figured some time in jail, with forced sobriety, might do the woman some good. But her grandchildren, especially the younger ones, fretted something fierce when their mother was in jail.

They didn't particularly miss their mom, as she was seldom home even when she was out of jail and on probation. But they were convinced that while incarcerated, Shirley would attack the sheriff or one of his deputies or try to escape down a knotted bedsheet, flub it, and hang herself, thus heaping even greater disgrace upon the family name.

Stella worried about those things, too. Shirley could be quite creative when she set her mind to it.

"At least you aren't here to bail anybody out this time," Sheriff Gilford said, as though reading her mind. He sat down at his desk and began to shuffle papers around, looking for something.

Finally, he found what he was searching for—a black notebook and a ballpoint pen. "Sorry to hold y'all up like this," he said, waving a hand toward Stella and her two grandchildren, who sat on equally unattractive and uncomfortable folding chairs on either side of her. "But I couldn't leave until I was sure the crime scene was secure."

"Of course you couldn't," Savannah piped up. "Your deputies probably put that yellow tape stuff all around it to make sure nobody goes inside there. You wouldn't want anybody contaminating your evidence, touching anything they shouldn't, moving stuff around, and getting their fingerprints everywhere."

Sheriff Gilford studied the child thoughtfully for a moment. Stella could tell by the glimmer of humor in his pale gray eyes that he was stifling a grin. She silently blessed him for it.

With a show of great solemnity and respect, he nodded and told Savannah, "You seem to know a lot about law enforcement procedures, young lady. I'm quite impressed. Most people three times your age don't know as much as you do about how to process a crime scene. Some cops, too, for that matter, I'm sorry to say."

Waycross gave an impatient, derisive sniff. "Ha. It's just that she reads a lot of them Nancy Drew books. Always got one of 'em in her hands. Thinks she's gonna be a policeman when she grows up someday. But she can't, 'cause she's a girl."

"That's not true!" Savannah retorted. "We women got ourselves liberated, and now we can be whatever we want. I can be a policewoman when I grow up, if I want to. Huh, Granny?"

"Yes, you can, granddaughter. You can be anything you want when you grow up. Or even right now, for that matter."

"She can't be Mr. T," Waycross continued, unwilling to concede the fight. "Or Magnum, P.I."

Savannah bristled. "Oh, for heaven's sake, Waycross Reid. I don't wanna be Mr. T! I don't wanna be Magnum, either." Her face softened into a sappy smile. "I'd rather just look at him."

"That's enough, you two," Stella said. "We're not here to debate the ins and outs of women's liberation or the attractiveness of Mr. Tom Selleck. Sheriff Gilford here is trying to conduct an investigation. The sooner we get it over and done with, the quicker we can go home and relieve poor Elsie of her duties. She probably thinks we ran off to Timbuktu, leaving her with a passel of young'uns to contend with for the rest of her life."

"And the sooner we get back, the sooner you can gobble down that piece of apple pie she set back for you," Savannah added, grinning slyly.

"That too," Stella admitted. "I ain't gonna pretend I'm not looking forward to it. That toasted cheese sandwich and tomato soup I had at noon done wore off ages ago."

Sheriff Gilford opened his black notebook and clicked his ballpoint pen. "Okay. Let's get this done, so you can go home to the rest of your family and your apple pie. If Elsie made it, I can understand your eagerness."

"Thank you, sir. I appreciate it," Stella told him.

She saw a frown appear on her grandson's face and braced herself for what she knew was coming.

Waycross was known for carrying a grudge long past its time. This wasn't going to be pretty.

"Sheriff Gilford's mighty partial to Miss Elsie's apple pies," the boy grumbled under his breath. "I, of all people, know that. I know it all too well."

Gilford looked up from his notebook and saw the disgruntled look on the child's face. "What's that, young man?"

"Drop it, Waycross," Stella told her grandson. "Now's not the time."

"No, that's okay," the sheriff told her. "If this young fellow has a grievance against me, he's welcome to state it."

Stella rolled her eyes and sighed. "Okay, Waycross. Go on."

Waycross eagerly plunged into the deep end, happy to finally air his long-held grievance. "Okay, Sheriff. I'm gonna tell you. The thing is, you bid against me for one of Miss

Elsie's apple pies at the church social last summer. And you beat me, too, by a quarter."

Sheriff Gilford's eyes widened. He cleared his throat and rubbed his hand over his mouth before answering. "I'm mighty sorry to hear that, son. I didn't notice it was you that I was competing with. I suppose I was blinded by the thought of that pie. I didn't realize you were as eager to sink your choppers into it as I was."

"That's just the point," Waycross said, his lower lip protruding in what would have been a humorous pout if not for the fact that the child had tears in his eyes. "It wasn't for me. It was for my grandma. For her birthday."

Gilford glanced over at Stella. A look of profound guilt and remorse appeared on his handsome face. "Oh, my goodness," he said. "That's awful. I had no idea."

"Well, that's the ugly truth of it," Waycross commented. "You see, I knew that Miss Elsie would bake one of her apple pies for the auction, like she always does. I knew my gran would rather have that apple pie for her birthday more than anything else on earth. So, I washed Judge Patterson's big old Cadillac back to front and top to bottom, even though I had to stand on a chair to get the top good. I vacuumed out the insides and cleaned the windows, too, so's I'd have the money to buy it for her. But all the judge gave me was two dollars."

"And I outbid you by raising it that extra quarter?"

"You did, sir. But you didn't know the whole story. You was just thinkin' 'bout the pie and how good it was gonna taste once you got it home."

"I was. I admit it. I'm sorry."

"Then I forgive you, Sheriff."

At that point, Stella could have sworn she saw a small glimmer of light in her grandson's eyes . . . a mischievous twinkle, which made her grandma's instincts stand up and take notice.

Waycross continued to reassure the lawman, who looked like he was feeling lower than a snake in a well. "Don't worry about it, Sheriff. Really. If somebody does a bad thing and doesn't realize that it's a bad thing, you'd have to be a pretty mean, low-down skunk to hold it against them. That's what I've always said."

Gilford lifted one eyebrow and studied the child with his most suspicious, penetrating gaze—the one he had perfected on hard-core felons over the years. "That's what you've always said, huh? *Always said*, as in all nine years that you've been alive, right?"

"That's right, sir. It's a personal motto of mine." He grinned, showing off a bright smile, even with a front tooth missing. "It's a good motto, don't you think, Sheriff?"

Gilford continued to give the kid a skeptical, piercing look. "I suppose so," he finally agreed, his tone less than enthusiastic.

Stella stole a quick look at Savannah, who was sitting quietly in her chair, playing with her expired flashlight. But the smirk on her face spoke volumes.

"I think we better get back to the subject at hand," Stella said.

"Good idea," the sheriff replied, jotting something in his notebook. "If you could, please, Mrs. Reid, I'd like you to tell me everything you did and everything you saw from the time you and your grandchildren arrived at the town square this evening until, well, until I joined you. Let's start off with the time you first got there."

From the corner of her eye, Stella could see Waycross squirm in his chair.

She drew a deep breath and cleared her throat. "I believe

we got there about eight thirty, more or less." She watched as Gilford began to scribble in the notebook. "I parked the truck there on the street, across from the pool hall. We sat there for a while and—"

"For how long?"

"About thirty minutes."

Gilford stopped scribbling and looked up at her. "You sat in your truck for thirty minutes?"

"Yes, sir. About that."

"That's a long time to just sit in a truck. Especially with a couple of kids on a cold winter night."

Stella said nothing, and for what seemed like forever, neither did the sheriff.

Finally, he asked, "What were you doing, Mrs. Reid, while you were sitting there . . . the three of you?"

"Looking at the Christmas decorations on the street. Watching the people coming and going from the stores. Talking."

"About what?"

"Stuff."

Again, he stopped writing and looked up at her. His eyes searched Stella's with such intensity that it made her most uncomfortable.

She had known Manny Gilford for more than half a century, and this was the first time she had ever felt uneasy in his presence.

Not just uneasy. A bit afraid.

"Okay," he said. "You sat there for thirty minutes. By then it was about nine."

"It was."

"What did you do then?"

"We got out of the truck and . . ." She looked over at her grandson, whose face was a fierce shade of red. His freckles were practically standing out on stems. "And we went about our business."

"Which was?"

"We were there to do a bit of restoration." She looked down at her hands, which were folded demurely in her lap. Anything to avoid looking into those intense, truth-seeking, predatory eyes of his.

"You see, Sheriff," she continued softly, weighing every word, "we felt bad about what happened to the nativity scene. So bad that I went over to Florence's house earlier in the evening and got some paints. The ones she used when she restored it the first time. We thought we'd paint over the . . . you know, the damage that'd been done."

"You decided to do a good deed on behalf of the town," Gilford said, but with a less than congratulatory tone.

"Somethin' like that."

"But you decided to wait until the stores had closed and everybody had gone home to do this good deed. As in, you didn't want to get caught doing a good deed."

Stella gulped. "Like the Good Book says, 'Be careful not to practice your righteousness in front of others to be seen by them.'"

He gave her a look that cut straight through to her heart, and in a gently reproving tone, he said, "I'm not sure that now's the best time to be quoting the Good Book, using it in this circumstance, if you know what I mean, Mrs. Reid."

She did know what he meant. Exactly what he meant. And she instantly felt guilty. Tears sprang to her eyes. "We did want to do a good thing, Sheriff," she said, pleading. "Truly, I swear to you, we felt real bad about what was done to them figures there, and we wanted to set things right. Put things back to the way they were before. Before *that* got done."

The sheriff looked over at Savannah. He observed how she was nervously clicking the switch on her dead flashlight over and over.

He turned his attention to Waycross, whose face had gone from red to a strange shade of purple, almost matching his sister's warmest coat. A coat that was covered with splotches of flesh-tone paint, along with streaks of brown and white.

The boy's hands were similarly stained.

"As I recall," Gilford began, "about a month ago, a bunch of signboards around here were vandalized in a similar fashion as those statues. Big curly mustaches painted on all the faces. I also saw a couple of WANTED posters in the post office that had the same, um, decorations. I asked around and managed to compile a physical description of the culprit."

Both Stella and Savannah shot quick looks at Waycross, who was suddenly fascinated by his shoelaces.

"It's a pretty distinctive description. The suspect was described as male, about four feet tall. A dangerous-looking fellow with wild red curls and freckles galore."

Waycross looked up quickly, met the sheriff's eyes for an instant, then went back to studying his shoes.

"Then the vandalizing stopped. No more incidents. So, I figured it was a drifter, some sort of hobo, who'd moved on. I closed the case. I decided that as long as there weren't any new offenses, I'd just turn my attention to some of the other unsolved crimes here in my jurisdiction."

He stared long and hard at Waycross, who eventually raised his head and said, "That drifter probably moved on, like you said."

"Reckon so." Gilford gave him a half smile. "Or maybe the culprit didn't realize that what he was doing was bad, and when he did, he decided not to do it. *Ever. Again.*"

"I'm sure that's the case," Stella softly interjected.

"If it is," Gilford said, "and the vandal has truly seen the error of his ways, I wouldn't want to be a mean, low-down skunk by holding it against him."

"Exactly," Waycross said with far too much enthusiasm.

Gilford picked up his pen and turned back to Stella. "Out of the goodness of your own hearts, the three of you set about repairing the damage to the figures done by some unknown four-foot, red-haired, freckle-faced drifter, and then what happened?"

"We saw Principal Neville's big, fancy Chrysler station wagon go driving by," Savannah offered. "We were sure it was his. We'd know that big car anywhere."

Gilford began to scribble furiously. "Where exactly was the car when you first saw it?"

"Coming south on Main Street," Stella replied. "We first saw it when it was about even with the drugstore. For a minute, we thought it was your cruiser, both bein' big cars and all."

He looked up at her knowingly. "That must have been exciting, under the circumstances."

"It was. A bit," Stella admitted.

"Do you think Jake noticed you?"

"I don't think he would have. We weren't exactly in plain view," Stella admitted.

"No, I don't imagine you were. And then?"

"He drove on past us and pulled into the space between the tavern and the pool hall."

"Where did he go from there?"

"He disappeared into the alley. Back there behind the tavern."

Suddenly, the sheriff seemed both excited and intensely serious at once. "Okay, now, this is very important," he said.

"Could any of you tell whether he stopped in the alley or not? Did you hear a car door open or close?"

All three shook their heads.

"No," Stella said. "Can't say as I did. But the wind was blowing pretty bad by then. I'm not sure if we would've heard, one way or the other."

"Did you see the car again after that? Like driving back out the way it came in or maybe out the other end?"

"It didn't come back out the way it went in. As for goin' out the other end, I can't say, Sheriff," Stella replied. "Sorry."

"We was busy paintin' to beat the band," added Waycross.

"'Cept me," Savannah said. "I was the flashlight holder. But I didn't see him anymore, either. Wherever he went, he stayed gone."

"Then, when I finished painting the baby Jesus, that's when we heard it," Waycross said. "The person holler."

"It was awful," Savannah told the sheriff. "Made me feel scared and sick and sad all at the same time."

"Was it a man's or a woman's voice?" Gilford asked.

"We couldn't tell," replied Stella. "But you knew they were in trouble. Terrible trouble. And I didn't know what it might be. That's why I brought the kids here to the station—so's they'd be safe, and they could let y'all know what was goin' on."

"Good thinking. Then you ran straight back there?"

"I did. I hurried back to the alley and walked into it."

"What did you see?"

"Not much of nothin'. It was dark as the inside of a cow in there. I couldn't make out a blamed thing. Or hear anything. But then Elmer hit me."

"What?" Gilford nearly dropped his pen. "Elmer Yonce *hit you?*"

"More like ran into me. Full tilt. He darned near knocked me right off my feet!"

"Are you telling me that Elmer Yonce was running out of that alley behind the Bulldog Tavern?"

"Like somebody had lit his tail feathers afire."

"Are you absolutely sure it was him?"

"When he collided with me, I wasn't. But once he got to the street, then I was sure. He was limpin', you know, like he does. And the four-way traffic blinker gave off enough light for me to see his face. It was him. No doubt about it."

"Did you see anybody else back there in the alley?"

"At first, I couldn't see anything, on account of the darkness. But then I heard Priscilla moaning. And I heard her death gargle." She glanced over at her grandchildren, thinking she didn't want to get overly graphic with them listening. "You know," she said, "like they do when they're about to . . ."

"Yes. I understand. Did she say anything to you?"

"Just my name. I told her it was me there with her, and she repeated my name back to me. I asked her if she'd fallen down the stairs accidentally, and she shook her head no. I asked if someone had hurt her, and she nodded."

"Are you absolutely sure about that?"

"I had my hands on her face. I felt her move her head. Very deliberate like. Yes. I'm positive."

"Did you think to ask her who it was that hurt her?"

"Yes. I asked her, but by then . . ." She looked over at Savannah and saw tears in the girl's eyes. "By then, it was too late. She was already, you know, going."

Stella felt her own eyes filling as she recalled the exact moment when she felt Priscilla leave her body.

Priscilla's departure hadn't been a peaceful, sweet passing, like those Stella had attended when she'd sat with people whose long, painful battles with sickness were ending.

No, Priscilla Carr hadn't passed gently.

She had fought, clinging to life and feeling it slip away from her long before she was ready to let it go.

"I want you to catch whoever did this awful thing, Manny," Stella told the sheriff. "Promise me you will. I swear, I'll do everything I can to help you. Whoever took Prissy's life, they can't have the chance to do something that awful to someone else."

Sheriff Gilford rose from his desk, walked over to his friend's chair, and pulled her to her feet.

He wrapped Stella in a tight, strong embrace, hugged her close to his big, broad chest, and said, "Don't you worry, Stella May. Nobody takes a life in my town and gets away with it. Nobody."

He pulled back and looked down at her, his expression soft, kind, affectionate. Gently, he brushed one of her dark curls out of her eyes and said, "Thank you, Stella, for all you and your family did tonight."

"You're welcome. We were glad to help."

"We'll get him. You and me and my deputies. We won't stop until we do. I promise."

"Good," Stella said, feeling a bit better already. "That's a promise I'm going to hold you to, Sheriff."

Chapter 8

When Stella finally made it home with a sleepy Waycross and an uncharacteristically quiet Savannah, she expected to find Elsie weary and ready to go home. But her friend was quite the opposite—bright eyed, bushy tailed, and as hungry for gossip as Stella was for the apple pie.

The moment they walked through the door, Elsie jumped up from Stella's avocado leatherette recliner and rushed over to them. "I heard all about it! I can't believe it! Is it true?"

"If you're talking about what I think you are," Stella said, slipping off her shoes and placing them behind the door, "then I reckon it's true."

"We had us an honest-to-goodness murder right here in McGill?" Elsie asked, shaking her head in disbelief. "And you guys all saw it? You were official witnesses?"

"We were witnesses. I don't know how 'official' we managed to be," Stella admitted. "I didn't see the murder happen, thank goodness. I saw the aftermath, and heaven knows, that was bad enough."

"I didn't see nothin' at all," said Waycross. "Me and Savannah was coolin' our heels in the sheriff's station while Gran was gettin' to do all the excitin' stuff."

"I wouldn't call it *exciting*, Waycross," Savannah told her brother in a curt, reproving voice. "*Christmas* is exciting. *Halloween* is exciting. Somebody lost their life tonight. That's just puredee sad."

But Waycross wasn't prepared to surrender so quickly. "I reckon it's a mite sad, like you say. But that woman who died, that Prissy Carr, she wasn't a very nice person. Mama said she was the worst woman in town. If Mama saw her comin' down the sidewalk toward us, she'd make us walk across the street, so's we wouldn't meet up with her."

The weariness that Stella had been feeling since she left the sheriff's station suddenly increased tenfold at hearing her grandson's words. "Waycross, I know you're just a child repeating what you've heard from grown-ups," she told him. "And you're probably gonna hear those exact words too many times in the next few days. When you do, I want you to remember something. Miss Priscilla Carr did some bad things in her lifetime, some things that weren't wise or kind to other people. That's true. Most of us do things we shouldn't at one time or another. That doesn't make us bad people. It just makes us human beings."

She reached over and pulled the boy to her. She smoothed his tousled hair and continued. "Whatever bad things Miss Carr did, she didn't deserve to have that happen to her. Nobody does. Taking a person's life . . . Crimes don't get any worse than that. You know how you made restitution tonight, fixing what you'd done wrong?"

"Yes, ma'am." The boy's face was solemn but peaceful— the peace of a person with a clean conscience.

Stella continued, "Murder's a lot different than most crimes.

If you steal a person's money, you can work hard, get some more money, and give it back. If you lie to someone, you can tell him the truth and apologize to him. But there's no way to make murder right. No way to undo it. That's what makes it such an awful sin. You understand?"

He nodded, his eyes red rimmed from crying and fatigue.

She hugged him close and luxuriated in the warm, loving way he returned the embrace. Just for a moment, Stella believed that perhaps the world wasn't such a bad place, after all.

"I know you're tired, sugar," she told him. "Why don't you go lie down for a while there on my bed? If you go to sleep, I'll carry you in here and put you on the couch, once me and Miss Elsie are done talkin' and I'm ready for bed. Does that sound good?"

"It sure does." He wasted no time heading for her bedroom and her big, comfy featherbed.

Stella reached for Savannah and patted her shoulder. "How about you, babycakes? Aren't you tuckered out, too?"

"I am," Savannah admitted. "I'm going to go hit the hay myself. But there's just one thing I've gotta do first."

Without another word, the girl disappeared, heading toward the back of the house.

Stella sank onto the sofa, exhausted. Finally, she turned her attention to Elsie, who had been waiting patiently for her to finish addressing her grandchildren. One look at her friend told Stella that Elsie was about to burst with anticipation. Stella couldn't blame her. If the house slipper were on the other foot, Stella would be just as eager to hear the gory details as Elsie.

"I didn't want to say so in front of the kids," Stella told her, "but it was bad, Elsie. Really bad."

Elsie hurried over and sat next to her on the couch. "How

in tarnation did they do it? Did somebody shoot her or stab her? How did they kill her?"

"I don't exactly know for sure. It was dark, and I couldn't see her very well. But she was lying there, all crumpled up, at the bottom of her stairs in the alleyway."

"Oh, Lordy. How awful."

"There was blood, lots of it, all over her head. I had a bunch of it on my hands, but the sheriff let me wash it off when we got to the station house, before he questioned us."

She looked down at her fingers and saw that there was still plenty of Priscilla's blood under her fingernails. She shuddered, reached over to the end table, pulled open its small drawer, and took out a nail file. She ran the tip of it under each nail and dug deeply to get out every bit of the dark red gore.

"If I live to be a hundred, I won't forget tonight, Elsie. I couldn't if I tried. Being with that young gal when she died, I tell you, it'll haunt me for the rest of my days."

Elsie nodded knowingly. "I understand. I really do. It would've scared me half to death if I'd been there. That ain't all. If I was you, I'd be worried about her haunting me, too. You know, they say a murdered spirit is a restless one. She won't be resting in peace, that one."

"Oh, mercy, Elsie. Did you have to go and say a thing like that? I reckon I've got enough on my plate, worrying about the living, let alone the dead."

"Are you worried about the killer?"

Stella shrugged. "I don't know. Should I be?"

"I would be, for sure. What if he's afraid you'll identify him?"

"But I can't identify him. I don't know who he is. Unless it's Elmer Yonce. I did see him running away from the scene of the crime. But it's hard to imagine him killing somebody— him all old and rickety like he is."

Elsie laughed. "He ain't all that old. Not much older than we are, Sister Stella. And I'm pretty rickety myself, especially when there's a storm a-comin' and my joints act up."

"I guess we could kill somebody if we had to. Some folks claim I darn near killed Bud Bagley that day with my skillet."

Elsie gave a sniff and said, "Too bad you didn't hit him just one more time and a wee bit harder. This old world of ours would be a better place without Bud Bagley in it. Oh, and speak of the devil, Florence called about an hour ago. She'd heard about Prissy's demise, too. She wants you to call her back and give 'er the whole rundown on it. Said to tell you it doesn't matter how late you get in, that she'll wait up for your call."

Stella stifled a groan. "I love Flo," she said. "But all I want right now is to go to bed and put an end to this miserable day."

"That's not all you want, Granny," said a sweet voice behind her.

Stella turned to see Savannah standing in the doorway. In her hand was one of Stella's nicest china dessert dishes, and on the plate was a gloriously large piece of Elsie's famous apple pie, almost completely covered with French vanilla ice cream.

"You want *this*," Savannah said, handing her the plate, a fork, and one of Stella's Sunday-best lace-trimmed napkins. "You've been waiting for this all evening, and you deserve it. Every delicious bite of it. And if you want me to call Miss Flo and tell her how tired you are, I'd be glad to. I'm sure she'd understand that you'd rather talk in the morning, after you've had some rest."

Stella thought her heart would beat right out of her chest as she took the plate from her granddaughter and saw the love shining in the child's eyes.

If even one person in the whole world loved you that much, surely life was worth living—every single minute of it.

"Better yet," Elsie piped up, "I'll call Flo and explain it to her." To Savannah, she said, "You look like death warmed over, child, what with the awful night you've had. I'll get along home, and when I get there, I'll call Flo and tell her to give y'all time to rest and recuperate from your ordeal."

"Oh, thank you, Elsie," Stella said, digging into the luscious dessert. "All I want in life right now is to eat this pie and then get myself horizontal before I faint dead away and fall on my face."

To Savannah, she added, "And you, Miss Savannah, are the very best granddaughter who ever walked God's green earth. What do you suppose I did to deserve having you for my own?"

Savannah laughed, her eyes shining from the praise. She bent down and gave her grandmother a kiss on the forehead. "Nighty-night, Granny," she said. "If you get scared tonight or have any bad dreams, you let me know, and I'll come sleep with you."

"Okay. I will," Stella replied. How quickly they grew up, these precious grandchildren. One day you were checking under their beds to make sure there were no bogeymen lurking beneath. Then, the next, those same grandkids were offering to comfort you, should you be visited by nightmares of your own.

Stella never failed to be surprised at how life unfolded. How many surprises it held along the way. Thank heavens, most of those surprises were good ones, she had decided long ago. Otherwise, it might not be worth the bother.

An hour later, Elsie had left the Reid house, Savannah had retired to the upper level of one of the two bunk beds in the childrens' room, and Waycross was sound asleep on the sofa, curled up in his G.I. Joe sleeping bag.

When Stella kissed him and turned out the living-room lights, she thought he looked like one of the cherub ornaments waiting in a box in the corner to be placed on their Christmas tree, when she could find the money to buy one. No one but an exhausted child with a recently cleansed conscience could slumber so deeply and peacefully.

Stella hoped she would fare as well once she was settled in bed, but she had her doubts.

While she wasn't worried about Elsie's warning of an actual visitation from Prissy's troubled spirit, she had a feeling that once she lay down and closed her eyes, all she would see was Doc Hynson and Sheriff Gilford lifting Prissy's limp, lifeless body and putting it on a gurney, the whole scene, including her pale, once-pretty face, lit by the harsh, cold glare of the cruiser's headlights.

"No nightmares tonight, if you please, Lord," she murmured as she climbed into her own bed and pulled her precious wedding ring quilt around her shoulders, the one sewn by her Cherokee grandmother and given to her and Art on the day they married. "Just a nice, peaceful sleep," she whispered, "to get me through the trials of tomorrow. That's all I ask."

Her prayer was answered, but not in the way she would have liked. She had no nightmares, but only because she couldn't go to sleep.

Tossing and turning on her featherbed, Stella felt more alone than she had in a long time.

Those first few years without Art had been terrible. At times she had doubted she would survive them. With the passage of time, she hadn't gotten used to him being gone—she was sure she never would—but the sharpest edges of the pain had dulled ever so slightly, making the loneliness almost bearable.

Tonight, more than ever, she missed him, wished he was there to hold her, longed for his wise words and compassionate advice, which had afforded her so much guidance and comfort during the years they were married.

"I miss you, honey," she whispered. "I wish I could talk to you about what happened today. I imagine you'd tell me that I was brave and that you're proud of me. Boy, I could sure stand to hear that right now."

As always, when she spoke to her departed husband, there was no reply. At least not the kind human ears could hear. He was nearby; she had no doubt whatsoever. But only her heart itself could hear any message he had to give her.

She felt him tonight, even more clearly than she had sensed that terrible, sinister presence in the alley. But instead of feeling oppressed, suffocated, and threatened, as she had earlier, Stella found that her husband's residual love for her did the opposite. She felt warm, uplifted, and protected, in spite of the terror caused by her experience in the alley.

The two sensations fought for purchase in her spirit as she lay there alone in the darkness.

Good and evil.

Dark and light.

Fear and love.

Then, suddenly, Stella was aware of yet another presence—a slight tugging at the sleeve of her flannel nightgown. She turned over and saw her oldest granddaughter standing beside her bed, looking down on her with affection and concern on her lovely face, mixed with a bit of fear of her own.

"I was worried about you, Granny," Savannah said, patting her arm. "I was afraid you were in here having nightmares, dreaming about what happened to that poor lady in the alley."

Something, probably a grandmother's intuition, told Stella that it was the child herself who was having nightmares.

But Savannah was a tough girl—at least in her own estimation. The last thing she would ever admit was that it was she who was afraid and needed some comfort and reassurance. That sort of thing was for the babies in the family, certainly not for the oldest daughter.

Stella reached over and peeled the quilt and sheet back from the other side of the bed. "As a matter of fact, I *was* having a tough time," Stella told her. "I'm glad you came in to check on me." She patted the sheet next to her. "I'd really appreciate it if you would sleep in here with me. Just for tonight, of course."

Savannah wasted no time scrambling into bed and snuggling beneath the quilt, like a squirrel seeking refuge in a tree hollow during a snowstorm. "Of course," Savannah said. "We wouldn't want to make a habit of it. And we sure as shootin' wouldn't want to tell the other kids that a nasty ol' nightmare was the cause of it."

"Most certainly not. Otherwise, the little ones will all be in here, claiming to have nightmares galore. We'll be eight to a bed, and then none of us will get any sleep."

"We can't have *that*!"

"We certainly *cannot*."

Savannah rolled toward her grandmother, slipped her arm around her waist, and laid her head on her shoulder.

After a moment, the girl said, "Remember back when I was little?"

"I most certainly do, sugar."

"I remember when Gramps had just died, and we were all feeling really bad."

93

"Yes, darlin', I recall those times, too. Very well. Those were hard days for all of us. Nights even worse."

"They sure were. I was scared a lot back then. About a bunch of things."

"Me too, hon."

"Every time it stormed and I was sleeping here at your house, you'd let me come get in bed with you."

"I do remember that. Nobody's fond of lightning and thunder, but you took a particular dislike to them back then, as I remember."

"I did. But that was because I was just a little kid. I'm much more mature now."

Stella smiled. "Yes, you certainly are, sweetheart. You're almost a grown-up lady now. And, boy, you sure behaved like one today. I was never prouder of you."

Savannah reached for her grandmother's hand and squeezed it. "I was never prouder of you, either, Granny. The way you talked to the sheriff today, not telling him any lies but taking up for Waycross as best you could . . . I know that was hard for you, but you did it. You did just fine."

"We're family, sweetheart. We stick together and look out for one another. That's how it's gotta be."

"But the thing I'm most proud of you for, Granny," Savannah continued, her voice tremulous and sweet, "was the way you helped Miss Carr when she was dying and needed somebody. She must have been awful scared, but I know she felt better with the likes of you there."

Stella felt hot tears sting her eyes as her grandchild's words found a special soft place in her heart. "Thank you, darlin'. But I didn't do anything that anybody else couldn't have done."

"That's just the point. There's a lot of people in this town who *could* have helped Miss Carr if they'd been there, but they probably wouldn't have. At least not in as nice a way as you did. I love a lot of things about you, Granny, but the thing I love most is that you do nice things for people who don't even deserve it."

Stella hugged her close. "Everybody's deserving of human kindness, darlin'. And besides, we don't treat people according to who *they* are. We treat them according to who *we* are, and we try our best to be decent people, even if we do come up short lots of the time. It's the tryin' that counts."

Stella could tell that her granddaughter was considering her words long and hard, because it was a while before Savannah looked over at her grandmother, a twinkle of humor in her eyes, and said, "Except for that ornery ol' Bud Bagley. I don't reckon that was human kindness that you were doling out there in the kitchen with the frying pan."

Stella chuckled and found the laughter to be healing to her sad, exhausted spirit. "Kindness comes in many forms," she replied. "And as I recall, I was more interested in being kind to Miss Flo that day than ol' fart head Bud."

They both giggled hysterically, and once again, Stella felt the dark, ugly coldness that had taken up residence in her heart earlier in the evening continue to melt away.

"Can I call Marietta an old fart head sometime?" Savannah asked as they snuggled closer, enjoying the warmth and companionship that unconditional love offered.

"No."

"Why not? You just called—"

"She's your sister, and what did I just say about family?"

"Can I call her a pee-pee brain?"

95

"No."

"Bottom burp? That's a nicer word for *fart*."

"Vannah Sue, don't make me have to—"

"But she *is* one. Seriously, have you gotten a good whiff of that girl lately?"

"*Good night*, Savannah!"

"Good night, Granny."

Chapter 9

Stella had to admit that she was relieved to drop her grandkids off at school the next morning. As much as she adored them and enjoyed their company, she had plans today. She intended to accomplish a lot before they got out of school, and the places she would go, the people she would see, and the things they would talk about weren't for young eyes and ears.

Her first stop was at Florence's house. She had called Flo that morning, before taking the children to school, and they had agreed that Florence would drop by for coffee later in the morning. But no sooner had Stella hung up the phone than she realized she could have scheduled her time with Flo more wisely.

Florence tended to linger wherever she was parked, sometimes for hours, and Stella wanted to do more with her day than entertain her curious friend with every grisly detail of yesterday's miserable experience and listen to her complaints about ol' bottom burp Bud.

So as soon as she had delivered the children to the big, ancient brick elementary school, which Stella and the previous three generations of her family had attended, she headed for Flo's house.

She figured if she was the one dropping by, she could leave as soon as she wanted to and get on with her day's activities.

After having Bud nearly run her down the night before, Stella was hoping to avoid him. But unlike a lot of people in town, she had never been afraid of Bud Bagley, and she wasn't about to start now.

Since he was her next-door neighbor, she didn't see the point in trying to avoid him, either. Their paths were bound to cross on a daily basis, as they had for thirty years, and she was determined not to let him intimidate her the way he did his wife.

However, when Stella drove up the driveway to the house and saw that his monster truck was nowhere in sight, she had to admit that she felt a bit relieved. Still quite shaken from the drama of the past evening, she wasn't inclined to invite more today.

She parked her truck in front of the house, got out, and hurried to the front door.

Usually, she went to the back door, opened it, and hollered for Florence. But today she felt like being a bit less informal. Her last talk with Flo hadn't been a particularly pleasant one, and her friend had sounded a bit cool on the phone earlier. She wasn't sure Flo was ready to welcome her with open arms.

Another reason to hate Bud Bagley, Stella thought as she waited for Florence to answer her knock.

Convinced that you shouldn't harbor animosity in your heart against anyone, Stella worked hard not to hate Bud. It wasn't easy, since the guy gave her reasons on a daily basis.

Finally, the door opened and Florence appeared, looking disheveled and distraught, and not in the mood for company.

"I thought I was coming over to your house later," she told Stella, sounding quite testy.

"That's what we said," Stella admitted. "But when I was dropping the young'uns off, it occurred to me that I could just swing by here on my way into town."

"Wasn't exactly on your way."

"Wasn't that far outta my way."

Stella could tell by the suspicious, disapproving expression on her best friend's face that Flo wasn't buying it. Or liking it.

After so many years of being friends, if anyone could tell when Stella was fudging the truth a bit, it was Florence.

"If it's not a good time for you, I'll skedaddle," Stella offered. "I don't want to interrupt you if you're—"

Florence burst into tears, with sobs that were so deep and racking that Stella was alarmed. She rushed through the doorway and put her arms around her friend.

"What's the matter? Flo, what is it? What's going on?"

When Stella received no answer, she gently shook her. "Flo, stop your bawlin' and tell me what's happened."

"It's . . . it's Bud," Florence finally managed to say.

Stella held her at arm's length and looked her up and down, searching for any telltale bruising or other marks. "Has that bastard beaten you again?"

"No! It's worse than that."

"Worse? How could it be worse?"

"He's leaving me. For sure. For good."

Stella didn't know what to say. Her first inclination was to jump up and down and yell, "Yippee!" but she figured that would be inappropriate, so she said and did nothing.

"He means it this time," Florence said, as though Stella wasn't believing her. "He's at the bank right now, cleaning out our accounts."

For the first time, Stella noticed some suitcases stacked haphazardly at the bottom of the staircase. The flicker of hope inside her flared to a soul-warming blaze.

Could it be true? It seemed too good to be believed.

Stella held her emotions in check. *No point in raisin' your hopes sky high*, she told herself. *It's a long way to fall if it ain't so.*

"Are those your bags, Flo?" she asked. "Is he throwing you out? Because if he is, I can help you find a—"

"No! He's moving out himself. He said I can stay here till he sells the place. He's leaving town. Says he's done with me, the town, his whole life here. He wants a new start."

"He's almost sixty."

"I know. Stupid, huh? But that's what he wants."

"A bit late for a midlife crisis."

"I told him that. He told me to shut my face if I wanted to keep it."

Among the suitcases, Stella saw several matching boxes made of finely polished mahogany. She knew what they contained, having seen Bud's extensive collection of valuable coins more times than she cared to. Bud was as proud of his coins as most men were of their children.

"He's taking his coin collection, too, I see," she observed.

"He's taking everything we have that's of any value," Florence complained. "I'll be lucky if I get to keep my mama's china. He tried to empty out my jewelry box, too. Said he gave the stuff to me, so he could take it, and I told him no way. I was surprised when he put it back. That was the first time he ever did what I told him."

First time she ever called his bluff, Stella thought, confirming her own suspicion that Bud was a two-bit bully.

Standing up to some bullies could cost a person their life, Stella had learned the hard way long, long ago. But most garden-variety bullies would back down in the face of stern opposition.

She had always suspected that Bud Bagley was one of those run-of-the-mill, dime-a-dozen tormentors who could dish out far more than they could take.

After she listened to Florence's story about the jewelry, it occurred to Stella that if her friend had made a habit of standing up to Bud years ago, when the relationship was newer, the dynamics a bit more pliable, they might've had a different marriage.

Probably not a good one. But at least Florence might have received fewer busted lips.

Stella reminded herself, she might've wound up in the local cemetery instead. No one really knew what went on between a husband and wife behind closed doors.

"I'm glad you stood up to him for your jewelry, Flo," Stella told her. "I know how much some of those pieces mean to you—gifts from your mom and your sisters and such."

"Gifts from you," Florence said, her tears subsiding a bit.

Stella shook her head. "I never gave you any jewelry worth having. Never could afford the real thing."

"You gave me some earrings and bracelets that you made out of shells and flowers you'd pressed. Things like that mean just as much as the rest when they're given from the heart."

Stella looked at her friend, whose red, swollen eyes were filled with affection—as well as more fear than Stella had ever seen in Florence. She reminded herself that even though she thought Flo would be better off without Bud, this didn't appear to be what Florence thought.

It was a wife's perception, not a neighbor's, that mattered at a time like this.

"Are you going to be okay?" Stella asked her.

After a long pause, Florence said, "I guess so. I don't have much of a choice, do I?"

"I reckon not. But you know that people love you in this town, and we'll all be scrambling to find ways we can help you. Bud might be leaving you with precious little, but he ain't leaving you alone. Don't you forget that."

Florence nodded and seemed a bit more confident of her shaky future.

"I won't forget it, Stella. I'll never forget what a good friend you've been to me. Maybe with Bud gone and all his torments, I won't be crying on your shoulder so much. Maybe I can be as good a friend to you as you've been to me."

"Don't you worry about that," Stella assured her. "Life's a long journey with lots of twists and turns. I'm sure the day will come, as it has before, when I'll need you as much as you need me. It'll all work out even in the long run, I'm sure."

Florence glanced around the room, at the luggage and the coin boxes. A worried look crossed her face. "You'd better get going, Stella. Bud's bound to show up any minute now to collect this stuff, and you don't want him to find you here. Considering the way he's felt about you since the skillet affray, in the mood he's in right now, I couldn't guarantee your safety."

"Don't concern yourself with me and Bud. We reached us an understanding a long time ago. You just keep yourself safe. Don't be afraid to call Sheriff Gilford if a situation arises. And if it's serious enough, call me first. I can get over here with my skillet a lot faster than the sheriff can with his gun."

Florence promised that she would be careful, the two friends embraced, and Stella was on her way.

It wasn't until Stella arrived at the town square and parked across the street from the Bulldog Tavern that she realized how upset her old friend really was.

Gossipy Florence hadn't thought to ask her one single, solitary question about the murder.

Oh goody. Just what I need, Stella thought as she walked past the tavern door on her way to the alley and ran nearly headlong into her daughter-in-law. *A strong dose of Shirley first thing in the morning. Now, ain't that a delight and a half?*

She could tell from the look on the other woman's face that Shirley was just as thrilled to see her. Maybe even a little less.

"How are my kids doing after all that rigmarole you put 'em through yesterday?" Shirley demanded, her hands on her hips, jaw jutting out and lifted a notch with indignation.

"And a very good morning to you, too, Shirley," Stella replied, reminding herself of the Good Book's admonition, "A soft word turneth away wrath."

"I leave them with you for ten minutes, and you get them mixed up in a damn murder. What kind of grandmother are you, anyway?"

Okay, Stella thought. Apparently, when King Solomon wrote that particular proverb, he hadn't met Shirley Reid yet.

"Your kids, my grandchildren, weren't mixed up in any murder. They weren't in danger at all last night," Stella told her, keeping her voice low and soft, while imagining how much fun it would be to just pinch Shirley's head off and thump it into the gutter. Considering how scrawny her neck was, it probably wouldn't take much of an effort at all.

"That's not what I heard!" Shirley flipped her long black hair from one shoulder to the other—a practiced gesture, which Stella was pretty sure she employed to better show off her latest shoulder-duster earrings.

"Then you heard wrong. Two of them were safe and sound in the sheriff's station, and the other five were back home, bein' watched by Elsie Dingle, the best babysitter in the county."

"Yeah, yeah. Good old Elsie. Couldn't you find a babysitter who ain't a . . . well . . . Couldn't you find somebody who's the same color as—"

"That's enough! Stop right there, Shirley Reid!" Stella could feel her face turning hot and the blood pounding in her temples. "Don't you dare to—"

"Okay, okay. I know *you* ain't particular about who *you* associate with, and I guess that's your business. But when it comes to my kids, I worry about what you're exposing them to."

"The people I *expose* them to—like Elsie Dingle, who's one of the best women that ever walked this earth—are a sight better than the mangy, horny mutts you drag home every Saturday night from that there bar," Stella said. She pointed to the tavern as her patience and Proverbs-inspired good intentions evaporated.

Shirley sputtered a moment or two, obviously flustered, waving her hands around like a duck that was having a hard time taking off from a pond.

That was another mannerism that Stella was pretty sure Shirley employed to show off new jewelry. This time it was rings, enormous silver ones set with turquoise.

Shirley was proud of her Native American collection.

She couldn't afford fresh fruit for her kids. But she always seemed to have money for beer and turquoise-studded silver jewelry.

Stella watched as her daughter-in-law's black, penciled-on eyebrows knit into an ugly frown. "Yeah. Once in a while, I invite a gentleman back to the house for coffee on a Saturday night," she countered. "Why shouldn't I? It's not like your worthless son's ever home to keep me company. But at least there ain't no murderers in the batch."

"That you know of."

Shirley hiked her large fringed leather purse—also studded with silver and turquoise—higher onto her shoulder and tossed her head. The earrings danced, and her rings flashed, as did the four necklaces and eight bangle bracelets.

"All I know is this," she said. "With all that tender lovin', 'butter wouldn't melt in my mouth' grandma care that you supposedly give my kids, you nearly got 'em kilt. Thanks to you, they could've all been strangled to death, like that stupid slut Prissy Carr."

Stella watched as Shirley whirled around and strutted back into the tavern, her buttocks twitching from side to side in her ultra-tight jeans with every step.

The jeans were also accented with medallions of silver set with turquoise.

"Girl, you better hope you never fall into the river," Stella muttered. "With all that jewelry on, you'll sink like a rock, never to be seen again. So, keep wearin' it."

Chapter 10

As Stella continued her walk between the buildings, heading for the alley, she tried to think of a reason why that would be such a bad thing—Shirley sinking into the river, minus even one bob up for air.

You should be ashamed of yourself, even thinking somethin' like that, Stella May Reid, she told herself. *She's your grandchildren's mother.*

"For all the good she's worth to 'em," she couldn't help adding.

Rounding the corner, Stella discovered that she was unable to go into the alley—at least legally. As Savannah had predicted when speaking to the sheriff, bright yellow crime-scene tape had been strung across the entrance, warning the public not to cross into the space.

Stella stopped, as the tape instructed, and watched the action taking place within the restricted area.

Like almost every day spent in McGill and every square inch of the tiny town, little was unfamiliar here. Stella knew every person she met, whether in the grocery store, the pharmacy, the bank, or on the school grounds. Therefore, she wasn't surprised that she knew every person inside the yellow tape, every member of law enforcement who was involved in the investigation of Priscilla Carr's murder.

In a town where no one had met their death through foul play for many years, there was no need for a full-time coroner. Long ago, Herbert Jameson, the mortician, had been elected to the job, and since then, no one had challenged him for the position.

For as long as Stella could remember, Herb had been the coroner in name only, never having to actually lift a scalpel and perform an honest-to-goodness autopsy.

When Larry Kramer's cocker spaniel had suddenly dropped dead during the Easter parade, the unpopular mayor had suspected that someone might have poisoned his poor dog. Weeks before, Mayor Kramer had made the unfortunate decision to close the boat ramp on the river, east of town. Kramer felt that the town had hauled one too many trucks, belonging to drunken fishermen, out of the water after the intoxicated drivers had experienced difficulties navigating the algae-slick ramp. Fishermen, drunk and sober alike, had been livid. Some had made threats. Hence, Larry's paranoia.

At the mayor's request, mortician/coroner Herb Jameson had examined Frisky's remains, only to find that the poor creature's manner of death was "accidental." His cause of death was ruled "eating rocks."

That was the extent of Coroner Herbert Jameson's hands-on experience.

Stella was concerned that if the identity of Priscilla's killer turned out to be less than blatantly obvious—like if he hadn't left his driver's license at the scene—the murderer might just get away with it.

She watched as Herb knelt at the bottom of the stairs and stared at something of interest on the asphalt. Sheriff Gilford stood next to him, taking pictures of the spot with his fancy new waterproof Olympus camera—a gift from the town on the occasion of his twentieth anniversary of being sheriff.

On the other side of the alley, opposite the tavern and staircase, Deputy Augustus Faber and Deputy Mervin Jarvis were collecting bits and pieces of miscellaneous litter that had been tossed there, mostly by patrons of the Bulldog, who often stepped outside into the alley to have a private chat, to catch a breath of air that was slightly less stale than that inside, or, rumor had it, to purchase various types of contraband.

Wearing gloves and bored, disgruntled looks on their faces, Faber and Jarvis were placing each piece of "evidence" into a small brown paper bag the size of those that Stella used for packing the grandchildren's school lunches—peanut butter and grape jelly sandwiches and a banana.

For a moment, Stella thought of how eager little Savannah would have been to perform such a menial task. The girl would have been thrilled, not annoyed like these law enforcement officials.

Long ago, Stella had decided that she wouldn't be at all surprised if her oldest grandchild grew up to become a police officer. Considering where she came from, that was a mighty high aspiration.

Standing outside the tape, Stella found herself wishing that she had a badge of her own to help her legally cross the barrier. She would have loved to hear what Herb and Sheriff Gilford were saying as they examined the spot of ground where, only hours before, Prissy had died in her arms.

Stella was thinking about how much more informed she was about the situation than either of those men.

No sooner had the thoughts crossed her mind than Sheriff Gilford seemed to sense her presence. He turned and looked in her direction.

The moment he saw Stella, he left Herb and hurried over to join her.

"Good morning, Mrs. Reid," he told her, lifting the yellow tape and motioning for her to step inside the restricted area.

She did as he indicated, experiencing a mixture of contradictory emotions. She was honored that he would allow her this liberty and curious about what she might see in the daylight that she had missed in the darkness. But she was surprised at how strong the fear and the awful helplessness from the night before felt when they resurfaced.

"How are you today?" he asked, his eyes searching hers for an honest answer.

She gave him one. "Not so good. It was hard to get to sleep last night."

"I've had a lot of those nights myself over the years," he admitted. "That's the worst part about this job. At least it is for me. You see things that you can't unsee."

Stella thought of Prissy Carr's face—ghastly white in the headlights. "I understand. You get those pictures in your head, and they stick around for the rest of your life."

"They do."

"You must have a pretty big collection after all these years."

"That's for sure. I wouldn't wish them on anybody. Not my worst enemy."

Stella thought of the stickiness of Priscilla's blood on her hands. "The pictures in your head, Sheriff, the things you felt and heard and smelled—does any of it fade with time? Even a little bit?"

He hesitated, and for the first time his eyes wouldn't meet

hers when he replied, "A little bit. But then you see a new sight, hear a new sound, and it brings it all back. Sometimes even worse, 'cause now you've got one bad experience piled on top of the other."

Nodding, she said, "I understand. Leastways, I think I do. I don't envy you."

He gave a dry chuckle. "Most people don't. But that's okay. It's not such a bad job."

"Compared to what?"

Again, he laughed, but this time he had a twinkle in his eye, as well. "Oh, lion taming, cat herding, bullfighting."

"Ballerina."

"God forbid. Too rough on the toes, and don't get me started about those scratchy tutus."

He reached out, took her arm at the elbow, and guided her toward the staircase. "Would you mind speaking to Herb for a few minutes? He's got a couple of questions for you." He lowered his head closer to hers and whispered, "I think he's little overwhelmed."

"No surprise there. Who wouldn't be? All he's got to compare this to is the case of the rock-eatin' cocker spaniel."

"Exactly. I'd appreciate it if you'd help him out any way you can."

A deep sense of satisfaction swept through Stella, from her head to her toes. The thought that she could help, actually be of service in this dreadful situation, pleased her enormously. Maybe the awful experience she'd had the night before could be used for good and, therefore, cause it to be worthwhile in the long run.

"I'd be happy to, Sheriff. I don't know what I can add to your investigation, but I'll sure give it my best shot."

"That's all anybody can ask."

When Herb Jameson saw them coming, he stood and hurried over to meet them halfway.

Stella had always thought that Herb had an unlikely appearance for an undertaker. His complexion was deeply tanned, as he spent many hours chasing a golf ball around the back lawn of the mortuary when no "guests" were lying in state. His thick, wavy auburn hair had a mind of its own. In spite of the copious amounts of oil he used to slick it back, several strands insisted on hanging down his forehead and getting in his eyes, creating a less than solemn, polished appearance.

Herb's wife had died a few years back, leaving him with three young daughters to raise. In the opinion of the townsfolk, Herb was doing a fine job of it. His girls were happy, healthy, and respectable in every way, their clothes clean and crisp, their hair carefully styled.

Herb had always been a better hairstylist than the town's two beauticians. Some women had considered asking him to give them a special hairdo for their wedding or anniversary or a "glamour shot" photo session. But in the end, they had decided against it.

There was something a bit creepy about having an undertaker mess with your locks. Besides, sending the dearly departed of McGill on their way and raising three daughters kept Herb busy.

Stella couldn't recall a time when he hadn't looked plumb worn out.

He always had a somber expression on his face, which Stella assumed was part of his job description. A body couldn't go around looking jolly while conducting funerals.

Today he had been looking particularly grim. But when he saw her, something akin to a smile's second cousin appeared on his face.

It occurred to her that he, too, seemed to think that she could help with the investigation. Once again, she found that to be comforting.

Maybe she had been put there in that alley last night to serve a purpose. A very good and important purpose.

Maybe she could help find justice for Priscilla Carr and somehow be instrumental in taking a very bad person out of society and putting them behind bars, where they couldn't hurt anyone else ever again.

"Good morning to you, Sister Stella," Herb greeted her.

The two of them had attended the same church for years, and addressing each other as "sister" and "brother" had been a long-standing tradition for as long as either of them could remember.

They weren't likely to forgo the habit. Not even in the midst of something as serious as a murder investigation.

"Mornin', Brother Herb," she said. "Looks like you've got your hands full here."

"I sure do. Who'd have ever thought that we'd have to contend with such a thing right here in little ol' McGill? I thought those boys putting outhouses up on top of barns was as bad as it'd ever get around these parts." He shook his head sadly. "Now look at this. It's a shame."

"It is," Stella agreed. "A cryin' shame. Enough to melt a heart of stone."

Herb gave her a doubtful look. "Well, it's a shame, all right. But a *cryin'* shame? I wouldn't go all that far, considering who it was and all."

"Who it was?" Stella bristled. "Are you telling me it's less sad because Prissy wasn't the most popular gal in town?"

Herb gave an ugly little snicker. "Reckon she was popular, all right. Not with the womenfolk, but with a lot of their husbands." He drew himself up and straightened his tie. "There's a word, more than one word, in fact, for women like Prissy. I won't use it, of course, because I'm in the presence of a true lady such as yourself, Sist—"

"Shut up, Herb," Gilford barked. "If you talked crap like that at your funeral home, you'd lose all your customers."

Herb looked confused. "No I wouldn't. I'm the only mortician in town."

"We'd start building pine coffins and burying our own." The sheriff waved Herb back toward the staircase. "Go take blood samples off that pavement, like you're supposed to."

"What for? You took pictures."

"You can't test pictures, now can you?"

"Test? Test the blood? For what?"

Stella forced herself not to shake her head.

The sheriff displayed no such self-restraint. "For God's sake, man! Use your brain! First, you have to check it to see if it's even human."

"But we know it is. That's where the Carr woman was when Sister Reid here tended to her."

"I'd appreciate it if you didn't call me 'sister' no more," Stella told the mortician with a sad, disappointed tone of voice. "I always thought well of you, Herb Jameson . . . the way you're raisin' them girls of yours on your own, the kindness you showed me and mine when my husband passed. But it don't sit well with me, what I just heard you say. About a dead woman, at that."

Herb seemed surprised and puzzled by her statement, but rather than answer her, he turned his attention back to Gilford. "I don't have anything to check blood like that."

"Then get something. We don't want to arrest somebody, bring them to trial, and then have some defense attorney say it was the blood of some cat or dog that got hit back here in the alley."

"Okay." Herb didn't look convinced, but he did seem leery of Gilford, who appeared to be getting more annoyed by the moment.

"You're also going to have to check the blood type."

"What?"

"You know . . . O negative. A positive. The blood type."

"I don't have a way to—"

"Get a kit. Some equipment. Whatever you need."

"That stuff's bound to be expensive."

"Give me the bill, and I'll pass it along to Kramer. He owes you one for that necropsy you did on Frisky."

Herb hesitated a moment, but a stern look from Gilford sent him back to the staircase, where he opened a black briefcase he had left there and began to swab the asphalt.

"Lord, help us," the sheriff muttered. "Before this is all said and done, he might be our second victim. I don't know how much of this I can take."

Stella smiled. "If you get desperate, I could send Savannah over. She probably knows just how to collect a blood specimen and how to test its type with stuff from the drugstore."

"I wouldn't be the least bit surprised. 'Twasn't a very windy day when that apple fell from the tree. She's the spitting image of you at that age . . . looks *and* brains."

"Why, thank you, Manny," she said, allowing herself the rare liberty of using his first name since they were strolling down memory lane.

"Would you like to come into Miss Carr's apartment with me?" he asked, suddenly all business again. "I'd appreciate a female's sharp eye looking over the woman stuff that's in there."

"Of course. I'd be glad to," she told him. "Like I said, I'll do anything I can for Prissy. I don't feel the same way about her as Herb there does."

"That's a good thing, and I respect you for it, Stella," he replied. "But more people think like him in this town than you'd want to believe."

"I know. People like to jump on folks who commit the obvious sins more than on ones who commit the less obvious. They'll get all in a bother about fornication and the occasional curse word, and they forget about pride and greed and gossipin'."

On their way to the staircase, they passed Herb, who was on his hands and knees, scrubbing blood off the pavement with cotton swabs.

Halfway up the steps, Stella whispered to Gilford, "Once you figure out who did this, you'd better squeeze him hard for a confession. 'Cause if you have to rely on physical evidence . . ."

"Exactly what I was thinking. I'd better dig out my cat-o'-nine-tails and my set of Christmas nut-cracking utensils."

He opened the door and let her into the apartment ahead of him.

"Was it unlocked when you got here?" she asked.

"Yes. Wide open, in fact."

She paused and carefully studied the doorknob, lock, and frame. "No signs of it being forced."

"None that I could find."

Stella walked to the middle of the small room that served as a modest studio apartment—a living room, eating area, kitchenette, and bedroom all in one. After looking around, she pointed to two doors on the back wall. "And those lead to . . . ?"

"The right one is a closet. The left is the bathroom."

Taking in the overall dishevelment of the room, she said,

"It's hard to tell if there was a fight in here. Everything's so topsy-turvy."

"I know. But look at that hand mirror over there on the bed."

He didn't have to tell Stella not to touch anything in the room. She had listened to Savannah extol the virtues and procedures of Nancy Drew, the world's best crime investigator, for hours on end.

She walked over to the bed and saw among the crumpled sheets and blankets a silver hand mirror. Probably solid sterling. It looked antique and expensive. Among the mostly simple, poorly constructed furnishings, it seemed out of place.

Stella couldn't recall anyone ever mentioning that Prissy had a job of any sort or a reliable way to support herself. Stella couldn't help wondering how she might have afforded such a pretty and valuable accessory.

The mirror's glass was broken, and when Stella bent over to look at it more closely, she saw blood and some blond hair stuck to the frame, with its ornate baroque ornamentation.

More blood was spattered on the bedspread, the stains mingling with the orange rose print.

"Wow!" she exclaimed. "You might have your murder weapon there."

"If that's what killed her," Gilford said. "We won't know for sure until Herb examines the body."

"He's a good mortician, but if he's as good at doin' an autopsy as he is at blood collectin' and testin'—"

"I know. I'm getting an ulcer just thinking about it."

"Other than the bleeding, were there any other signs of violence on the body that you could see?" Stella asked, dreading the answer. In the middle of the night, she had considered the fact that Priscilla might have been sexually assaulted. The woman's clothes hadn't appeared to be in disarray, but it had been so dark in the alley that Stella couldn't be sure.

"I looked her over good there in the mortuary first thing this morning," the sheriff replied as he took some photographs of the mirror from numerous angles. "I saw several bruises on her neck. Looked like where fingertips had dug in."

Stella shuddered and said, "When she spoke my name, her voice was real hoarse and gravelly sounding. She was having a real tough time breathing there at the end, too."

"Then it might be hard to establish whether it was the blow on the head or getting choked that killed her." The sheriff slipped on a pair of surgical gloves, gingerly picked up the mirror, and slid it into a paper bag that was slightly larger than the ones being used by the deputies in the alley.

"Or being pushed down a flight of stairs."

"That, too."

"Seems like we got us several causes of death and a couple of suspects." She glanced at her watch. "And it ain't even ten o'clock in the morning."

"Sounds like famous last words."

"Speaking of suspects, were you able to find Elmer?"

Gilford taped the top of the bag closed. "I was. In fact, I had him in custody within an hour after you told me that you saw him here."

"In *custody*? Does that mean you've charged him with the murder already?"

"No. I charged him for exposing himself to Myrtle Hickok when she was carrying her garbage out to the curb last night there by the old folks' home. She called it in to the station about nine forty-five, right after he did it. At least we know where he was at that point in the evening."

"*Okay.* Elmer Yonce, showin' off his shortcomings. Thanks for sharin' that, Sheriff. Talk about nasty images that'll stay with a body for the rest of their life."

"Sorry. It's a dirty little habit that Elmer has. I'm surprised he hasn't 'made an ugly face' at you before."

"Nope. I've been spared that particular indignity. Thank goodness."

"I figure it's because he's heard about the Stella Reid Skillet Massacre."

"Reckon he didn't want to take a chance on losing his, uh, mind."

Gilford laughed, and Stella continued to look around the room as he wrote his signature and the date on the bag containing the mirror.

"Reckon we can rule out robbery," she said, pointing to an open jewelry box on the nightstand beside the bed. "There's some pretty nice pieces in there, and it doesn't even look like it was rifled through, let alone that anything was taken."

"Yes, I saw that and agree. There's also twenty dollars over there on the other night table, lying there plain as can be. In this day, with the economy like it is, that's a fortune to some folks."

As she continued to work her way around the room, Stella noticed there was a full array of makeup spread across the top of the dresser. The collection included everyday basics like mascara, lipstick, and eyeliner—products that Prissy wouldn't have been seen in public without.

"Prissy wasn't going anywhere—not for an overnight or anything like that," Stella observed. "She wouldn't have left without her makeup essentials. Not a woman like that, one who wouldn't let the mailman see her without her face painted on."

Stella walked to the bathroom door, opened it, and looked inside. She sniffed and detected an acrid odor that she recognized, having smelled it before at Florence's house. She glanced into the small garbage can next to the toilet and saw a box, some stained plastic gloves, and an empty squeeze bottle that had recently contained a platinum blond shade of hair color. An old, threadbare, stained towel hung haphazardly over the shower curtain rod.

When she walked back into the main living area, she saw Sheriff Gilford photographing the contents of Prissy's purse, which he had spread across the bed.

"When you looked at the body this morning, Sheriff, did you notice if she was wearing old clothes?"

"Yes, as a matter of fact, she was. Tattered jeans and a torn-up T-shirt. It kinda surprised me. She was usually dressed up when she was out about town."

"I believe she'd just colored her hair," Stella told him. "That's somethin' a woman does if she figures she's gonna be alone for the evenin'. It stinks up the house, and you look right awful doing it. You gotta wear old clothes that you don't mind gettin' stains on. It's certainly not something you plan to do if you're fixin' to have company. Especially a male visitor."

"Okay. Good to know. Thank you."

She watched as he placed the items back inside the purse, then slipped it into an evidence bag, as well. "Did you get a chance to talk to Jake Neville?" she asked.

"Yes, I questioned him late last night, after talking to you and before arresting Elmer. Jake's living in his mama's basement now."

"I heard."

"She gave him an alibi. Said he'd been home all evening."

"He was not. We saw that big ol' station wagon of his clear as I'm seein' you right now. He drove into that alley. No doubt about it."

"I believe you. Which means he was doing something he's not proud of or happy about, otherwise he wouldn't be lying about it."

Stella propped her hands on her hips and gave a defiant toss of her head. "You just haul Jake Neville's backside into your station house, and I'll come over and confront him face-to-face with what I saw. We can both watch him squirm like a worm on a hot sidewalk."

Sheriff Gilford laughed, then gave her an affectionate smile that, just for a moment, made her feel like she was a fifteen-year-old girl all over again.

"You know, Stella May," he said, "I believe you could break him, even without using my nutcracker. I think you could scare a man into confessing that he'd shot President Lincoln, if you were sure he did it."

She gave him a half-coquettish smile. "Why, Sheriff, keep talkin' like that and you could turn a girl's head."

"On a good day maybe," he replied softly, "if I was real, real lucky."

Chapter 11

When Stella and the sheriff finally left Priscilla's apartment, he had several boxes filled with evidence bags in the backseat of his cruiser and two deputies who were eager to move on to the more glamorous duties of protecting and serving their community.

"Ain't it about time for a break?" Mervin asked, leaning heavily on the cruiser's hood. "I'm about done for, and this alley's the cleanest it's been since this was all part of the Garden of Eden."

Stella watched him wipe the sweat from his brow with his forearm, and it occurred to her that Deputy Mervin Jarvis might be the only person she'd ever known who could perspire profusely in the middle of a snowstorm.

Gilford looked at his watch. "It's eleven o'clock, Mervin. It's a bit early for lunch, even for you."

Augustus spoke up. "You know Mervin, boss. Two hours—that's about his limit when it comes to hard physical labor. What would you like us to do next?"

"Canvas the stores, every one of them, up and down Main.

Find out who was in their store the last hour before they closed, and when the owners actually locked up and left. Ask if they saw anything suspicious. Anything at all."

Stella considered speaking up and mentioning that all the stores were dark, the streets were deserted, and not a soul was in sight last night. But she doubted the wisdom of highlighting the fact that she was all too aware of those facts. It wasn't something your run-of-the-mill downtown visitor would have paid such close attention to.

"Okay, boss." Augustus gave Gilford a most officious, curt nod, spun on his heel, and marched away.

Stella kept an eye on Gilford as he watched Augustus leave. While she might have expected the sheriff to appreciate his deputy's highly professional attitude and admirable work ethic, Gilford's expression was more suspicious than grateful.

Rumors around town suggested that Deputy Augustus Faber had every intention of being Sheriff Augustus Faber one day soon.

Stella couldn't imagine that Manny Gilford was a man who would go gently into the good night of retirement. Even though she had known him as a quiet child and a gangly teenager, he had become a sheriff before turning thirty, and Stella couldn't picture him wearing anything but his uniform. She couldn't imagine him driving an ordinary vehicle to the grocery store or fishing by the riverside on a lazy summer afternoon.

No. Augustus Faber could whirl on his heel, march like a marine, and solve the Black Dahlia murder, but Sheriff Manny Gilford would never retire and hand Augustus his badge.

Gilford turned to Mervin and said, "Unless you'd like to wash and wax that vehicle, Deputy, I suggest you stop using it as a La-Z-Boy recliner and carry on with your duties."

With exaggerated effort, Mervin pushed himself off the cruiser. "What duties would those be, sir? I could go back to the station and keep an eye on Elmer for you."

"The last time you offered to keep an eye on a prisoner at the station, I came back to a deputy who reeked of pizza and a petty-cash drawer without a single quarter in it."

Mervin shrugged and looked down at the ground sheepishly. "I think I got me one of them *Pac-Man* addictions, sir. I heard on the news last night that some folks are startin' to think it's a real disease, and it's sweepin' the nation."

"I'm going to give you a broom," Gilford told him, "and you'll be the one *sweepin' the nation*, or at least this county, Jarvis, if you don't get to canvassing those shops with your fellow deputy."

"Yes, sir."

"Stay away from that pizza parlor and its *Pac-Man* machine."

Mervin trudged away, moving as though he had fifty pounds of lead weights sewn into his boxers.

Gilford turned his attention to Stella. She couldn't help noticing that his face softened the moment he did.

She was touched and somewhat pleased. But, for reasons she couldn't quite understand, it made her uneasy.

"Mrs. Reid," he said, "I can't tell you how much I've appreciated your help last night and this morning. Most people don't step forward to aid law enforcement, like you and your family have. They're even less likely to if the victim is somebody they aren't particularly fond of."

"That's a shame," Stella replied. "Even the less loved among us deserve our protection. In fact, they might need it more than most, them not always having family to back 'em up."

She thought for a moment of what she had seen—and not

seen—in Priscilla Carr's apartment. "Speaking of family," she said, "did Prissy have any family around here? I can't recall hearing of any, and she's been here in McGill about five years, if I remember correctly."

"She *has* been here five years. Moved here from Chesterville when she was twenty."

"Didn't get far."

"I heard she walked most of the way. She'd been raised in foster homes. Got married young. Left him because she was sick and tired of getting beat up."

"Some might say the poor girl never had a chance."

"Everybody gets a chance. Some kind or the other. It's what they decide to do with it that counts."

"I just meant that some have an easier time than others."

"I don't disagree with you," he said. "I just get tired of people blaming fate for their own mistakes. Sometimes good people get a bad break. I won't deny it happens. But a lot of times, the trouble folks find themselves in . . . it's just chickens coming home to roost."

"Except murder," Stella said, gently insisting on Priscilla's behalf.

"Yes. Except murder."

Sheriff Gilford brushed his hand over his eyes and sighed. It occurred to Stella that his face was gray and his eyes were dull.

"Are you okay, Sheriff?" she asked. "You're lookin' pretty peaked. You feelin' poorly?"

"Naw. Just a bit tired. That's all."

"How much sleep did you get last night?"

"Sleep?"

"Reckon that answers my question. Maybe you should go home and catch a few winks."

He shook his head. "I have to get that evidence back to the station. Though it won't all fit in the safe. I may have to lock it up in one of the cells. Out of Elmer's reach, of course."

"Of course. And don't forget, if you need somebody to rough him up and ring a confession out of 'im, I volunteer for the job."

He gave her a quick glance over. Not a long, lingering lecherous look—the kind that Elmer Yonce gave women. Gilford didn't linger on her bustline, making her feel like a rump roast being sized up in a butcher shop.

No, Sheriff Gilford's evaluation and the approving look in his eye made her feel appreciated, admired, and respected.

Stella had to admit it was a good feeling, one she hadn't experienced much in the past six years.

"There's something I was meaning to ask you," she said. "If you don't mind and have the time."

"Of course I do. What is it?"

"I was wondering, did you happen to mention to anybody that Priscilla was strangled to death?"

"No."

"Are you sure?"

"Absolutely sure. Why would I tell someone that when I don't even know for sure if it's true?"

"That's what I figured." She took a deep breath. "Do you reckon anybody else might've mentioned that?"

"No. Herb didn't see the marks on her neck until I pointed them out to him there at the mortuary. I've been with him since then, and I had him so busy swabbing blood off the pavement that he hasn't talked to anybody but you and me. Not even Augustus or Mervin."

"Again, are you real sure about that?"

"Completely sure. Why are you asking me this stuff, Stella?"

"Just somethin' I was thinkin' about. I'm sure it's not important. If you're finished with me, I think I should get going now," she said, suddenly eager to leave.

She told herself that she was uneasy with being at the scene of the crime. But Stella Reid knew herself pretty well, and she was aware that at least part of her eagerness to get going had to do with Sheriff Gilford, how good he looked in his uniform, his thick silver hair, and the affectionate gleam in his gray eyes when he spoke to her.

For as long as she could remember, he had looked at her that way. The idea that Manny Gilford might have a bit of a crush on her was hardly a new one. She had suspected that since second grade, when he slipped her a bit of paper with a red heart on it for Valentine's Day.

But Manny had been one of her husband's best friends. To her knowledge, Manny had never been the sort of fella to make a move on another man's woman. *Any* man's woman. And certainly not if she was involved with one of his best friends.

Of course, Arthur was gone now. Had been for some time. But only in body. Not in spirit.

That was why Stella wore Art's wedding ring on a chain around her neck—a chain long enough that the ring was situated directly over her heart.

As far as she was concerned, she was still a married woman and always would be. Even the slightest bit of flirting with an old friend like Manny Gilford felt wrong to her. Adulterous even.

Those feelings—not the blood on the asphalt—were the reason she wanted to get out of the alley as quickly as possible.

"If you need me for anything, Sheriff," she said, "don't hesitate to ask. Just gimme me a ring or stop by the house. I know how important this investigation is. I'll drop anything I'm doin' to help you with it."

Again, he gave her that smile that seemed to go directly to her knees and make them wobbly. "Thank you, Mrs. Reid, and I want you to know, if you ever need anything, anything at all, you or your family, just let me know and I'll come running. I'd consider it an honor to help you any way I can."

Just for a moment, Stella allowed herself to return his smile. She heard a slight trembling in her own voice when she replied, "I know that, Manny. I've always known it, and I depend on it. On you. Thank you, Sheriff."

With that, she turned and left.

Quickly.

Before she made the mistake of doing or saying something that she would regret later that night in the dark silence of her bedroom, with her husband's spirit nearby.

Stella Reid wasn't in the habit of going into taverns.

But when she did, it was almost always to fetch her daughter-in-law when there was some sort of emergency and she had no other choice.

It wasn't that she felt she was too good to mingle with the folks inside those doors. She knew that being in a bar didn't make you a drunk any more than parking in a garage made you a car or sitting in a church pew made you righteous. But she was allergic to the smoke and didn't like the loud music, or the way the other patrons looked at her when she walked through the establishment. As though she didn't belong there. As if she wasn't one of them and, therefore, wasn't particularly welcome.

Stella had felt that way most of her childhood—lonely, separate from those around her—and she didn't fancy repeating the experience as an adult if she could avoid it.

She felt that same sense of alienation when she stepped inside the Bulldog's front door now. She sensed every eye in the place turn and lock on her—scrutinizing, evaluating, and somehow finding her wanting.

As always, the smoke was thick and acrid. It irritated her eyes almost instantly, and the odor was so strong that she could taste it.

She would have to change clothes the moment she got home and maybe even wash her hair to avoid getting a headache from it.

When her eyes finally adjusted to the dim light, she spotted Shirley, seated in her usual place—the last stool at the end of the bar, beneath an eight-by-ten black-and-white head shot of Elvis Presley.

Everybody else might have moved on from Elvis, embracing the Beatles and subsequent rock bands since. But Shirley would be an Elvis fan until her dying day.

In her early twenties, Shirley had frequented a different tavern, one just outside of town, down by the river. That was where she had asked the owner to hang a picture of Elvis over her favorite stool, enhancing her view and, ultimately, her mood.

But when she was permanently banned from the riverside bar, she brought the photo with her to her new watering hole. From that day forward, Shirley Reid swore that she would never drink a beer in any tavern that was unadorned with a picture of "the King."

It was known in every drinking establishment within fifty miles of McGill that it was to the owner's advantage to post a picture of Elvis. Shirley Reid's bar bill more than compensated the owner for their effort.

Stella walked over to Shirley, took a seat on the stool next to hers, and laid her purse on the bar, well away from Shirley's ashtray.

"I'm surprised you'd show your face in here," Shirley said, her cigarette dangling from the corner of her mouth, "after the rough things you said to me outside."

Stella couldn't remember saying anything particularly "rough" to her daughter-in-law, though she did recall being accused of nearly getting her grandchildren murdered.

But she hadn't come here to argue with Shirley. Quite the contrary. Stella preferred to live in peace with her fellow man, as much as they would allow and she could manage.

Though, so far, her "live and let live" philosophy hadn't worked with Shirley. She was sure that girl could start a fight in an empty room or win an argument with a fence post.

Some people seemed to thrive on conflict. It was one of their basic food groups, and they didn't seem to be able to live without it.

Shirley's silver bangle bracelets jingled as she tapped the bar, signaling for the bartender to bring her another beer. She half turned on her stool, and when her eyes met Stella's, the older woman was surprised to see the amount of animosity burning there.

Stella couldn't recall when she and Shirley had first argued all those years ago. But their relationship had gotten off to a rocky start from the very beginning, and it had gone downhill since.

Stella had to admit that she could have been far more patient with her daughter-in-law. More loving and accepting, to be sure.

She should have given less unsolicited advice and over-looked a few more chocolate-smeared faces, since such things seldom mattered much in the long run.

But there was no pretending that Shirley had been a diligent, devoted mother. Stella couldn't bring herself to lie about such a thing, not even to herself. She found it much easier to forgive her daughter-in-law for any offenses she might have committed against her than for those she had inflicted upon her grandchildren.

"I didn't come in here to start a fight with you, Shirley," she said, trying to keep her tone as even and calm as possible. "Truly, I didn't."

"Then what *did* you come in here for? Got a hankering for a scotch on the rocks, or do you take it neat?"

Stella wasn't well versed in bar terms, but she had no problem interpreting the ugly sneer on the younger woman's face.

"I came in here to ask you a question," Stella told her. "Just one question and then I'll leave you to finish your . . . breakfast . . . in peace."

"Oh, I had my Bloody Mary breakfast a long time ago," Shirley told her as she hefted her beer. "Now I'm working on lunch. Go on. Ask your question so I can get rid of you."

"Out there in front, when we were talking earlier," Stella whispered, "you told me you were worried about your kids almost gettin' strangled, like Priscilla did."

"Yeah? So? That'd worry almost any mother, now, wouldn't it?"

"I'm sure it would," Stella replied, "if that's what happened. But what I wanna know is, why would you say she was strangled?"

Shirley's cockiness vanished in an instant. Suddenly, she looked afraid, like a rabbit caught in a cage trap.

130

"Well, she was. Wasn't she?"

Stella couldn't remember ever seeing her daughter-in-law so scared. Shirley usually had enough alcohol running through her system to avoid such an emotion.

"I don't think anybody knows for sure how she got killed," Stella said, choosing her words carefully so as not to violate any of the sheriff's confidences.

"I must've heard it somewhere." Shirley shook a cigarette from her pack, then dropped her silver lighter with its turquoise butterfly onto the bar. It landed with a clatter, and Shirley jumped.

"Think hard, Shirl," Stella coaxed her. "It's important. Who do you reckon you heard it from?"

"I don't know! Somebody must've said something about it sometime. Or maybe I just dreamed it up. Leave me alone and let me finish my beer before it goes flat."

Stella looked around and realized that the other patrons were giving her looks that were even less friendly than the ones they had sent her way when she'd first arrived.

Yes, she had definitely worn out her welcome in this establishment. She looked into her daughter-in-law's eyes and saw a degree of hatred that seared her heart.

With all those beautiful children that we share in common, not to mention Macon, how did we wind up here? she asked herself.

Time to go.

Stella retrieved her purse off the bar, stood, and said softly, "Thank you, Shirley, for your time. I'm sorry to have disturbed you. If you happen to remember the answer to that question of mine, I'd sure appreciate it if you'd let me know. You have a good day now, hear?"

A grumble was Shirley's only response as she lifted her beer to her lips. But Stella heard enough to know that she had just been told where to go—and it wasn't a five-star vacation destination.

As she made her way out the tavern's front door, Stella realized with a heavy heart that she was carrying more questions and misgivings out of the Bulldog Tavern than she had carried in.

Chapter 12

When the school bell rang and the Reid children raced to catch the bus to their grandmother's house, they found her waiting for them in her old panel truck near the bus parking lot.

Stella thought they would be happy to see her, especially when they discovered that she had brought along their grandpa's old thermos, which she'd filled with hot cocoa, and some cups.

They did appear pleased, although Stella thought she detected a mood that was less than festive when they climbed inside and buckled themselves into their appointed seats.

Being the oldest, Savannah sat in the front passenger seat, next to Stella. One look at her granddaughter told Stella that, indeed, something unpleasant was afoot.

"Everything okay?" Stella asked.

Too quickly, too cheerfully, Savannah responded, "Sure! Everything's fine! Just fine!"

Okay, Stella thought. *Either somebody died or Christmas got cancelled.*

Stella turned in her seat and saw a truck filled with glum faces.

"What's going on?" she asked. "Y'all look like somebody done licked the red off your candy canes."

"I'll tell you what's wrong," Marietta piped up. "Everybody at school has already got—"

"Marietta, you hush your mouth," Savannah barked.

"I will not!"

"You will, too, if you know what's good for you."

"Girls!" Stella glanced from Marietta's pouty face to Savannah's stern one. "Let's keep civil tongues in our heads when we speak to each other."

"Marietta's got nothing to say," Savannah replied, looking deeply distressed. "But she's bound to say it, anyway. No matter who it hurts, because that's the way she is."

Stella looked at Waycross, who was fidgeting with the library book he held in his lap. His big eyes met Stella's. "That's true. Marietta's that way. Yes, she is," he said. "She don't care who she hurts as long as she gets her say."

Turning to Marietta, Stella said, "Granddaughter, is that true? Are the words you want to speak likely to hurt somebody?"

Marietta stuck her chin out indignantly and puffed herself up until she looked like she was about to explode out of her winter jacket. "*I'm* the one who's hurt, so why should I be quiet about it?"

"How did you get hurt, darlin'?"

Stella saw Savannah shoot Marietta a fierce warning look. She also saw it fly right over Marietta's head and land somewhere in the back of the truck.

"It was me who got hurt, standing there on the playground,

listening to everybody talk about what kind of Christmas tree their family got this year, when I got no kind at all."

"None of the rest of us have one, either," Vidalia noted, rubbing at the paint stains on her jacket. "But you didn't see us making a scene, standin' there on the playground, bawlin' like a calf without a mama and telling the whole world about it."

"That would've been a sight," Waycross said, "if we'd all pitched a hissy fit like you did. We'd probably been on the news."

"Family makes complete jackasses of themselves," Savannah muttered under her breath. "Film at eleven."

"I don't want to hear you use that word, Miss Savannah Sue," Stella whispered back.

"It's in the Bible."

"You heard me."

Stella began to pour the cocoa into the cups, being careful to fill them only halfway in case of spills. As she handed one to each child, she said, "It's funny that y'all should bring up the topic of a Christmas tree. 'Cause that's where we're going right now. To buy one. We'll set it up tonight there in the front room, and you kids can put the lights and ornaments on for me. The icicles, too, if you promise to hang them straight. You know I don't abide crooked icicles."

There was so much cheering inside the truck that Stella feared the cocoa would be spilled before it was even tasted.

Everyone from little Jesup to Marietta was positively overflowing with holiday cheer.

Only Savannah sat quietly, staring off into the distance, with an inscrutable expression on her pretty face.

Stella didn't have to ask why. Sadly, her eldest granddaughter was far too well informed when it came to the inadequacies of the Reid family budget.

Stella decided to set her mind at ease.

Turning to the gang in the rear of the truck, Stella said, "Hold on to your hot chocolate. We're off to Mr. Anderson's Christmas tree lot to get the best tree we can find. But first, we have to stop by the house just for a second, while I run inside and get something."

"Like money?" Savannah whispered.

Stella simply nodded as she started the truck and pulled out of the parking lot, driving carefully so as not to jostle the hot chocolate drinkers and their treats.

A few moments later, they had reached the little shotgun shack. Stella left the children waiting while she ran inside.

It was as she was dumping the coffee can from under the sink into a pillowcase that she glanced up and saw Savannah standing there, looking confused and surprised.

Finally, the child said, "I thought that money was just for bailing Mama out of jail."

"It's for emergencies."

"I know. Like bailing Mama out of jail."

Stella drew a deep breath. "I'm the one who saves it up, one nickel at a time. So, I'm the one who decides what it's used for. And I say this family's got itself an emergency. It needs a Christmas tree."

The grandmother and the girl stood, searching each other's eyes, for a long time.

Then Stella said, "What do you think of that, Miss Savannah?"

Her granddaughter gave her a small, sly smile and said, "Reckon it might be the first time that Mr. Anderson ever got paid for a tree with a pillowcase full of nickels."

"He's a nice man, and a sale's a sale. Somethin' tells me he won't mind a bit."

Together, they walked out of the house, Stella clutching the heavy pillow slip to her chest.

Nearing the truck, Stella heard Savannah say, "Good idea you had there, Granny. I approve."

"Thank you, sugar. I'm glad you understand."

"I do. Probably better than you think. There's not much point in throwing somebody a lifeline if they're just going to keep on jumping back into the river over and over again."

"That's so true, darlin'. Especially when lifelines are scarce and there's others that need 'em."

Even with the Christmas trees being already picked over, Stella and her grandchildren had no problem scoring a fine tree—small enough for their tiny living room, but fresh and full and well balanced.

As Savannah, Waycross, and Vidalia helped Stella tie the tree to the top of the truck, Savannah told her grandmother, "Mr. Anderson gave us a deal on that tree, and you know why, don't you?"

"Because it's about the end of the season, and he was afraid he wouldn't be able to sell it to anybody else?"

"Nope. It's because he's sweet on you."

"That's not true, Savannah. I think you've been reading some of them romance novels along with your Nancy Drew books. Your imagination's workin' overtime."

"No it's not. I know what I'm talking about. Mr. Anderson likes you, and Sheriff Gilford likes you. Every man in town who's ol . . . I mean, your age, they're carryin' a torch for you. It's cause you're the prettiest lady in McGill who's, well, you know, your age."

"Hmm. Thank you. I reckon. But I do believe you're exaggeratin' the situation a mite."

"No, Savannah's right," Waycross interjected, tugging on a twine knot to make sure it was secure. "Mr. Anderson likes you, and the sheriff's got the hots for you big-time. No doubt about it."

"Waycross! You're not supposed to even know about stuff like 'hots' yet."

Savannah laughed, finally lighthearted and joyful with the festivities under way. "Don't kid yourself, Granny. Waycross knows a lot about stuff like that. We all do. We can't help it. That's all people talk about at school. It's all they hear in the songs on the radio and all they see on TV. Here's what everybody was singing at recess today. . . ."

To Stella's consternation, Savannah and Waycross began to bellow out Donna Summer's "Hot Stuff."

Stella clapped her hands over her ears and, with greatly exaggerated outrage, shouted, "No! Y'all quit it! I can't bear it! It's an abomination!"

The kids collapsed in a fit of giggles.

"Maybe we should try a Christmas carol," Savannah told Waycross. "We don't want Granny to blow a gasket before we even get the tree home."

Waycross agreed and launched into his own full-throated rendition of "Grandma Got Run Over by a Reindeer." They were all guffawing by the time they got the tree tied snugly.

As they were getting into the truck to join the rest and head home, Mr. Anderson came running toward them, carrying an enormous cake covered with coconut frosting and decorated with colorful gumdrops.

"Here," he said, shoving the cake through Stella's open window. "My sister, Charlene, bakes one of these every Christmas for me. But this year I'm on a diet. I was wondering if y'all know anybody who might like to have it."

"I know somebody!" Vidalia screamed.

"Yes!" Waycross yelled. "*We* would!"

"I'll take it!" Marietta cried. "I can eat the whole thing myself!"

Once Stella had the cake in hand, she gave Mr. Anderson her prettiest smile—the kind a fellow might appreciate if he was "sweet" on a gal—and told him, "Thank you so much, Mr. Anderson. You've no idea what this means to us. God bless you, sir."

"My pleasure, ma'am. A very merry Christmas to you and yours."

As he walked away, a big smile on his face, Waycross leaned over his grandmother's shoulder and whispered, "Hots, Gran. Major hot stuff."

She would have ruffled his hair, but her hands were too full of cake. "There's an empty cardboard box back there somewhere. Find it and pass it up, would ya, grandson?"

A moment later, the box was put on Savannah's lap, and the cake was lovingly placed inside it.

"There you go, darlin'," Stella told the girl. "You hang on tight to that beautiful cake, and I'll try not to make any sudden stops."

But when Savannah didn't reply, Stella gave her an inquisitive look and saw that she was staring straight ahead out the windshield at something in front of the truck.

Instantly, the child's alarmed expression caused Stella's heart to skip a beat. She looked to see the cause for concern, and she understood instantly.

Shirley had gotten out of an old pickup and was walking toward them. Stella recognized the vehicle, with its enormous snarling bulldog logo on the side, as the truck that the tavern owner used for deliveries.

One look at Shirley's face and Stella felt her stomach spasm. She had seen Shirley in some bad moods before, even throwing complete and utter conniptions. But she had never seen her like that.

Contorted with rage, Shirley's face reminded Stella of every horror movie she had ever seen involving people who were possessed by demonic spirits.

Shirley looked as though at any second her hair would burst into flames, her head would start to spin, and fire would shoot out of her mouth.

She figured it out, Stella thought. *She knows that I know that she was lying this morning. She knows more about Priscilla's death than she's saying, and she knows I know it.*

Stella was also aware that she was about to pay dearly for her insight.

"Get outta that truck!" Shirley screamed as she approached them. "You kids get outta there this minute!"

At first, the children, like Stella, were too shocked to move or speak.

But when Shirley made her way to the back of the truck and pulled the doors open, they began to cry.

To Stella's horror, Shirley began to yank them out, one by one, pulling them by their arms and tossing them onto the ground like they were so many old rag dolls.

"Stop! Shirley, no!" Stella scrambled out of the truck and raced to the rear, where her grandchildren were screaming with pain and fear.

"Mama, no! Don't!" Vidalia cried as she was dragged out.

"Ow! That hurts!" Waycross yelled.

Marietta was lying on the ground, where she'd been thrown, shrieking like she was dying. Alma lay beside her, terrorized into complete silence.

When Shirley took hold of little Jesup, the child began to shake violently and sob.

Stella grabbed Shirley by the shoulders and spun her around to face her. "Shirley!" she screamed in her face, trying to jar the woman out of the rage she was in. "Stop it! What in tarnation are you doing?"

Shirley shook off Stella's grip, but she released Jesup, who climbed down from the truck herself and collapsed into the arms of her oldest sister. Like Stella, Savannah had rushed to the rear of the truck to protect her siblings.

"I'm taking my kids home, where they belong," Shirley yelled back. "You wicked old witch, telling them bad things about me! You've got a lot of nerve when your son's nothing but a worthless piece of—"

"Shirley. That's enough. Please, let's settle down and talk about this." Stella fought to calm herself, to catch her breath. There for a moment, she had thought that she and her daughter-in-law were going to come to blows right in front of all seven children.

"There's nothing to talk about," Shirley said. "I'm taking them back home with me, and it'll be a cold day in hell before you get to see 'em again."

Savannah reached over and put her hand on her mother's shoulder. "Mama, Granny doesn't talk bad about you to us. She's never said one bad thing about you. She wouldn't do that. You're our mother and—"

"Yeah, yeah, she's a damned saint, this one."

"I never claimed to be a saint," Stella said, "but I want to make peace with you. Right here, right now. You're my daughter-in-law, the mother of my grandchildren. I don't want trouble with you." Stella forced a smile to her lips.

What choice do you have but to play nice? she told herself, feeling like a liar and a hypocrite as she stood there, smiling at someone she'd prefer to take apart at the seams.

But Shirley was holding hostage the seven people Stella loved most in the world. Precious, innocent children—the perfect weapons in the hands of someone who didn't care who got hurt as long as they won every battle and maintained control over those around them. One of the oldest, cruelest, and most effective tactics available to someone with a stunted conscience had to be, "Do what I want, or I'll hit you with someone you love. They'll get hurt, and it'll be your fault."

Both Stella and Shirley knew that Stella would submit, because of her love for her grandchildren. An otherwise strong woman would back down, paste a fake smile on her face, and speak gentle words of peace when she felt like screaming and striking out, because sweet, innocent hostages were being held.

But Stella was old enough to have seen the game played many times, and she knew how it ended. Those who won so many battles using such despicable means lost the war and ended up bitter and alone, because eventually, one way or another, the hostages broke free.

As Stella looked into Shirley's eyes, she knew exactly what her daughter-in-law wanted. Control. Pure and simple.

Shirley had yet to learn that control wasn't power. Love was power.

So, Stella gave her daughter-in-law the control she craved, knowing that the law of sowing and reaping would provide justice for her and the children someday.

Just not today.

"We were fixin' to go back to the house and put up this Christmas tree," she told Shirley, looking around at the sobbing, frightened children. "We've even got us a Christmas cake to eat while we're doing it. Why don't we all go back to the house together? You too. We'll have a nice evening and make some sweet memories for the kids to remember."

For a couple of seconds, Stella thought Shirley was considering it. She seemed to be.

The children waited breathlessly to see if this Christmas miracle might happen. But . . .

"No! I'm not going to your house for no tree and cake, just so's you can look like a Miss Goody Two-shoes in front of the kids. I'm not that stupid, Stella. I see right through you, and someday, the kids will, too. They'll see you for the mean, evil bitch that you—"

"Mama! No!" Waycross shouted. He scrambled up from the ground, where she had thrown him, and confronted her, getting as face-to-face as he could, considering that he was a foot and a half shorter. "Don't you talk to Gran that way. Don't you call her bad names. We're not gonna have that."

"*We're* not gonna? Who's *we*, little Mister Smart Mouth?"

"All of us," he said, waving his hand to indicate all his siblings. "We're family, and we stick up for each other."

Shirley turned on Stella. "See there? That's what I mean. You turn my kids against me, and I'm supposed to let you see them? Let them stay with you for days on end?"

Stella bit her tongue, not allowing herself to remind Shirley that the extended grandkid visits were almost always at Shirley's request. Shirley made the most of her kid-free time by inviting men over for drunken parties that went on all night or until the neighbors complained.

"Go on, you kids." Shirley waved a hand toward the Bulldog delivery pickup. "Go get in the back of that truck. You're going home."

"But the tree," Marietta whined.

"You don't need no tree. There's plenty of Christmas decorations around town for you to look at. The damned things are everywhere."

Stella looked at Savannah and saw tears streaming down her granddaughter's face.

At that moment, Stella despised Shirley. Try as she might, she couldn't help it. Moments before they had been so happy. Now everyone was heartbroken, all because Shirley was jealous that her children were receiving some happiness that wasn't coming directly from her own hand.

"Come on, you guys," Savannah said, gently pulling her brother and her other siblings to her side. "Let's go. That's the way it's gotta be."

"But you can't put them all in the cab," Stella protested. "There isn't room for seven kids in a—"

"Get in the back!" Shirley shouted at her brood. "It ain't that far, and it ain't that cold. It won't kill ya."

"Shirley, please," Stella pleaded. "If you won't come back to the house with me, and you won't let them . . . then let me take them back to your house. My truck's got a seat and a belt for each one of them. It's safer and warmer than the back of a pickup. I won't come into your house. I'll just drop them off. Okay?"

"I told you, we don't need your help, Stella Reid! We don't need anything from you!"

"Yes we do. We need the Christmas cake. It's got gumdrops on it and everything," Marietta said, getting up off the ground and brushing the dirt from her clothes and her skinned knees.

"You don't need *her* cake. As far as I'm concerned, Stella knows exactly what she can do with that cake. I might do it for her, if she don't look out."

Stella watched as her grandchildren left, heading for the pickup, their heads low, their spirits wounded.

If they hadn't been there, Stella hated to think what she might have done to Shirley. The whacks that Bud had received from her were a schoolboy's spanking compared to the havoc she wanted to wreak upon her daughter-in-law at that moment.

Stella considered running into Mr. Anderson's office, calling the sheriff, and asking him to intervene on her behalf.

But she knew how fruitless that would be. Unfortunately, there was no law that forbade Shirley from doing exactly what she had done to her children. Stella considered it strange that the statutes that would send Shirley to jail for assaulting some numskull in the tavern wouldn't protect a child who received the same abuse.

She walked back to the driver's door of her truck, opened it, and got inside. She turned the key in the ignition but shut off the heat. If her grandchildren would be riding in a cold truck without heat, so would she.

She turned and looked at the cake sitting in the box on the passenger's seat, where Savannah had left it.

Savannah. Her first grandchild. Her heart.

She watched as the girl, already forced to be a woman, helped her smallest sisters into the cab, then lifted the others into the rear of the pickup.

Just before she climbed in herself, Savannah stopped, looked back at Stella's truck, and made eye contact with her grandmother. They held the gaze, suffering not only their own pain but each other's.

145

"Get in the dadgum truck, Savannah! I haven't got all day!" Shirley bellowed.

Savannah did as she was told.

Stella thought she saw the child blow her a kiss, so she sent her one in return. But she couldn't be sure if Savannah saw the answering gesture.

Stella couldn't see that clearly. Her eyes were too full of tears.

When Stella set the Christmas tree in the corner of her living room, it was all she could do just to place it in the stand and water it. The thought of decorating its branches without her grandchildren brought her more sorrow than she could bear.

As did the sight of Mr. Anderson's cake sitting in its cardboard box on the coffee table. He had given her family that treat to bring them happiness. But thanks to Shirley's rejection of it, the gift only added to the grief of the moment.

Stella didn't know what to do with it. She had no desire to eat it herself.

Then she remembered there was one other person within her immediate vicinity who was probably even more miserable than she.

Long ago, Stella had learned that few things lifted a heavy heart more effectively than generosity. Many times, during her darkest moments, she had found a ray of sunlight in a simple act of charity.

Once the tree was situated, bare and cheerless though it might be, she snatched up the cake and headed out the door with it.

She was determined that Mr. Anderson's Christmas gift, bestowed with such goodwill, would find its way to someone who needed the love it represented even more than she did.

It didn't take Stella long to drive to Florence Bagley's house. Once there, she looked around to see if Bud's big, fancy pickup was parked by the front door or around back.

If he had returned home and sweet-talked Florence into some sort of "rubber band and duct tape" reconciliation, as he had done so many times before after breaking her heart and abusing her, the last thing Stella wanted was to interrupt their happy reunion.

Not because she was such a considerate neighbor, but because she didn't think she could stand to see the look of sly glee that Bud always wore after such a "triumph."

Bud might be stupid, but he was no dummy. He knew that Stella had his number. Even if Florence wasn't aware of his all too deliberate manipulations of her, Stella knew. He enjoyed flaunting the control he had over Florence, knowing how much it frustrated and upset Stella. After the day Stella had just endured, if she had to watch Bud strut around, his nose in the air, she was afraid it just might compel her to commit violence.

As Stella took the cake from the truck and carried it up the steps to the veranda, it occurred to her, not for the first time, that she was having a hard time stomping out the little fires of hate that were continually springing up here and there in her spirit lately.

That was the problem with those little fires. Once ignited, they grew into brushfires, and all too quickly, when you least expected it, they exploded into raging infernos that destroyed everything and everyone in their path.

All too well, Stella knew that the first victim an out-of-control forest fire claimed, scorching them with mindless, heartless ferocity, was the person whose spirit had harbored the initial spark.

Stella found it almost impossible not to hate the likes of Shirley and Bud, who continually hurt the ones she loved and, instead of feeling remorse, appeared to thrive on their own cruelty.

To Stella's dismay, no amount of praying seemed to help.

She would start off humble enough, but then her temper would get the better of her, and her righteous entreaties would quickly disintegrate into words like, *Lord, please put some of your divine love in my heart for Shirley, 'cause I can't seem to conjure up any of my own. Meanwhile, you best keep that weasel-faced, pecker-head Bud Bagley away from me, 'cause if I see him anytime soon, I'm liable to jerk a knot in his tail, then beat him to death with it.*

Though she wasn't proud of herself after such spiritual discourse, Stella figured the Lord forgave her. He knew Shirley and Bud Bagley even better than she did.

After knocking three times on the front door, Stella started to debate the pros and cons of nabbing the house key that Florence had told her was stashed under the geranium pot on the windowsill and just letting herself in.

Pros: She'd get in the house a lot faster and spare her knuckles.

Cons: When she and Florence were teenagers, she'd spent a summer teaching Flo how to shoot a .22 rifle. As a result, her friend was a darned good shot. In Florence's present emotional state, she might get overly excited to find someone rambling around inside her house at night.

A body could wind up dead like that, and Stella couldn't bear the thought of Florence having to live with all that guilt.

Finally, she reached a compromise. She took the key out from under the geranium pot, unlocked the door, opened it, stuck her head in, and yelled, "Flo, it's me, Stella. I know you're there, and I know you heard me poundin' on your door. Get your butt in here, girl. I've got coconut cake."

She knew that would do it. Flo had a weakness for sweets that was almost as fierce as Stella's.

It wasn't thirty seconds before a disheveled Florence, dressed in an old bathrobe and scruffy house slippers, her hair standing on end, and without a smidgen of makeup on, came trudging down the staircase.

She stopped halfway down and stared at Stella and the cake. "Is it one of Elsie's?" she asked.

"No. It's Harry Anderson's sister's."

Florence stood still, said nothing.

"Flo. It's *cake*."

Florence plodded down the remaining stairs and through the foyer, leading the way to the back of the house and the kitchen. "I'm not hungry," she said. "Haven't eaten a thing all day. That's why I'm going to force myself to have a slice."

Stella took the cake from the cardboard box and set it on the marble counter. "I understand," she said. "You gotta keep your strength up."

"That's right. I've lost the love of my life—may the lousy, good-for-nothing sonuvabitch fall down a flight of stairs into a pit of rabid crocodiles—but I've got to keep going."

"That's the spirit. Have you heard from the sonuvabitch in question?"

"Not since this morning. No sooner had you left than he came by for the rest of his stuff. You just missed him."

"Lucky me."

"He took all the guns with him, too. Didn't even leave me that twenty-two you gave me to protect myself and the house with."

"Well, shoot. I could've just gone ahead and let myself in with the key."

"What?"

"Never mind. Cut me a piece of that cake. I'm not hungry, either, so a medium-size piece'll do 'er."

Florence took two of her crystal dessert dishes from the cupboard, cut two ridiculously large pieces of the cake and plated them, then carefully arranged any wayward gumdrops in an attractive pattern on the top.

A linen napkin for each and a tumbler of iced sweet tea, and they were ready to chat and eat away their problems.

Or at least put a decent dent in them.

Florence led Stella to the table situated in a cozy breakfast nook that was about the size of Stella's entire kitchen. They sat across from each other, the delectable dessert between them.

"I heard you had a battle royal with your daughter-in-law at the Christmas tree lot this afternoon," Florence said, digging into the cake with greater gusto than one might expect of a woman who had just been dumped by her husband of over thirty years.

"Who told you?"

"Gay Copeland. Her sister-in-law, Becky Davis, was visiting from Chattanooga, and the two of them were driving by just as Shirley was flinging those young'uns right and left out the back of your truck. They contemplated pulling over and putting a stop to it, but then they saw that you were taking the situation in hand. Sounded plumb awful, to hear them tell it."

Stella shook her head and sighed. "Just once," she said, "I'd like to not have the entire town know my business before I do."

"That's the joy of living in a small community. Everybody knows what everybody else had for supper, and they've all got an opinion on it."

Stella popped a cherry gumdrop into her mouth, but it had no flavor, and she nearly choked on it, just thinking about the joy it would have given her grandchildren.

It didn't seem right, her eating this cake when they couldn't, after them being so thrilled to get it.

She pushed the plate away and decided to just drink the tea instead. "Yes, me and Shirley had it out right there on Mr. Anderson's property. It was plumb ugly. I thought we were gonna clean each other's clocks for sure right there in front of the kids."

"I'm sorry. That woman's given you nothing but grief since she and Macon started keeping company. I remember you telling me even back then that she was a heap of trouble, and you were right."

"In those days, I thought Macon could do better. But now I'm not sure he could've. I wouldn't admit this to just anybody, Flo, but Macon's been a heartache to me. I know he neglects his family. He's probably part of the reason why Shirley's the way she is."

Stella took a long drink of her iced tea and noticed that her own hand was shaking. "If I'm honest," she said, "I'd have to admit that since Macon's daddy was the best man who ever walked the earth, I must be the reason why Macon turned out bad. I don't know where I went wrong, but I must've. I try to remember that when I get too mad at either one of 'em. Reckon there's enough blame to go around for everybody."

"You and Art wouldn't be the first good parents to turn out a rotten kid," Florence countered. "Look around you. Happens all the time. Then you have the opposite—two lousy parents whose children are the salt of the earth. Like Shirley and Macon and your grandkids. They say that goodness and badness skip generations. I'd say that's the case with your situation. Look at that little Savannah. She's the spitting image of you. If you're gonna take the blame for Macon, you've gotta take the credit for her."

As much as Florence's words were soothing to Stella's spirit, she'd come to her friend's house not to be comforted, but to console.

"I didn't come over here to burden you, Flo, but to lift you up a bit. I was worried about you, hon." She reached over and squeezed Florence's hand. "I couldn't go to bed till I knew if you were okay."

"Bless you, Stella." Tears began to roll down Florence's cheeks again, and her voice choked when she added, "You're the best friend anybody ever had."

"Oh, hooey. You wouldn't have said that the day we were clowning around down by the river, and I pushed you into that blackberry patch."

Florence chuckled. "That's true. I had to go to the eighth-grade graduation party looking like I'd tangled with a bobcat and *lost*!"

"I remember we stole your mama's makeup and tried to cover up those scratches. We used the whole bottle, and it didn't do a bit of good." Stella smiled, remembering, cherishing the memories—good and bad. "We've made it through a lot, Flo," she told her old friend. "We've got the scars to prove it, inside and out. But what didn't kill us made us stronger."

Florence thought it over for a moment. "So they say. But

I'm not sure it's true. Do you feel stronger, Stella, for all the crap you've been through?"

"Not particularly, now that you mention it. Mostly, I just feel tired and pissed off at people who've made my life harder than it needed to be. Right up to today. Shirley had no call to pitch that hissy fit in front of her children and hurt 'em like that. I swear, if they hadn't been there and I'd had a billy club in my hand, I'd have plowed that gal's field for her then and there."

Florence looked a little shocked and a bit uneasy with Stella's confession. She said nothing, just stared down into her glass of tea.

Finally, Stella said, "I'm sorry, sugar. I didn't mean to dump all that ugliness on you. You've had trials aplenty yourself today. The last thing you need is to hear me gripe about mine."

"No, no, don't apologize. You're just speaking your heart, and I'm here to listen. That's what friends are for."

Stella rose to her feet, which ached, reminding her of how exhausting the past twenty-four hours had been. She took her plate with its uneaten cake and her glass from the table and set them on the counter. "I'd best be heading back home," she said. "Tomorrow's another day, and if it's anything like yesterday or today, I'm gonna need some rest before I tackle it."

"Me too. I don't know for sure where Bud went. He wouldn't say. But it sounded like he was leaving town tonight. Said he's going to sell the grocery store and gas station and the pool hall, just like I was afraid he'd do. But until he does, I guess I'll keep working at the store. What else am I going to do with myself?"

Stella gave her a playful grin. "I guess if times get rough, you could buy yourself a red purse and hang out by a lamppost downtown. Sell your 'wares' to the old farts stumblin' outta the Bulldog."

Florence smiled back. "I suppose I could. But my 'wares' are pretty worn, and those nickels don't add up so quick."

Both women laughed and hugged each other long and hard.

Stella patted her friend on the back and said, "You'll figure it out. We may be tired old gals with worn-to-a-frazzle wares, but we're tough. It'd take a lot more than this to kill either one of us."

Chapter 13

Other than missing her grandchildren and worrying about how they were doing, the next day passed peacefully for Stella. At least, more peacefully than the two before it.

Wouldn't take much, Stella told herself when contemplating the fact on her way to choir practice that evening. *I'd rather get beat with a wet squirrel then relive those two days all over again.*

As soon as she pulled into the parking lot, she saw that attendance was up. Taking a quick tally of the cars, she realized that everyone who had ever attended choir practice in their life was there.

In a small town like McGill, there was nothing quite like a morsel of juicy gossip to draw folks to a house of worship. Or any other gathering place, for that matter.

Tonight they had way more than a morsel. They had a mouthful to chew on.

No sooner had she walked into the sanctuary than Stella saw Elsie Dingle sprinting down the aisle in her direction, an eager gleam in her eye.

"Sister Stella! Just the person I wanted to see! I hear you

and Shirley had a knock-down-drag-out right there on the Anderson Christmas tree lot. Heard you ripped out a hank of her
hair and knocked a bunch of her teeth so far down her throat
that she'll have to sit on a bologna sandwich to chew it!"

Okay, Stella thought. *Word's done got around, and now we have*
two *tasty mouthfuls to chew on.*

It hadn't occurred to her that the Christmas Tree Lot
Ruckus could compete with Priscilla Carr's murder.

But nothing was discarded. Drama and the gossip it gener-
ated were precious commodities to McGillians. Every tidbit
was to be ruminated and savored to the fullest. Or at least
until the next delicious morsel came along.

"That is the highly embroidered version of the story,"
Stella admitted. "I hate to say it, but I much prefer it to the
real one."

Elsie was genuinely disappointed. "Then what's the real
one?"

"Shirley's still got all her hair and teeth. She's got the grandkids, too, and says that I can't see them, maybe ever again. That
I'm a bad influence on them."

Elsie shook her head in disgust. "If that ain't the pot callin'
the kettle black. Not that you're a kettle, Sister Stella. Just to
say that Shirley's got no room to talk 'bout bad influences on
children. I hear tell that she was at the bar last night, drinkin'
herself stupid—which we all know wouldn't take long, in her
case, bless 'er heart."

Stella winced. "I guess that means my grandchildren were
sitting at home by themselves, instead of being at my house,
decoratin' the tree and eatin' cake, like they wanted to be.
Breaks my heart, Elsie. Breaks it plumb in two."

Elsie gathered Stella into her arms and squeezed her tightly
against her ample bosom. "I know it does, sugar. Breaks mine,

too. Them kids are the sweetest things I ever saw. She don't deserve 'em. Never has, and now she's gettin' worse."

Toward the front of the church, Connie O'Reilly, the pastor's wife, was attempting to gather the group into some semblance of order.

"Sister Connie's tryin' to corral the chorale," Stella observed, happy to end the conversation about Shirley. "Guess we should take our seats now."

"Reckon so. We can talk about this after practice."

Oh, goody, Stella thought. *So much for escaping the aggravation of drama, even in God's front room.*

As Stella and Elsie took their seats in the choir pews at the front of the church, Stella couldn't help noticing that Allison Neville had shown up. She was a regular choir member and was faithful in her attendance. But considering that her family was the subject of at least one major rumor at that moment, Stella was surprised that she would appear.

Even Stella herself couldn't look at the woman without thinking about those Grinch drawers floating down the street. Now she couldn't help picturing the Chrysler station wagon driving into the alley—right before a murder had been committed.

Stella wondered if word had gotten out that Jake had been spotted in the vicinity that night. She had told Sheriff Gilford, and the sheriff had questioned both Jake and Jake's mother.

Somebody must have seen or heard something about it.

In McGill three people could keep a secret only if two of them were dead and the last one was mute and had his mouth duct-taped shut.

Stella assumed that by now, everybody in town was fully informed.

Judging from the covert suspicious looks being shot in poor

Allison's direction, it was clear that the members of the church choir were among the enlightened.

Allison stared straight ahead, her face drawn into a somber, pained expression.

"He did it, you know," someone whispered in Stella's ear.

She turned to see that Velma Milton had parked herself beside her and had the gleam of gossip in her eye.

"Who did what?" Stella asked. She knew what was coming, but she wanted Velma to have to actually state her accusation. Maybe when she heard it coming out of her mouth, she'd realize how bad it sounded.

"Jake Neville. *Her* husband." Velma gave a not very subtle nod toward Allison. "He killed that Prissy Carr gal in the alley behind the bar."

"I don't believe we know that for sure. I wouldn't—"

"It's true! I heard it from Monique Alan, and she always tells the truth. Not like the rest of these blabbermouths, who exaggerate a hundred times before they even get out of bed in the mornin'."

"Monique's fine character and truthfulness aside, I think until somebody's actually been charged with something, we shouldn't cast aspersions on—"

"And him, the principal of a school, too. Shameful!"

"Innocent until proven gui—"

"I'll bet he's a child molester, too. Have you heard what kind of undershorts he wears? Disgusting!"

Something snapped inside Stella. She suspected it was her last strained nerve.

She jumped to her feet, and the next thing she knew, she was running past the startled preacher's wife and down the center aisle of the church, toward the back door.

Enough was enough. She had enjoyed the company of her

fellow human beings as much as she could stand for the moment. If she missed choir practice and sang a sour note during the Sunday service, so be it. One bad vocal performance from alto Stella Reid wasn't likely to usher in the Apocalypse.

She took a long drink of water from the fountain in the foyer, then made her way outside to the parking lot and her truck.

She was going home. No, the grandkids wouldn't be there. The tree would be standing, bare and undecorated, in the corner, reminding her that the grandchildren weren't there. Reminding her that she wasn't sure when she would see them again.

But it was her home, and she wasn't about to allow the likes of Shirley Reid to turn her against her own home.

She had spent many a lonely hour there before, and she was bound to again.

So be it. She wasn't the first widow to suffer from loneliness. She wouldn't be the last.

For that matter, there were plenty of married people who were lonely every day of their life, coupled with partners too busy to speak to them, too self-centered, or too burdened with troubles of their own to realize how badly their spouse needed them.

While Stella had never suffered that fate herself, she had seen lots of folks who had. She had always thought that must be the deepest and most painful form of loneliness of all. To be with someone yet be alone.

So absorbed was she with her thoughts as she walked across the parking lot to her truck that she didn't notice someone was inside it.

It wasn't until she was climbing in herself that she saw Savannah sitting in the passenger seat.

The interior of the vehicle was cold. The child's teeth were chattering. She was wearing only a thin, ragged denim jacket, which Stella recognized as one of Shirley's throwaways.

"Oh, darlin', you 'bout scared me to death." Stella leaned over and kissed her granddaughter's cold cheek. "What are you doing, sitting out here on a chilly night like this?"

Savannah shrugged. "Waiting for you. I knew you'd be out sooner or later, after your practicing." The girl gave an unconvincing half smile. "I didn't think you'd be out this quick, though."

Stella switched on the engine and cranked the heat up full force. "I didn't exactly stay for the whole thing. Good thing I came out early, before you turned into a Savannah-sicle."

The child giggled, but the laughter was fleeting.

Stella reached for her cold hands and enclosed them between her own. "Does your mama know you're here, sweetheart?" she asked.

Savannah shook her head.

"That's what I was afraid of. You walked all the way here?"

She nodded.

Stella looked down at her granddaughter's feet and saw a pair of rhinestone-studded flip-flops. More of Shirley's castoffs.

Now that Savannah was almost as tall as her mother, Shirley had decided she no longer needed to buy clothing for her daughter. Her own hand-me-downs would do nicely.

Stella did a quick mental tally of her personal finances, then counted the days until she would be receiving her pension check. Three weeks. Far too long for a child to be running around in the winter, wearing flip-flops. Rhinestone studded or not. "Sparklies" didn't keep the toes warm in December.

She'd have to find a way to get her hands on a pair of warm shoes. Fast.

"How did you get out of the house?" Stella asked, fearing the answer.

"I went out my bedroom window," was the straightforward reply.

"But your bedroom's on the second floor!"

"I've got my ways."

"I'll just bet you do. Make sure that your 'way' don't include you fallin' and crackin' your head like Humpty Dumpty."

"I've slipped and fallen a bunch of times. The bushes down below are soft. They cushion my landing. I pretty much just bounce."

"Oh. Well. Now I feel so much better." Stella rolled her eyes. "Have you had anything to eat this evenin'?"

Savannah avoided her eyes. "I had a big lunch at school."

"School lunches aren't enough to feed a bird on a diet. Let's get you something to eat."

Suddenly, Savannah looked frightened. "No. I don't want anybody to see me with you. I mean, not that I'm ashamed of you, but Mama . . ."

"I know, baby. You don't need to say another word. How's about we go to Burger Igloo's new drive-up window and grab us a couple of burgers? You can get down on the floorboard while I'm ordering."

Savannah brightened momentarily, then turned her face away from her grandmother and didn't reply.

Stella knew her granddaughter, knew the tender maternal feelings that she held toward her siblings.

"Do you reckon," Stella added, "you could carry a bag with six more burgers when you're climbing back up to your bedroom window—without diving into those bushes, that is?"

Instantly, the girl was all smiles. "I sure could, and Mama was asleep when I left. She will be when I get back, too. The kids can eat them in their bedroom or the bathroom, and she'll be none the wiser. I'll make sure the wrappers get thrown away where they won't be seen."

While Stella was proud of Savannah's concern for her siblings, she hated to see an otherwise honest child having to connive and scheme just to get food for her family.

Stella looked down at the worn-out flip-flops, then at the tattered, thin jacket. This couldn't continue. It simply could not.

After pulling the truck out of the church parking lot, Stella chose darker, less traveled streets to drive to the burger joint. The last thing she wanted to do was make her granddaughter's already difficult life even worse.

"Is there a particular reason, sweetie, why you came to the church to see me today? I mean, other than that you miss me?"

"I do miss you. I miss you anytime I'm not with you."

"Same here, darlin'. But is there another reason?"

Savannah hesitated, then murmured a soft *yes*.

"Do you want to tell me now?"

"No. But I have to. I didn't want to, because it'll worry you, and I know you already worry a lot about us. I don't want to make you feel worse."

"That's okay, honey. If you can stand to live it, I can at least stand to hear about it. Say what you gotta say."

Stella steeled herself for what she was sure would be bad news. Was there any other kind when Shirley Reid was involved?

"It's about Mama," Savannah began.

"I figured as much."

"You know that she drinks a lot."

"I noticed that. Yes."

"She's drinking a lot more now."

"I noticed that, too."

"Well, now she's not just drinking. She's doing other stuff, too." Savannah started to tremble, and her breathing became rapid and uneven. "She's doing drugs."

Stella felt as though she'd received a blow to the diaphragm. Not that she hadn't considered the possibility long ago. She had actually been watching for signs of drug addiction in Shirley, but not having experienced narcotic problems herself, she hadn't known exactly what to look for.

"What kind of drugs? Do you know?"

"White powder. She's sniffing it. She left her purse open, and I saw some little plastic bags with it in there. Like sandwich bags, but smaller. And I've seen white powder on the inside of her nose."

Stella flashed back to the day before, to the crazed look in Shirley's eyes, her shaking with rage as she yanked her children from the truck, her irrational anger, and her nonsensical accusations.

"How's she been actin' lately, compared to before?" she asked.

"She's all nervous and shaky. She's not eating anything at all, just drinking beer. She wakes us up at night, because she's rushing around, doing stuff fast as she can. But mostly, she's real mad. All the time. And mean! So, so mean! We're scared of her. All of us. We've been hiding in our room, hoping she'll forget we're there. She usually does . . . forget, that is."

Again, Stella's heart broke.

Sometimes she wondered how many pieces one heart could break into before the damage was irreparable.

"That's not all," Savannah said.

"Then tell me the rest. Tell me everything."

"She buys the white stuff—I think it's called coke—from a man."

"Okay. How do you know this?"

"He comes to our house."

Horrified, Stella pulled the truck to the side of the road and parked at the edge of a fallow cotton field. "She has a drug dealer who comes to your house? When you kids are there?"

"Yes. He's come two times that I know of. The other day—but I didn't know who he was then—and last night. I think she thought we were all asleep. But I heard a man's voice in the kitchen, so I snuck out and looked. I saw him. A big, fat guy with long, dirty hair and a long, dirty beard. He looked like a nasty, mean Santa Claus. She gave him some money, and he gave her three of those little bags with white powder in them."

"I'm so sorry, darlin'. You shouldn't have to see something like that, let alone worry about it."

"I'm not worried about the powder. I mean, I wish she wasn't using it, but it's what he said to her that's got me worried. That's why I came to see you tonight. Something's bad wrong, and I'm scared."

"What did he say that scared you, honey? Tell me exactly what you heard."

"He said, 'You haven't told anybody about last night, have you?' Then she said, real nervous like, 'No! I told you I wouldn't tell nobody what I saw. Nobody even knows I was back there when it happened. Really. I swear.'"

Suddenly, Stella felt as though a lump of coal had been shoved down her throat, blocking her breathing. "What else?" she managed to say.

"He told her, 'That's good. Make sure you don't, unless you

wanna get hurt. Real bad. Worse than hurt. You and your brat kids, too."

The two sat in silence for a long time.

Stella's head swirled with thoughts, none of them less than terrifying.

"I'm scared, Granny," Savannah said, her voice and her lips trembling. "I'm mighty scared. He looked real mean, and he sounded like he meant it when he said he'd hurt Mama and us. Mama thought he meant it, too, 'cause when he said it, she started to cry. What are we gonna do, Granny?"

Stella reached for her granddaughter and hugged her close. So close that she was afraid the child would feel her heart pounding in her chest and know how frightened she was.

"What we're gonna do," she said, when she finally found the words, "is this. . . . We're going to go get burgers for you and your brother and your sisters. Two each. Then I'm going to take you home so you can feed them while the food's still hot. You're going to have to be a good little actress and act like nothin's wrong. Nothin' at all. As soon as I've dropped you off at your house, I'm gonna hightail it over to the sheriff's office and tell him all that you just told me."

"But if you do that, I'll get in big trouble with Mama!"

"I know, honey. But try not to worry about your mama and let Sheriff Gilford take care of her. She's not the biggest problem right now."

"She's not?"

"No. But I don't want you to worry about that, either. I want you to trust me and the sheriff. Between the two of us, we'll do whatever we have to do in order to keep you kids safe. Okay?"

"Okay."

Stella saw the trust in her grandchild's eyes. The trust of an innocent who believed what they were being told by someone they loved.

An innocent who hadn't yet learned that no one could truly keep another person safe at all times, not even one who meant more to them than life itself.

Sadly, the cruel world offered no such guarantees.

But a grandmother's promise—a Southern grandma, whose inclination was to fight tooth and claw for those she loved—that was about as good as it got.

Chapter 14

After dropping Savannah discreetly down the street from her mother's house, Stella headed directly to the sheriff's station. She found the front desk manned by a bored, sleepy Deputy Mervin Jarvis.

A solitaire card game was in progress on the desk. From the way he was slumped forward in the chair, his face nearly in his cards, Stella surmised that he was losing.

But then, something about Mervin Jarvis just seemed to announce to the world that he lost most challenges that life threw his way.

She asked to speak to Sheriff Gilford and was told, "The boss went home for a couple of hours. Said he had to get something to eat and would maybe catch a nap if he could. I'd leave him alone, if I was you."

Figuring that was all she would get out of Deputy Mervin, Stella left him to his card game and hurried out the door.

Once back in her truck, she did a U-turn on the street and headed toward the river.

Many years ago, Manny Gilford and his wife, Lucy, had

bought a decrepit little fisherman's cabin set high on a bluff overlooking the Pine River. They had refurbished it with every spare penny they could save from his job as a deputy sheriff and hers at Sherry Ann's Bakery in downtown McGill.

Once the house had been converted into a charming, cozy cabin, they'd set about attempting to raise a family. Their efforts had been short lived, like Lucy Gilford.

One hot July day, while Manny was away on a drunk-and-disorderly call at the tavern, Lucy decided to take a swim in the river, probably to escape the heat.

When Manny returned an hour later, his pretty Lucy was nowhere to be found.

It was three terrible weeks before her body was finally located downstream.

Lucy had never been known as a strong swimmer. Manny was, but of course, he had been out on a call.

The county's handsome young sheriff had never forgiven himself.

The town of McGill grieved with him and for him. When he refused to answer the door, cakes galore were left on the cabin's porch, along with casseroles and fried chicken, condolence cards, and every flower that the local florist had in stock.

Widow Maxwell even crocheted a little cross bookmarker.

Manny buried it with Lucy.

But, although their grieving deputy performed his duties impeccably, as though nothing at all had happened to shatter his heart and his world, Manny Gilford held all his well-meaning neighbors at arm's length.

Even his two closest friends, Arthur and Stella Reid, had never been invited to the cabin again.

If Stella wasn't so worried about her grandchildren, she would never have invaded his privacy by just dropping by unannounced. Plus, with a murder investigation under way, she knew he had to be exhausted, and heaven only knew when he had eaten his last solid meal.

But Stella reminded herself of the sincere look in his eyes when he had told her not to hesitate to ask, should she need his help.

She had never needed help more, and she had no doubt that he would understand her desperation.

A flood of nostalgia swept over her as she drove down the narrow, winding road. On either side of her, the forest grew more dense and dark as she drew closer to the river.

Her headlights illuminated the stately slash pines, some of them from eighty to one hundred feet tall, their long dark needles glistening against their red bark. Their sweet fragrance filled her truck, invoking even sweeter memories.

She remembered the long summer evenings when they enjoyed Manny's barbecued ribs; corn on the comb, seasoned with Lucy's special blend, wrapped in foil, and nested among the coals; and Stella's strawberry shortcake for dessert.

She recalled Monopoly games that stretched into the wee hours of the night, Lucy's squeals of indignation when she discovered that Manny had moved one of her hotels from her property to his, her own outcries when she caught Art pilfering a five-hundred-dollar bill from the bank.

Such good times, never to be forgotten.

Sadly, never to be re-created.

When Stella reached the cabin, she was dismayed to see there were no lights on, other than the porch lamp beside the door.

Sheriff Gilford was getting a well-deserved rest. If he was lucky, even some sleep. But her momentary pangs of guilt for disturbing him vanished when she thought of her grandchildren living in a home with hard-core drugs and visits from a dealer who had no qualms about threatening to harm them.

She parked the truck, got out, and hurried past the fire pit, with its comfortable Adirondack chairs; the hot tub, its cover blanketed with pine needles; and the stone grill, which Manny himself had built with river rock.

In another lifetime.

So urgent were her present concerns that she pushed the memories, good and bad, to the back of her mind—possibly to be considered at a more peaceful, less anxious time.

She knocked on the door and, only afterward, realized how hard and how loudly she had done so.

Such a simple action, knocking on a door, but simplistic as it might be, the sound communicated a definite sense of urgency.

A drowsy and disheveled Sheriff Gilford threw open the door and peered down at her with sleepy eyes.

He was wearing only a pair of jeans, his chest and feet bare.

Stella hadn't seen Manny shirtless since the four of them had gone tubing in the river together so many years ago. She was surprised to see that his physique hadn't changed much since then. If anything, he was even more heavily muscled than he had been as a younger man. She was also surprised that she would even notice such a thing with so much else on her mind.

"Stella," he said, instantly alert when he saw the worried look on her face. "What is it? What's wrong?" After flinging the door wide, he reached for her arm and pulled her inside.

"My grandkids," she began. "They're in danger."

A serious, officious look came over his face. He gave her a gentle push toward the sofa, then reached for his uniform shirt, which was hanging over the back of a chair at the nearby dining table. He tugged his shirt on, then walked to the stone fireplace, stirred the embers to life, and added a few pieces of firewood.

When he turned back to her, he noticed that she was shivering. He grabbed a red wool blanket, woven with Native American patterns, from a nearby chair and wrapped it snugly around her shoulders.

Then he dragged the footstool from an easy chair closer to where she was on the sofa. He sat on the footstool and, with his elbows on his knees, leaned toward her and grasped her hands.

Deeply concerned, he studied her face intently. "What's happened?" he asked. "Tell me everything."

For the next five minutes, Stella poured her concerns out onto him like a hot torrent that had been pent up too long.

She told him about Shirley's drinking problem, which she could tell he already knew far too much about.

She told him about the filthy house, the lack of food, about Savannah wearing rhinestone flip-flops in December. She watched his face grow darker and angrier by the moment.

But it was when she told him about the packets of white powder that he finally spoke. "Damn," was his simple but angry reply. He groaned with exasperation and ran his fingers through his silver hair. Stella could have sworn that she saw his hand shaking.

"I know," she said softly. "I was always afraid she might go in that direction."

"Me too. I've been keeping a close eye on that one for a long time."

"You have?"

His face softened. His eyes searched hers. What he was looking for, she couldn't be sure.

Finally, he said, "Of course I have, Stella. She's a troubled woman, and she's raising *your* grandchildren."

Stella looked down at her hands, covered by his. She could feel a heat rising in her cheeks that had little to do with the warmth coming from the stone fireplace or the cozy red blanket around her shoulders.

In one small corner of her mind, a tiny space that was less consumed by the urgency of the moment, she realized that she was alone with a man, a man who obviously cared deeply for her, for the first time in six years.

She was aware of his home, which was so different from when she had visited years ago, when Lucy was still living there. The soft, frilly feminine touches were gone, along with Lucy's creative clutter: her fabric stashes, yarn baskets, and her sewing machine.

Instead, the place was tidy, a bit sparse by comparison, but masculine and tasteful, with heavy leather furniture that had simple lines but appeared comfortable and inviting. The cabin's knotty pine walls were decorated with a few nicely framed paintings and photographs that reflected the beauty of mountains, forests, rivers, and lakes.

Behind the door sat a well-stocked, well-locked gun cabinet, and in the corner, some fishing equipment—still shiny, new, and neglected.

There was something about the cabin now that made Stella, even in her time of trouble, feel sheltered and protected, as though nothing truly bad could happen within these walls.

The man who lived here simply wouldn't allow it.

For the first time since Stella had shared her disturbing news, she felt a bit of hope that, with Manny Gilford's help, this terrible situation might reach a satisfactory conclusion, after all.

Nevertheless, she steeled herself before continuing. "Manny . . . there's more."

"Okay. Let's hear it," he replied, tightening his fingers around hers.

"Shirley's drug dealer comes to the house. Savannah's seen him twice."

She saw the anger flare in his eyes, but he quickly banked it and said in an even, professional tone, "Did Savannah mention what he looks like?"

"A big, fat guy with long, dirty hair and a long, dirty beard. 'Like a nasty, mean Santa Claus.' That's how she described him."

Instantly, Gilford's face hardened. "I know him."

"Really?"

"Yes. Let's just say I've 'dealt' with him before."

"*Is* he mean?"

He hesitated, and she had the distinct feeling that he was deciding whether or not to be fully candid with her.

Finally, he said, "Yes. He is. Worse yet, he's stupid, and that's a bad combination. You don't want him anywhere near your grandkids."

"He threatened to hurt the kids."

Her words hung in the air like a violent storm, heavy and ominous, about to break over their heads.

"When?"

"Last night. Savannah saw him and Shirley talking in her kitchen. He sold Shirley some packets of white powder—Savannah thinks they were coke, though it bothers me something fierce to think she'd even know such a thing—and then he asked Shirley if she'd told anybody what she saw the night before. That'd be the night of the killing."

"I see. Go on."

"She told him no, that nobody even knew she was 'back there when it happened.' He told her if she did tell anyone, she and her brat kids would get hurt. 'Worse than hurt.'"

"Okay."

It was one simple word, but Stella could see a change in her old friend's face, specifically in his gray eyes, which had suddenly gone icy. She saw a distinct transformation from Manny, the sweet guy, to a fierce predator who had just caught a whiff of prey.

"One other thing," Stella continued. "I was talking to Shirley, and when we spoke of Priscilla's murder, she mentioned that Prissy was strangled."

"Is that why you asked me if I'd told anybody that, Stella?"

She hung her head, blushing. "Yes. I'm sorry. I should have told you then and there. But I'd just had some ugly words with her, and I was afraid that if I told on her, she'd think it was on account of that. Besides, I couldn't really believe that she'd actually have anything to do with somethin' so awful."

"I understand."

"You do?"

"Sure. You've helped me out a lot already, and you've got to put your family's welfare first."

"Thank you. I appreciate your patience."

"Stella May Reid, a lot of people in this town try my patience. You aren't one of 'em."

"Glad to hear it."

He stood and began to pace in front of the fireplace. "All right. Game plan. The first thing I'm going to do is talk to Shirley. Then, depending on what she tells me, I'll decide how I'm going to deal with Leland Corder."

"Leland who?"

"Santa's evil twin. He's from Hooter Grove. He used to come

174

here to McGill to sell his dope. I put the fear o' God in him last year, but it seems it's worn off. He's in need of another dose. Worse than a dose, if I can manage it."

Stella cleared her throat and said, "Manny, I know you've gotta do your duties, but when you talk to Shirley, can you please leave my little Savannah out of it? Shirley's off her rocker lately from those drugs, and she's been bein' mean to the young'uns already. If she knew Savannah—"

"I'll just tell her that I know she was there in the alley that night. I won't tell her how I know. Shirley doesn't strike me as the soul of discretion. She's probably told a few people there at the bar already. She'll assume it was one of them who told me."

"Shirley's pretty loose lipped, for sure. She figures the definition of a *secret* is 'something that you tell to only one person at a time.'"

"On the other hand, if she picked an inconvenient time to suddenly become discreet, she's going to know it was you. I may not be able to keep *you* out of it."

"Better me than poor Savannah. That child carries a heavy enough burden as it is."

They were silent for several moments, both of them thinking.

Finally, Gilford said, "I've got an idea. I could bring her to the station, make sure nobody else's there but you."

"But *me?*"

"Yes. I could stash you in my office and close the door. Then bring her in and question her there at the front desk, like I did you and your grandkids. I'll interview her while you listen in."

"How am I going to listen in if I'm in your office and the door's closed?"

He looked right, then left, leaned closer, and whispered, "If you put your ear on the radiator, which I'll make sure is turned off, you'll hear every word. But if you tell anybody that, I'll have you run out of town and dumped in the desert."

"There aren't any deserts in Georgia."

"I'll find one."

She laughed. "I'll keep mum. Promise. But why would I be in your office, eavesdropping?"

"That way, if Shirley really didn't tell anybody but you, I can haul you out, confront her with her accuser, face-to-face, and with any luck, scare her into spilling everything she knows."

Stella thought it over, then gave him a grim smile. "I wouldn't mind confronting Miss Shirley right now. I'd rather do it with a frying pan, but since you'll be there . . ."

"Just wiggle your right earlobe and I'll excuse myself to the little boy's room. But make sure you've cleaned up the scene before I come back."

"Or if she refuses to talk, you could always use that 'dump you in the desert' threat."

"Scared *you*, didn't I?"

She rolled her eyes. "Plumb terrified."

"I'll wait until tomorrow morning, pick her up after your grandkids are off to school."

"Okay. If you think that'll be soon enough. I can't help but worry about that dirty Santa Claus, Leland fella."

Gilford smirked. "Don't fret about Leland Corder. I plan to contact the chief of police there in Hooter Grove. He's an old friend of mine from way back. Leland'll be in custody in half an hour."

"Half an hour? How can you be sure he'll find him that fast?"

"'Cause Hooter Grove's a small town like McGill, and there

are only three places Leland would be—the tavern, the pool hall, or his trailer."

"What if he's here in McGill?"

"Then I'll already have him in jail."

She looked confused.

He stood and began to tuck his shirt in. "You see, Mrs. Reid, I'm fixin' to walk you to your truck right now, and then I'm taking a run into town. If Leland's there, I'll find him and lock him up."

"What for?"

"I'll think of something."

"What if he's not and your chief of police friend can't find him, either?"

"Then I'm going to park outside your daughter-in-law's place, just to make sure he doesn't come anywhere near the house. I'll sit there till I hear Hooter Grove's got him behind bars."

"Even if it takes all night?"

"It won't, but yes, even if it does. Nothing's going to happen to your family, Stella. Not on my watch."

She jumped to her feet and nearly burst into tears of relief. She moved toward him to hug him, and he met her halfway.

For a few seconds, she allowed herself to lean against him, to feel the comfort of someone else's strength buoying her up in her moment of weakness. To feel protected. Maybe even loved?

When she pulled back and looked up at him, the expression on his face answered her question.

Yes, Sheriff Manny Gilford loved her. Very much. There was no mistaking the look in those pale gray eyes.

Stella might have had only one lover in her lifetime, but that was enough for her to know what that look meant.

While they stood there for only a few moments, searching each other's eyes, many questions were asked and answered without a word spoken.

Stella knew that her relationship with Sheriff Manny Gilford would never be the same again. But with her grandchildren in jeopardy, there was no time to discuss it or even think about it.

"We've gotta go," he whispered, reaching up and brushing one of her dark curls away from her face.

"Yes," she replied a bit breathlessly. "Right now."

She threw the blanket off her shoulders and onto the sofa.

He picked up his weapon and holster from the dining table and grabbed his coat.

Together, they raced for the door.

Chapter 15

"Just have a seat over there by the desk, Shirley. If you'll answer a few questions for me and do so truthfully, you'll be back to your Bloody Mary in no time."

Stella wouldn't recommend the ear-against-the-radiator method of eavesdropping to anyone, comfort-wise. But she had to admit that, even though it triggered a serious crick in the neck in less than a minute, it was most efficient. She could hear every word that Manny was saying. She even knew when Shirley tossed her heavy, fringed, and turquoise-spangled purse onto the front desk.

Stella also heard the scraping of the metal folding chair when Shirley sat down on it.

"You don't care if I smoke in here, right?" Shirley asked.

Stella grinned, knowing what the answer would be. As a former pack-and-a-half-a-day smoker who had suffered to give up his habit years ago, Sheriff Gilford was death on cigarettes.

"You answer my questions quickly and honestly," she heard him say as he settled into the squeaky desk chair, "you can return to your Bloody Mary *and* your smokes. Got it?"

There was only a grumbled response.

As Stella slid down to a sitting position on the floor, to relieve some of the strain on her neck, she heard the sheriff begin.

"I need to know where you were three nights ago, between the hours of eight and ten."

It took Shirley a long time to answer. Stella wished she could see as well as hear what was going on in the other room. One facial expression told a lot, and she was dying to know what sort her daughter-in-law was wearing at that moment.

Finally, she heard her say, "That was a long time ago. How am I supposed to remember that particular night?"

"It's the night Prissy Carr was murdered. Does that ring any bells?"

"Oh, yeah. I was the same place I usually am. There in the Bulldog."

"Doing what?"

"What do you suppose? Just what you do in a bar. Drinking and socializing."

"Who were you socializing with?"

"Just the usual gang. Nobody in particular."

"You were there in the bar the whole time? You didn't leave, even once, for any reason?"

"No. Why?"

"I understand you spent some time back there in the alley."

There was a long silence. Stella could feel her own heart pounding. She could only imagine how Shirley's must be racing.

"No," Shirley finally answered. "I was inside the whole time."

Stella heard Manny sigh. She knew the exasperated look he must be giving Shirley at that moment.

A lot of people gave Shirley Reid that look.

"Your Bloody Mary is gonna go flat and warm, you keep this

up, Shirl," he told her. "At this rate, by the time I let you leave here, you'll be having the nicotine fit to beat all."

"Look, Sheriff! I was at the Bulldog between eight and ten, and I stayed there, didn't go anyplace else. That's all I got to say to you. What's all this about?"

"It's about a young woman losing her life. About somebody deciding that they could kill her and get away with it."

"Yeah, yeah. That's a bummer."

Shirley didn't sound all that bummed to Stella.

Apparently, Gilford didn't think so, either, because his voice was raised and harsh when he said, "It's more than a bummer. A person getting murdered is a downright tragedy."

"Well, with some more than others."

"No! With *anyone*! Prissy Carr did some rotten stuff. She ruined families, hurt a lot of people. She deserved to get told off, loud and clear, by some angry wives. If some of them decided to box her jaws for her, I'd say she had it coming. But nobody, *nobody*, gets to strangle the life out of anybody in this town without me seeing to it that they pay for it."

Stella heard him slap his hand down hard on the desk's surface. "Now, you think very seriously about how you're going to answer this next question, Shirley Reid, because if you don't tell the truth, you'll be in deep trouble with me. Years-in-jail kinda trouble. Now . . . how do you know that Priscilla Carr was strangled?"

Stella didn't dare to breathe as she waited. Waited for Shirley to do the right thing.

Finally, she heard an indignant Shirley blurt out, "I don't know what you're talking about, Sheriff Gilford. What makes you think I know anything about anything?"

"You were overheard telling some people that she was strangled to death. That's not something you'd know unless you'd been there and seen it happen. You were outside in the alley when she was killed."

"I was not!"

"You were. How else would you know her cause of death? Nobody knows that but me."

"Ohhh! I see now. That bitch of a mother-in-law of mine's been talking to you, hasn't she? She'd say anything at all to get me in trouble. She hates me. Always has. You can't believe a word that comes out of her lyin' mouth! Specially about *me*!"

"What makes you think it was your mother-in-law?"

"'Cause I never told nobody else. Just her. She was the only one, so it has to be her who—"

Stella nearly yelped with glee. Shirley had been so busy condemning Stella that she had put her own foot into the sheriff's trap.

They could all practically hear it snap around her scrawny ankle.

"As a matter of fact, it *was* your mother-in-law who brought this information to me," he said, "as she should have. Everyone should be doing all they can to help me solve this murder."

In a much louder voice, he called out, "Mrs. Reid, would you please join us in here?"

Stella scrambled to her feet, smoothed her skirt and, with mixed emotions, hurried out of the office. As she exited, she saw the sheriff and Shirley sitting at the front desk, just as she'd pictured them.

Manny's elbows were propped on its surface; his fingers laced together in a pseudo-casual pose.

Shirley was leaning back in the folding chair—so far back that Stella predicted she would topple over backward at any minute. Her arms were crossed over the front of her denim jacket, and a scowl was on her gaunt gray face.

The instant Shirley saw Stella, she sprang to her feet and charged across the room toward her. "You bitch!" she screamed. "You're just trying to get me in trouble 'cause you—"

But she didn't finish her attack or her insult, because Gilford had reached her, grabbed her, and twisted her arms behind her back.

She struggled only a moment, until it was obvious that fighting would cause her only more discomfort.

"Get back in your chair," Gilford told her in his best sheriff voice.

When she didn't move quickly enough to suit him, he said, "Go back to your chair, Shirley, sit down, and calm yourself, or I'm gonna handcuff you."

She didn't take her eyes off Stella, but she did as he said, glaring at her mother-in-law with undiluted hatred as she obeyed.

The sheriff grabbed another chair and placed it on the opposite side of the desk from Shirley's. "Have a seat, Mrs. Reid, and let's get back to business here. I'm in the middle of a murder investigation, and daylight's burnin'."

Shirley jabbed an accusing finger at Stella with all the ferocity of an attacker stabbing someone with a knife. "I told her that in confidence!" she shouted. "She had no right to repeat it to nobody."

"There was nothin' confidential in nature about you tellin' me that," Stella returned, settling onto the chair. "You just opened your blabberin' mouth, and it fell out. Like right now."

"I don't care. You still should've kept it to yourself. You would have, too, if you didn't hate me. If you weren't just tryin' to get me in trouble."

"That's enough!" Gilford roared, his deep voice filling the room. "Shirley, it doesn't matter if she swore to you on a stack

183

of Bibles not to tell a soul. Stella coming to the law with information about a homicide case is praiseworthy, not a felony, like obstructing justice or committing murder. If you don't start talking some truth to me in the next five minutes, I'm going to arrest you on one of those charges. Maybe both! You hear me, woman?"

Shirley seemed to have gotten the message. She all but melted into her chair, her body sagging, like someone about to surrender during a long, hard battle.

Stella could have sworn that she even saw some tears brimming in her daughter-in-law's eyes.

In all their years of knowing each other, Stella couldn't remember ever seeing Miss Tough Cookie Shirley cry over anything. Scream, yes. Cry, no.

"Okay, Sheriff," she said. "You don't have to charge me with murder. Or anything else. I'll tell you what you wanna hear. But you have to promise to keep me safe."

Stella couldn't help noticing that Shirley had said, "Me," not "Us," as though her children hadn't been threatened at the same time.

"I'll keep you safe," Gilford assured her. "You help me solve this case, I'll make sure you don't pay a price for it."

Shirley gave him a suspicious, doubtful look. "Even if I did somethin', um, kinda against the law?"

"Did you kill her?"

"No!"

"Did you tell somebody else to or pay them or talk them into it?"

"No!"

"Did you hold her down while somebody else did?"

"Of course not!"

"Then you're in the clear. Tell me whatcha got."

Shirley drew a deep breath, threw another hateful look Stella's way, then plunged in. "I did step outside, out back, for a few minutes that night."

"Okay. Good. Go on."

"I went out there to, well, to talk to a friend about somethin'."

"Who?"

"Just this guy I know."

"And his name is . . . ?"

"Leland."

"Leland Corder?"

"Yeah. How did you know?"

Gilford smirked. "I know only two Lelands in the county, and the other one's a preacher. He wouldn't be hanging out with a woman who ain't his wife behind a tavern." He hesitated. "I don't think he would, leastways."

He reached for his notebook and pen and started scribbling. "So, you and Leland Corder were in the alley behind the bar about what time?"

"Around ten, more or less."

"Doin' what?"

"I was sorta, like, paying him some money I owed him."

The sheriff looked up from his scribbling and gave her a piercing look. "You weren't gonna lie to me about anything at all, remember? Otherwise, we might add some drug charges along with obstructing justice. That'd get your kids taken away from you, wouldn't it?"

Shirley shot another look in Stella's direction, only this time there was fear in her eyes.

Ah, Stella thought. *The thought's occurred to her that the state might take the kids away from her and give 'em to me.*

The thought pleased Stella. Enormously. Let Shirley worry

about losing the kids to her. If she didn't love her children enough to take care of them, maybe she hated Stella enough to do the right thing by them, if it meant keeping them out of her hated mother-in-law's hands.

"I know Leland Corder," Gilford continued, addressing Shirley. "I know what he does for a living. Let's just state for the record that you and he were back there doing a drug deal in the alley that night. Shall we?"

Shirley didn't reply. She just nodded slightly.

"Like I told you," Gilford said, raising his voice, "this is for the record. Answer me out loud. You and Leland Corder were doing a drug deal back there in the alley about ten o'clock?"

"Yeah. You got me. Happy now?"

Rather than rise to her bait, Gilford continued in a calmer tone. "Tell me everything that happened from the moment you walked out into that alley until you left. Don't leave anything out."

"Okay." Shirley drew a deep breath. She began to run her trembling fingers through the fringe on her purse. "We walked out the back door together. He pulled out his cigarettes, I bummed one off him, and we lit up. Then I paid him the money. He gave me, you know, the stuff."

"Cocaine?" Gilford asked.

"No. Just some pot."

The sheriff brought his hand down on the desk again. The sound reverberated off the walls. Shirley jumped like she had been poked with a cattle prod.

"I told you that I know Leland Corder. I know him well. He ain't a pot dealer. If you exchanged money with him for drugs, it was cocaine, maybe heroin."

"Okay, okay. It was coke. Just a little. A tiny Baggie."

Gilford rose to his feet and leaned over the desk until he was nearly face-to-face with Shirley. "Leland Corder doesn't mess with one Baggie. If you lie to me one more time, this interview is over, and your butt is gonna be upstairs in one of my cells. I guarantee you, it won't be for your usual one-nighter, either."

"Three Baggies."

Shirley looked genuinely afraid. While Stella would have felt a bit of pity for almost anyone else in her situation, all she had to do was remember the look on Shirley's face when she threw her children out of the truck onto the ground. And the expressions on theirs.

No, Stella told herself. *If I have any sympathy to spare, I'll spend it on the grandkids. They deserve it.*

"All right, you and Leland lit up smokes," Gilford continued. "You bought three Baggies of cocaine from him, and then what?"

"That's when we saw him."

Stella sat upright in her chair. She noticed that Manny did the same.

"You saw who?" Gilford wanted to know.

"Elmer Yonce."

"What was he doing?"

"Just walking around back there, like he does sometimes. But he was moving kinda sneaky."

"Elmer limps," Gilford said.

"I know. But this was different, even for him. Like maybe somebody was after him. Or he didn't wanna be seen. Like he was hiding or whatever."

"How does somebody move sneaky? Or like they don't want to be seen?"

Shirley threw up her hands. "I don't know, Sheriff. You asked me what I saw, what he was doing. That's it. It's really dark back there, since the lightbulb went out. You can't see much."

"How long's the bulb been out?"

"Oh, I don't know. A month, maybe more."

"Where was Elmer, exactly?" Gilford asked.

"Over by the foot of the stairs. The ones leading up to Prissy's apartment." She gave an ugly little snicker and added, "Them stairs got a lot a use while she lived up there. Grand Central Station, in fact."

"What was Elmer doing, besides acting sneaky?"

Shirley gave a shrug and a dismissive wave. "I don't know. We didn't pay him much mind. We got our, you know, business done. We put out our cigarettes there on the ground. We went back in. We were still standing there, just inside the door, when we heard it."

"Heard what?" Stella exclaimed without thinking.

She knew she really should keep her mouth closed during the sheriff's interrogation. But while Stella Reid was good at many things, maintaining tightly closed lips for any length of time wasn't one of them.

"We heard a yell," Shirley said, "like somebody had got hurt real bad. Then there was a racket—someone or something tumbling down the stairs. I thought about it later, and I'm sure that's what it was. Prissy Carr was taking a header down those mighty popular steps of hers. Yep, that's what it was, all right."

"But you didn't see who pushed her?" Gilford sounded disappointed.

"No."

"Then how do you know about the strangling part?"

"I was curious, so I opened the door back up, just a crack. I peeped out, and that's when I saw him."

"Who?"

She shrugged. "Don't know. He had his face turned away, and all I saw was his back. I could tell he was making a strangling motion. Had somebody by the neck and was bearing down on them, you know, like they do in the movies."

"Was it Elmer?"

"Can't say one way or the other. It was really dark out there."

Manny sighed. "So you've mentioned. You keep saying 'him.' Are you sure it was a man?"

"Not really. Reckon, now that I think about it, it could've been a woman."

Stella could feel her heart sinking by the moment.

From the look on Sheriff Gilford's face, she knew he was feeling the same.

He tossed his pen onto the desktop with an exasperated groan. "Then it might have been Elmer, but you can't say for sure."

"Right."

"And it wasn't you or Leland?"

"Of course not. We was both inside at that point."

"Did you mention to Leland that you'd just seen somebody murdered?"

"Of course! Wouldn't you? That's not somethin' you see every day! I was all scared and excited and shook up! I had to tell somebody."

"What did Leland say when you told him?"

"He told me to shut the damned door and mind my own business. I told him we should call you and tell you about it, but he said I was dumber than dirt. Said you'd go askin' what we were doin' back there, and it might come out that we'd been, you know, buyin' and sellin' . . . stuff. Then him and me would be in trouble."

"You could've dropped a dime anonymously, you know," Gilford told her. "Told me what you saw."

"Why bother? I just told you, totally poured my guts out, and you're not a bit closer to knowing what happened than you were before."

"Thanks," Gilford said, running his fingers through his hair and looking more tired than Stella had ever seen him. "I appreciate you reminding me."

Shirley sank lower in her chair. Stella noticed she was shivering in spite of the warmth of the room.

"Now that I've told you all this stuff, Sheriff," Shirley said, "I'm gonna have to be lookin' over my shoulder ever' minute. If Leland gets wind of it, he'll knock me into next Sunday. If I'm lucky."

"Leland Corder won't be knocking anybody anywhere," Gilford replied. "He's cooling his heels in a cell in Hooter Grove right now."

"In jail?" both Shirley and Stella exclaimed.

The sheriff looked more than a little pleased with himself. "Yes, indeed. An anonymous tip last night led the police chief over there to his trailer, where he had a ton of cocaine stashed in a coffee can in his freezer. How original." He chuckled. "Leland's a second cousin twice removed from Albert Einstein's nephew's neighbor."

"Really?" Shirley looked puzzled. "He didn't seem that smart to me. Just goes to show, you never know."

Gilford sighed, folded his notebook, and shoved it into a drawer. "Leland was booked into the Hooter Grove jail by three this morning. Nobody's going to have to worry about him for a very long time."

The sheriff stood and walked around to stand beside Shirley's chair.

"Gimme your purse," he said, holding out his hand.

Shirley clutched it to her breast like a mother protecting her infant from a charging grizzly bear. "No! Why?"

"You've just confessed to buying cocaine from a known drug dealer. You're the mother of seven children, the oldest being only twelve years old. Do you really think I'm going to let you walk out of here with drugs in your purse?"

Shirley tried to stare him down with one of her best "hate Stella" looks, but it had no effect at all on Sheriff Manny Gilford. He returned it as he said, "Gimme that purse, Shirley Reid. Now!"

She stood and shoved it at his chest as hard as she could.

"Thank you, Mrs. Reid, for your cooperation," he said, his tone unmistakably sarcastic.

He dumped the contents of the purse onto the top of the desk.

Stella wasn't surprised to see most of the items spread before them, the standard Shirley paraphernalia: a copious amount of makeup, several packs of cigarettes, some breath spray, three different hairbrushes, hair spray, some backup turquoise jewelry, and numerous different brands and styles of condoms.

Stella supposed that she should be indignant to see that her daughter-in-law was using birth control when her husband was on the other side of the country and not expected back for months. But instead of outrage or surprise, Stella felt a bit of relief. At least Shirley was being careful, showing a little responsibility—a rare occurrence, but a welcome one.

Two other items bothered Stella far more. The first was a small plastic bag containing white powder.

It was one thing to hear about the drugs from Savannah and Shirley. It was quite another for Stella to see it with her own eyes.

She thought of her grandchildren, especially the smaller ones, who were innocent and blissfully ignorant of such things. Unbidden images crossed her mind of them finding a Baggie like that. Playing with it. Maybe tasting it or inhaling it. The possible tragic outcome.

Then there was the other item. A roll of cash, bound with a thick rubber band.

Where had Shirley gotten her hands on that much money? Heaven knows, she hadn't earned it by the sweat of her brow. Sitting on a barstool under a picture of Elvis didn't work up a lot of sweat or pay that much.

Stella thought of the empty refrigerator at home and Savannah wearing worn flip-flops and a thin, cast-off jacket in December.

Her rage rose, hot and fierce inside her. Rather than try to tamp it down with reminders to "Love thy neighbor," she allowed the anger inside her spirit to go unchecked. If ever there was such a thing as "righteous indignation," surely this was it.

"I assume," Sheriff Gilford said, "that this is one of the bags that you scored off Leland the other night."

Shirley gave him a curt nod and sank back down onto her chair.

She and Stella watched as he took a small brown evidence envelope from his desk drawer and scribbled Shirley's name, the date, and the time on the front. Then, using the tip of the pen, rather than his fingers, he flipped the Baggie into the envelope and sealed it.

"I'm going to be keeping this somewhere special," he told Shirley. "Under lock and key. If you behave yourself, that's where it'll stay. But I better not hear one more report of you mistreating your children, of you throwing a temper tantrum in front of them, yanking them around, doing drugs, driving drunk or, in general, not acting in a manner appropriate for the mother of seven children. If I do, I'll be taking that Baggie of cocaine, along with some pretty sad stories about you, over to Judge Patterson. He takes a dim view of people who expose children to that kind of malarkey. You'll wind up behind bars. Not the ones upstairs, either. Prison bars. Not for days or weeks, but for months or years, where there's no alcohol, no men, and no turquoise jewelry."

Shirley said nothing. She just sat and fumed.

"What's even worse," he continued, "at least in your estimation, I'd bet, is that the state would take away those kids of yours and would give them to your mother-in-law here. Something tells me you'd absolutely hate that. Not so much because you'd be pining for your children, but because you'd know *she* had them."

Shirley shot a .45 caliber glare at Stella.

"Keep that in mind," the sheriff continued, "the next time you decide to hang out in dark alleys and score cocaine, or drive drunk with those kids in the back of a pickup truck."

Shirley brushed some imaginary lint off her jacket, lifted her chin, and said, "Are you quite done with me, Sheriff? I gave you all I've got in the way of information, and you promised you'd cut me loose if I did."

"Go."

"Good."

She began to pick up her belongings from the desk and

shove them into her purse. Stella couldn't help noticing that the first things she put away were the condoms.

The second thing she picked up was the cash roll, but before she could stick it in her purse, Gilford snatched it out of her hand.

"Hey! What do you think you're doin'?" she yelled as he removed the rubber band and began to peel bills off the roll. "That there's my rent money!"

He gave her a withering look. "Sure it is, Shirley. We both know you were getting ready to score with that money. But now you don't need to, because you just turned over a new leaf. Right?"

He replaced the rubber band around the remaining bills, put a paper clip on the ones he had taken, and shoved them into a drawer. "Are you going to be home about four o'clock this afternoon?" he asked.

"Um, I don't know. Usually I—"

"I know. I know. Usually, you're still at the bar at that hour. But your kids will be home from school, right?"

"Yeah. Why?"

"Because Deputy Jarvis is gonna take that money and go grocery shopping with it. He'll drop by about four with a bunch of nutritious food for those children."

"But what if I'm not there?"

"Your kids'll let him in, and I'm sure they'll help him put away the groceries. You better hope he doesn't find that house of yours looking like a rat's nest, the way it did the last time I took you home drunk."

Stella could see Shirley practically squirm inside her denim jacket. While she had to admit that she enjoyed seeing her daughter-in-law having to account for misbehavior, Stella received no real comfort from it.

With Shirley, any improvement was bound to be temporary.

But Sheriff Manny Gilford was trying. She had to give him that.

He took a few steps closer to Shirley, until he was quite literally breathing down her neck. "You better listen to me, woman, and listen good. Your kids are gonna start having a better life. I'm gonna see to it. I'm gonna watch you day and night, and the minute you step out of line, that's it. You'll lose everything that ever meant anything to you."

He leaned even closer, until they were nearly nose to nose. "Look into my eyes, Shirley Reid. Go on. Do it. Tell me I don't mean it."

Shirley looked up and winced at what she saw.

"Yeah," he said. "You remember that. Now, pick up the rest of your crap and get the hell out of my station."

Shirley wasted no time when shoving her remaining belongings into her purse. In seconds, she was heading out the door, slamming it behind her.

Stella sighed and turned to Manny. "Not exactly overcome with remorse, was she?"

"Nope. I've seen more repentant serial killers."

"You've seen serial killers?"

He grinned and shrugged. "On TV."

"Oh, well, yeah. Who hasn't?"

She stood, walked over to stand beside him, and placed her hand on his forearm. Even through the cloth of his sleeve, she could feel his warmth.

For reasons she didn't have time to examine then and there, she recalled the moment he had held her there in his cabin. Something told her he was remembering it, too.

"I sure appreciate all you did, and all you tried to do, for me and mine here today, Manny. I'm never gonna forget it. I owe you."

He placed his hand over hers and gave it a squeeze. "You don't owe me anything, Stella May Reid. I'm just doing my job."

"I know you are, Sheriff, and I know you do your job well. But I can't help thinking you went some extra miles for me, like sitting in a car outside my grandchildren's house until three this morning, making sure Leland Corder was behind bars and they were safe. That's above and beyond."

He shrugged, and she was surprised to see that he was even blushing a bit beneath his perpetual sheriff's tan.

She removed her hand from his arm and instantly felt a slight loss, as though something very nice, very special was gone.

At least for the moment.

"I should get going," she said.

"Me too. I'm fixin' to run over to Hooter Grove to talk to Leland. I'll put the squeeze on him and see if his story lines up with your daughter-in-law's."

"Reckon it will?"

"I think so. How about you? Do you think she was being truthful? You always did have a truffle pig's nose when it comes to sniffin' out a liar."

"I think she told it the way it happened. Shirley's pretty easy to catch in a lie. She's not good at spinnin' yarns on the spur of the moment. I don't think she's creative enough to come up with those details, like Elmer lookin' like he was hiding from somebody."

"He *was* hiding from somebody. Me. I chased him away from the old folks' home where he'd shown his . . . ignorance. Lost him a few blocks this side of there."

"Looks like he's your number one suspect at the moment."

"Yeah. I'll have a friendly chat with him once I get back from Hooter Grove." He hesitated a moment, then said a bit tentatively, "You wanna come with me? You know, just so we can talk about the case on the way there and back."

She smiled up at him, her dimples deep. "I'd enjoy that, Manny. But I'll have to take a rain check. I've got somethin' I gotta do at three fifteen, and you might not be back before that."

He looked disappointed, but his voice was soft and kind when he said, "You can have that rain check, Mrs. Reid. In fact, you can have as many as you want for as long as you want."

She must have looked as startled as she felt, because he quickly added, "You know, because I appreciate your input. You're good at this investigation stuff. That's why I said . . . I mean, why I—"

"Of course," she interjected. "You'd rather have me workin' beside you than ol' Jarvis."

He gave her a quick appreciative glance up and down that made her glad she'd put on one of her best floral-print dresses before leaving the house that morning.

"Yes, ma'am," he said. "I'd much rather have you beside me than Jarvis, or anybody else that I can think of. For more reasons than one."

Again, she saw the look, felt the warmth of the affection behind it.

"I'll see you tonight, Manny," she said softly. "At Prissy's visitation. You'll be there. Right?"

"Gotta be. I have to watch and see how different people 'take it.'"

"Who's cryin' and who's dancin' in their bloomers?"

197

"You got it. I'd appreciate it if you'd pay close attention yourself and then report back to me."

A sly grin brightened Stella's face. "That sounds a lot like spyin' on folks and then gossipin' about 'em."

"Welcome to the world of law enforcement."

"And you get paid for this?" she mused as she headed for the door. "Sounds more like fun than work to me."

Chapter 16

Early in life, Stella Reid had learned to observe people's habits. Everyone had a routine, and she had discovered a great deal about those who lived around her by observing their rituals.

Everyone in the little town of McGill had activities that they performed daily, weekly, monthly, or annually. Those pastimes defined who they were. In their own eyes, and in the opinions of those around them.

The way they chose to spend their time, especially their free time, spoke louder than words about their character, their values, their joys, their heartaches, and their dreams.

Every single afternoon April Pomeroy could be seen walking down Main Street to the edge of town and St. Michael's Cemetery, carrying some flowers from her garden in one hand and a small picture frame in the other. April would place those flowers on a young man's grave, sit next to his tombstone, and talk to the soldier she had wanted so desperately to marry—much the same way as Waycross Reid talked to his grandfather.

April would have married her young man, and been happy to do so, had he not perished in the jungles of Vietnam.

Every woman in McGill knew better than to invite April to an afternoon social. Every eligible bachelor in McGill knew better than to ask her out on a date.

April's daily ritual said it all.

Then there was Stephen. . . .

Stephen Oldring's entire family on his father's side had died of heart attacks before celebrating their forty-fifth birthday. Every day on the highway leading to Hooter Grove, Stephen could be seen running, running, running. Like with April and her graveyard visits, weather mattered not one iota. Stephen never missed a day, ever.

Some folks speculated that he was trying to outrun the Grim Reaper himself. Others, less dramatically inclined, said they respected his discipline and his determination to remain healthy. Some admired his efforts but criticized his attire.

His T-shirt was tie-dyed. The colors had been brilliant in the sixties but after years of constant wear, they were now only faded pastels. Likewise, the sun had faded his running shorts, which had been black when he began wearing them but over the years had morphed to dark purple, then brown, and finally to a drab green.

Some folks were heard to say, "Who cares how long you live or how healthy you are if you can't dress proper? Just imagine if a bus hit 'im and he died in that gitup!"

As a result, Stephen was known as the healthiest and worst-dressed man in McGill—the most likely to be run over on the road or to die of a heart attack, in spite of his best efforts.

Stella knew everyone's habits: where they would be, when they would arrive there, what they would be doing at their destination, when they would leave and why.

So, she knew exactly where to go and when in order to have a private talk with her oldest grandchild.

Stella parked in front of the town's library, got out, and walked up the sidewalk to the old Victorian mansion. Donated to the town by a well-to-do lady named Mildred Hodge, the home was a beauty, with a round turret, colorful stained-glass windows, and the delicate, ornate gingerbread trim so popular in its era.

The library was Savannah's favorite place on earth, and it didn't take a lot of grandmotherly intuition for Stella to figure out why.

The child led a mundane, often difficult life. Other than school, nearly all her waking hours were spent caring for her siblings, catering to her mother, and being trapped in a house with no television or radio.

From the cage those walls created, there was no escape for the girl's curious, adventurous spirit—except through books.

While Savannah had no books of her own to provide the excitement she so desperately needed, she had discovered a portal into one thousand worlds inside the walls of that mansion.

Every Wednesday afternoon at 3:15 p.m., Savannah treated herself to a trip to the library. When she first discovered the place, she had told her grandmother, "I can't believe it, Granny! They've got a zillion books in there, and they'll let you borrow them for free! You read them, and then you take them back and get more! It's the best thing in the whole wide world!"

Stella Reid had no doubt whatsoever that for her grandchild—her insatiably curious, life-embracing, courageous granddaughter—it *was* the best thing in the world.

Stella opened the elegant front door, with its oval beveled-glass window, and walked into the foyer. Above hung a gorgeous crystal chandelier, which bathed the room in a clean golden light. Below, the floor was covered with hand-painted terra-cotta tiles.

She found her granddaughter, as always, beneath the graceful curving staircase, tucked away in a cozy alcove, sitting on a tiny, made-for-children chair.

At twelve, Savannah was big for her age, tall and strong, like her grandpa Art had been. Stella couldn't help noticing that it wouldn't be long before she would be too large for that miniature chair.

Nothing stayed the same. Everything was constantly changing, including Stella's grandchildren, and that was both a source of joy and sorrow to her heart.

So deeply engrossed was Savannah in her Hardy Boys mystery that Stella was reluctant to disturb her. The poor girl had so little time to herself that it seemed a shame to interrupt her. But Stella knew she was bringing welcome news to someone who received too few happy updates. The intrusion would be welcome.

"Hey, sugar," she whispered as she bent down and stuck her head into the alcove, near the dragonfly stained-glass lamp that lit the cozy cubbyhole for any solitary reader sitting in it.

Savannah started at the sound and looked up with troubled eyes. Once she saw who her visitor was, she appeared overjoyed and relieved.

Stella cringed to see her granddaughter's reaction. Savannah was scared, and understandably so. A thug had threatened her mother with harm to the entire family. How could the girl be otherwise?

"I'm sorry to bother you while you're reading," Stella told her as she sat on the floor beside the tiny chair.

Savannah reached over, put her arms around Stella's neck, and gave her a warm, lingering hug. "That's okay, Granny. Don't ever say you're a bother. I'm always tickled to see you."

Glancing around, Stella whispered, "Where's Miss Rose?"

"In there." Savannah nodded toward an adjoining room, which had once been the old mansion's parlor. "Sitting at her desk. I already did the filing for her."

"What a precious girl you are. You make me mighty proud, Savannah."

"That's okay. I like helping Miss Rose. I think I might become a librarian someday. A volunteer one on my days off." She looked down at the book in her hand. "But, of course, the rest of the time, I'll be a policewoman. A detective policewoman. That way I can sleuth all the time, like Frank and Joe, or Nancy."

"Speaking of sleuthing, I've been on the prowl myself since I saw you last. And I have some news for you. But you can't tell anybody that you know. Nobody at all. Promise?"

"Sure! Double-dog promise!"

"Okay. Mostly, I came in here today so I could tell you that you don't have to worry no more about that dirty old guy with the nasty beard who threatened your mama."

"I don't?"

"Nope. He's in jail."

"For real?"

"As real as those iron bars get."

"He didn't get arrested for hurting my mom, did he?" she asked, suddenly fearful.

"No, of course not." Stella leaned back as far as she could and saw Rose Clingingsmith sitting at her desk, working on some book cards, totally absorbed in her task. "He was arrested for having a lot of drugs in his house. Somebody tipped the police off that he had a bunch, so they raided his trailer and found them."

Savannah eyed Stella suspiciously. "That 'somebody' wasn't you, was it?"

"No, it wasn't. Him getting arrested wasn't connected to you in no way, punkin. He got his ornery backside tossed in jail all because of his own wrongdoings. It had nothin' to do with what he said to your mom."

Savannah lowered her eyes. "Or that he sold her stuff, and she bought it?"

"That either, darlin'. Like I said, there's nothing at all to worry your noggin about. Not just that, but Sheriff Gilford gave your mom a very serious talkin'-to. She's not to take any more drugs or drive when she's drinking, especially with you kids in the car. She's not supposed to go jerkin' you kids around, being over rough with you, like she was the other day at the Christmas tree lot. If she does any of those things, the sheriff will find out about it, and he'll be on her like a duck on a june bug."

Savannah gazed at Stella with bright, happy eyes, which were filled with wonder at such good fortune.

While Stella was pleased to see her granddaughter over-joyed, it hurt her heart that the child would be so happy just to be safe—a right that, thankfully, most children were blessed with every day.

Once again, Savannah wrapped her arms around her grand-mother's neck and hugged her tightly. "Thank you, Granny," she whispered. "Thank you so much."

"I told you, sweet cheeks, us Reids had nothing to do with this fine turn of events. Truth be told, it was Sheriff Gilford who took control of the situation. If you want to thank somebody, maybe one of these days you could thank him. But not in front of anybody. He gets all bashful if you praise him too much."

Savannah gave her a playful, knowing look. "Sure, Granny. We both know why he gets all bashful in front of you."

"That'll be enough of that, young lady. You and your smarty-pants brother already made your opinion known on that subject."

"And we're right!"

"I told you, enough hooey. Now, hush up your foolishness, 'cause I got something else to tell you. Some more good news."

"More? I can't take it! All this and it ain't even Christmas yet."

Stella glanced at her watch. "It's twenty minutes to four, so you better skedaddle and get yourself home."

Savannah nodded and reluctantly closed her book. "I know. I shouldn't leave them alone like this, not even once a week. Someday, when we least expect it, Mari and Vi are gonna kill each other over who gets to wear that stupid red hair bow. They don't have a lick o' sense between them, when it comes to that hair bow."

"My news ain't about a hair bow. Or your sisters whuppin' each other's tails. It's way better than that—the reason why you gotta get back home. You have to be there at four o'clock because the sheriff is sending his deputy around with a bunch of groceries for you kids."

Again, Stella watched her granddaughter's face light up with joy over the prospect of receiving what other children took for granted.

"Oh, Granny, really? That's so cool!"

"Sheriff Gilford's got two deputies," Stella told her. "Don't mention that I said this, but as it turns out, one's a lot brighter than the other one."

Savannah tucked her book under her arm, stood, and wriggled out of the alcove. "Let me guess," she said as she took Stella's hand and they strolled out of the library. "The one who's bringing the groceries is the one who—"

"Could ihrow hisself on the ground and miss."

"His porch light's on, but nobody's home."

"His corn bread ain't quite done in the middle."

"He's a macaroni short of a tuna casserole."

They both laughed long and hard, relishing the lightness of spirit that only those who had recently been deeply frightened could experience.

When they'd finally collected themselves, Stella said, "Bless his heart. We shouldn't poke fun at Deputy Jarvis. It ain't nice."

"Yeah, we shouldn't laugh at somebody who might be bringing us ice cream."

"That's for sure."

They looked at each other and again collapsed into fits of giggles.

"You better watch out. Be careful . . . ," Stella said.

"That he don't stick the ice cream in the oven!"

Chapter 17

When Stella slipped into her navy blue "funeral dress," she couldn't help thinking of the times she had put it on in the past and feeling a predictable sadness.

Certainly, she had worn it on many other occasions, too. With her limited wardrobe, no garment was exclusive to one event.

But Florence had bought it for her when Arthur died. Therefore, it would forever be her "funeral dress."

Once she had it on and zipped up the back, she turned and looked at her reflection in the mirror on the back of her bathroom door.

She saw a tired woman whose skin had lost the summer glow it received from daily gardening.

But when she took a closer look, she pretty much liked what she saw there. The woman in the mirror had a sparkle in her eye that showed she treasured life, difficult as it might be from time to time. She looked strong, with a slight up-tilt to her chin that spoke of determination and confidence.

Stella thought she also seemed at peace with herself and

basically contented with where she was, what she had, and who she was.

It didn't get much better than that.

However, for some reason, Stella wanted to look just a little nicer than usual tonight. On any given day, she spent hardly any time on her appearance. She'd twist her unruly dark curls into a big roll at the nape of her neck and secure it with whatever barrette or clip was handy. Maybe a swipe of lip gloss and she was out the door. But as she prepared to pay her respects to Priscilla Carr, Stella wanted to look a tad more polished.

She spent a bit more time on her hair twist, making sure all the stray wisps were neatly tucked. Then she secured it with a leather bun barrette with the Cherokee symbol for love cut into it. The barrette was one of Stella's most beloved possessions, the only thing she owned that had once belonged to her mother—a woman who had had even fewer personal treasures than her daughter.

Her hair done, Stella searched in the back of the medicine chest for a tube of red lipstick she had stashed there ages ago.

Priscilla Carr would never have gone out in public without her famous ruby-red lipstick.

Stella found it, and as she carefully applied it, she tried to convince herself she was doing so for Prissy.

I guess that's for Prissy, too, she thought as she dabbed a bit of the Blue Waltz cologne that Savannah had given her for Christmas last year behind each ear. *Get real, Stella darlin'. We know each other a little better than that, and Prissy's past smelling anything now, bless her heart.*

Her grooming completed, Stella headed to the kitchen and made a quick phone call.

"I'm on my way, Flo," she said. "You ready?"

"As ready as I'll ever be, I reckon," was the lackluster reply.

"Okay. Skedaddle on outside. I'll swing by and getcha in a minute."

As Florence climbed into the truck, she gave Stella a quick perusal. "I see you're wearing the dress I gave you," she said.

"Yes, Flo." Stella managed not to sigh or sound cross. That was one thing about Florence—she was generous to a fault, but if she gave you something, she never let you forget it. In fact, by the end of the day, the entire town would be well informed of her liberality.

Flo was a nice gal with a good heart, but it would never occur to her to leave money anonymously in somebody's mailbox or to give them a dress without telling them how much it cost and letting them know that she'd had to do without in order to give it to them.

After reaching over and feeling the fabric of the skirt, Florence said, "Yeah, that dress has held up good over the years. But then, you get what you pay for, and Lord knows I paid enough for that. Didn't have time to wait for it to go on sale, what with Art's funeral coming up in just a couple of days. Plumb ruined my clothes budget for the month. I had to wear an old raggedy dress myself, but like Jenny at the beauty shop said, it was more important that you looked good, you being the widow and all."

"You're just too good, Flo. That's what's wrong with you."

"I know."

They rode along in awkward silence, the elephant in the truck all too obvious. Finally, Stella had to ask, "Well, have you heard from him?"

Florence stared straight ahead out the windshield, her jaw tight. "Nope. Not a word."

Stella couldn't quite discern the look on her friend's face. "Is that good news, you figure, or bad?"

Florence shrugged. "Don't know. Maybe a bit of both."

"How's that?"

"I don't like being all alone in that big house. Bud wasn't one for talking, but at least he was there, taking up space."

"He ain't yelling at you or threatening you anymore."

"That's true. There's something kind of peaceful about that—not having to worry if you're gonna get hit for putting dinner on the table a little late, 'cause the beans were taking a bit longer than you'd thought to cook, or for looking at a body the wrong way."

Florence's matter-of-fact tone when she talked about Bud's abuse had always surprised Stella—as if getting hit or screamed at by one's mate was as predictable as a change in the weather.

Regarding anybody who might dare to lay a hand on her in anger, Stella's motto was, "Hit me once, and the next time you see me will be in court—after you get out of the hospital."

She had made sure that even gentle-tempered Art had known that before she walked down the aisle with him. Stella knew all too well what some men were capable of doing to a woman they had sworn to love and protect for the rest of their lives.

"I checked with the bank this morning," Florence said, "to see if he's made any moves toward selling the store or the house."

"Well, has he?"

"Lora Schuster said she hasn't heard anything about it. You know how she is there at the bank, her ears on the stretch to hear everybody's business. If anything was going on, she'd be one of the first to know."

"True. Lora's got superpowers. She can hear through the thickest wall and read lips from across the biggest room."

"I asked her to let me know if she finds out anything."

Stella searched her mind for any way that she could help her friend. "Tell her, if she does come up with something worthwhile, I'll bake her an apple pie."

Florence chuckled. "If I offer her that, she'll just make up something on the spot."

"I hadn't thought of that."

"That's because you're not as devious as most of us, Stella. You're a good person. A fine friend. I'm lucky to have you."

Stella reached over and patted Florence's shoulder. "The feeling's mutual, darlin'," she said. "I figure we're both mighty blessed."

As they pulled into the parking lot of Herb Jameson's mortuary, Flo looked around at all the cars and said, "You reckon they're here because they harbored a deep and abiding affection for Prissy?"

"I suspect that most of these people have come to gawk, to make comments about how much makeup Prissy's wearing, even when she's dead, and to swap opinions about who murdered her."

Florence nodded solemnly. "That's one thing I'll say for you, Stella May Reid. You're an astute judge of human behavior. Maybe a bit cynical, but . . ."

"I ain't particularly gifted or overly cynical. Figuring out your fellow man ain't hard. Just assume on any given day that the average person's up to no good. Most of the time you'll be right."

Stella found an empty spot and parked near the edge of the lot. As she and Florence climbed out of the truck, Stella felt a bit apprehensive about the upcoming ordeal. Gathering to pay homage to the town's primary floozy was bound to be an event fraught with tension. She wasn't looking forward to it.

As they walked across the parking lot, heading toward the mortuary's front door, Stella spotted a familiar figure coming toward them—Sheriff Manny Gilford, still in his uniform, still looking especially nice. He had a pleasant look on his face as he locked eyes with Stella.

"Good evening, ladies," he said. "I see we happened to arrive at the same time."

For some reason, Stella got the feeling that perhaps Sheriff Gilford had been waiting in his cruiser somewhere out of sight, intending to arrive at the same time she did.

One part of her said that she was vain to even think such a thing.

A second part told the first part, *Shut up and enjoy the notion.* How often did a widow in her fifties enjoy the attention of such a nice-looking man of good character and high standing in the community?

One glance at Florence told Stella that her friend might be thinking something similar. All of a sudden Flo was wearing a knowing little grin and had a twinkle in her eye.

She leaned closer to Stella and whispered, "Oh. *Now* I see. I was wondering about the red lipstick and the neat hairdo."

"Shhh!" Stella hissed, giving Florence a pinch on her arm. "Hush up. You don't see squat."

"Anything wrong?" the sheriff asked as he joined them.

"Nothin' at all," Stella replied. "Except that we're about to attend a funeral, of course."

"Of course." Gilford glanced around, as though looking for someone. "Bud's not with you tonight?" he asked Florence.

"No. Just Stella," was her abbreviated reply.

"Oh. Okay."

Stella could tell by the way Manny was studying Florence that he was curious about her answer. If Flo wanted to keep her and Bud's separation a secret for much longer, she was going to have to get better at answering the inevitable questions.

"I'm gonna go on inside," Florence said. "You two take your time, and I'll meet up with you later."

Manny watched as Florence hurried up the stairs and through the big double doors of the mortuary. Then he turned to Stella and said, "What's got into her? Bud been smacking her around again?"

"Let's just say there's a bit of trouble in paradise," Stella replied. "But keep it to yourself."

"Can't tell me any more than that?"

"No. Sorry. I really can't."

He considered her words, then said, "I respect that. Keeping a friend's confidence is a good thing. I was just asking in case I need to intervene. Bud's a mean guy. He can get pretty rough when he has a mind to."

"Ain't no secret in that. The whole town knows that about him. He makes sure they do."

"That reminds me—I saw Bud heading out of town the day before yesterday. You can spot that monster truck of his a mile off with that god-awful sparkly blue paint job. He caught my eye because he was on the river road, heading north toward the county line. Most people don't use that road much in the wintertime. In all the years I've known him, I can't recall ever seeing him on it before. Most of Bud's business is here in town or south of here."

Stella silently told herself to file that bit of information away for Florence. It might give her a clue as to where her husband had absconded to.

Manny pressed his point a bit more. "You wouldn't happen to know where he was headed, would you, Stella?" he asked.

"I have no idea where he'd be headed, if he was going in that direction. Any particular reason you're asking?"

He laughed. "No reason. Except that if I get a feeling somebody doesn't want me to know something, I suddenly develop a burning curiosity to find out all I can about it. I'm just nosy that way."

"Then we're all nosy that way, Sheriff." She pulled her coat collar up around her neck as a particularly biting wind whipped across the parking lot. "Speaking of being nosy," she continued, "I was wondering if you've got anything new on the murder. How did your interview with Leland Corder go?"

"Let's sit in my car," he said, "and I'll turn on the heater. Don't want my right-hand gal freezing to death on me. I'll fill you in on everything, but let's do it someplace where you're not going to get frostbite."

On their way to his vehicle, which, as she had suspected, was a bit farther down the street from the mortuary than was necessary, Stella wondered which pleased her more, the fact that he was concerned for her comfort or the fact that he considered her his "right-hand gal."

She decided it was the latter.

Manny opened the passenger door for her, waited as she settled herself inside, then walked around and got into the driver's seat.

When he turned on the car ignition, the radio began to blast a popular disco song. He quickly switched it off and looked a bit embarrassed.

Stella laughed. "I didn't have you pegged as a guy with disco fever."

"The Bee Gees, the Steve Miller Band, Olivia Newton-John, Chicago, Willy Nelson—I'm a fan of all of them. You spend as much time in a vehicle as I do, you get less picky."

"I imagine you do. Now, tell me about Leland. Did you squeeze him hard?"

"Harder than a mustard bottle gets squeezed on the Fourth of July. It was fun. I'm not overfond of Mr. Corder. He's a most unpleasant fella."

"Did he back up Shirley's story?"

"All the way. Except for the drug deal. He wouldn't own up to that."

"He probably figures he's got enough trouble in that department already."

"My thoughts precisely."

"But he said he saw Elmer in the alley?"

"He did, same as Shirley. But after they went back inside the Bulldog and heard the fall down the stairs, he says he didn't look out the door like she did. So, he didn't see anybody strangling anybody."

"That's too bad."

"Sure is. But even if he didn't help much with this case, he'll be going away on the drug charge for a long time, this being his fourth offense. You and your family can forget about him."

"How about Elmer?" she asked. "Did you get a chance to talk to him yet?"

"Absolutely. He's my number one suspect right now—lucky him."

"Did you get anything good outta him?"

"Nope. I got squat outta the old pervert. And I did everything short of holding him up by his ankles and shaking him till the change fell out of his pockets."

"More likely, his dentures would fall out before any money would. Elmer's too broke to pay attention. Always has been."

"He admitted to being in the alley," Manny said. "He didn't have much choice, since three people saw him. Tried to say he was just hanging out back there. But I got him to admit he was hiding from me after I chased him away from the retirement home."

Stella thought it over for a moment. "If he flashed his dick-do at Myrtle, then ran down the street and into an alley, with you after him, then raced upstairs to Prissy's apartment, smashed her over the head with that fancy mirror, threw her down the stairs, ran down after her, and strangled her to death . . . I gotta tell you, Manny, that's the hardest day's work Elmer Yonce ever did. Personally, I don't think he's able."

"Does sound a bit ambitious for him, now that you mention it."

"Did he say if he saw anybody else?"

"Says he spied two people smoking outside the tavern door. Didn't get a good enough look at them to tell if it was Shirley, and I don't know if he's acquainted with Leland. But he said it was a fat man and a skinny woman."

"Sounds like those two."

"It does. Elmer also saw Jake Neville's Chrysler cruise through the alley. Says it stopped for a few seconds there at the bottom of the stairs, then drove on out the other side. I had a little talk with Allison this afternoon, and she admitted to me that it was her. Seemed she just wanted to see if Jake was there with Prissy. But she couldn't see anything from the car, so she just drove on."

"Guess that takes Jake outta the runnin'."

"Maybe. I'm trying to keep an open mind about everybody and everything at this point."

"Did Elmer hear somebody scream and fall down the stairs?"

"Yes. He claims it scared him so bad that he hid behind that big Dumpster back there and didn't come out until he figured the coast was clear. Says that's when he ran into you."

"Don't tell me he didn't hear Prissy's death gargles. I sure did. If he was back there, he couldn't have missed 'em. He had to know somebody was hurt and in trouble."

"Actually, he admitted to me that he heard the scream, the fall, and the choking. He said he heard her making those awful dying sounds. But he said he was afraid to come out and try to help." Manny paused and wiped his hand wearily across his eyes. "I believe him, Stella. The man had tears rolling down his cheeks when he told me. He's all broken up about it. Feels guilty. I guess there's a speck of decency in everybody, if you look hard enough for it."

"I'd like to think that's true."

Stella thought about the scream and how she had felt it deep in her soul. She recalled Prissy's final breaths and knew she'd be haunted by those sounds for the rest of her life.

Yes, she had been able to put her fear aside and help the woman, anyway. But what if Elmer Yonce had reached into his soul and simply hadn't found the strength to do the same? What if it just wasn't there?

Could she really blame him?

"That leaves you with a whole lot of nobody and nothin', huh, Manny?" she said.

"I'd say that about sums it up, Stella May." He turned the

ignition off and shoved the keys in his pocket. "Whatcha think, kiddo? Shall we go pay our respects?"

"I'd rather chew bumblebees than go inside there and hear all the malarkey that's gonna be said about that girl. But I suppose we might as well get 'er done."

Chapter 18

As Stella and Sheriff Gilford walked up the circular brick driveway to the mortuary, it occurred to her, not for the first time, that Jameson's Funeral Home was one of the prettiest buildings in town, if not in the entire county. Other than Judge Patterson's antebellum mansion, of course.

Both were colonial style, white with massive columns and elegant black shutters. But the judge's home was the real thing. Jameson's was a facade.

Inside Judge Patterson's mansion, some Civil War soldiers had been nursed back to health, while others had perished on the long oak dining table that had been pressed into service for surgeries. Some said the ghosts of the soldiers who had suffered and died there still haunted the place.

While the funeral parlor had always seemed a bit creepy in Stella's estimation, she doubted there were any actual ghosts there. She figured the suffering that might have incited spectral visitations had occurred before the earthly remains of the departed had arrived at this place.

Still, when Sheriff Gilford opened one of the double doors and ushered Stella inside, she felt a wash of emotions that caused her to wish she could turn around and run back out.

No matter how soft the navy-blue carpet under her feet might be, or how tasteful the finely polished mahogany wainscoting on the walls, Jameson's Funeral Home was and would forever be the place she had seen her husband's face for the last time. The place where she had stroked his hand and said good-bye.

She would always love this place and hate it for the same reason.

As though sensing her thoughts, Manny placed his hand gently on her upper back as they walked along the hallway toward the viewing rooms in the back.

"Are you okay?" he asked.

She turned, looked up at him, and saw tears brimming in his eyes. Whether they were for his best friend, Arthur, or his wife, Lucy, she couldn't tell.

Probably both, she decided.

A door to the right opened, and Herb Jameson stepped into the hallway. He smiled, as though happy to see them, and said, "I was hoping I'd run into you, Sheriff, Sist . . . I mean, Mrs. Reid. Can I have a quick word with you before we go in?"

Gilford looked down at her, as though asking her permission. She nodded, and they both followed Herb into his office.

Like the rest of the mortuary, this was an elegant, quiet, dark room. Several comfortable chairs were gathered around a heavy desk.

All too well, she recalled sitting in one of those chairs, talking to Herb, looking at pictures spread across his desk. Photos of caskets. She had been attempting to make final arrangements for her vital, still young husband, whom she had kissed good-bye just before he left to work in the fields less than forty-eight hours before.

At that time, she could hardly breathe, let alone pick out a coffin.

Stella sat in a chair, as directed, but hoped that Herb Jameson would say his piece quickly and let her escape the suffocating confines of the room.

"Are you okay?" Manny softly asked again as he sat on the chair next to hers. "Because, if you aren't, we can—"

"I'm okay. What's up, Herb?"

She knew she was being a bit abrupt with the funeral director. So, he hadn't shown a lot of aptitude in the alley, and he'd said some unpleasant things about a young woman who had passed. She had no reason to hate him or to act like she did.

"First," Herb began, "I want to apologize to you both. You being a lady, I'll start with you, Mrs. Reid. The things I said about Miss Carr were inappropriate. I should never have said them in front of anyone, let alone a lady like yourself. I never should have even thought them. They were unkind and judgmental. I hope you can forgive me."

Stella searched his eyes and saw genuine remorse. "I can, Brother Herb," she told him. "I accept and appreciate your apology."

"Thank you." Herb turned to the sheriff. "And you, Sheriff Gilford . . . I behaved like an idiot the other day, not knowing the simplest things that a coroner should know. To be honest with you, when I took the job, I never dreamed I'd ever have to investigate a murder. I didn't study up like I should have. At least on the basic procedures. I was wrong. But I've been making up for lost time now, and if, God forbid, you should ever need me to fulfill my duties as a coroner again, I'll be much better prepared."

Gilford seemed as impressed as Stella. "Happy to hear it, Herb. Does this mean you've got those blood-type tests done for me?"

"I do." Herb grabbed a folder off his desk and shoved it into the sheriff's hands. "Priscilla was A negative. Only six percent of people here in the United States are A negative. Of those ten swabs I took there at the foot of the stairs, all ten were A negative."

"Then she was probably the only bleeder at the scene," Gilford replied. "Good to know."

"Also," Herb continued, "the samples I took from the bedspread and the brush upstairs were A positive. The hairs on the brush were microscopically similar to Miss Carr's, enough to say they were most likely hers."

"Thank you, Herb. This is all helpful," Manny said, looking over the paperwork. "I also see you found more evidence of strangulation."

"That's right!" Herb said enthusiastically, quite proud of himself. "Besides the bruising that you saw on her neck, her hyoid bone was definitely broken."

"What does that mean?" Stella asked.

"The hyoid bone is deep in the neck and not easily broken," Manny replied. "Since she wasn't in a car accident and had no gunshot wound, she was almost certainly strangled. That makes her manner of death strangulation, and her cause of death homicide."

"But she was still alive when I got there," Stella said, trying to understand.

"Barely," Herb replied. "Strangulation doesn't always mean instant death. The throat can continue to swell after a choking. People have died minutes, hours, days, or even months after they've been choked, all from the damage it causes."

"Oh, I see." Stella felt sick inside, thinking of Priscilla fighting for breath through swollen passages that were narrowing by the moment.

"That's impressive work, Herb." Manny handed back the folder. "Is that all?"

"One more thing. She has a little girl."

"What?" Stella stared at Herb. "Prissy was a mother?"

"She was. I was trying to find out if she has any next of kin there in Chesterville, where she's from . . . someone who'd like to say how and where she should be buried. She has no siblings, and her parents are gone. But her aunt's been raising her five-year-old girl, hoping that Priscilla would get her life back on track. Seems that at one time Prissy wanted to be a nurse, but . . ."

"I'll need the name of that aunt and any contact information you might have for her," Gilford said. "I'll have to find out if Prissy had any enemies in Chesterville that we don't know about."

"Here's her phone number, Sheriff," Herb said, handing Manny a piece of paper. "I already asked the aunt when I talked to her if she had any idea who might have done it, but she had no clue."

"Then she isn't here tonight?" Stella asked.

"No. She thought it would be better if she stayed with her great-niece. But she paid for the funeral and asked that I do a nice job for Prissy. I did. The best I could."

Stella stood along with Manny, and Herb walked them to the door.

For a moment, she reached over and touched her church brother's arm. "Thank you," she said. "I'm glad we're on good terms again. I don't like being on the outs with people I care about."

"I feel the same way," he told her. "Life's too short."

Stella nodded. "You, of all people, should know that."

When Stella walked into the visitation room with Sheriff Gilford and Herb Jameson on either side of her, the first person to greet her was Elsie Dingle.

It took only seconds for Elsie to cross the room and enfold Stella in a warm, comforting embrace. Stella melted against her comfy, cushy friend, savoring every moment.

When Stella finally pulled back and looked down into her friend's beautiful, dark eyes, she said, "What would I do without you, Sister Elsie, and those hugs of yours?"

"Don't know," was the cheerful reply. "But you'll never have to find out, 'cause I'll always be nearby when you need one."

Manny and Herb drifted away in opposite directions, leaving Stella and Elsie to mull over the more mundane topics commonly discussed at visitations.

"How does she look?" Stella asked, nodding toward the coffin at the end of the room.

"Pretty as a picture," Elsie told her. "Brother Jameson did a fine job on her. Her hair in particular. Herb always has been good with hair, you know."

"Yes," Stella agreed. "He's downright gifted when it comes to hair. That's for sure."

"Prissy looks like Snow White, only with bleached blond hair, lyin' there all prettied up, just waiting for her prince to come along and give her a big kiss to wake her."

Stella winced just a bit at Elsie's choice of metaphor. Looking around the room, Stella could see numerous couples who had come to pay their respects. She was a bit surprised, considering the rumors about previous visitations of another sort—the ones to Prissy's apartment.

Stella couldn't imagine how awkward it was for those men to accompany their wives on this somber occasion. To see one's mistress lying in a coffin would be bad enough. To have to do so while holding your wife's hand in a room full of your neighbors had to be even worse.

Stella tried to drum up some sympathy in her heart for them, but she couldn't. As far as she was concerned, an awkward evening at a funeral home was a small price to pay for breaking one's marriage vows.

"I'll tell you who *don't* seem so good tonight," Elsie whispered. "And that's Flo. She looks downright peaked, and she's cranky, too. Noni Wilde asked her where Bud is, and Flo 'bout bit her head off and spit it back at her. What do you reckon's wrong with her?"

Stella stifled a groan and wished that Florence would make some sort of public proclamation about her and Bud's separation. Trying to cover for her was getting to be wearisome.

She glanced over at Florence, who was talking to Pastor O'Reilly and his wife, Connie. They seemed deep in conversation. Stella could tell that Florence was having a hard time appearing cheerful. She never had been very good at hiding her feelings. At least not the bad ones.

"Flo's got some problems at the moment," Stella told Elsie, choosing her words carefully. "I'm sure she'll share them with you and everybody else once she's got everything all settled in her mind."

"That's exactly what I thought it was." Elsie shook her head, disgusted. She made a clucking sound with her tongue. "That good-for-nothin' weasel done left her, and him bein' tighter than the skin on bologna, he's probably gonna take her for all she's worth. I don't know why I'm surprised. That's just the sort he is, to take off and leave a good woman behind, like she is nothing but a sack of half-rotten potatoes."

Stella stared down at Elsie and said, "How on earth, Elsie Dingle, did you get that outta what I said? All I told you was—"

"Oh, I heard what you said. Ever' word. And I know exactly what you meant. Bud's done gone and dumped Flo. Lord o' mercy. Here ever'body thought when the time came, *she'd* be the one doin' the dumpin', what with ol' Bud being short on understandin' and long on mean."

Eager to divert the topic of conversation away from Florence, Stella looked around the room and saw Allison and Jake Neville walking up to the casket hand in hand.

"Glory be!" Stella exclaimed. "Just look over yonder at that! Principal Neville and his wife have made up!"

Elsie shrugged. "That's old news. Ever'body in town knows that already. Where you been, girl?"

"Busy, apparently. When did it happen?"

"Around suppertime."

"That was less than an hour ago."

"Sounds about right. Seems he got sick and tired of livin' with his mama. You know her. Can you blame him? So, he drove all the way to Atlanta and bought Allison one of them fancy diamond bracelets—though Rayleen Shields says it looks more like that cubic zirconia stuff to her—and he got down on his knees in front of Allison, like he was proposing or something, and cried and begged her to forgive him. As you know, Ally's always set great store by jewelry, so she finally told him she'd give him one more chance and ..." Elsie waved a hand in their direction. "Bob's your uncle."

"That's mighty big of her, forgiving him like that, bracelet or not," Stella observed. "But then, unlike other wives with wayward husbands, she won't have to worry about the other woman rearin' her ugly head again."

"True. Course, if he's that kind, and Jake is, it won't take him long to latch onto another one."

"Ain't it so? They're like egg-suckin' hounds, men like that. Once they get a taste, you have to shoot 'em to git 'em to quit."

Both women bowed their heads solemnly in homage to unfortunate women everywhere who were cursed with wayward husbands.

Suddenly, the sacred peace of the visitation room was shattered by a scream, then another, followed by total bedlam!

Stella jumped and grabbed Elsie. "What on earth?" she exclaimed, trying to discern the center of the commotion.

"It's up front!" Elsie answered, her voice shaking with fear and excitement. "By the coffin!"

From the corner of her eye, Stella saw Sheriff Gilford rushing from the back of the room to where the casket and the guest of honor were displayed.

Emboldened by the fact that he was on the way and would have things under control in a minute, maybe two, Stella put her fear aside and decided to indulge her curiosity. "Come on," she told Elsie.

Elsie needed no additional coaxing. Together, they fought their way through the agitated, confused crowd to the front. They arrived shortly after Gilford, just in time to see him receive a hearty right jab to the face.

Delivered by Allison Neville.

"You get your hands off me, Manny Gilford!" she was screeching. "You'll stay outta this if you know what's good for you!"

Seeing that blood was pouring from Manny's nose, Stella decided it might take a bit longer than a minute or two for the sheriff to seize control of the situation.

"Honey bun, don't!" Jake Neville was yelling in his enraged wife's face. "You just assaulted an officer of the law! You can't be doin' that, darlin'!"

Allison froze, fixing a most evil eye on her husband. The crowd was silent, watching, waiting to see what would happen next.

They didn't have long to wait.

Allison pulled back a fist, let it fly, and clobbered her husband, too, landing a good one squarely on his right eye.

Onlookers gasped, then stared in complete amazement as she whirled around to face the coffin.

Before anyone could stop her, she leaned over the casket and made a violent snatching motion in the vicinity of Prissy's neck.

When she turned back around to the multitude, she lifted her right hand and displayed her prize, like Attila the Hun, in the heat of battle, lifting a severed head.

"This necklace is *mine*!" she screamed to the crowd. "Mine! My husband gave *my* necklace to a *whore*!"

"Sugar, don't—" Jake wasn't able to finish his sentence, because his wife was on him again, swinging at him with the fist holding the heavy gold chain.

When Gilford tried to pull her off, he got a mouthful of the chain, too. In seconds, his lip was bleeding as much as his nose.

"I was looking for this necklace for better'n six months, you sumbitch!" Allison shouted at her husband as she dangled the chain a few inches in front of his eyes. "I turned that house upside down and inside out. The car, too, and you stood right there and said nothin' the whole time. Even pretended to help me look. I oughta kill you! Kill you *dead*!"

"Mrs. Neville, please," Manny said, his voice muffled because he was holding his hand over his nose and mouth. "I can understand that you're upset, but this isn't the time or place to discuss a private family matter."

But Allison paid him no attention as she continued to rail at her husband. "You just wait till I tell your blessed mama about this. She thinks the sun rises just to hear her son crow! And you in charge of a school full of innocent children."

That got the crowd riled up. Instantly, they were nodding and discussing it among themselves, and they became louder and angrier by the moment.

Stella even heard snippets of conversations that included phrases like "I figured Jake was the one who killed her."

"Murdering a pretty young woman like that . . ."

"Oughta string him up here and now."

"I got a rope in my truck."

"Okay," Stella heard Manny say. "That's it."

She saw him reach down to his duty belt and retrieve a pair of handcuffs. "Mrs. Neville, I'm arresting you for disturbing the peace. You have the right to—"

But he had no time to finish informing Allison Neville of her rights, because another woman had made her way past the affray to the casket.

Gina Wallace leaned over the body, took a closer look, and began to scream, too. "She's wearing my earrings!" Gina shouted, whirling around to address the sheepish-looking fellow behind her. "You gave me those for Valentine's Day!"

"You never wore 'em," he offered in weak defense.

"Because they are ugly! But that's not the point!" she screamed, her eyes bugging out like those of a demon-possessed troll doll.

A second later, Prissy's earrings had been snatched from her as unceremoniously as her necklace.

Gina began to pummel her husband's chest with her fists. In the process, the unattractive heart-shaped red earrings went flying across the room.

"And that's my bracelet she's wearing!" Melinda Hicks yelled. "The one my mama gave me when I married you, Daryl, you no-good piece of crap on a cracker! Don't you run away from me, Daryl James Hicks! When I get my hands on you, boy, you and me are gonna *mix*!"

Much later that night, in the quiet of her own home and the comfort of her easy chair, Stella would recall the moment Melinda Hicks chased Daryl James Hicks from the room, the moment the mayor's wife spotted her watch on Prissy's wrist, and the moment the mailman's longtime girlfriend noticed her hair barrette decorating Prissy's golden locks.

That was when the *real* trouble began.

Chapter 19

"**O**w! That hurts, Stella May! What the hell's in that stuff? Carbolic acid?"

Manny Gilford sat next to his desk, grasping the arms of his chair like a fighter-plane pilot who had just pushed the EJECT button. Stella stood beside him, holding a bottle of Merthiolate and some cotton balls that were stained with the red tincture and the lawman's blood.

"Oh, for mercy's sake, Manny. In the line of duty, you've been shot, beaned with a baseball bat, knocked down a well, shocked with a cattle prod, and run over by a bull. I think you can handle having a little bit of Merthiolate smeared on your boo-boos."

"Yeah? Well, that junk hurts worse than all those others put together. When are you gonna be done torturing me, woman?"

She dabbed a bit more of the liquid on his cut lip. He groaned, stomped his feet and, when she had finished, shook his head like a dog with a big sticker burr in its ear.

"Not the sort to suffer in silence, are we?" she said with a grin as she replaced the bottle top, with its long glass applicator wand. "But then," she added under her breath, "you being male and all . . ."

"What was that?"

"Nothin'. Didn't say a thing." She tossed the soiled cotton balls into a nearby waste can as he pulled a mirror from a drawer and examined his wounds.

"That one on your lip's gonna leave a scar," she said.

"Won't be my first. Or my last," he replied, deepening his voice half an octave.

"*Now* we're gonna play the manly man." She winked at him. "A bit late for that."

"Watch that sharp tongue of yours, gal. I've had a rough night."

"You have. I'll give you that. About the roughest I've ever seen in this little town of ours."

They both paused and listened to the cacophony of shouts, curses, shrieks, and sobs drifting down the stairs from the cells above.

"When's the last time you had ever'one of your cells full like that?" Stella asked.

"Never. That's when. There's a first time for everything, and tonight we broke an all-time McGill record."

"When are you figurin' on lettin' 'em out?"

"As soon as I know they aren't gonna be killing each other."

"That might be a spell."

"It'll take as long as it takes. I'd rather be having them cool their heels in jail than make national news about a bloodbath here in little McGill."

"I can see it now, the footage of all the men's bodies bein' carried out, and the women holdin' their bloody knives in one hand and their retrieved jewelry in the other."

Manny sighed and shook his head. "I never saw the like. If

you and Elsie and the others hadn't jumped in to help, I'd have had a wholesale slaughter on my hands."

Suddenly, Manny thought of something, and a frightened look crossed his face. "Damn! How am I going to feed all those people?"

"You'll have to ask the mayor to appropriate some funds to . . . oh . . . never mind. I forgot."

"Yeah. He and his old lady are upstairs with the rest."

"You can forget about keepin' it outta the papers. You'll be famous by sunrise."

He looked horrified. "You think?"

She laughed long and hard, until tears streamed down her cheeks and she could hardly breathe. After collapsing onto a chair near his, she finally collected herself and said, "Time will tell, Manny. I've stopped speculatin' on how things around here are gonna go lately. I've been surprised at every turn in the road."

"Me too," he admitted. "From all I've ever heard—contrary to what you see on television—most murders are pretty easy to solve. Generally, the killer's somebody closest to the victim, and everybody around them saw it comin' a mile off. It's usually a woman getting murdered by a husband or boyfriend that she just kicked to the curb. Or some bad-tempered dude, who's lived his whole life bullying and hurting people, stabs his brother with a steak knife because he grabbed the biggest T-bone off the grill. But this one . . . It's a stumper."

"Especially now, when you've got your cells filled to the brim and runnin' over with suspects. Could've been any one of those guys who was messin' around with Prissy. Or any of their wives, for that matter."

"A woman strangling another woman to death?"

"Could happen. It's not like Prissy necessarily put up a big fight. She'd already been hit on the head, bless her heart, and either fell or was pushed down a flight of stairs."

"True. Neither Herb nor I saw any scratches on her neck."

"Scratches?"

"Yes." A sad look crossed Manny's face. "Unless their hands are bound, strangulation victims usually claw at whatever's choking them, to get loose. They wind up scratching their own necks in the process."

"That's a sorrowful thing to have to know."

He looked down at the cuts and bruises on his own hands, compliments of the wives who were occupying his cells upstairs. "There's a lot of miserable stuff you find out in this job," he said. "Sometimes I feel old and exhausted just thinking about it."

"I'll bet you do. I don't think I'd wanna have your job, Sheriff." She reached over and smoothed his hair, as she often did Waycross's after he'd been out in the wind or roughhousing with his sisters.

He smiled at her, silently thanking her for the kind gesture. "It's not so bad," he told her. "It has its perks. Once in a while, you get to help a good person who truly deserves it. That feels pretty nice."

"I'll bet it does." She paused for a moment, then said, "Which reminds me, there's something I'd like to do for somebody. Two somebodies, for that matter. Only with your permission, of course."

"What's that, Miss Stella?"

Stella drew a deep breath. "I feel real bad for them women upstairs. I know they're suffering from what transpired tonight. In an awful public way, they found out not only that their husbands were unfaithful to them but also that the low-down skunks even gave away their jewelry to that woman."

"I'm sure they're in a world of hurt. Who wouldn't be?"

"But I also feel a bit bad for Prissy Carr," Stella admitted.

"Why? Do you really think she didn't know that jewelry was stolen? And who it was stolen from?"

"I'm not saying she was innocent. Obviously, she didn't mind setting aside the Golden Rule when it served her purposes. She probably knew or at least had an inkling where the stuff came from. But whether she did or not, it hurt me to see her gettin' the jewelry snatched right off her corpse like that."

"It *was* an ugly scene. I'll give you that," he admitted with a slight shudder. "What's this good deed that you need my blessing for?"

"The jewelry box that we saw there in her apartment—it had a lot of stuff in it."

He looked alarmed. "No! No, Stella May! I'm not going to put the contents of that box on display and have the rest of the women in this town going crazy when they find their things among them! I'm all for returning stolen merchandise to its rightful owner, but I got enough trouble housing the ones I've already got upstairs."

"There, there. Don't get your britches in an uproar. That's not what I was gonna suggest."

"Thank goodness. You had me worried there. What is it, exactly, that you want to do?"

"First, can you tell me if that jewelry box is still in her apartment?"

"I believe it is. Herb said he went by to pick out a dress and some jewelry for her to be laid out in. But to my knowledge, he left the rest of it there. Why?"

"Prissy took a lot of pride in her appearance. She always dressed nice and had her sparklies on when she was out and about town. With your permission, I'd like to go get that box, pick out a few items, and take them to Herb. He can put them on her right before he closes the casket, without anybody seein' or, heaven forbid, identifyin' them. I know she would have wanted it that way."

The sheriff thought it over for a moment, then said, "Okay. That's kind of you, Stella. If Herb doesn't mind, I have no objection. As long as no wives get a look at what's in that box."

"Thank you, Manny."

"What's the second thing?"

"I want to send the rest of the jewelry to Prissy's aunt, the one who's taking care of her little girl. I don't think Prissy owned much in this world. But what she did have should be handed down to her daughter. It's the only thing that child will have to remember her by."

"Good idea."

"I assume you've got the door to the apartment locked now."

"I do. The key was in her purse."

"Can I borrow it?"

He opened a desk drawer but hesitated. "I'm a mite uneasy about sending you over there by yourself."

"I know it's still a crime scene. I promise not to touch anything. I'll wear gloves if you want me to."

He smiled. "I'm not worried about you messing up my crime scene, Stella. I'm worried about you."

"You think the killer might come back there for somethin'?"

"It occurred to me."

"It occurred to me, too. But I'll not be dawdlin' once I get inside there. I figure it'll take me less than fifteen seconds to walk in, pick up that box, and walk out."

"You work fast."

"I can when I need to."

He placed the key in her hand. "I'd go with you if I could. But I don't dare leave that bunch up there unattended, and I don't know for sure when Jarvis is gonna show up."

"I understand, Manny. Really, I do. I swear I won't be in there longer than two shakes of a lamb's tail."

"Go along then. Promise you'll call me when you get to the funeral home?"

"I promise. Thank you."

"You're welcome. And thank you for the . . ." He waved a hand, indicating his injured but newly doctored face.

"For torturing you with Merthiolate?"

"Yeah. That. The next time you say, 'Hold on. This might sting a bit,' I'm gonna get myself a bullet to bite on."

True to her word, Stella took less than a minute to retrieve the jewelry box from Priscilla Carr's apartment. Even if she hadn't promised Manny, she wouldn't have hung around the place.

As before, when she'd been there with the sheriff, she sensed a heaviness in the air, which made her feel the need to literally run from the place once she had the box in hand.

No doubt, Elsie would have attributed the room's melancholy aura to the presence of "haunts." Stella wasn't sure what this feeling was, but she didn't want to be around there any longer than absolutely necessary.

With the door locked behind her and Prissy's treasures tucked securely under her arm, Stella headed back to her truck.

Even though someone had replaced the burned-out lightbulb over the tavern's door and, as a result, the alley was less dark and foreboding than it had been the night of the murder, Stella decided to lock her truck's doors for the first time since she could remember.

Spending time in a place where someone had just been murdered, while carrying a box full of a dead woman's jewelry—some of which was probably the real thing—wasn't something she did every day.

She had no desire to make a habit of it.

As she pulled out of the alley, passed between the Bulldog and the pool hall, and drove onto the street, Stella began to feel better already. With the worst part of the day behind her and only one simple task ahead, she would soon be resting in her comfortable recliner and reflecting on the day's events.

You are not likely to forget this one, she told herself as she tried to remember the date for future reference. Her brain was so tired, and her emotions were so scrambled, that it took a while.

That's not a good sign, Stella girl, she thought, *when it takes that long to remember what day it is. Especially when it's Christmas Eve.*

She felt a momentary jolt of panic as she considered the too-small collection of gifts on the top shelf of her kitchen cupboard, hidden away from curious grandkid eyes.

Since September she had been crocheting warm hats with pom-pom balls on the top, house slippers with pom-pom balls, and mittens without pom-pom balls. After completing the twenty-first ball and finishing the last hat and slipper, Stella had decided once and for all that she could happily live the rest of her life without making another pom-pom ball.

If that meant she was a less than perfect grandmother, so be it.

Her main present to the children this year was locked away in the shed next to her garden.

Last August she had found an old, rusted swing set at a

garage sale for a price that even she could afford. For the past four months, she had been restoring the sad mess to its original glory. Even better than original, she was proud to say.

She had found some old but perfectly passable white paint and had given the swing set three thick coats. Once those had dried thoroughly, she had striped its long steel legs and crossbeam with wide masking tape and had spray-painted the remaining exposed areas bright red.

She was thrilled to death with the results, and she knew her grand-angels would be, too.

That was one of the few blessings to being poor. Small things mattered so much to those who had nothing.

Yes, it'll be a fine Christmas with the grandbabies, she told herself. *We'll have ourselves a merry time decorating the tree and singing carols and making fudge.*

If that stinkin' Shirley lets you see them, added her darker, less positive side.

Shut up! she told the ugly voice. *I've been praying about it day and night, and the good Lord ain't deaf. He heard ever' word. Ever'thing's gonna be just fine and dandy. So, stick* that *in your pipe and smoke it!*

Stella had just reached the end of Main Street and turned left, heading toward the funeral home, when she heard a siren in the distance.

She had always hated that sound.

A speeding ambulance in a small town meant that somebody she knew was in trouble, heading to the hospital with a heart attack or a broken arm. Maybe an asthma attack.

She never knew what it was until word got around to her later. But unless somebody was in labor and about to bring a baby into the world, it meant worry and maybe even heartache for someone.

She ran over the short list in her head of the people in McGill who were quite elderly or very sick. Sam Brotherton's chest cold could have gone into pneumonia. Two months ago, Josephine Collin's cancer had reappeared, and her chemo wasn't working very well.

"Lord, whoever it is, help 'em out," she prayed as she drove. "Help them get to the hospital in time. Or if it's your will that they go, let their passing be a gentle one, for them and for their loved ones."

The siren continued to get louder and louder. Stella looked in her rearview mirror and saw the flashing lights coming up behind her.

Dutifully, she pulled over to the side of the road, onto the shoulder.

When the vehicle shot past her, going at a high rate of speed, she realized it wasn't an ambulance at all.

It was a big black-and-white cruiser.

Sheriff Manny Gilford's car.

But she had left Manny not that long ago at the station. He had told her he couldn't leave with a jail full of prisoners. Why was he racing down the highway like his life depended on it?

Or someone else's?

She checked her mirror again, to make sure no one else was coming, then pulled back onto the road.

She had to find out what the trouble was. For all she knew, he could be headed for a bad situation, like the one he'd been in earlier at the funeral home, and might need some assistance.

She stepped on the gas, driving faster than she was accustomed to, though she knew she'd never catch up with him.

Maybe it's just down the road a piece, she thought, her pulse pounding.

She rounded a curve and there, less than a quarter of a mile away, she could see the cruiser, lights still flashing, stopped in the middle of the road.

As she drew closer, she saw Manny rushing around, lighting and throwing flares onto the pavement.

She saw a vehicle in the ditch on the right, resting on its passenger side.

On the visible door was the large, distinctive logo of a snarling bulldog.

Chapter 20

"No," Stella whispered as she brought her truck to an abrupt stop in the middle of the road, near the cruiser. "No, no, no."

She got out of her truck and raced to Manny, who was on his hands and knees at the side of the road, talking to someone lying there.

"You're going to be okay. Do you hear me?" he was asking the still figure. "Say yes if you hear me."

"Yes."

Stella knew the voice. It was Waycross.

"No!" she heard someone scream.

Then she realized it was her.

Manny turned, saw her, and jumped to his feet. He ran to her and grabbed her by her shoulders. She could see tears in his eyes.

"The kids? Is it my kids?"

He pointed toward the person he had just been comforting. "Waycross is there. I think he's okay."

She felt like her throat had closed. She could barely manage to say, "The others?"

"Spread around." He waved his arm, indicating the road, the ditches on either side, the fields beyond. "The damned bitch had them loose in the back of the truck."

Stella didn't think to ask him where Shirley was.

She didn't care.

Peering into the darkness beside the country road, she couldn't see much, except what was illuminated by the cruiser's and the truck's headlights.

Other than Waycross, who was sitting up now, she saw no one.

But she could hear her grandkids crying, and she felt her heart shattering into what felt like a thousand jagged glass shards.

"Flashlight!" she screamed at Manny. "Gimme a flashlight!"

He disappeared for only a moment, then raced back with two heavy-duty lights and shoved one into her hand.

"Help's on the way, Stella," he said. "I called. They're coming."

The next few minutes were a blur, as she raced up and down the road with Manny Gilford, locating and trying to comfort her hurt, terrified grandchildren.

After a quick word of reassurance to Waycross, who appeared to be more frightened than hurt, they located Jesup and Cordelia, huddled in the pickup's cab, clinging to each other and softly crying. Manny yanked the driver's door open, then climbed down inside, gently pulled each one out, and gave them to Stella.

"Oh, babies, don't cry," she told them, kissing their wet cheeks as she ran her hands over their arms, legs, and torsos, searching for wounds. "Granny's got you, darlin's. You're gonna be okay."

She and Manny carried them over to where Waycross sat on the grass beside the road.

"Here, sugars. You two stay here with your brother and keep him company while we round up the rest of you kids."

Instantly, Waycross became the protective older brother, pulling his little sisters to his sides and hugging them tightly.

"I got 'em, Gran," he said. "You go help the others."

It didn't take long for Stella to locate Marietta, because she was shrieking her fear and indignation to the high heavens. Stella found her sitting in a large puddle of mud just off the road. Fortunately, it was soft mud, and other than a filthy, torn dress and a scrape on her elbow, she seemed okay.

Stella led her to Waycross and the two younger girls and told her, "Sit down there and stop cryin' if you can, sugar. You're okay, and you're scarin' your little sisters."

"My dress is all dirty!" Marietta replied.

Stella didn't have time to debate the matter with her.

She left to join Manny, who had located Alma deep in the ditch just in front of the truck. She was clinging to its bumper, her eyes wide with terror.

As Manny pulled her out and handed her to Stella, the child's teeth were chattering so badly that they could hardly understand her when she said, "Mama . . . Mama had . . . I think, a wreck."

"Yes, baby girl," Stella said. "I think so, too. But it's all done. The worst is over now."

"Are you hurt, honey?" Manny asked her, playing his flashlight beam up and down the child's small frame.

"Just here." She held up her small hand, and both Stella and Manny could see that it was bruised and badly swollen.

"Can you make a fist with your hand, Alma?" Manny asked.

She tried but yelped from the pain it caused her.

"That's okay," he told her. "You don't need to try that anymore if it hurts." He shot Stella a knowing look.

The hand was probably broken. Stella could tell, and so could he.

She hurried Alma over to the increasing knot of children and sat her down with the others. "Watch out for her hand," she told Waycross.

He took one look at it and said, "I will. Alma, come sit here by me."

Manny came running back from his cruiser with a large blanket under each arm. He tossed one to Stella, and they both wrapped several kids in each blanket.

"We've still got two missing," Stella told Manny breathlessly. "Vidalia and Savannah."

"Okay." He shouted, "Vidalia! Savannah! Where are you? Holler if you hear me!"

They paused to listen, and both heard a low moan from farther away, back down the road that the truck and they had traveled.

"Savannah?" Stella shouted. "Vidalia?"

Both she and Manny began running down the road, shining their flashlights into the dead weeds on either side.

The groaning seemed louder as they went.

"Vi? Vannah?" Stella shouted. "Where're you at?"

"Here. Granny, here."

The voice was soft and shaky, but Stella knew it well. "Savannah! Savannah! I hear you. We're coming!"

Manny's light found them first.

To the left of the road, in weeds that were so high that they nearly concealed the children, Savannah was kneeling beside Vidalia, who was lying on her back.

Stella stumbled and fell as she dove off the road and into the brush. She felt Manny's hand on her arm as he lifted her back onto her feet, then pulled her along until they both reached the girls.

Savannah's face was frightfully pale, and she had blood smeared on her cheek and neck. Her hands and arms were covered with it.

"Oh, sweetie," Stella said, reaching her first. "You're hurt."

"Not much. The blood's Vidalia's."

Savannah nodded toward her sister. Both Manny and Stella pointed their flashlights at Vidalia and gasped at what they saw.

Savannah had wrapped her thin denim jacket around her sister's leg and was holding it so tightly that she was shaking from the effort, the stress of the situation, and from the December cold.

The once blue garment was dark red, drenched in blood.

"Her knee's cut bad," Savannah told them. "I couldn't see it in the dark, but I felt the blood coming out somethin' fierce. That's why I put my coat around it."

"You did great, Savannah. No grown-up policeman could've done better," Manny told her as he peeled off his jacket and laid it over Savannah's shoulders.

"Or *policewoman*?" she asked softly.

He smiled and patted her head. "Or *policewoman*."

Stella dropped to her knees beside Vidalia and brushed her granddaughter's tousled hair away from her face so that she could see into her eyes. "Vidalia, darlin', it's Granny. I'm here with you. Can you hear me?"

Vidalia opened her eyes and nodded, but she looked weak, pale, and stunned.

"You're okay. Savannah took good care of you, and now we're going to help, too. Do you understand?"

Again, a feeble nod. Then Vidalia murmured, "What happened?"

"You had a wreck, sugar. But it's all done now, and ever'thing's gonna be okay from here on out. You just rest."

Manny knelt on the other side of the girl and told Savannah, "You can let go, if you want to rest. I can take it from here. If that's all right with you."

"It's okay," Savannah said, but she didn't release her hold on her sister's leg. "I'm afraid to let go," she whispered to Manny. "I'm afraid that if I let go, she might bleed to . . . you know. . . ."

"Gotcha," he said. "I'll hold it tight, too. Okay?"

"Okay." Savannah removed her hands from the bloody jacket, and for a moment, Stella thought she might faint.

"Lay back there and rest yourself a spell," Stella told her. "You been through a lot, too."

"The other kids," Savannah said, tears beginning to streak the blood on her cheeks. "Are they . . . ?"

"They're okay," Stella said. "We found 'em all. One hurt hand, some bumps and scrapes, but okay. You don't have to worry anymore. It's all over, and us grown-ups are gonna take care of the rest."

Savannah started to cry with relief but, just as quickly, got herself under control, wiped the tears away, and watched as Manny carefully unwound the jacket from Vidalia's knee.

She grabbed his flashlight, which he had laid on the ground, and held it steady, lighting her sister's leg. "I'm the flashlight holder," she said, giving her grandmother a silly, weak smile.

"And a fine one at that," Stella told her.

"Let's see what we're dealing with here before we move

her," the sheriff said as he unwrapped the last bit of the jacket, exposing the wound.

The knee was badly cut from one side to the other. Blood began to flow out of it again, so he quickly replaced the wrapping. "It's a long, deep cut," he said, "but I don't think it's down to the bone. If we get her and Alma to Doc Hynson's house, he can look at them both and tell us if he can handle it or if we'll need to get an ambulance to take them to the clinic in Chesterville."

"Okay. Thank you, Sheriff," Stella said.

"Yes, thank you, Sheriff," Savannah added shyly.

"You're welcome, ladies. Now, let's get Miss Vidalia up to the road and into my cruiser."

"Can I ride in it, too? Please," Savannah asked.

"I think you should," he told her. "If you're going to be in law enforcement when you grow up, you might as well get used to riding around in one now."

Stella silently blessed him when she saw the bright smile on her grandchild's face.

Gently, carefully, Manny scooped Vidalia into his arms and carried her to the road. Stella and Savannah followed, walking hand in hand.

When they reached the pavement, Stella thought she heard a siren coming toward them.

"Didn't you say you called for help?" she asked Manny.

"First thing when I got here," he said. "Augustus should've been here by now."

"Even if another policeman comes," Savannah said, suddenly looking worried, "we should probably take Vi in your cop car, huh, Sheriff? You can go faster than your deputy can, and you probably know the way to the doctor better than he does, you being a sheriff and all."

"Yes, I'll be taking your sister in my unit."

"And me, too?"

"You and some of the other kids can also ride with me. Okay?" he replied.

"Okay!"

The vehicle with the siren came whipping around the curve and headed toward them. Stella could see it was a cruiser.

Deputy Augustus Faber had arrived in all his glory. He came to a screeching, dramatic stop beside them, tires smoking, and rolled down his window.

"What have we got, Sheriff?" he shouted.

"What we've got, Deputy, is everything under control. Thanks anyway," Gilford replied. "Hang around, though. I might have a transport for you."

"Ten-four, sir."

As Manny headed for his vehicle, Vidalia in his arms, Stella and Savannah hurried over to the other five children, who were still huddled beneath the sheriff's blankets.

They were all overjoyed to see their oldest sister, except for Marietta, who was still crying about her dress being muddy.

When Waycross saw Sheriff Gilford carrying Vidalia, he said, "Oh, no! What's wrong with Vi? She's not dead, is she, Gran?"

"No, no. Nothin' so bad as all that," Stella assured him. "Her knee's cut, and she's gonna have to go see the doc to get it stitched up."

Stella reached down and stroked Alma's hair. "We'll get that hand of yours looked at, too, sweet pea. You kids have been through the mill tonight, but it looks like you all made it through okay."

They gave halfhearted nods.

Except Marietta, who sobbed. "I'm not okay. I'm not even a little bit okay. I need a bath and a clean dress."

"Yes, you do, darlin'," Stella told her. "And we'll get you both just as soon as we can."

The others looked almost as woebegone as their mud-covered sister. Stella couldn't blame them for being glum. It would be a while before any of them recuperated from this. She was sure that the scare had taken years off her lifespan.

At that moment, she thought she heard something, a noise coming from farther up the road.

It sounded like . . . singing.

"Oh, what fun . . . ride . . . in a one-horse . . . sleigh, hey!"

"Somebody's singin' 'Jingle Bells,' " Jesup said.

"O'er the fields . . . laughin' . . ."

"Yes," Stella said. "That's 'Jingle Bells,' all right. No doubt about it."

She was all too familiar with that drunken, off-key voice. She had heard it far too many times to be mistaken.

Rage and its accompanying adrenaline poured into her bloodstream. It was the closest she had ever come to literally "seeing red."

"You kids wait right here," she said. "Don't go nowhere till I tell ya. No matter what you see or hear."

She left them and started down the road, heading toward the gleeful, tipsy warbler.

Along the way she passed Manny, who was laying Vidalia across the backseat of his car and placing her head on Savannah's lap.

The singing continued. "Ohh, dashing through the snow . . . in a sled . . . to Grandmother's house we . . . no, no . . . not to that ol' bat's house . . . to . . . to walkin' in a winter wonderland!"

"That's Shirley, squallin' like a cat with its tail caught in a wringer," Stella told Manny. "She's singing gall-danged Christmas carols! At a time like this!"

He watched her, obviously deeply concerned. "You want to tend to Vidalia, Stella May, while I deal with Shirley?" he said a bit too eagerly.

"Just gimme one minute with 'er, and then she's all yours," was Stella's clipped reply. "What I got to say to her won't take long."

"Yeah, that's what I was afraid of," he muttered.

Stella strode down the road, a woman with a purpose, with Manny several paces behind her.

She could smell Shirley even before the woman stepped up from the ditch into the headlight beams. The stench of alcohol wafting from her daughter-in-law was overpowering. The stink went straight from Stella's nose to her stomach, making her nauseous in an instant.

She ain't just been drinkin' that whiskey, Stella thought. *She plumb took a bath in it.*

Apparently, the accident had caused Shirley to lose control of her bottle, as well as her vehicle, because the entire front of her blouse was drenched with booze.

But a great deal of it must have found its way down her throat before the accident, judging from the glassy look in her eyes. She blinked several times, stared at Stella uncomprehendingly, then gave her a big, cheerful smile.

"I know you! Merry Christmas! You're . . . you're . . ." Suddenly, the smile disappeared. "Oh, it's *you*," she mumbled.

"Yes, it's *me*, Shirley. Where are your children?"

Shirley froze in mid-step, looked around her, down at the ground, then up at the sky. She shook her head, the picture of confusion. "They were here just a minute ago."

A strange numbness took hold of Stella. It was a sensation

she had never felt before, and she welcomed it. She felt a switch flip deep inside her, a master switch that controlled many things—caution, restraint, and the fear of consequences, along with the basic rules of society.

She had gone past the heat of anger to a cold, thought-free place where nothing mattered anymore. Nothing but the next two seconds.

Stella took one more step toward her daughter-in-law, drew back her fist, and slammed it into her face.

Shirley collapsed like a cheap air mattress that had just been run over by a semitruck.

A whooshing sound came out of her as she hit the pavement, where she lay, utterly still and, thankfully, silent.

Stella heard a soft "Wow!" whispered behind her.

Manny rushed to Shirley, knelt beside her, and pressed his fingers to her neck, feeling for a pulse.

"Well? Is she dead?" Stella asked, somehow surprised by her own lack of interest in the answer.

He chuckled. "She's all right. But remind me not to ever piss you off, girl. That was one helluva shot."

Stella turned to walk back to her wounded, frightened grandchildren.

"It was a long time comin'," she said. "A *long, long* time."

Chapter 21

"See there," Stella told her grandchildren as they sat in the living room, sipping cups of hot chocolate with marshmallows floating on top. "I told you ever'thing would be okay in a few hours, and here we are, back to normal."

"Not exactly normal," Savannah said. "Nobody's talking."

"I'm too tired to talk," Marietta said, tugging Stella's rose-spangled satin bathrobe tighter around her and running her fingers through her wet, freshly shampooed hair. "All that mud—it took a lot outta me."

Waycross grimaced. "I can tell right now, that mud's gonna take a lot outta all of us. We'll be hearin' 'bout it till our dyin' day."

Stella pulled Alma, who was sitting on her lap, a bit closer to her. The girl's hand was in a cast—a cast that had already been signed by everyone present and decorated with Christmas bells, candy canes, and a crude attempt at a Rudolph, who looked like a cat with a red nose and a crooked TV antenna on his head.

Stella gave a warm Grandma's smile and a wink across the

room to Vidalia, who was lying on the couch, her head in Savannah's lap, her knee bandaged from mid-thigh to her calf. She looked a bit forlorn but seemed to be enjoying all the attention, especially having her big sister stroke her head and play with her hair.

"Now that we're all settled down," Stella continued, "I wanna take a minute to thank each and ever' one of you for the fine job you did tonight. Our family went through a ferocious ordeal, and we couldn't have come out, reignin' victorious, at the end without the contributions of each of you."

She turned to Jesup. "Bein' the littlest, our Jesup usually comes last, so we'll thank her first. Miss Jesup, you might be the baby of the family, but you sure didn't behave like one today. You and Cordelia were all hemmed in there in the cab o' that truck, cold and scared, but you weren't bawlin' your heads off or pitchin' fits and makin' things worse. Cordelia, y'all behaved better than most grown-ups would've. And once we hauled you outta there, you did exactly what we asked you to, with no complaints at all."

She turned Alma around on her lap so that she could look into her big, innocent eyes. "Miss Alma, you were hurt bad—a broken hand that must've been smartin' somethin' fierce. But you didn't squall, neither. You sucked it up and stuck it out with grace and dignity, like the little lady you are, and you made me mighty proud."

"Thank you, Granny," the child replied, snuggling closer.

"Waycross," Stella said, "you braved your own pain and fear and took good care of your little sisters while the sheriff and I were trying to find the rest of 'em. You're the man of our house, and we all feel safer because you are."

Stella was happy to look at Vidalia and see that she was smiling, knowing she was next in line. "Our sweet Vidalia, you

254

were hurt the worst of all tonight. Thirty-nine stitches ain't nothin' to whistle Dixie about. But while Doc Hynson was stitchin' you up, you sat there quiet as a well-behaved church mouse and didn't holler once."

"She cried, though," Marietta said, suddenly deciding she wasn't too tired to talk. "I saw tears rollin' down her cheeks aplenty."

"Oh, hush, Mari," Savannah snapped. "Crying's allowed when you're getting stitches. At least she wasn't pitchin' a hissy fit over getting dirty."

"As I was sayin'," Stella continued, "Miss Vidalia, you were brave as brave gets tonight. In the days and years ahead, when you look down at the scar you're bound to have on that knee, you remember that it's a badge of courage and be proud of it!"

Stella turned to Marietta and frantically searched her brain for some virtuous act to praise on her second granddaughter's behalf. She felt bad that it was such a challenge.

"Miss Marietta, I thank you for the sacrifice that you made tonight by riding in our old truck with me, instead of in Sheriff Gilford's big, fancy cruiser or the deputy's."

"It's not like I had a choice," Marietta said, pouting. "You made me. Pushed me right in, like I was a sack of flour."

"I explained to you before," Stella said, summoning her last modicum of patience, "I didn't want you to get either of the lawmen's cars dirty."

"Vidalia got the sheriff's all bloody, and that's way worse!" Marietta argued.

Stella turned to Savannah, her eyes soft and loving. "Savannah, dear, what would we do without you? You may have saved your sister's life tonight, bandagin' her up like you did with your jacket and keeping her bleedin' under control till we got there. Then, in the doctor's office, you and Waycross did such a good job of keeping everybody calm and entertained while Doc took care of Vidalia and Alma. We are truly blessed to have you in this family."

Stella paused, composing her next words carefully before she spoke them. Finally, she said, "And all of us need to give a special thanks to the person who helped us so much tonight in so many ways, and he ain't even part of our family."

She waved a hand toward the corner, where Sheriff Manny Gilford sat on one of her dining-room chairs, which he had brought in from the kitchen, quietly taking in the scene before him.

He smiled and gave a quick nod as the roomful of children and their grandmother cheered and clapped uproariously, demonstrating more enthusiasm and energy than they had shown all evening.

When the applause finally died down, he said, "You're all welcome. It was an honor to help such fine folks. I'm just glad it all turned out okay in the end."

"You arrested our mama."

Everyone turned to stare at little Jesup. Her eyes were wide, and her face was solemn, as her words hung in the air.

Manny shot Stella a helpless, troubled look. He seemed to be searching his mind for an appropriate answer and finding none.

"Yes, he did," Stella quickly interjected. "He had to. It was his duty as sheriff. He didn't have a choice in the matter."

"Mama broke the law, Jesup," Savannah softly said.

"Because she drove the truck into the ditch?" asked Alma.

"No," Manny replied. "Driving a truck into a ditch isn't necessarily against the law. That's usually just an accident."

"Mama was drunk," Savannah said. "You all saw how much

she was drinking there at the house. She could hardly even walk when she loaded us into the truck. I asked her not to, but—"

"I did, too," Waycross said. "She was talkin' but not makin' sense."

"She was laughing a lot," Alma added. "And Mama never laughs unless she drinks a lot of whiskey."

"She drove drunk," Savannah said, "and that's the part that's against the law. Huh, Sheriff?"

"You're absolutely right, Savannah," Manny agreed. "The law about not driving drunk is a really important law."

"Yeah, and we know why," Waycross said. "Look at what happened tonight."

"That's right," Manny told him. "And what's worse, she had you kids in the truck with her. That broke another very, very important law. Grown-ups can't put kids in danger like that without getting in a whole lot of trouble."

"Did you take her to jail again?" Alma wanted to know.

"Deputy Faber did, because I told him to," the sheriff answered.

"She was screamin' like she was gettin' kilt when he was puttin' her in his car," Waycross said. "I've heard her pitch a duck fit before, but not like that. That one was a doozy!"

"Deputy Faber wasn't hurting her," Savannah said. "Not one bit. She was just mad."

"Madder than a hornet in a Coke bottle," Waycross added.

"Are we gonna have to get the coffee can out from under the kitchen sink, Sheriff?" Jesup asked. "Do we need to give you what we got in there so's she can get out of jail?"

Manny looked sad as he said, "No, sweetie. I'm afraid there's not enough change in that can to bail her out this time."

Stella shot a quick look at Savannah. The girl returned the

look with what Stella was pretty sure was a bit of a relieved smile.

"Is Mama gonna have to stay in there for a long spell?" Alma asked, her voice trembling.

Stella hugged her close.

"She probably will," the sheriff replied. "I'm sorry, but we have to make sure she doesn't cause anybody else to get hurt. But for the grace of God, you all could have been hurt way worse or even killed tonight. Sheriffs and prosecutors and judges, we take that kind of thing very seriously."

Alma looked up at her grandmother, tears streaming down her face. "Does that . . . does that mean we get to stay here with you, Granny?" she asked.

Stella hugged her close. She looked around the room at seven little faces, eyes wide, waiting to hear her answer.

It was with more gratitude than Stella had ever felt in her life that she said, "That's what it means, sweeties. It means you get to stay here with me."

"For how long?" Waycross asked, his face practically shining with joy.

"Can we stay a long time?" Vidalia asked.

"Yeah, a long, *long* time?" Jesup echoed.

"If I have anything to say about it," Sheriff Gilford said under his breath, "it'll be forever and a day."

Stella waited until after the sheriff had left and the last child had gone to sleep before she crept into the kitchen, got herself a glass of buttermilk to soothe her stomach, and pulled a slip of paper from between the pages of her cookbook.

She had filed it next to her fudge recipe, knowing that if she was ever going to use the information written on that paper, it would be at Christmas.

Christmastime was fudge time, so it had made sense to her when she'd put it there months before.

She set her buttermilk on the kitchen table, punched the number on the slip of paper into the phone on the wall, and sat down as it rang the party on the other end.

Feeling her pulse begin to pound from anxiety, Stella couldn't help feeling resentful. For a task that should be simple, even pleasurable, to cause her such angst—it just wasn't right.

Finally, someone answered on the other end. It was a woman with a voice as tired as Stella felt. "Sleepy Time Motor Inn. Can I help you?"

"Yes, thank you," Stella replied with as much courtesy as she could muster. "Do you have a Macon Reid staying with you?"

"Um, I'm not sure. May I ask who's calling?"

"His mama."

"Hang on. I'll check."

Stella waited for what seemed like forever. Finally, the woman returned.

"He ain't here. Sorry."

If there was anything Stella could do other than bake an amazing German chocolate cake, it was spot a liar. Folks in McGill said her gift was downright divine, and most of them went out of their way to tell her the truth rather than get caught with their pants on fire.

"He's there," she said with great confidence. "Tell him it's important. Tell him his kids were in a car wreck. Nobody's dead, but I need to talk to him, so he better pick up the damn phone."

"Yes, ma'am. Right away."

A moment later, a voice with a thick Southern drawl said, "Hey, Mama. What in tarnation's goin' on back there?"

"Shirley was drivin' drunk and wrecked a pickup truck, with the kids loose in the back. They went flyin' everywhere. Vidalia's knee got laid open. Took thirty-nine stitches to close it. Alma's hand got broke. Shirley's in jail. Other than that, nothin' much. How 'bout your neck o' the woods?"

Stella could hear the sarcastic, bitter tone in her own voice, and it didn't make her proud. No wonder her son didn't like to call home anymore. No wonder he pretended not to be in his hotel room when she reached out to him.

It seemed the only time they spoke anymore was when something went wrong. Badly wrong.

She wished she'd done better by him. She wished he'd do better by her. But wishing hadn't gotten either one of them any closer to the other.

She'd said many a prayer, too. Thousands. They hadn't worked either, though she clung to her faith that they would. Someday.

When he didn't respond, she said, "I'm sorry, son, for takin' such a harsh tone with you. It's been a long day."

"I imagine so." There was a long, tense pause. Then he said, "But ever'body's okay . . . other than all that."

"Yes. Thank goodness it wasn't worse."

"Sounds like it coulda been. Easy."

"Coulda been."

Another lengthy, awkward silence ensued. Stella's love of her son and desire to have this talk turn out somehow different than the others warred with her desire to just put the conversation out of its misery and spare them both.

"You ready for Christmas?" he finally asked.

"I got a stack of crocheted caps, mittens, and house shoes put away. And some candy canes for 'em."

"They'll like that."

"I got hold of an old swing set and painted it up. Turned out nice."

"I'll bet it did, if you did it, Mama."

There it was—an affectionate tone in his voice that told her all wasn't lost between them. She had to fight to keep from bursting into tears.

"Thanks for all you do for the young'uns," he added. "Wish I could've sent some money, but times are tough."

"Yes, they are. For everybody, son."

"I send Shirley what I can, but I reckon she just drinks it away there at the Bulldog."

"She won't be darkenin' the Bulldog's doors anytime soon. Sheriff Gilford arrested her for drunk drivin'—that's her fourth one now—and endangering a minor. Seven of 'em, in fact. She'll be doin' some serious time."

"Reckon I'm not surprised."

"No. We've seen this one afar off." She paused and decided to broach a sensitive topic. "Reckon you'll be callin' the kids Christmas Day? They'll be here at my house. That's where they're stayin' now."

She heard him clear his throat and shuffle around a bit before he replied. "Um, I'll try to. But I'll be on a stretch of road that don't have a lot of truck stops with phones."

Stella cringed. He trotted that one out at least once a month for holidays and birthdays. She wished he'd come up with a new one, if for no other reason than that it angered her that he thought she was dumb enough to believe it every time.

"Your kids would love to hear from you, son," she said. "Especially Waycross. He misses you somethin' fierce. So, if you do happen to run across a telephone anytime in the next forty-eight hours or so, you'd make your young'uns happy by lettin' them hear your voice. They've been through a lot lately."

"Haven't we all, Mama? Haven't we all?" He coughed, then took a deep breath and said, "I'm gonna have to get to bed now. Gotta head out at first light tomorrow mornin'. Merry Christmas, Mama."

"Merry Christmas, Macon. I love you, son."

"You too, Mama. Tell the kids I say hey."

"Okay."

"Bye."

Stella stood, walked to the wall, and replaced the phone in its cradle. Then she returned to the table and sat down. She picked up her buttermilk and drank it down without stopping to catch a breath.

"I tried, honey," she whispered to her husband, just in case he might be listening. "Maybe not hard enough. Maybe too hard. I never know with that boy."

Then she propped her elbows on the table, buried her face in her hands, and cried.

She wept for the son who slipped farther and farther away from her with every passing year.

She wept for the daughter-in-law who was now behind bars and would be for heaven only knew how long.

She wept tears of relief that she wouldn't have to worry anymore about that daughter-in-law hurting or killing her grandchildren with her foolishness.

She wept tears of happiness just to know that they would all be under her roof, at least for a season, and she could make sure that they had warm, nutritious meals on time every day, that they would dress in clothing that was appropriate for the weather, that they would be told good things about themselves rather than what a nuisance they were.

By the time Stella finished crying and headed off to bed to end this terrible, wonderful day, she had decided that she might have her trials, but all in all, she had been blessed beyond belief.

Her heart was overflowing with gratitude and joy.

Chapter 22

Stella stood at the stove, stirring a pot of her famous fudge. She had beaten it until her arm was aching, waiting for it to lose some of its glossy look. It had only been minutes, but her wrist was complaining that it had been hours.

"Aren't you about done with that fudge, Granny?" Savannah asked as she sat at the table, shelling pecans and keeping an eye peeled for any progress on the fudge front.

"I wish I was," Stella replied. "My arm's about to fall off."

"Then why don't we call it good and eat it?"

"Because this is one of the most important steps. If I beat it too much, it'll get all hard and sugary. If I get lazy and don't beat it enough, we'll have chocolate syrup instead of fudge."

"I'll eat it with a spoon," Savannah offered. "I'd suck it through a straw, if need be, and enjoy every sip."

Stella laughed. "I know you would, darlin'. You were born with a sweet tooth, just like your granny. No denying it. Would you butter that pan over there, the one lined with foil? When I'm done, I'll let you lick the spoon for your troubles."

Savannah shot up off her chair and headed straight for the refrigerator.

Stella wondered, not for the first time, at the power of chocolate to motivate a female to action.

"Oh, that fudge smells good, Granny," Savannah said as she carefully smeared butter over every square inch of the foil lining the pan.

"It sure does, darlin'. I can hardly hold back myself."

"I love Christmas," Savannah said dreamily. "I love it so much that I don't know which part I love the most. The pretty lights, the music that you get to hear only one time a year, the food—especially the candy—Santa and, of course, the story of Mary, Joseph, and baby Jesus. It's the only time when magic seems real."

"Now you're sounding like Alma," Stella said as she grabbed the buttered, foiled pan and began to scoop the heavenly concoction into it.

"Yeah," Savannah replied. "I can't imagine where we got such fancy notions. Wouldn't have been handed down from you, would they?"

Stella thought of Shirley, who, to her knowledge, had never once played Santa to her children or bought a tree or cooked a Christmas dish of any kind.

She did sing carols if she was drunk enough, but it took a lot of whiskey to get her in the Christmas spirit.

She thought of Macon, whom she hadn't seen at her holiday table for more than ten years. The father who couldn't pull over to the side of the road and use a pay phone to call his children to wish them a Merry Christmas.

But all the Reid kids loved the season and savored every moment of it every year.

Perhaps curly dark hair and bright blue eyes weren't the only things she'd passed down to her descendants.

She finished spreading the fudge in the pan, making sure not to remove too much from the wooden spoon in the process.

"There ya go, puddin'," she said, handing the spoon to Savannah. "Take a taste and tell me if I got it right."

Savannah licked the spoon, rolled her eyes ecstatically, and proclaimed, "It's plumb fit to eat!"

"Then let's cut it up, so's we can give it to them scalawags in the front room. Have they got the icicles on the tree yet?"

"They're on the second boxful. Waycross says you like a lot on there."

"I like 'em hangin' down straight like the real ones do. So no just standin' back and hurlin' 'em willy-nilly at the tree."

"They know that, too, Granny. We're all well acquainted with your icicle-hanging standards."

"Most things that are worth doin' at all are worth doin' well."

Savannah paused in her fudge cutting and looked at Stella, confused. "I thought the first part of the saying was '*Anything* that's worth doing at all.'"

"That's for overly persnickety folks. The truth is, there's a lot that's not worth doing at all, let alone worth doing well."

Stella set the empty fudge pan in the sink and ran hot water in it. "Wouldn't you rather be in there with your brother and your sisters, decorating the tree, than hanging around in the kitchen with an old lady?"

"You're not old. You're Granny."

"Why, thank you, sugar."

"You're welcome. Can I ask you for a favor?"

Stella smiled, thinking that it was nice that the child was

highly intelligent but not overly cunning. At least not yet. She was still delightfully transparent.

"Butterin' me up first, huh? Okay, what's this favor of yours?"

"I heard you talking on the phone this morning to Sheriff Gilford about the box of jewelry that you took from Miss Carr's apartment."

"Oh, you did, huh?"

"Yes, ma'am. I heard you say something about picking something out for her to be buried in."

"That's right. Is there anything you didn't hear me say?"

Savannah grinned. "I didn't hear you say it'd be something that goes good with pink, since her dress is pink."

"What's your point, kiddo?"

"I was wondering if I could take a stab at picking something outta there. If you don't think I did a good job, then you could choose something else. But I'd like to give it a try."

Stella studied the sweet little face, thinking it over. "Can I ask why you wanna do it?"

Savannah shrugged and blushed. "Miss Carr was nice to me one time. I'd like to do something nice for her. This'll be the last chance I'll ever have."

"What did she do for you?"

"I was in the drugstore, looking at the paper dolls. They had some real pretty Barbie ones, but I didn't have enough birthday money to buy them, so I was gonna buy the cheap ones that looked like Barbie but 'tweren't."

"I see."

"Miss Carr was standing nearby, holding a red lipstick that she'd just picked out and was fixin' to buy. It was like she read my mind about the paper dolls. She said to me, 'You'd rather buy the Barbie ones, wouldn't you?' So, I said, 'Yes, ma'am. I would.' And she says, 'How much more do you need to buy the good ones?' I said, 'Forty-nine cents.' That's when she looked in her purse, counted her money, and gave me two quarters. She put the lipstick back on the shelf and told me, 'Enjoy your paper dolls, dumplin'.' Then she walked out and didn't buy her lipstick. I don't think she had enough money after giving me her quarters."

Stella felt a lump in her throat as she thought of the beautiful young woman who had been kind enough to give a poor child a gift of paper dolls, when she couldn't afford a tube of lipstick for herself. She thought of how her corpse had been mistreated the night before by angry women. Women who had good reason to be angry. But it still didn't sit well with Stella, the way it had all happened.

"I think that's a fine idea," Stella told the girl. "I think Miss Carr would've liked to have you pick out her last jewelry for her. Earrings, a necklace, and a bracelet. Maybe two, if you think they go together nice."

"Guess she don't need a watch anymore."

"No. Reckon not."

Stella walked to the refrigerator and opened the cupboard above it. Carefully, she took down the jewelry box that she had stashed there last night.

As she placed it on the kitchen table, she said, "There's just two things, Savannah, and they're both very important. You can take every piece of jewelry that's in the box out and look at it all you want, if you need to, so's you can make your decision. But you're responsible for seeing to it that every bit of it goes back inside when you're done, other than what you pick out for her. Is that understood?"

"I promise I'll take good care of it."

"Good, because it's going to Miss Prissy's little girl, for her to remember her mama by. And the other thing is important, too. Nobody will ever know that you saw what was in that box, and you don't need to tell anybody that you did."

"How come? Is it some kind of secret?"

"It is, kinda. And I'm sorry I can't explain it all to you, but it's a grown-up thing. A worrisome thing that kids shouldn't have to know about or be concerned with. You'll just have to take my word for it, okay?"

"Okay. I won't tell anybody. It'll just be our own deep, dark secret."

"You've been reading too many of those mystery books." Stella laughed and slid the box in front of her. "I'll go help the kids with the icicles and keep 'em all outta your hair while you conduct your mysterious business in here."

No sooner had Stella joined the rest of the children in the living room than she saw Florence driving up. Normally, Florence stopped in front of the house and knocked on the front door. But this time she continued on until she was near the back door.

Stella walked over to the side window and saw her friend getting out of the car with a box in her hand. Smiling, Stella thought it kind of Florence to come bearing a gift of some sort, considering all the troubles she had on her mind lately.

"How are we gonna get the star on top, Gran?" Waycross asked. "The tree's too big. We're gonna need a step stool to reach that far up."

Stella glanced out the front window and saw yet another car turn off the highway and head down the dirt road in their direction. "Lordy," she said, "it's Grand Central Station round here all of a sudden."

"It's Sheriff Gilford!" Waycross said, terribly excited. "He's real tall. He can stick the star on the tree for us."

Stella turned and saw Savannah standing behind her, an enormous smile on her face. "Miss Flo brought us something," she said breathlessly. "Something really special. But it's got a little something wrong with it, and she has to fix it before she brings it out here. She wants everybody to sit down and close their eyes."

It took a few moments to get everyone seated, as Vidalia had her hurt leg elevated on one of the extra chairs. But finally, they were all in position, with closed eyes, when Stella heard Florence say in a bright, cheery voice, "Open your eyes! Merry Christmas!"

They did, and what a wonder they beheld.

Florence stood in the middle of the living room, holding a beautiful white coconut cake decorated with gumdrops. It looked just like the one Mr. Anderson had given them, only larger and fluffier. Stella would have recognized the baker's handiwork anywhere.

"It's one of Elsie's!" she shouted without thinking.

Florence's lower lip shot out in a pout. "Well, yes, but I bought it from her. Um, actually, I didn't wind up paying her for it, 'cause she wouldn't take my money once she knew I was giving it to you, but it was my idea!"

"And a fine idea it was, too." Stella grabbed the cake from Florence before one of the children, who were now on their feet and were jumping up and down for joy, knocked it out of her hands.

"Be careful there," Florence told her. "The gumdrops keep slippin'. They were all down on the plate by the time I got it in here. I had to reposition 'em before you saw it."

"Don't worry about it," Stella told her. "This cake isn't long for this world. I guarantee you, nobody's gonna care where the gumdrops are ten minutes from now."

A hearty knock at the front door told them that Sheriff Gilford had arrived.

"Savannah, would you let the sheriff in? I'm gonna take this back to the kitchen and—"

"But . . . but I . . . ," Savannah stammered. "I got to finish something I started back there in the kitchen."

"Oh, right." Stella handed her the cake. "You take this back there and put it on the counter. Then finish what you were doing. Flo, sit yerself down and take a load off. I'll put on a pot of coffee, and in a few minutes, we'll cut the cake."

"No, no. I wasn't intending to stay. I've got things to do, it being Christmas Eve and all. I just wanted to get the cake to you while it's fresh. You visit with the sheriff and tell him Merry Christmas for me."

A second later, she was heading toward the back of the house and Manny Gilford was coming in the front.

He was wearing a broad smile and was carrying a paper bag in one hand and two bright yellow roses in the other.

For a moment, Stella thought the roses were for her, and the idea that they might be didn't sit well with her.

But he quickly put her mind at ease when he handed one to Vidalia and the other to Alma. "Those are for our two ladies who got the worst end of the deal last night. And there's one of these for everybody."

He reached into the bag and began to produce one Rubik's Cube after another, which he pressed into each eager hand in turn.

The toys were an instant hit. The kids squealed and jumped around like wild jackrabbits on a date, until Jesup got too close to Vidalia's wounded leg.

"Okay! That's enough!" Stella told them. "Everybody thank Sheriff Gilford, sit down, and play with your new toys."

Within seconds, the sheriff had been thanked, they had all found a seat, and they were as entranced by the complexities of the cube as the rest of the nation.

"Listen to that," Stella said, hardly believing it.

"Listen to what?" Manny asked.

"Exactly. They aren't even that quiet when they're asleep." She looked up at him, gratitude shining in her eyes. "Thank you, Manny."

"You're most welcome."

"Would you like to come into the kitchen with me for a moment?" she asked. Looking around at the children, she added, "I'm pretty sure they won't even miss us."

When they entered the room, she saw Savannah frantically toss a dish towel over some items on the table.

"That's okay," Stella told her. "We can let the sheriff in on what we're doing. He won't mind."

"Oh, all right." Savannah removed the towel, exposing at least twenty items of jewelry, which she had placed in neat lines, divided into categories. Necklaces, earrings, rings, and bracelets. There was even a brooch or two.

"Wow, that's some haul," Manny said. "It's a good thing we didn't let the public see that stuff. It would've caused—" He glanced over at Savannah and cleared his throat. "Um, problems."

"It's all right," Stella told him. "I told Savannah that she wasn't to mention this box or anything in it to anybody, and she promised not to. My granddaughter is a girl of her word."

"Just like her grandma," Manny added.

"I'm not just playing with it, Sheriff," Savannah said. "I've got a good reason to go through it. Granny says I can pick out the jewelry that Miss Carr's going to be buried in."

Manny gave Stella a questioning look.

"She has good taste," Stella said. "And besides, she feels she owes a debt to Miss Carr, and this'll be her last chance to pay it."

"Then by all means," Manny said. "Have you decided on something yet?"

"I have." Savannah picked up a pair of pearl earrings, a pearl necklace, a small gold ring, and a matching gold bracelet. As she showed the pieces to them, she said, "The ring and the bracelet are because she had a heart of gold. Some people may not have seen it, but I did, when she was nice to me. I picked out the pearls because they go with everything. But mostly because I heard that pearls stand for purity. I'm thinking maybe now that she's passed on, her spirit is all pure. Maybe she didn't know no better when she was here on earth, but now that she's in heaven, she's smarter about some stuff."

Stella took the pearls, the ring, and the bracelet, held them tightly in her hands for a moment, then wrapped them in a clean napkin. "I think that was a fine choice, Savannah girl. Fine, indeed. Well done."

Turning to Manny, Stella said, "I'll get these over to the funeral home right away. I know he intends to bury her this afternoon."

Manny held out his hand. "I'm going right by there. Let me take care of it. One less thing for you to concern yourself with."

Gratefully, she gave the folded napkin to him, and he tucked it into his inside jacket pocket.

Savannah began to gather up the jewelry and replace it carefully, piece by piece, in the box.

Stella grabbed the coffeepot and started to fill it with water. "How's the case going, Sheriff?" she asked.

"Frustrating," he replied. "I feel like a rubber-nosed woodpecker in a petrified forest."

"That bad, huh?"

"I had a jail full of suspects and not one shred of solid evidence on any of them."

"*Had*? You let 'em go?"

Manny shrugged. "It's Christmas Eve. They've got families."

"I understand."

"Besides," he said, "most of the wives aren't even speaking to their husbands, so they probably won't murder 'em. Unless they glare 'em to death."

Stella looked at Savannah and realized she was all ears. She decided to change the subject. "You're gonna stay and have some cake with us, aren't you?"

He glanced over at the cake on the counter. "It's tempting, to be sure. It's one of Elsie's, isn't it?"

"It is. Compliments of Florence."

He consulted his watch. "I really can't, Stella. I've gotta get back to the station. I just came by to drop off those cubes and to give you some good news."

He glanced over at Savannah, then looked questioningly at Stella.

"You can speak in front of my eldest," Stella told him. "About most stuff, anyway. As you can tell, she's old beyond her years."

Manny gave the girl a kind, sympathetic look. "You've had to be, haven't you, honey?"

"Kinda," Savannah whispered.

"Well, as it turns out, you're going to get the chance to just be a kid and not have to worry about grown-up problems anymore." He turned back to Stella. "I just came from Judge Patterson's house. He let me bend his ear for nearly an hour, even though it's Christmas Eve. I told him about last night. I filled him in on everything that's been going on with Shirley. I even let him know that your son, being such a hard worker and all, is hardly ever around. Anyway, when all was said and done, the judge said I could assure you that if you want sole custody of your grandkids, he'll make sure you get it."

Savannah gasped and clapped her hands over her mouth.

Stella nearly dropped the coffeepot.

"Really?" Stella set the pot on the counter and ran over to him. "Are you sure, Manny? Not just them staying with me while she's in jail, but real custody?"

"Real custody, Stella May," he said, smiling down at her. "Yours, all yours. To love and to raise as you see fit."

She threw herself into his arms, nearly knocking him off his feet. "Oh, Manny! Bless your heart! Thank you!" she cried, burying her face in his chest.

He laughed and stroked her hair. "Wow! I haven't been tackled that hard since homecoming my senior year, when Jimmy 'the Refrigerator' Scognamiglio nailed me on the ten-yard line!"

A moment later, he had another Reid female to contend with. Savannah had grabbed him around the waist and was sobbing along with her grandmother.

He held them both for quite a while. The weeping didn't abate. In fact, it got harder and louder.

Finally, he pulled back, looked down at them, and said, "You two are crying because you're *happy*, right?"

275

They both nodded vigorously.

"Oh, okay," he said, pulling them back into his embrace. "Just checkin'. Carry on."

Half an hour later, Stella and Sheriff Gilford had informed the living-room troops of the good news, which had received the same enthusiastic reaction as had occurred in the kitchen.

Having placed the star upon the Reids' Christmas tree, Manny was ready to go.

"I'll walk you out to your car," Stella told him, grabbing her coat.

"I won't keep you from it," he replied.

After giving and exchanging hugs all the way around, he was on his way, escorted by Stella.

"I'm glad you came out with me," he told her as they walked to his cruiser. "I don't know how to say this, but . . . I was wondering if I could help you in any way. I looked around Shirley's place to see if maybe she'd stashed some toys away for the kids, but there wasn't anything there."

"That's how she is. How she's always been," Stella replied. "I crocheted them some stuff. Got 'em some candy treats."

"I was wondering if you could use some, I mean, if I could help with . . ."

"They love the Rubik's Cubes, Manny."

"I'd like to do more, if you'd let me."

"That's plenty, really. But thank you so much for offerin'."

He looked so disappointed that she searched her mind for an answer and found one.

"There is one thing," she said.

"Name it."

"I was stupid and got myself in a bit of a pickle."

"You? Stupid? I find that hard to believe."

"Believe it. You see, I bought this old, used swing set at a garage sale. I brought it home in bits and pieces and painted it and put it together there in my storage shed, so's they wouldn't see it."

"It's too big to fit through the door?" he asked, smirking.

"No, Mr. Smarty-Pants. I took that into consideration. What I didn't think about was how heavy and awkward it'd be to move. I don't reckon I can shift it on my own."

He laughed. "Is it made of steel?"

"It sure is."

"Then no, I don't suppose you could." He thought for a moment. "What time do they go to bed?"

"Eight thirty for the little 'uns. Nine for the three oldest."

"Then about nine thirty or ten, I'll get Jarvis to come here with me, and the two of us will get it out of there and put it . . . Where do you want it?"

"On that patch of grass between the garden and the chicken coop."

"Consider it done."

"Are you sure it's not too much trouble, it bein' Christmas Eve?"

"No trouble at all. Jarvis doesn't have a life, so he won't mind. As for me, I always wanted a chance to play Santa Claus."

Stella thought of Lucy. Of how they had been hoping to start a family.

It was a shame, she thought, because Manny Gilford would have made a wonderful father.

"Thank you, Manny," she said. "I owe you so much."

"I'd like to have your friendship for the rest of my life. But you owe me nothing." He bent his head and gave her a quick kiss on the forehead. "Merry Christmas, Stella."

"Merry Christmas, Manny," she replied.

As she watched him drive away, Stella wondered why she felt sad rather than happy. Heaven knows, she had every reason to be shouting about her latest blessings from the rooftop. Whose life had ever turned so quickly for the better than hers just had?

But she couldn't stand there and wonder for long.

She turned and walked back to the house.

She had seven children to raise.

Chapter 23

Stella awoke on Christmas morning in the center of a bed filled with grandkids.

Having retired with only Alma and Vidalia, she opened her eyes to find the two of them still on either side of her. But Marietta and Jesup had shoved the two convalescing sisters toward the middle and climbed in beside them. Cordelia was perched precariously on the edge of the bed next to Jesup.

They were all sleeping deeply, no doubt because they had stayed awake so late, straining to hear the jingling of sleigh bells.

Stella wasn't surprised that Waycross had not joined his sisters. He was taking that "man of the house" business quite seriously these days, and part of his duty was sleeping in the living room, where he could fend off the super-villain, Skeletor, if he should come charging through the front door.

Lying there on the soft featherbed, her grandchildren safe and snug around her, Stella felt a bit like Farmer Buskirk's old calico cat.

When Stella was a child, Mr. and Mrs. Buskirk were her neighbors. One day, Mr. Buskirk found a litter of puppies left in a box by the side of the road near his farm. He rescued the pups and introduced them to his old barnyard cat, who happily accepted them as her own and raised them in a snug box filled with hay in the horse stable.

Farmer Buskirk proudly showed young Stella the cat and her adopted babies when Stella brought his ailing wife some pumpkin bread. Stella had never seen a more contented creature in her life as that mother cat.

Stella had always wanted to feel as happy and peaceful as that old calico at least once in her life.

That Christmas morning, she remembered the cat, remembered her wish, and reveled in the fact that it had been fulfilled.

Other than the fact that a couple of the pups grew into dogs who occasionally mewed when they begged for food, all of them lived happily ever after. Stella hoped she could do as well with her "litter."

Feeling something warm and soft at her feet, Stella looked down and saw that Savannah was stretched across the foot of the bed, her eyes wide open, watching her.

"Merry Christmas, sweetheart," Stella whispered.

"Merry Christmas, Granny," was the soft, somewhat subdued reply.

Since when wasn't her oldest grandchild a giggling mess of excitement on Christmas morning? Stella wondered. Being a giddy wreck of happiness on the morning of December 25 was practically mandatory in the Reid clan.

"You okay?" Stella asked.

"Yeah," was the unconvincing reply.

Stella searched her mind for what might be bothering the

child, then decided that she must be worried about what Santa might have brought—or not brought—last night.

Savannah had never been materialistic, had never demanded or even expected a bounty of her own. But every year for as long as Stella could remember, she had worried that her younger siblings, who still believed in Santa, would be crushed if he didn't pay a visit to their house.

Most years, he would have bypassed their place if Stella hadn't dropped by late on Christmas Eve with gifts and sneaked them to Savannah, who had carefully arranged them on the sofa, to be discovered the next morning.

Savannah was a bright kid, and Stella was sure it had occurred to her that the dramas of the past few days might have interfered with any preparations for a visit from jolly ol' Saint Nick.

Carefully, trying not to disturb Vidalia or Alma on either side of her, Stella sat up in bed. She crooked her finger, beckoning Savannah closer.

With her mouth an inch from Savannah's ear, she whispered, "Santa Claus came last night. He left something in the backyard."

Savannah looked moderately pleased, a bit relieved, but it wasn't the happy reaction Stella had hoped for.

She decided to try again. "Are you happy about what the sheriff told us yesterday, darlin'? Do you think it's a good idea, you all living with me from now on?"

There it was. The dimple-deepening grin that she'd been hoping for.

"It's the best ever, Granny! I've been hoping for this my whole life, and now it's happened. Like a Christmas miracle!"

"It *is* a Christmas miracle! We have a lot to be thankful for today."

"We do."

It took only a few seconds for the newfound smile to disappear, replaced by the same sad, worried look the girl had worn before.

"Is something troublin' you, child?" Stella asked.

Savannah hesitated, and Stella's grandmother intuition told her that she was trying to find an answer that was truthful but not revealing. "I'd like to get up and go to the kitchen," she said at last. "I could use a drink of water."

"Okay."

No point in pressin' that any further, Stella told herself. *When that child has a mind to, she clams up tighter than a bullfrog's keister in a bucket of ice water.*

Savannah wasted no time getting out of the bed and making her way to the kitchen.

Stella decided to follow her. She could use a cup of coffee herself, and maybe a mug of hot chocolate would loosen the kid's lips.

It took her a while to wriggle out from under the covers, down to the foot of the bed, and across to the side without waking the "puppies."

They'd be live wires soon enough. A few moments of peace would be nice before the Christmas morning mayhem began.

To her surprise, when Stella entered the kitchen, she found Savannah on her hands and knees under the table.

"Whatcha doin' down there?" she asked.

Savannah jumped and looked up at her with guilty eyes. "Nothin'!" She reconsidered. "I mean, I was just looking for something, but . . . it's not . . ." Scrambling out from under the table, she headed for the sink. "I'm gonna get that glass of water now, Granny. You want one?"

"No, sugar," Stella replied, studying her with as sharp an eye as Sheriff Gilford had ever used on a suspect. "I'm gonna make myself some coffee. How about a cup of hot chocolate with some marshmallows on the top as a little Christmas mornin' treat?"

"That'd be nice, Granny. Thank you."

Stella walked to the window and looked out at the backyard. The swing set was sitting exactly where she had requested, glowing like a handful of giant red-and-white candy canes.

They would be pleased with it, she was sure, and that made her happy. So did the fact that during the night, a few inches of snow had fallen, decorating everything with sparkling white frosting, like that on one of Elsie's coconut cakes.

What a nice Christmas this was shaping up to be.

Or at least it would be once she figured out what was wrong with her granddaughter, who was sitting quietly at the table, a troubled look on her face.

Yes, she was in bad need of chocolate . . . a female's cure for most of life's ills.

But no sooner had Stella set the coffeepot on the stove and filled the teakettle than there were rumblings from the rest of the house.

"Oh, well. So much for our calm before the storm," she told Savannah. "They're gonna be shriekin' like a pack of hyenas in ten seconds."

It took only five for the house to erupt into utter chaos. Stella heard them racing to the living room to see if there was any treasure to be had beneath the tree.

Knowing that nothing new had been added to the simple homemade gifts of hers, she hurried into the room and announced, "Santa came!"

"No he didn't," Marietta argued. "There's nothin' here but those presents from you, and we all know what they are. Silly ol' hats and mittens and—"

"Marietta Reid, you shut up!" Savannah yelled. "You don't have the sense God gave liverwurst, and your heart's nothin' but a thumpin' gizzard. Granny works hard on what she gives us, and the rest of us love her presents!"

Some of the more tenderhearted among them jumped in.

"Yeah, Mari, if you can't say something nice, keep your trap shut," Waycross told her.

"A Grinch and a Scrooge all rolled up into one stingy green ball of humbug," Vidalia added. "That's what you are, Marietta."

"You're probably the reason Santa didn't come," Cordelia whined. "He found out that *you're* livin' here now!"

"Hey, hey, hey!" Stella shouted to be heard above the din. "Quiet!"

Once the room was silent, she said, "It just so happens that Santa Claus *did* stop by this house last night. He left y'all somethin' in the backyard. But you're gonna have to put on your coats and shoes and bundle up good before you go out. Look outside and you'll see why."

They all ran to the window, looked, and went crazy.

"Snow! Snow! It snowed!"

"I wanna make a snowman!"

"I'm gonna hit Marietta in the face with a big, wet snowball for sayin' that mess about Gran's mittens," Waycross muttered.

"Nobody's hittin' nobody with nothin'," Stella said as she hurried to her closet and pulled out her warmest, most substantial pair of shoes. She handed them to Savannah and said, "Here, sugar. Wear these."

"I can't. They're your good Sunday shoes."

"And you're my good everyday granddaughter. They'll be too big, but if you get some thick wool socks outta my dresser drawer and put 'em on, they should do. Hurry up! Time's a-wastin'."

Seconds later, they were pouring out the back door and into the yard.

It took them no time at all to locate the swing set and start climbing all over it, shrieking like a family of monkeys who had gotten hold of some fermented coconut milk.

Even Vidalia was having fun as Waycross settled her onto a swing seat and held her injured leg straight as she gently rocked back and forth.

Jesup brushed an inch of snow off the other seat and helped Alma onto that one. Jesup steadied her sister as she gently swung to and fro. The swing moved less than a foot in each direction, but it was enough to delight Alma, who giggled all the while.

Savannah stood beside Stella, watching rather than participating. Whether her lack of involvement was due to the fact that she had grown a bit too old for candy-cane swing sets or to her inexplicable lack of holiday cheer, Stella couldn't tell.

"Don't feel like playin' with the rest?" Stella asked her.

Instead of replying, Savannah started to walk toward the shed.

"What is it, honey?" Stella asked.

"Look! There's something on the door," Savannah called back. "A piece of paper."

Stella caught up with her and saw that she was right. Someone had thumbtacked a piece of bright red paper to the shed door.

As they got closer, Stella could read what was written there in large bold print.

ALL NICE KIDS,
LOOK INSIDE!
LOVE, SANTA

Savannah turned to her grandmother. "What's in there? What is it?"

"I have absolutely no idea whatsoever."

"You don't?" Savannah looked doubtful.

"I swear, Vannah Sue. I don't have a clue what's on the other side of that door."

Chapter 24

Stella looked around her living room at her grandchildren, who were knee-deep in what appeared to be the contents of an entire toy store. Each had several gifts, appropriate to their age, gender, and interests. Even Savannah had a stack of assorted children's mystery classics, as well as a Barbie doll and a carrying case filled with clothes. She also had a pair of warm fleece-lined boots, which she was wearing.

Stella predicted she would sleep in them that night.

With the children all deliriously occupied, Stella sneaked off to the kitchen to make a phone call.

She debated whether to dial the station number or Manny's home phone. Something told her that since he had no family within driving distance and had a penchant for hard work, he would be on the job.

She was right. He picked up after the first ring.

"Sheriff's station. Gilford here."

"Hello, Gilford here. Reid here," she said, imitating his deep, authoritative tone.

"Stella! Merry Christmas!"

"It most certainly is over here."

"Oh, good. Glad to hear it."

"Like you had nothin' to do with it."

"Uh, well . . . maybe not as much as you might think. I had a lot of help."

"Hooey. If it hadn't been for you, my shed would not have been stuffed to the gills with toys and warm clothes this Christmas mornin'. If it wasn't for you, my grandkids wouldn't be sittin' in my front room right now, playin' with things they've only dreamed of havin'." Her voice cracked. She had to fight to add, "Thank you."

"You're welcome, honey," he said softly. "You're well thought of in this town. Dearly loved. By a lotta folks. Word got around about what happened there on the highway, and that you've got the kids now. Everybody jumped at the chance to help you out."

"Yeah, and I know just how 'word got around' and how that stuff got bought and carted over here and set up all nice like that. Them kids' eyes 'bout bugged outta their heads when they opened that door a while ago. Last time I saw a bunch of people so happy was when that MoonPie truck dumped its load all over Main Street that summer in sixty-eight."

He laughed, and they sat for a few moments in companionable silence.

"What're you doin' for Christmas dinner?" she asked, her heart in her voice.

"Oh, I don't know. I'll catch a bite somewhere."

"We're havin' Florence and Elsie over. Florence's bringin' ham, and Elsie'll have her apple pie and a pecan one, too. You're more'n welcome to join us. We'd be proud to have you."

He waited so long to respond that she thought perhaps he hadn't heard her.

"I appreciate your kind offer, Stella," he said at last. "You have no idea how much. But I'd best pass."

His refusal surprised her. She could tell he wanted to accept.

"I never thought I'd see the day you'd turn down a piece of Elsie's apple pie. Waycross'd be plumb flabbergasted to hear it. Are you sure?"

"I'm pretty sure it's best. Under the circumstances."

She wondered what circumstances in particular he was referring to, but the sadness in his voice kept her from asking.

"Okay," she said. "But I'll put a piece of that pie back for you and get it over there to the station sometime tomorrow. How does that sound?"

"That sounds wonderful, Stella. I'll look forward to the pie. And to seeing you."

"Thank you again, Manny. I'll never forget this Christmas. Or what you did for me and mine."

"It's not a Christmas I'm likely to ever forget, either. Not if I live to be as old as Methuselah's great-granddaddy. Goodbye, Stella."

The moment she heard the phone click on the other end, Stella felt lonely.

With a house filled with seven rambunctious grandchildren, she felt alone.

Eventually, years after Art had died, she'd begun to feel a bit less lonesome. There were moments when she could almost bear to realize that the man she loved was alive in memory only.

Now she noticed that when Manny Gilford wasn't in the room, she missed him. But not the way she missed Florence or Elsie if she didn't see them for a day or two.

This was a new kind of loneliness, and she didn't like it.

289

She couldn't afford the distraction.

Maybe she could have handled it before. But her life had changed so drastically in the past few days. Everything was so different now.

She heard someone knock on the front door, and the children scramble to let them in.

It was Elsie with her pies. In a few minutes, Florence would be there, too.

Stella had a Christmas dinner to prepare.

She also had a granddaughter with a knee that needed re-bandaging and another child with a broken hand to contend with.

She had seven grandchildren to raise; and arthritis in her left knee and right thumb; and a roof that needed to be replaced, because it leaked like a sieve with a hole blown in the bottom of it; and a pension that wasn't enough to support both her *and* a goldfish.

She had a daughter-in-law headed for prison, and she had court appearances ahead, which racked her brain and her nerves just to think about.

Lord only knew, Stella Reid had problems and complications up to her eyeballs.

The last thing she needed in her life right now was a man who made her feel lonely all over again just by hanging up the telephone.

"I thought the best part of Christmas was the toys, especially now that I got me them sparkly high heels I been wantin'," Marietta said as she pushed her plate away from her and rested her hands on her belly. "But now I've decided it's the food. I'm full as a tick and too tired to move a muscle."

"What a convenient time to declare that you're paralyzed,"

Savannah muttered. "Just when there's dirty dishes to be done."

"That was a fine meal," Waycross said in his most grown-up voice. "Thank you, Granny and Miss Elsie and Miss Flo."

Once the "Thank yous" and "You're welcomes" were finished, Elsie rose and started gathering up the dishes from the table.

"Come along, Marietta and Savannah," she said. "You two hard workers help me out, and we'll have these dishes done in a jiffy."

"We'll all lend a hand," Stella said, doing the same, "and we'll be in the front room, singin' carols and eatin' fudge, before you know it."

"I'm afraid I've gotta go," Florence said. "Y'all divide up the ham among you. I got another one in the freezer for Easter."

Stella watched as Florence walked away from the table, not a single plate in her hand, and sauntered toward the back door.

Since Stella could remember, Florence had offered to bring the main dish to any feast—usually a ham or a turkey—and apparently, she seemed to feel that excused her from any menial cleanup chores. No sooner had the last bite been taken from the last plate than she would skedaddle out the door.

On her way out, Florence stopped and kissed the top of each child's head and wished them a Merry Christmas.

Stella couldn't help noticing that when Florence bent down to kiss Savannah, the girl seemed to shrink away from her touch. That surprised Stella, as Savannah had always liked Miss Flo. For the past five summers, since Savannah was seven, Florence had hired the child to come weed her flower garden. Flo had paid her well enough, and Savannah had been grateful for the money. Once, Florence had even given Savannah a pretty headband that Flo had grown tired of.

Stella couldn't think of anything that might have caused the change in the child's opinion of her neighbor.

Stella decided that Savannah's reaction was just part of the girl's moodiness. After all, she was approaching adolescence. The sulking and irritability were bound to show up soon.

Having just gone through the reverse of adolescence, menopause, Stella had already decided she would cut the kid some slack.

Hormone fluctuations weren't for sissies.

As they cleaned the kitchen, Stella kept a close eye on her oldest grandchild and noticed that, if anything, her mood was deteriorating. Quickly. She snapped at Marietta even more than usual and left food on the plates she was washing.

When she finally dropped and broke a glass, Stella took her by the arm and said to the kitchen crew, "Y'all please excuse us for a minute or two. Savannah and I are going to sit out on the porch for a while."

"In the cold?" Marietta asked.

"It ain't that cold, and we wanna look at the snow some," Stella replied.

She grabbed a wool blanket and her coat, which she handed to Savannah, and got a heavy sweater for herself. Then she put a hand on Savannah's shoulder, and as they headed for the front door, she said, "Okay, darlin'. Let's go sit and swing a spell. Ain't nothin' quite like it to clear the head."

Stella and Savannah settled onto the front porch swing and leaned back against the soft floral-print cushions. After spreading the thick wool blanket that she had brought with her over both of their laps, Stella tucked it around them snugly.

"There," she said, taking her granddaughter's hand in hers and pushing the swing with her feet. The chains began to creak, a sound Stella had always found most comforting. "Just look at them pretty fields," she said, "all covered with snow and tell me that ain't a lovely sight to behold."

Savannah looked and said, "It *is*, Granny. It looks like a Christmas card with glitter on it."

"Even prettier than when the cotton's open."

"Yes, and you don't have to pick it."

They both chuckled. A little. Picking cotton in the hot Georgia sun wasn't much of a laughing matter, as both of them knew all too well.

"Have you had a nice Christmas, sweet cheeks?" Stella asked, turning so that she could watch the girl's ever-changing expressions.

"I have. The best ever. Except . . ." Her lower lip began to tremble, and tears sprang to her eyes.

Stella thought Savannah was going to talk about the accident and how badly it had frightened her, so she was taken aback when she heard Savannah say, "Except for something that happened yesterday."

"What's that, honey? What happened?"

Savannah turned to look at her with eyes filled with anguish. "I have to tell you something, Granny. Something bad that I did and something, maybe bad, that somebody else did."

"Savannah girl, don't you worry about nothin'. We're gonna talk this out, and all will be well. Okay?"

"Okay."

"All right. Tell me all about it."

"Remember when you said that if I looked through the jewelry, if I picked out the pieces for Miss Carr to wear, I had to take really good care of them? You said it was my responsibility."

"Yes. That was the deal."

"But I didn't."

"Okay. What happened?"

"I'm not sure. But yesterday, when I took the things all out and sorted them and looked them all over, there was this one piece that was extra pretty, and I noticed it. I thought it might be a nice one to choose for her, but then I thought of the pearls and the purity thing, and I decided against it."

"I see. And then . . . ?"

"Then, later, when I was putting the stuff all back into the box, it was missing. Gone! I thought I must have dropped it, so I looked under the table and under the cabinets and inside my sleeves and pockets and everywhere I could think of, but it just wasn't anywhere."

"I understand. Is that what you were doing this morning there in the kitchen?"

"Yes. I couldn't get to sleep last night, worrying about it. So, I went in there again when we got up to see if maybe I'd just overlooked it. But it wasn't there."

"What was it, this missing piece?"

"A necklace. I think it was real gold, too. It was probably expensive. I'm sure Miss Carr's little girl would want it, and she would have wanted her to have it. I tried to do something for Miss Carr, but I messed it up." She began to cry. Stella put her arm around her shoulders and drew her closer.

"Don't cry, sugar. I'm sure Miss Carr would understand. You didn't lose it on purpose. We've talked before 'bout how a body shouldn't feel too bad about somethin' that went wrong if it wasn't done on purpose or in carelessness."

"But I *was* careless. It turns out, I didn't lose it, after all. But I left it in the kitchen, unattended, and it got stolen."

"Got stolen? What on earth do you mean? Stolen outta our kitchen?"

"Yes, Granny."

"If one of your little sisters nabbed it, they probably just wanted to play with it. But either way, we'll find it and—"

"'Twasn't one of us."

"Then who? Waycross wouldn't—"

"Miss Flo."

"Miss Flo?" Stella was dumbfounded. Surely, the child was mistaken. "Honey, that's a serious accusation to make against an adult, a person who's old enough to know that what they're doin' is wrong. A crime even. What makes you think she stole it?"

"She was wearing it today. When she bent down to kiss me good-bye, I saw it around her neck. She had it inside her blouse, but I saw it hanging there, clear as day."

For once, Stella wasn't happy to have her special power of discerning the truth from falsehoods. Her granddaughter was telling the truth. No doubt about it. Which meant that one of her best friends was a thief.

She put her own shock and disappointment aside. Savannah's concerns needed to be addressed first.

"Savannah, I want you to listen to me. You did nothin' wrong. Nothin' at all. There was no way that you could've known that Florence would take the necklace when you left the items unattended there in the kitchen. I woulda done that myself in a heartbeat. You don't ever have to feel bad about that again. Okay?"

Savannah smiled. "Okay. Thank you, Granny."

"Now, tell me, what did this necklace look like?"

"It was a pretty little gold cross on a fancy chain. It had a purple stone in the middle of it."

Stella felt her stomach lurch and thought she might be sick.

"I know that necklace," she told Savannah. "I was there at

Florence's thirteenth birthday party, when her aunt Lovenia gave it to her. Flo was real close to her aunt, and that necklace meant a lot to her."

Savannah brightened. "Oh! Then it was her necklace, anyway. If it already belonged to her, she didn't really steal it."

"That's right," Stella said, still feeling nauseous.

"Then it's okay that she took it."

Stella nodded, distracted, as the wheels of her brain whirred like a cotton gin at full speed.

"But how did Miss Flo's necklace get into Miss Carr's jewelry box?" Savannah mused. Then a look of awkward realization dawned on her face. "Oh. I guess Mr. Bagley was one of Miss Carr's 'special' friends. He must've given it to her."

"Yeah. He must've."

"Why didn't he come to Christmas dinner today, Granny? Not that I wanted him to, 'cause I've never really liked him that much, but seems like he'd want to eat Christmas dinner with his wife."

"Just between us, darlin', Miss Flo and her husband aren't doing so well right now."

"Well, yeah. If he's giving her jewelry away to other women, it's not likely they're gonna get along so good. Did she know he gave it away?"

"I'm not sure," Stella said, trying to remember the conversation she'd had with Florence about Bud trying to take her jewelry when he left.

"Where's Mr. Bagley at now?" Savannah asked.

"I'm not sure about that, either. Sheriff Gilford said he saw Bud's big monster truck on the river road, heading north toward the county line, a few days ago."

"What's up north? Why would he go up there?" Savannah asked.

Stella could see that Savannah's brain was doing some spinning of its own.

"I don't know," Stella replied. "There's not much up there by the county line except farms."

"Mr. Bagley never seemed like a farmer kinda guy."

"No, he's a town guy. Florence is the one who loves farms. She lived on one for a while when she was little and—"

Stella gasped as her searching mind found what it had been looking for. She turned and looked at Savannah. "Her family owned a farm up north. She took me there a couple of times when we were teenagers. She still owns it, loves it. Couldn't let it go."

"That must be where Mr. Bagley was going the other day. Up to her old farm. But why would he go there, you think?"

Abruptly, Stella stood and gathered the blanket into her arms. "Come along, sugar. I know it's Christmas, but if I can get Elsie to watch you young'uns for me, I'm fixin' to take a drive. It ain't that far. I shouldn't be gone long."

Savannah gave her a suspicious look, then said, "I know where you're going."

"No you don't."

"Yes I do. You're going to Miss Florence's old farm. The one she took you to when you were teenagers."

Stella stared down into the little face, with its know-it-all grin. "Don't tell anybody."

"I know what you're doing, too."

"Okay, Miss Smarty-Pants. What am I doin'?"

"You're going *sleuthing*."

Stella started to deny it, but she knew that Savannah had an internal lie detector that was almost as accurate as her own. There was no point in even trying to deceive the girl. "Okay. I am. Don't tell anybody that, either."

"I won't."

"Promise?"

"Yep. I promise. Don't worry. I won't have a chance to tell 'em, 'cause *I'm* going *with* you."

Chapter 25

As Stella drove the truck through the wooded areas that lined the riverbank north of McGill, the forests of pines mixed with hardwoods thinned and gave way to meadows. There was hardly any snow here. With no evergreens to add color, everything looked the same muddy shade of brown— the trees, with their bare limbs, and the bushes and grasses, dormant and dead, that lined the narrow two-lane road.

Savannah stared out the window, taking in every bit of the scenery.

"I've never been this far north," she said. "I love going places I've never been before. I wish I could go around the whole world and see everything. Maybe even go all the way to California, where they have palm trees."

"You have an adventurer's spirit inside you, Savannah girl," Stella told her. "That's a fine thing. Promise me that you'll always have adventures in this life of yours. They're more important than fancy cars or big houses or even pretty clothes."

"Unless you're Marietta." Savannah snickered and made a

face. "Clothes and hairdos are all she thinks about. How she looks."

"Marietta lives in a world of her own inside that head of hers. Try to be a bit nicer to your sister for me, Savannah. It ain't easy bein' her."

"No, I don't reckon it is. The smell alone would—"

"Stop! That's the kind of ugliness I'm talkin' about."

"I wouldn't say stuff like that if she wasn't so mean."

"Like most folks, Mari can be contrary sometimes. But we treat people—"

"I know. I know. According to who *we* are, not who *they* are."

"That's right."

They rode along in silence as the meadows turned into small farms with ramshackle houses and barns that looked like they might collapse at any moment.

It won't be long now, Stella told herself. *Just a few more miles and then we'll know.*

She hoped she could live with what she discovered.

"Are we about there?" Savannah asked.

"Another mile or so."

"Did you remember to bring the camera?"

"Sure did. Did you remember the flashlights?"

"I did. We're all set to sleuth. All we need is one of those big magnifying glasses, like Sherlock Holmes has. But why do we need the flashlights? It's not dark yet. Won't be for a few more hours."

"We might want to look in the house or the barn. I don't think Florence keeps the power on anymore, since she's never there."

"You don't think cranky ol' Mr. Bagley will be there, do you?"

Stella hesitated, then said, "No, sugar. I don't 'spect we'll be runnin' into him."

Since they had left the house, Stella had entertained some misgivings about whether or not she would recognize the farm when she saw it. After all, it had been nearly forty years since she had been there.

But when she spotted the weathered sign on the side of the road, with its rearing white stallion and the words PALE HORSE FARM scrawled across the top, she turned to Savannah and said, "We're here. You ready?"

Savannah held up the flashlights, one in each hand. "Ready!"

"It's a darned good thing we brought them flashlights," Stella said once she had climbed through the bathroom window and pulled Savannah in with her.

They were standing in the tub, which Stella had discovered was a particularly uncomfortable place to land when one miscalculated one's "boosting jump" and fell headfirst through a window.

"Here." Savannah handed her a light. "What are you gonna use it for? To look for some sort of treasure?"

"First, I'm fixin' to make sure my face is still in one piece."

Stella shuffled to the mirror and examined herself. Other than a slight bruise forming on her chin, she appeared to be all right.

"Okay, kiddo," she said. "Let's get this detecting business on the road. We'll start with the downstairs."

"What are we looking for?"

"Won't know until we find it."

"O-o-kay."

Actually, Stella had a feeling she knew what she would find here on Pale Horse Farm. But there was no point in raising Savannah's suspicions any higher than they already were.

Stella desperately hoped that this impromptu Christmas Day trip would turn out to be for naught. Nothing would please her more than to discover that her own imagination was working overtime.

As she and Savannah made their way through the old, abandoned farmhouse, Stella shuddered to see the state of the home, which she had enjoyed visiting as a child.

Florence's parents had brought the girls to this place for a few long weekends in the summer. Though it was no longer a working farm by that time, Stella and Florence had enjoyed running through the fields, exploring the woods, and swimming in a nearby pond.

Florence's mother and father were long gone, along with the rustic charm of the place. Now it was just an empty, crumbling deserted building, inhabited only by vermin, a fact made all too obvious by the rodent droppings scattered across the half-rotten wooden floor.

"You were right," Savannah said. "Mr. Bagley wouldn't live in a place like this. There's not a stick of furniture in it. Plus, it's way too grubby and gross. He's big on things being clean. When I was working in Miss Flo's garden last summer, I could hear him yelling at her because he thought he saw some dirt somewhere."

"He ain't all that worried about dirt, darlin'. He's never picked up a rag or a broom to clean nothin' in his life. He just likes bossin' other folks around. Makes him feel strong for a minute."

"If that's the only way you know to make yourself feel strong, you're not strong at all."

"My dear, you are wise beyond your years."

They walked through the living room, the bedrooms, and the kitchen. Stella checked the pantry thoroughly, even the top shelf, thinking that was one of the better places to hide something if one had a mind to.

"It's not easy to hide things in an empty house," she murmured, more to herself than to Savannah.

But Savannah heard her and said, "We're looking for something that's hidden?"

"Sure. That's more fun than lookin' for something that's lyin' out in plain sight."

"True."

Stella was about to give up and declare the trip a write-off when she remembered something.

She recalled the summer when she had smoked her first and only cigarette. Florence had stolen a pack from her father and had hidden it in her room. One afternoon, when her parents had gone into town for some groceries, Florence had produced the pack. They had each smoked a cigarette and become violently ill as a result.

Neither had ever smoked again.

"Let's check that front bedroom one more time," Stella said.

"Did you forget something?" Savannah asked.

"No. I remembered something."

Once inside the bedroom that had been Florence's, Stella went straight to the bay window and the window seat, which had once been cushioned but was now bare. She knelt on the filthy floor and shone her light on the seat.

"Wait a minute," Savannah said, directing her own beam onto the floor. "Somebody's been here."

"How do you know?"

"Look on the floor in front of the window. The floor's got clean places, where the dirt's been messed with. Somebody besides us was walking there. Quite a bit, too."

Although the child's description lacked sophistication, Stella could instantly see that she was right. Someone had been there. Recently.

Her heart started to pound when she saw the scuff marks on the front panel of the window seat—the very panel that she had been about to remove.

"Hand me the camera," she said. "And hold my flashlight on that spot right there. I want a good picture of those scratches."

"Somebody moved that board there, huh?" Savannah said, producing the camera from her pocket.

"I think so." Stella took a few pictures, then set the camera on the seat.

Carefully, she pulled at the panel and was surprised to see how easily it came off. She set it aside and shone her light into the alcove.

"Look, Savannah girl. That's what I was afraid I'd find."

Savannah bent down, pointed her light under the seat, and gasped. "It's Mr. Bagley's gold coin collection inside those fancy wood boxes! He showed them to me once."

"And his guns," Stella said. "Along with Flo's twenty-two rifle. The one I taught her to shoot back there in that pasture. And his suitcases."

Again, Stella reached for the camera and took numerous shots of the items under the seat.

"What does all this mean?" Savannah asked. "Why did Mr. Bagley put his gold here in this icky old house, and his guns, too? They're worth a lot of money. Somebody could steal them."

"People do all sorts of foolish things, honey," Stella told her as she replaced the panel, leaving everything exactly as it was. "Especially when they're trying to cover up what they did wrong. Let's go check that barn now."

"Hopefully the barn won't be locked," Savannah said as they headed for the door. "Then you won't have to fall through . . . I mean, climb through the window and break your face off."

"Next time I wanna hear from you, young'un, I'll yank your chain. Understand?"

Savannah giggled.

"The kid's scared to death o' me," Stella muttered as they went out the front door. They were careful to lock it securely behind them.

"Yeah. I'm plumb terrified."

Chapter 26

The next morning Stella replaced the kitchen phone on its wall hook and turned to Savannah, who stood nearby, looking up at her with eager eyes.

"Okay," Stella said somberly. "That's done. Are you sure you're up for this, Savannah girl?"

"I sure am!"

"Don't think I'm gonna be lettin' you skip school ever' day to do this sorta thing."

"Come on, Granny. Like we would do this sorta thing every day? This is a once-in-a-lifetime event!"

"I certainly hope so." Stella walked to the cupboard and pulled out a Tupperware container filled with fudge. She checked the coffeepot on the stove to make sure it was still hot.

Then she turned back to her granddaughter. "Remember, the second we hear the knock on that front door, you hightail it outta here. You don't come back inside till you get the signal."

"Then, once I come back in, *I* give *you* the signal, one way or the other."

"That's right. But what's the most important thing I told you to remember?"

"At the first sign of trouble, even a smidgen bit of trouble, I make a beeline out the back door, run to the shed, climb up into the rafters, and wait till it all blows over."

"That's exactly right." Stella looked over at the envelope on the table. "I reckon we got it covered. All except sayin' a prayer that it all works out the way it's supposed to."

"How do you figure it's supposed to work out?"

"I have no idea. That's the point of the prayer—droppin' the whole darned complicated, tangled-up mess in the hands of somebody way smarter than us."

As Stella hurried to answer the front door, she heard Savannah scurry out the back, just as she'd been instructed.

Not for the first time, Stella worried that she was placing too much responsibility on a child's shoulders. But then she reminded herself that her oldest granddaughter was more capable than most adults she knew.

Besides, if it hadn't been for Savannah, her honesty and keen eye, Stella would never have gone to the farm or made the discoveries she had. It seemed only fair to allow the girl to continue, if she chose to do so.

"Well, here we go," she whispered as she hurried to the door and opened it.

"Good morning," she said a bit too brightly.

"If you say so," Florence replied. "I'm not feeling so good, but you said it was important, so here I am."

"I appreciate it." Stella opened the door wider. "Come on in and set a spell with me. I've got just the thing to perk you up."

"What's that?"

"Fudge."

"For breakfast?"

"I won't tell if you don't."

"Yeah, okay."

Stella led her friend into the kitchen, with a pang of guilt that felt a bit like a bad case of indigestion. She was seldom false to people, and it didn't sit well with her when she was.

By the time both women had sat down at the table, Stella had dropped the casual, cheery tone. She poured Florence a mug of coffee and one for herself, then slid the plate of fudge in front of her.

"I gotta tell you, Flo, I didn't invite you over just for coffee and fudge," she said.

To Stella's surprise, Flo dropped her own facade and looked at her with haunted eyes. "I had a feeling there was something in particular on your mind."

"There is. Somethin' that kept me awake, tossin' and turnin', till the mornin's light."

Florence's hands curled around the mug so tightly that Stella was glad she'd given her one that was sturdy earthenware. "Are you sure you have to talk to me about this, Stella?" she asked. "Do you suppose it's a conversation we could avoid . . . just put it aside, forget about it, and go on?"

"That's what I was wonderin' last night, while I was doin' all that wrasslin' around between the sheets. I was wonderin' if I could live with myself if I just never brought it up." She took a deep breath and searched her old friend's eyes. "I was wonderin' if you could live with it."

"I was gonna try."

"How's it workin' so far?"

Tears filled Florence's eyes. "I do a lot of tossing and turning myself at night, too."

"I 'magine you do."

Florence looked down at the envelope lying in the center of the table. "Have you got something to show me there?"

"Yes."

Stella reached for the envelope, opened it, and showed Florence that it contained numerous photographs. "The drugstore's gettin' fast when it comes to developin' pictures. Used to take 'em days. Now it's hours. I took these yesterday and picked them up this mornin'."

Florence watched, a look of ever-increasing anxiety on her face, as Stella removed a photo from the envelope.

"Me and Savannah took a drive yesterday," Stella continued, "to a place that holds some sweet memories for you and me, Flo."

She laid a picture on the table, in front of Florence. It was of the Pale Horse Farm sign. "The place is fallin' apart at the seams now, but there was a time it seemed like paradise to a poor kid who loved to visit there with her well-to-do friend."

Florence blinked, and the tears spilled down her cheeks. "I remember, Stella. They *were* good times. Some of the best of my life."

"That's where we decided we weren't going to be smokers when we grew up. Those cigarettes that you hid there in the window seat . . . just one each was all we had, but that made our minds up for us once and for all." Stella laid a picture of the window seat on the table. "That was a great hiding place you had. I remember you also kept those naughty books you liked to read in there, and your love letters from Chris Franke."

"I should've married Chris. He was poor as a lizard-eatin' cat, but he loved me, and he would've been good to me."

"Chris didn't own any gold coin collections back then." Stella put a picture of some of the alcove's contents on the table, namely, the coin boxes and suitcases. "He probably still doesn't, but you're right. He'd have been good to you. No point in torturin' yourself about the past, Flo. Those days are gone. We're here. That's all that matters."

Stella flipped another picture down. "I remember how good you were with that twenty-two after I taught you how to use it."

Again, Stella searched her friend's eyes. "Please tell me, Flo, that I'm not gonna be sorry I taught you how to use a gun, that I'm not gonna regret it for the rest of my life."

Florence looked down at the tabletop, sniffed, and said, "You're not going to regret teaching me how to use a gun, Stella."

"Truly?"

"Truly. I promise."

Stella pulled another picture from the envelope. "I remember all the hours we played in that old barn, wallowin' around in the hay, talking about which boys we'd kiss and which ones we wouldn't look sideways at."

Stella placed a photo of the outside of the barn on the table. Next to it, she laid a picture of the barn's interior—where Bud's monster pickup was parked. It was partly covered by a tarpaulin. But the canvas had been cut for a much smaller vehicle, and Bud's blue metal-flake paint job was all too identifiable on the exposed fenders.

Florence closed her eyes and shook her head, as though denying what she was seeing.

"I remember," Stella continued, "when I visited with you those summers, sometimes we'd catch the bus there at that stop down the road a piece, and we'd go into Hooter Grove. We'd look at all the comic books and paper dolls there in the five-and-dime and buy a candy bar to bring home and split between us."

"Those simple pleasures were the best," Florence said, taking a tissue from her purse and blowing her nose.

"They were. Nothin' ever tasted quite as good as that shared candy bar."

Stella pulled the last picture from the envelope and laid it down beside the others. It was of the bus stop that was "down the road a piece."

"I was kinda surprised to hear that bus is still runnin'," Stella said. "Goes north to Hooter Grove, like it always did. Comes south all the way to Pine Hollow. It stops in McGill on the way, at that diner on the highway."

Stella paused a moment, then added, "I called Mike Kenman today and asked if he ever picks folks up from the diner and takes 'em wherever they've a mind to go. Like home. He assured me that he does that exact thing from time to time. Has recently, in fact."

Florence was shaking so hard that Stella could feel the vibration in the table they were both leaning on.

"Sounds like you've got it all figured out, Stella," Florence said.

"Most of it," Stella replied. She rose from her chair and walked over to the kitchen window. Looking outside, she saw her oldest grandchild standing in the snow, watching the window with a deadly serious look on her face.

Stella reached up and adjusted the geranium plant that was blooming on the sill.

Instantly, Savannah headed across the yard to the back door. A moment later, the door opened, and the girl walked in, snow all over her new boots.

Florence jumped, startled by the sound, and looked surprised and confused when she saw Savannah.

"Why aren't you in school today?" she asked the child.

"She's helpin' me today," Stella said, quickly moving to stand between Florence and her granddaughter.

Stella led Savannah to the opposite side of the room and gave her a questioning look.

Savannah nodded.

"Are you sure?" Stella asked.

"Real sure," was the reply. "The big flower bed next to the wishing well. Even with the snow on it, you can tell. Freshly dug."

"Thank you, darlin'." Stella returned to the table and began to pick up the photos, one by one, and put them back into the envelope.

Florence sat and silently watched, her face growing whiter by the moment.

"We don't have it all figured out," Stella told Florence. "For instance, I don't know why. But you can tell the rest to the sheriff. It's time somebody had a nice, long talk with him. Either you by yourself, or me and Savannah, or all three of us. Your choice."

"Is that it?" Florence said. "Those are all the options I've got to pick from?"

"I'm afraid so." Stella reached over, placed her hand on her friend's, and gave it a squeeze. "It was just before dawn this mornin' that I decided it wasn't somethin' I can live with. I've known you most of your life, Florence. I don't think you can, either."

Florence thought for a moment, then said, "You're right. I'd pretty much decided that myself, and about the same time. Just before dawn." She stood and picked her purse up from the table. "I'd like to go in alone. That's my choice."

Stella studied her, evaluating, deciding. "You're going straight to the sheriff's station from here right now?"

"Yes."

"Okay. I'll call the sheriff and tell him you're on your way. I'll tell him you'll be there in about seven minutes."

"Tell him six. I've always driven faster than you."

Chapter 27

"This is nice," Manny told Stella as they sat on her front porch swing, sipping coffee and watching the kids build snowmen in the yard.

"It sure is," she replied. "Anything that keeps them busy and gives me a chance to sit down—that's a fine thing in my book."

Waycross had rolled the largest snowballs for the base, torso, and head of his snowman. They were so large that he was having difficulty lifting the middle one onto the bottom one.

"Should I go give him a hand with that?" Manny asked. "We don't want him to be the only fourth grader in his class with a hernia."

"Naw, he can do it. Just watch. He's a lot stronger than he looks."

Alma was smoothing the face of her snow-woman with her good hand as Savannah tied a colorful scarf around its neck for her.

Marietta was experimenting with pine needles, trying to create long eyelashes on her snow lady, who already sported pinecone earrings, an enormous rock of a ring, a big blue bow on her head, and bright red lips, cut from wrapping paper. The paper was getting wet from the snow and starting to bleed its redness into the white snow surrounding it.

"Your snow gal's lips look like Widow Barker's," Vidalia shouted to her sister from where she was sitting in the red wagon she had received from "Santa" and supervising the snow people–building operation.

Cordelia was on her knees, trying to sculpt some sort of animal from a pile of snow. The species was yet to be determined . . . if ever. Waycross was known to possess most of the artistic talent in the family.

Stella turned and saw that Manny's mug was nearly empty. "Looks like you're ready for a refill."

"Naw. I gotta get back to the office. I promised Flo I'd give her a ride home once her bail bondsman finishes her paperwork."

"That'll be a few hours yet. I heard his wife's got him taking the Christmas lights off the roof. Some people just can't abide past-its-prime holiday décor."

"I guess she's one of them that can't." He drained his mug. "I'm glad Florence decided to plead self-defense. I don't think it'll be hard for her to prove. After all, it's Bud."

Stella had been dying to ask him the particulars of his interview with Flo ever since he arrived half an hour before, but she had been reluctant to pry.

It didn't take long for her curiosity to override her restraint.

"Can you tell me what she said?" she asked. "If it's not confidential or an invasion of personal privacy, that is."

He looked confused. "Personal privacy? There's no such thing as personal privacy in McGill."

Laughing, she said, "Of course. Silly me. So? Can you tell me?"

"I'll tell you what's going to come out in court, anyway, which is pretty much everything."

" 'Everything' would be nice."

"Apparently, the night Priscilla was killed, Flo and Bud had a row over her not bringing home enough beer or some such nonsense. He hit her and stormed out of the house."

"I know that much. He nearly ran me over when he was driving away," Stella added.

"That's what I heard. He went to Prissy for some, shall we say, recreational sex. Seems he'd been doing that off and on for quite a while. But apparently, Prissy had other ideas. She told him she was tired of having him show up only when he was 'in the mood.' She wanted more than a twenty-dollar bill shoved in her bra 'after the lovin'.' "

"I can't imagine a pretty young woman wanting *more* of Bud Bagley, but there's no accountin' for taste."

"I don't think it was so much Bud's charming self she was after. She wanted him to get a divorce and put a ring on her finger. She wanted the fine brick house, the nice car, the grocery store, the gas station, the pool hall. She wanted to be Mrs. Bagley and have what Flo had."

Stella thought of the misery she had seen her friend endure for so long and shook her head. "If she only knew *what* Flo had."

"Seems she threatened to rat Bud out to Flo, ruin his marriage and his reputation around town. Bud didn't take that well."

"No, I reckon he didn't."

"That's when he hit her with the mirror. They tussled across the room and out the door, and she fell down the stairs."

"Fell? Or was pushed?"

He shrugged. "We'll never know for sure. The only account we'll ever hear is his, by way of Florence."

"Okay. Go on. . . ."

"When he got to the bottom of the stairs, he could tell she was hurt bad, and figured he couldn't take the risk of her telling on him."

"So he strangled her."

"He did."

"How come nobody saw that big, nasty pickup of his in the alley?"

"He always parked around the corner, behind the hardware store, when he went calling on Prissy."

"Oh. Then, after he killed her, he went straight home to Florence?"

"Apparently so."

"How did Flo know all of this? He wasn't fool enough to tell her, was he?"

"Guess he was *drunk* enough to. She said he came home and spilled his guts. When she heard it all, she told him she wanted a divorce. That's when he attacked her again, worse than before, and said he was gonna kill her. She figured, if he'd just murdered another woman, he was likely to kill her, too. She grabbed a butcher knife and stabbed him once. Got him right in the heart."

Stella felt her throat tighten and her eyes burn. "She was right. I don't have to feel guilty for teaching her how to shoot."

"Pardon?"

"Nothing. Go on."

"She dragged him out to the garden, which she says was no easy task. She dug a big hole there in the flower bed by the wishing well, the one your granddaughter with the keen eye

317

found, and buried him. Then she piled some of his stuff in the foyer, where you'd see it when you dropped by."

"The whole thing about him packing up and leaving was a lie."

"It was. She loaded the stuff in his big pickup and drove to the old farm."

"She was the one you saw, not Bud, driving on the river road that day."

"Yes, but I'd never seen her drive his truck before, so I assumed it was him. Anyway, she took the stuff to the old farm and stashed it where you found it. She didn't want it in the house in case I came by to check on his whereabouts, him having disappeared and all. She knew I'd never believe that he left without taking that precious coin collection of his and his guns. She figured she'd sell the stuff later, after the dust settled."

"Then she caught the bus to the diner and a taxi home from there."

"I already talked to Mike Kenman. He says he picked her up and dropped her off that night."

Stella shook her head. "I wish she'd just called you after she stabbed him, told you all about it, and let you handle it."

"I'm sure she does, too. But I think by the time I get done testifying about how many nights I was called out to the house to get him off her—"

"And I'll testify about the incident with the frying pan."

"Exactly. I think she'll get off without serving a day."

"Are y'all gonna give Bud a proper Christian burial or leave him there in the flower bed?"

"Oh, he'll get dug up, autopsied, and planted in a cemetery. Though, if we left him where he is, he'd fertilize the flowers, and that's more good than he ever accomplished above-ground."

"That's for sure."

Manny looked out across the yard at Waycross, who was still struggling to lift the middle ball of his snowman into place. "Let me go help that child," he said, rising and handing her his mug. "I can't bear to watch him anymore."

A few moments later, Stella was standing at the stove, pouring her own blend of steaming, fragrant coffee spiked with chicory into their mugs, when she turned to see Manny standing behind her, watching her, with a strange expression on his face.

"Did you get Waycross and his snowman settled?" she asked.

"Yes."

"That's nice. I'm sure he appreciated the help."

In seconds, he crossed the floor, took the mugs from her, set them on the table, and pulled her into his arms, all in one quick, smooth movement.

Wow! Sheriff Gilford's mighty fast on his feet, was the thought that went through her mind, right before her mind went blank.

It went blank because he was kissing her. Slowly at first, softly, tenderly, sweetly. Her knees went weak, and she sagged against him. He put his right arm around her waist and pulled her even closer, until she could feel the heat of his body through their clothes. His hard muscles pressed against her softness.

The difference was delicious.

So was the taste of him. The smell of him.

His fingers, running through the curls at the nape of her neck, sent lovely shivers throughout her body, as did the sound of his deep voice murmuring her name when he deepened the kiss.

This was exactly what she had decided she didn't want. Exactly the sort of complication that her family didn't need right now.

But it was impossible to convince herself of that when something that she had fantasized about countless times was happening, and it was far, far better than anything she had imagined.

Finally, he pulled away, leaving them both breathless and shaken.

She leaned back against the counter for support and stared down at the floor, trying to collect her thoughts, to quiet the feelings burning inside her. He waited silently, until she finally looked up at him.

"I'm sorry, Stella," he said, "but I had to do that. Once. I know you're still in love with Art, and I don't blame you. He was a wonderful man, and you two were soul mates. I know you've got the world on your shoulders right now and don't have the time or energy for anything or anyone extra. Like me. But I've been wanting to do that since third grade, and I couldn't put it off any longer."

She didn't reply. She couldn't. Her mouth wasn't working. Her lips were still feeling the warm fullness of his.

"Don't worry," he said. "I won't ever do it again."

I'm not worried, she thought. *"Worried" is definitely not the word for what I am.*

"But there's one more thing I have to do," he was saying. "I have to do it right now. Just once." He paused to draw a deep breath, then said, "I have to tell you I love you, Stella. I've loved you for years. I'll love you for the rest of my life."

She still couldn't speak, but he didn't seem to mind.

He smiled and said, "Okay, I've got my kiss and said my piece, so I'm gonna go. I'll see you later."

With that, he was gone, leaving an enormous, aching emptiness in her kitchen and in her heart.

Her knees still shaky, Stella sank onto a chair and leaned her elbows on the table. "Lord have mercy, but that man can kiss," she whispered. "I'm glad I didn't know that years ago. I'd have been in deep trouble."

She sat there a long time and was only vaguely aware of the front door opening and closing and of hurried footsteps coming in her direction.

"Granny?" an excited voice said. "Granny, look! Look what Sheriff Gilford gave me!"

Stella turned and saw Savannah standing in the doorway, a big smile on her face and something that looked like a clear ball in her hand.

"It's a Christmas ornament! 'A day late,' the sheriff said." She held it out for Stella to see. "It's a special one that he made just for me."

Finally, Stella was able to concentrate on what she was seeing. It looked like a clear plastic ball, approximately three inches across. A red bow was tied on top and a small wire to hang it by. Inside dangled a silver object.

"It's a handcuff key, Granny! A real one! He gave it to me because I said I want to be a policewoman when I grow up. He said every cop needs a handcuff key. He put it inside a Christmas ornament, Granny, so I can hang it on my tree every year and remember the first time I helped solve a real, honest-to-goodness case! Is that awesome or what?"

"It's awesome, Savannah girl. Better than awesome!"

Savannah hugged her prize to her heart. "Sheriff Gilford is awesome, isn't he, Granny?"

Stella smiled. "He is, honey. Indeed, he is."

"And this was the best Christmas ever, in the history of the whole world. Well, since the first one, anyway."

Stella thought of all that had happened in the past few days, the light and the dark, the bitter and the sweet, the pain and the joy. The sweet, joyful light had definitely triumphed over the bitter, painful darkness.

"Yes, child," she told her happy granddaughter, "this *was* the best Christmas ever!"

Epilogue

Sitting before the Christmas tree, her great-granddaughter cuddled in her lap, Stella gazed at the round, clear ornament with its red ribbon on the top and silver key inside. She reached out, touched it with her fingertip . . . and remembered.

She didn't realize that her oldest grandchild was watching her until Savannah reached over and stroked her hair. "It wouldn't be my Christmas tree without that particular ornament on it," Savannah said. "I love hanging it every year and thinking of him, and what he did for us."

"He was special." Stella tried to keep her voice even, strong. "He sure was."

Savannah reached over and, as her grandmother had done, touched the ball, setting the key inside it to swinging. "Every year when I was growing up, I looked at that and thought, *Don't give up on your dream! Don't let go!*"

Stella decided not to say what she had thought each year when she looked at that ornament.

"But mostly," Savannah said, "I remember how much that

Christmas meant, because that's when we came to live in *your* house, surrounded by *your* protection and *your* love."

Stella kissed the sleeping baby in her arms. She kissed her granddaughter. She looked around the room at her family and the friends their hearts had adopted along the way. She looked at the most cherished ornament on the tree. "When it's all said and done, that's what life is about," she said. "It's all about the love."

The roots of the Moonlight Magnolia Detective Agency reach back to the 1980s in the little town of McGill, Georgia—where Stella Reid and her seven grandkids enjoy some spooky Halloween fun and stumble into murder . . .

It doesn't take cash, just some good old-fashioned creativity, to turn a pillowcase into a ghost costume or a trashcan into a suit of armor. So even if she has to stick to a budget, Stella Reid always makes holidays like Halloween memorable for twelve-year-old Savannah and the rest of her grandchildren.

After joining the other townspeople for trick-or-treating and the annual parade down Main Street, Granny Reid and the kids head to Judge Patterson's antebellum mansion, where a corn maze awaits. Most of the youngsters are too terrified to make it all the way to the middle. It's lucky for them, because when Savannah and Granny get there, it proves to be even scarier than they expected—half-buried in the mud at the center of the maze lies a human skull.

The grisly discovery uncovers a mystery that stretches back decades—and seems to be related to the long-unsolved murder of Granny Reid's own part-Cherokee mother. After all this time, the culprit may be long gone . . . or still hiding among them. It'll be up to Granny to dig into this Southern town's history and a mess of old family secrets . . .

Please turn the page for an exciting sneak peek of
G.A. McKevett's next Granny Reid mystery
MURDER IN THE CORN MAZE
coming soon wherever print and e-books are sold!

Chapter 1

"Who woulda thought a shaggy ol' brown rug could change a nice little boy into a snarlin', spittin'-mad grizzly bear?"

Stella Reid stuck her needle into her pin cushion, sat back in her recliner, and admired her handiwork. Taking her praise to heart, her nine-year-old grandson, Waycross, cranked up the drama by lunging at his oldest sister, paper claws "shredding" the air a few inches from her nose.

"Watch yourself there, Mr. Grizzly Bear," Savannah warned him with all the authority of a precocious sixth-grader. "*I'm* the one carryin' the gun, and I'm death on soup cans on a fence. I could take you down with one shot."

"Could not neither!" Waycross stood on tiptoes in a vain attempt to be eyeball-to-eyeball with his sister. "That's nothin' but a silly BB gun you got there, and it ain't loaded! Even if it was, it couldn't bring down a rabbit, let alone a snarlin', spittin'-mad grizzly bear like me."

He turned to his grandmother, his freckled face almost as red as his mop of curly hair, which was sticking out from under the cap with round bear ears—also made from what had formerly been Stella's kitchen sink rug. "She couldn't take down no grizzly bear with a dumb ol' BB gun, huh, Gran?"

Some days, Stella felt like ninty percent of her time and energy were spent acting as judge and jury to settle disputes between her grandchildren. With all seven of them living beneath her roof, there was seldom a moment when there wasn't some sort of "trial" under way.

She liked to tell herself that she was "growing in understanding" along the way. She figured by the time she got to the Pearly Gates, she'd be able to give King Solomon himself a run for his money in the wisdom department.

"It's Halloween, Mr. Waycross," she said with a tired sigh. "So, your sister's as much of a real hunter as you are a real grizzly bear." She reached over and tucked some of his copper curls back beneath the cap. "And I reckon her gun's about as deadly as your claws. You both better show each other some heartfelt respect, if you intend to get through that parade tonight still alive and kickin', let alone with the prize!"

Both kids giggled, and the argument was ended, at least for the time being. Stella savored the momentary peace.

But her golden silence was short-lived.

A few seconds later, a series of bloodcurdling shrieks erupted from the children's bedroom. It sounded like someone's hide was being removed, inch by inch, with red-hot pinchers.

Or perhaps, one of the girls had grabbed eleven-year-old Marietta's favorite hair bow. With Miss Mari it was often hard to tell if she was being tortured or just pitching a hissy fit.

Stella jumped to her feet and ran from the living room into the bedroom, ready to apply a tourniquet, fetch the fire extinguisher, or remove sharp objects that had been manually inserted into a kid—who might or might not themselves be innocent—by a malicious, mischievous sibling.

Fortunately, the latter didn't happen often, but it wasn't exactly unheard of in the Reid household.

The last incident was when ten-year-old Vidalia had snuck beneath the bed and stabbed the sleeping Marietta in the rear with a hat pin.

The injury was worse than what Stella could treat with her bottle of Merthiolate and had required a trip to the doctor's office for a tetanus shot. Then there was a follow-up visit for antibiotics when the wound got infected.

Vidalia had spent some meaningful, educational time with her grandmother behind the henhouse for that infraction.

As Stella charged into the bedroom, she hoped that whatever the crisis might be, it would prove less expensive this time. Doctor visits, shots, and penicillin didn't come cheap these days, and she did well to afford oatmeal, bologna, and potatoes.

The vision that greeted her inside the tiny bedroom was one of mayhem. She had arrived not a moment too soon, because Marietta was trying to pull Vidalia off the top berth of one of the three sets of bunk beds. Only a year younger than Marietta and nearly as large, Vidalia wasn't making it easy for her.

Although she was completely off the bed, Vidalia's arms and legs were wrapped around the railing, and she was hanging on for dear life.

To make the scene even more bizarre, Marietta was attired in a red chiffon evening dress and Vidalia a tropical-print, satin sarong. Both dresses had been borrowed from Stella's next-door neighbor, whose extensive wardrobe was far fancier than her own.

The girls also wore paper crowns spangled with glitter and the occasional rhinestone.

In the four seconds it took Stella to rush across the room, pull Marietta off her sister, and lower Vidalia safely to the floor, Stella had plenty of time to wonder how those crowns had managed to stay on during the fight that would have put a St. Paddy's Day, Irish donnybrook to shame.

"That stupid-face, contrary Mari was trying to snatch my crown," Vidalia wailed. "She was fixin' to rip it right off my head after me spendin' all day long gluin' glitter and diamonds on it!"

"I need it more than she does!" Marietta yelled. "She's just a *princess*, and I'm a *queen*. I need to wear the bigger crown, or we'll both look dumb as gutter dirt, and folks will laugh at us tonight at the parade."

Stella stood for a moment, staring at her granddaughter, whose audacity never failed to amaze and alarm her. Not to mention the girl's vocabulary.

"Do you have any idea what 'gutter dirt' is, Miss Marietta?"

The child thought it over for a while, then shrugged. "No, but it's what Vidalia's made of. And rat tails and slug slime and maggot poop and—"

"Okay! That'll be *quite* enough out of you, young lady. Apologize to your sister for manhandlin' her, sayin' ugly things about her, and tryin' to snatch the crown off her that she worked so hard on, just because you like it better than the one you made."

"But—!"

"No buts! Apologize and mean it, or you and me's gonna continue this discussion behind the woodshed."

"We ain't got no woodshed!"

"As you know, the henhouse does fine in a pinch. You sass

me one more time, young lady, I'll be takin' you out there and introducin' you to Miss Hickory Switch. And believe you me, you won't like her one bit!"

Marietta weighed the pros and cons far longer than Stella would have liked.

I'm gonna have to find new ways to instill fear and trembling, or at least a smidgeon of respect, in that young'un or we're both doomed, she thought.

Finally, Marietta mumbled a lackluster, one-syllabled "Sorry," in her sister's general direction.

"That was one of the puniest apologies ever uttered in the history of the world," Stella told her. "Try again. Harder."

"S-o-o-o-r! R-e-e-e-e!" Marietta shouted in her sister's face. "I'm so, so, so sorry, Vidalia Reid . . . that your face looks like a skunk's rear end!"

"That's it!" Stella grabbed Marietta by the hand and escorted her out of the bedroom, through Stella's own bedroom and the living room, where Savannah and Waycross watched, eyes wide and mouths open.

"Wait! Granny! Wait a cotton-pickin' minute! Where're you takin' me? Are you gonna give me a beatin'?" Marietta asked when Stella pulled her out the front door and slammed it behind them.

Stella looked down at Marietta and saw traces of genuine fear in the child's eyes. She thought of the times she had seen her daughter-in-law raise her hand to the children. Violence and cursing were the only tools in Shirley Reid's parenting kit. They were all the children had known until the courts had removed them from their mother and placed them in Stella's custody.

"No, child," Stella told her granddaughter. "I would never beat you, and this time I'm not even gonna spank you, though sometimes you do stand on my last nerve and dance a jig. I'm fixin' to sit you down over here in a place of repose."

She led her to the large porch swing and settled her onto it.

"What's 'a place of repose'?" Marietta asked, flouncing about like a hen sitting on a nest made of barbed wire.

"A peaceful spot where you can rest and—"

"I ain't tired."

"You should be. After all that hullabaloo, you should be plumb wore to a frazzle. Rest, like I said, and compose yourself, and reconsider your ways."

"What's that?"

"Think about what you did wrong."

"I didn't do a blamed thing wrong! It's Vi who did wrong! She's the one you should be pushin' down on swings. She's too dumb to know that a queen needs a bigger crown than—"

"Hush, Marietta Reid. Just 'cause you're reposin' on the porch, don't mean that marchin' you off behind the henhouse ain't still a consideration if you keep smarting off to me. I am your *grandmother*, and I won't abide it!"

They glared at each other for what seemed, at least to Stella, a miserably long time before the child finally looked away and sighed. Her shoulders and her chin dropped a notch.

Stella had a feeling that was as much of a sign of contrition as she was likely to get this go-around.

"That's right. You sit there and think about how you could've handled the last ten minutes differently and had a better outcome."

Marietta opened her mouth to retort but seemed to think better of it and shut it.

As Stella walked back to the door, she added, "Don't you dare lift your hind end off that swing till I come back to fetch you."

As she walked inside the old shotgun house and closed the screen door behind her, Stella whispered a heartfelt prayer. "Lord, please fill my heart with patience for that child. Otherwise, I'm afraid that one of these days me and her's gonna tangle, and I'm not sure who'd win."

Chapter 2

A few hours later, as Stella stood with the crowd on Main Street in McGill, Georgia, watching the tiny town's annual Halloween parade go by, she couldn't help beaming with pride at the Reid children.

Her family was well represented, if she did say so herself. Unlike many of the other costumes that had been purchased through catalogues and on out-of-town shopping expeditions, her grandchildren's outfits were homemade. Gathering whatever they could find around the house and yard, they had used their imagination, thread, glue, and nails to transform themselves into characters they loved and admired.

The youngest, little first-grader Jesup, had chosen to be Tinkerbell for a night, in an old olive T-shirt, cut with a jagged hem. Cotton balls had been glued together to create large pom-poms that were then stuck to the tops of green flip-flops. Some coat hangers and panty hose had been transformed into translucent wings that bobbed nicely as she marched along, carrying a wand made of a broken broomstick, its tip dipped in glue, then glitter.

She was prancing down the street, dousing bystanders with her leftover "fairy dust."

But only the females.

Stella had warned her before the parade had begun that, "Menfolk don't cotton to gettin' glitterfied."

Between Jesup flinging magic here and there with wild abandon, and the two older girls' crowns, the glitter bill alone had laid waste to Stella's meager Halloween budget. But seeing the smile of pure happiness on little Tinkerbell's face, Stella decided it was money well spent.

Someone squeezed closer to Stella, then poked her in the ribs with a fingertip. She turned and saw it was her next-door neighbor, Florence. As always, Stella had mixed feelings about seeing her childhood friend. Flo was a good person— when it suited her purposes. She was always happy to do a neighbor a favor and was equally passionate about reminding them and everyone else in town about it from that day forward.

"Those two granddaughters of yours look mighty pretty wearing my dresses," Florence observed, pointing at Queen Marietta, dressed in the red chiffon number with a zillion yards of net petticoats, and Princess Vidalia, in the brilliant tropical sarong that Florence had bought last summer for a wannabe luau at Judge Patterson's antebellum mansion.

"They do," Stella said. "Thank you for the use of them outfits. It meant the world to the girls. They feel mighty glamorous in them."

"Well," Florence sniffed. "I knew the fanciest thing in your closet was your funeral dress, the one I bought for you when your Arthur passed away, all unexpected-like."

Stella winced. Good ol' Flo had a way of finding a person's

deepest, most painful wound, sticking her finger right in the middle of it, and twisting.

Discarding the first five possible retorts that ran through her mind, Stella settled on, "Thank goodness for you and your fancy dresses, Flo. Queen Marietta woulda hightailed it to Timbuktu if I'd suggested she wear my funeral dress. It's not exactly regal."

"No, but you're one of the best-dressed women at every funeral this town has, year after year."

Stella thought, *She's leavin' off the "Thanks to me" part. Reckon it's just understood.*

"Thanks to me," Flo added.

Or not.

"Hey, look who's walking over here," Florence said, jabbing her in the ribs again. "He's got a way of showing up wherever you are. Ever notice that?"

Stella looked around to see who Florence was referring to . . . although she had a pretty good idea. As a result of those suspicions, her pulse rate went up at least ten points.

Yes. There he was, strolling along the edge of the street, patrolling the parade, making sure no parent was too full of hard apple cider to keep their little ones out of the road and away from the floats and vehicles.

"Sheriff Gilford," Stella said when he stopped next to her and gave her a warm smile that caused her knees to weaken. "I see you're dressed in your usual Halloween costume."

Manny Gilford's celebratory attire was a running joke in the small town. Since he had joined law enforcement at the age of twenty-two, few McGillians had ever seen him in anything but his khaki uniform.

However, on major holidays he would exchange his mundane, chocolate-brown tie for some sort of colorful, outlandish monstrosity, befitting the occasion. Tonight, he was wearing one with glow-in-the-dark skeletons whose bony hands were outstretched, grasping for victims. At the bottom the word *Gotcha!* was dripping with "blood."

"Your clan's sure putting on a show," he said, pointing to the Reid kids, marching by. "They do you proud, Miss Stella."

"Mari and Vi are wearing *my* dresses," Flo interjected. "Heaven knows, they needed something fancy to wear if they were going to be royalty."

Stella couldn't help but be pleased when Sheriff Gilford chose to completely ignore Florence's declaration. In fact, she found it more deeply soul satisfying, on numerous levels, than she wanted to admit.

"Your little Alma's a cutie in that wig," he said. "She's Little Orphan Annie, right?"

"Reckon so. We worked on that headpiece for ages. Took three skeins of orange yarn and a ton of curlin' and sprayin' with starch. The worst part was, she kept sayin' 'Gee, whiskers' and 'Leapin' lizards' the whole time. You'd be surprised how quick hearin' that gets old."

He chuckled, and Stella couldn't help being aware, as she had been for years, of what an attractive man the sheriff was—tall, tanned, strong-jawed, and muscular, with intense, gray eyes that missed nothing. Only his thick silver hair betrayed his fifty-plus years.

Stella had known him since they were both skinny, knob-kneed teenagers. He had grown more handsome with each passing decade. She wasn't sure if she had grown more or less attractive over time, but Manny still seemed to approve of her looks. He'd had a crush on her when they were kids, and she had reason to believe, now that he was a widower and she a widow, that flame might have been rekindled.

Since her husband's passing, Sheriff Gilford had stayed close, offering friendship, help, and protection to her and her brood of grandkids.

Stella spoke a prayer of thankfulness every night for the gift of a friend like Sheriff Manny Gilford.

He looked puzzled when he saw Cordelia pass, wearing an old white shirt that had *Dr. Cordelia Reid* scrawled above the pocket with a black marker. Around her neck hung an old stethoscope she had borrowed from their family physician, Dr. Hynson.

"Cordelia doesn't look so scary," he remarked. "Who's she supposed to be?"

Stella grinned. "She said she just wanted to be herself, only a doctor, so she could boss everybody around and tell them what to do."

"Now *that's* a frightening thought."

"Yes. I'm afraid she's already known around town for bein' a bit overbearing and opinionated."

Florence snickered. "Runs in the family."

"Shush, Florence Bagley," Stella told her, "or you won't be getting any of my Halloween carrot cake later tonight."

Manny quirked an eyebrow, suddenly alert. "Carrot cake? I think I'll come trick-or-treat *your* house."

"You're more'n welcome to." Stella felt yet another jab in the ribs.

Having reached her tolerance level with Florence, she turned to her friend and whispered, "The next finger you poke me with, gal, you ain't gettin' back."

"The bear and the hunter are my favorites, though," Manny added, watching the marchers and unaware of the women's exchange. "Your Savannah looks mighty stern, carting that BB gun on her shoulder. It's not loaded, right?"

"Of course not. We'd run outta BBs," Stella assured him with a smirk. "I debated the wisdom of lettin' the child march in a parade with an empty BB gun, but I'd run plumb outta rock salt for my shotgun."

He laughed. "Good call. Don't worry. If he gets too outta hand, I'll cuff him. I've taken worse grizzlies than that one into custody. I bled some in the process, but so did they, and the job got done."

Stella laughed and watched her grandson's antics as he struggled to get away from his captor. She had to admit that she might have created a monster when she'd cut up her rug and fashioned that costume for the child. He was taking his role quite seriously. She had tied a large, thick rope around his waist, and Savannah was leading him by it—or was at least trying to—the chore made more difficult by the BB rifle propped on her shoulder.

Meanwhile, the boy growled, snarled, and clawed the air as he fought against the rope that held him, and occasionally lunged at those sitting on the curb.

Some of the onlookers appeared to be genuinely afraid . . . much to the ferocious bear's delight.

With pride, Stella noticed that her softhearted grandson didn't unleash his ferocity on the smallest members of the audience, but saved it for their older siblings and parents.

Nodding toward Grizzly Waycross, Manny said, "The way that boy's hamming it up, I figure he's a shoo-in for first prize. Not only that, but he would've given Mr. Michael Douglas a run for his money for that 'Best Actor' Oscar."

Something farther up the street caught Manny's eye. A group of teenage boys was darting across the street. They only narrowly missed being struck by the McGill fire engine with a gigantic tarantula and webs on its hood. Astride the spider was the fire chief, wearing a Ronald Reagan mask and an enormous cowboy hat. Waving vigorously to the bystanders, he shouted, "Mr. Gorbachev, tear down this wall!"

"Gotta go. Good luck with the judging," the sheriff said as he hurried away to deal with the miscreants.

"That Manny's downright sweet on you," Florence said in her ear. "He's carried a torch for you since third grade."

Stella felt another sharp poke in her ribs.

Half a second later, Stella grabbed the offending finger and gave it a considerable twist.

Florence yelped and pushed away from her. "O-o-w! Dadgum, Stella May, that *hurt*!"

"Good. I was intendin' for it to." Stella pointed to Cordelia. "Go tell it to my doctor granddaughter there. She'll listen to that finger with her stethoscope, give you a diagnosis, then offer you some good medical advice, like, 'Don't go pokin' my granny no more. Next time your finger might get broke!'"

Connect with US

Visit us online at
KensingtonBooks.com
to read more from your favorite authors, see books
by series, view reading group guides, and more.

 Join us on social media

for sneak peeks, chances to win books and prize packs,
and to share your thoughts with other readers.

facebook.com/kensingtonpublishing
twitter.com/kensingtonbooks

Tell us what you think!

To share your thoughts, submit a review,
or sign up for our eNewsletters, please visit:
KensingtonBooks.com/TellUs.